PARKER DUQUE

PROGRESS

(a sophomoric case for optimism)

First published by LaJefa 2021

To contact Parker Duque email him at: parkerduque@gmail.com

First edition

ISBN: 978-1-7369809-1-0

This book was professionally typeset on Reedsy.
Find out more at reedsy.com

Contents

Acknowledgement

The author would like to thank his family and friends for support and encouragement that technically, spans two decades.

A special thank you to the early readers for their encouragement and feedback, you guys kept me going— Dr. Suz Wagner, Rebecca Perkins, Charles Noback, Gary Sheehan, David Hicks, Todd Grice, Dave Krugler and Ross Winkleman.

And a very extra-super special thank you to my wife CEW, for love and patience that technically, spans *three* decades. Your NBC *(near-brutal candor)* made this book way, way, *way* classier. Well, let's just say *less gross.*

1

SELF-MADE

Atlanta, Georgia (2006)

You know what you can't stop? Progress. Do I believe that? I guess so, but like everything else, it depends on how you look at it. Regardless, I found myself repeating the phrase more and more.

Believing in my own personal progress was harder. I still hadn't told my wife I was closing my "Big Deal," yet there I was, white knuckled at the closing table, a week *early*, and she thought it was a Wednesday. I'd been calling it my Big Deal because it felt silly using a cool name like *Operation Condor* for a real estate deal, but mostly because I couldn't come up with a cool name.

Closing the actual deal would be, and I use a technical term here, a *shit-ton* of progress. And sure enough, I hadn't even finished *thinking* my optimistic phrase about progress when I realized my soon-to-be ex-boss and his imbecile son were serving up a big bag of dicks for lunch.

I forgot to mention the buyers in my Big Deal were also my bosses. I also forgot to mention I was the seller, selling to my bosses, and yes, it did make for an excruciating dynamic on my part. With my hands tied behind my back, it had taken me over a year of relentless effort to finesse this deal, and this was my day to *finally* end my employment/partnership, whatever you'd like to call it, with these douchebag turds.

It felt too good to be true, I was actually excited to be there, in that shitty conference room, in that shitty office building, sitting across the table from equally shitty people; Thomas "Tommy" Thomas Jr., his son Thomas "Thom" Thomas III, and The Thomas Family Trust attorney, Biff Whogivesafuck.

I mean, what kind of person starts, let alone *perpetuates*, a double-named person? Thomas Thomas? *Come on.* I kid you not, as we live and breathe there's a Thomas Thomas the *fourth*. Little Tommy's perpetually drunk mother Teagan, a fankled former stripper, nearly set the family on its ear when she insisted he be named "Jay" instead, an unexplainable event I found confusing, sad, and fantastic to watch, all at the same time.

Hicks and I had come to refer to the father and son combo as Penis Penis and Penis Penis the third. I was disappointed we couldn't weave those titles into the Big Deal's contract, referring to them collectively as "The Doucherie" or something like that. Morale wise, that would have been incredible for me.

Signing the closing papers would sell my share of a reasonably successful apartment portfolio to the aforementioned Doucherie; a portfolio I had, largely on my own, cultivated over the last decade. It was literally my life's work up to that point, all the late nights, weekends, every hard-fought victory, all rolled up into one agreement, all cash at closing.

"Wait." I sighed, pulling back from the table, motioning for my attorney and best friend, Hicks Krugler, to join me.

As we found the corner of the conference room, I whispered to Hicks, "The closing statement has the title company wiring Rose's allocation to the Doucherie to distribute."

"You don't want Rose to get her money from Penis Penis?"

"I want Rose to get the money."

"He took it well when we told him it was Rose, I thought there'd be yelling," Hicks said, seeming a step behind, "There's money allocated for her. She should get a check."

"Right. She should. Who's cutting it? When? They'll try to weasel out of paying her or worse, vest it over four years." I was pissed, "I'm not signing

2

this until they cut her a check. I'd rather not do the deal than let them dangle money in front of Rose's face. It's *my* money. I'm as serious as a heart attack, Hicks. Does the contract not specify how she's paid?"

"Not specifically, remember we were trying to be discrete. I just assumed yours was a wire transfer, and Investor One proceeds would be disbursed as a check at closing because we were withholding her identity until the last minute. We only discussed the amount."

"Well, the title company has them distributing Investor One proceeds," I nodded over my shoulder at the Doucherie.

"Parker, hear me out," Hicks whispered, "as your attorney, I have to ask you, is this worth it? They're contractually obligated to pay her. It's not that much money to them. Remember, we're right there. You sign that paper, and we are done. Done, done. As in I have their signature pages, done. We can ink this deal and set you free from these guys and this depressing hell hole of an office. This deal hasn't been easy, it would be a lot to throw away over something they're contractually obligated to do. Is it worth it? Couldn't you trust them to pay her? I can send them some threatening letters if they don't."

I quit listening to Hicks halfway into his lawyer-speak, *what would Rose say, if she were here?* I heard the answer in her Midwestern twang, *"Those turkeys are all gobble."* BOOM! I knew exactly what I was going to do.

"Well," I whispered, "it's a wheelbarrow full of money to her and she earned it, so I'm going to make sure she gets it today, from me."

Hicks looked pained, "Parker—"

I interrupted him, "I know, and I know you, and I'm telling you now, don't sweat it, I should have thought about this. This is on me. They'll cut a check; I know they will. I'm going to pound a stake in the ground, right here, right now, this is it. Pull up your panties, son."

"No. I was going to say, 'Parker, don't do this.' Are you willing to risk everything? All you have to do is sign this and we're done. Let's just get it closed and then fight for her check afterward. They're contractually obligated. They *have* to pay her. Of this I am sure."

He was right, but I was done with the Doucherie.

3

"Nope. This is it; they have good pricing on these deals and the only reason we're here early is because they want to close, they want me out too. Look," I nodded toward Biff, the trust attorney, "that eunuch ain't cheap."

After we sat back down, I announced to Penis Penis, "I'm not signing this until you bring me a check that I can give to Rose today. A check that will clear the bank. Let's just cut the crap, I've been your partner for too long. That's it, either pony up the check or we're done here."

That was it. I had just stood up to them for the last time. I instantly regretted it. The jaundiced old fart across the table did his best impression of an unaffected narcissist.

"Seriously, we'll pay her. You can't trust us to pay her?" Chirped the imbecile son Thom Thomas III, technically my current boss.

I locked eyes with Penis Penis the third and felt Hicks squeezing my elbow, reminding me to stay cool. *He was right,* I thought, *it's not time yet, this is too important, I've come too far and was too close. I'll just be quiet until they say, 'Yes.'* This lasted three seconds.

"There are two people in a car, one of them farts," I said loudly, then yelled directly at Penis Penis the third, "*both of them know who did it!*"

Then there was silence. A lot of it. If Penis Penis had an Indian name at that moment, it would have been Coyote Stoic Dickface. After a minute of deep thought, he folded his hands on his lap, laughed a singular chuckle, and looked at his shrugging trust attorney. He rose from the table and walked towards the conference room door.

"What does that even mean?" Genuine confusion filled Penis Penis the third's horse-like face and shit filled my drawers as Hicks Krugler's concerned look fed my *I just killed the deal* panic, "Where are you going Daddy?"

Penis Penis turned around, "To have Brenda cut a check, but then I want you right out of this office." He wagged a long, awkward finger at me like I'd just peed on his wife's flowers, "And pick up your litter," pointing at Hicks, "because we are done."

BOOM! My insides exploded with joy as I tried to execute my own form of stoicism while sliding my completed signature page to Hicks. I whispered in his ear, "You can give them this when they hand over the check, but not until they hand it over. I'm serious."

"Yes Sir. Where are you going?"

"I'm gonna grab my stuff and say goodbye to Rose. Can you bring the check back the minute you're finished?" Hicks nodded.

"What does that even mean, farting in a car? That's gross." Penis Penis the third asked, still confused and upset.

Hicks answered, "Triple, it means that there are certain situations where it's really, really obvious someone is lying, no matter what they say or how believable they are. Look at us! It's just like old times with me explaining everything to you," I could tell Hicks was holding back, "Parker can smell your fart."

"He farted then. I didn't fart! I don't get it." Poor Penis Penis the third was exasperated, "I have never farted in your car Parker, gross." The confidence in his voice was gone. I shrugged, it was fantastic, he knew he was no longer my boss. He looked directly back at Hicks, "That's why we have a new attorney."

Hicks squared up to Penis Penis the third, "Triple, I dropped you as clients because your Daddy's a cheap douchebag and you're incompetent. You don't even make sense sometimes."

Hicks looked at me, willing to pass the torch, knowing I had spent the last year dreaming of my opportunity to talk shit to Penis Penis the third. The opportunity to tell him we don't call him triple because he's Thomas Thomas the third, but because he was *born on third base and thought he hit a triple.* This was my chance.

But you know what? Nothing. There wasn't a fuck to be given. I had zero emotion for the ridiculous things I was forced to endure over the years. Embarrassing things, such as a grown man asking us to start spelling his name "Thom" instead of "Tom," because his knock-kneed wife thought it made him appear more *exotic.* Nothing.

Maybe it's because I'd just made a tiny fortune from *my own* hard work with *my own* money. Me, Parker Duque, self-made. Who'd a thunk? For the first time in my life, I felt like a legitimate businessman instead of a con artist who'd weaseled his way into the room. This is a hang-up most rich kids have, although most of them will deny it and spend their entire life trying to convince you otherwise.

I was an *extremely* rich kid until my dad lost it all. My dad's a prince though, Triple's dad is a cheap, douchey, turd. In a weird way, I felt grateful my dad tanked the family business, because trust me, I wouldn't have made anything of myself with a giant trust fund safety net. I had no choice, I was forced into making something of myself, and I did it.

This was the best fucking day of my life. It felt like there was a nuclear explosion inside of me and lightning might start shooting out of my fingertips. Feeling this degree of self-confidence was incredibly satisfying, and incredibly new.

A familiar cackle outside the depressing conference room redirected my focus and I sprang towards the door. I couldn't wait to tell Rose. As I moved past Penis Penis the third I laughed, "Good luck Triple."

2

EVERYBODY LOVES DICK

My now former secretary, Rose Williams, a 62-year-old Midwest transplant was waiting for me as I walked toward her desk. As always, Rose was dressed like a tourist; practical pockets, many of them used, dotted an ensemble that suggested, *I'm not from the South.* I loved that Rose was old school, she favored the title secretary over administrative assistant and together, we had *worked our asses off* for the last ten years. She was my favorite person at the company and one of the smartest people I'd ever met.

Rose was locked in on my approach, standing behind her desk at the end of the depressing vanilla hallway we had shared, it seemed like, forever. With a phone wedged between her ear and shoulder, and invoices in both hands, she spread her arms out as if to say, *what took you so long?*

"What took you so long?" She said.

"We got into a little dust up."

"I heard from here! Did you close?"

I nodded "yes" with my best shit-eating grin, posturing myself around the worn corner of my desk to discourage her tendency for well-meaning hugs, which I'd preferred to avoid. It didn't work.

"I'm so happy for you Parker Duque! You deserve this, congratulations!" Coaxing her off with a quick pat on the back, I saw she'd been tearing up but was able to pull herself back together, which I'd always appreciated. "I've never heard you yell. *Ever.* Why were you yelling, what happened? I thought

I heard..." she whispered across my desk, "did Thom pass gas?"

"No. A minor oversight, completely avoidable." I laughed, feeling even more thankful the deal was finally done, "Come on in, let's have quick talk, I have something for you and then I need to get out of this place pronto, at Tommy's request."

"*OK,*" she said as she plopped into the chair then popped right back out, "I forgot. You have a call waiting on line two."

"I don't work here anymore."

"He asked for you, by name. Parker Duque."

"Sit down then." I said, indifferent to the call, probably a suit salesman or some depressing cold-calling person. "They'll hang up. If they don't, I'll pick it up after we're done. Anybody I need to talk to—"

"Calls your cellular phone. I know, I know," she finished my sentence like she had a thousand times before. *Where was Hicks with that check?*

I needed to stall for a minute. The good news was killing time with Rose was easy and I knew how I'd do it. I also knew I'd miss this wonderful person, but not for long, "Hicks is bringing me back something for you, but let's talk about Dick first."

"*Yay, Dick!* I'm so excited, two more weeks!" She didn't miss a beat, ever.

"Dick's coming through in two weeks? Were you even going to tell me?"

Richard Williams, or "Dick" as he was known to all, was anything but a dick. Dick Williams was a gravelly voiced, charismatic widower with a pep in his step and a sparkle in his crystal blue eyes that made you feel like you've been lifelong best friends. Dick summered in Southern Illinois and wintered in Florida, often stopping in Atlanta on his way through to visit his kid sister, Rose. Several years ago, I had the pleasure of meeting him and couldn't help but fall for his charm and wit, all the while discovering just how entertaining an earnest, undetected, double entendre could be.

"I know you love Dick; he loves you too. Everyone loves Dick," she smiled, wiping a rogue tear from the corner of her eye, "He asks about you every time we talk."

"The ladies in Florida must be sad he's leaving?"

"I'm sure they are," she said, in her Midwest accent, "the ladies in Florida

8

love Dick. You can't blame them."

Seriously, how many *pure* people like this are there in the world? I have no idea, but I can tell you one thing, if you're like me and have a sophomoric sense of humor, they can really bring a double entendre to life. We'd had this discussion 4 or 5 times now, never in front of others because I didn't want to embarrass her, but the things that would come out of her innocent mouth... incredibly entertaining. To me, her earnest nature was a quality as refreshing and rare as her high-top Velcro Reeboks.

"And why wouldn't they?" I asked.

"He's as happy as a pig in slop too. I was down there for Christmas and those ladies couldn't get enough. They go crazy for Dick."

A crash on the window outside my office revealed a hand holding what I knew to be Rose's check and my closing papers. Hicks' beaming smile filled the open doorway. My heart leapt at the sight.

You know what you can't stop? Progress. I believed it now.

After Rose released Hicks from his unsolicited hug, he handed me the papered mass, "We're closed."

I nodded, stuffed the check into an envelope and wrote "1" on the front. I looked back up at Hicks and announced summarily, "The ladies in Florida love Dick." Rose nodded in agreement. I couldn't help it; I was in such a good mood. I fought back the smile I'd held so many times before, "I love Dick too."

Rose joined in, "Everybody loves Dick."

In scuba diving, you can tell your dive partner's in trouble when their eyes go wide, it turns out this works on dry land too. Hicks Krugler was standing, paralyzed, in front of me, ghost white with a smile frozen awkwardly under eyes as wide as hubcaps. I could tell as a true Boston gentleman, he was determined to avoid any future eye contact with the Dick loving midwestern grandmother.

He focused on me in a confused, but trusting manner and asked, "Umm, we're still on for trivia tonight then?"

9

3

A ROSE

I handed Rose two envelopes, "These are for you."

"Oh my gosh! I'm so happy for Hicks too. It was so much fun working with him again, he's such a nice boy. I just love the friendship you fellas have," she sat down. Rose was not only the smartest person in our office, she was also the nicest person in Atlanta.

I motioned for her to open the envelopes, "Open the one that says '1' first. I know you've wanted to say something to me for a while now, this is your opportunity."

"Seriously, what is this?" She said, pointing to the envelopes, looking afraid to open either.

"You can find out the old-fashioned way or I can tell you, but I'm not saying anything until you tell me what you've been dying to get off your chest. Remember, you don't work for me anymore, I'm done here. Get it out of your system, don't be polite."

She was looking at the wall farthest from me, "Your wife is a horrible human being."

"Um—"

"You should divorce her before you have kids, she makes you miserable," she added quickly, like she was barely beating a game show buzzer. I was shell shocked; I thought she was dying to comment on the price I negotiated for my interests, not my *marriage*. I wasn't upset at all, I knew she wasn't a fan of Margot's, they had absolutely nothing in common. I'm not sure my wife even knew what Reeboks were.

"Good grief. No. I didn't mean—" I tried to stop her.

"Ignore that part then, what I've really been dying to tell you is that you shouldn't quit real estate to be a writer. You'll never make it. You're not a good writer, that's all I have," she was looking at me now, as though she had thoroughly enjoyed herself, "That's what I've been dying to tell you. Phew!" She exhaled deeply, "Thank you for letting me get that off my chest. That was surprisingly satisifying."

I was exasperated, "No. Thank you for the confidence, but no, I meant about the deal I cut with the Thomas Family! I feel like you've been dying to comment on the price I negotiated."

The lights in her eyes came on, "Oh now, I've an opinion on that too. Those turkeys stiffed you, and you let them. You left close to a half million dollars on the table." I could see the disgust for them in her eyes.

"There! Did you enjoy that?" I asked, my heart skipping a beat, *because I didn't.* I understood her opinion of my wife (she wasn't too far off) and I knew I'm wasn't that great of a writer but what *really* bothered me was I thought her number would be *smaller.*

During the negotiating, Rose had made several passive-aggressive comments on the pricing I had negotiated for my interests. I had a feeling she thought I was discounting the value too much, but a half-million dollars? That was *five* times the discount I thought I gave the Doucherie.

"Yes, but not really, it's too late now," She said.

"Yep, well put, it is too late now. Just curious, did you know I was Investor One too?"

"No! Why? Oh, that is a relief! Oh gosh, I had it wrong. Investor One is 6%, so I assumed it was a fee they were charging you. It made me sick to my stomach, so I quit being a Nosey Nelly."

I was amazed she didn't figure it out, she figures everything out. Don't *ever* play trivial pursuit with Rose Williams, it's maddening. You ask what seems to be an impossible question and she'll methodically hunt down the right answer, build consensus, politely hold off outliers, and deliver the win.

"So, the half million dollars you think I was off didn't include the proceeds to Investor One?" I was feeling a tremendous amount of relief now. Investor One is what we used in the closing documents so Rose wouldn't figure out the surprise. I had to hide it from her, if she knew my plan, she wouldn't let me do it. Anytime she becomes the center of attention she starts to freak out. I could see her wheels turning now, she looked increasingly nervous.

"Nope. That did not include Investor One. I thought those turkeys were..." She trailed off into the math as she'd already popped a HP 12B calculator out of one of her pockets, quietly computing the new cap rate. "Not too shabby kid! What a relief! Sheesh! Much better pricing if you include Investor One proceeds. Is that it, Bubba?"

As the weight of selling too cheap was lifted from my chest, the inebriation of success and freedom took back any lost ground. I could feel lightning in my fingertips again, "Nope, envelope one was the reason for the dust up. Open it!" I motioned to the envelopes she was holding. "I knew the pricing was bugging you and this fixes something that's been bugging me, it's been a long time coming. The important thing is I got enough. I wanted out. You also have to factor in who can I sell my interests to? Who out there wants to be partners with these guys?" I thumbed the general direction of the Doucherie.

"I never thought of that, I was just thinking of the numbers..." She bowed her head, looking at the envelopes. I think she already knew what was in there, "Could we do this later?"

"Sure, I mean, this isn't a special occasion or anything." I said, my arms outstretched to frame our presence together. Rose was doing what she does, trying to avoid *any* positive recognition of her efforts by a sustained campaign of ignorance, diversion, or postponement. I let the cat out of the bag a bit more, "Do you have a mason jar? We could bury the big check in your backyard, and you could dig it up when you retire?"

Anyone else would be losing their shit the minute they figured out what was in that envelope. But not Rose, you'd have thought I told her a close family member would die if she opened it.

"Parker this is making me uncomfortable. How much money is it?"

12

I took the envelope marked "1" and wrote in block letters, "YOU ARE INVESTOR" right in front of the "1."

I watched her look down at the envelope and mouth, "*You are Investor One.*" A tear dropped from her cheek onto the envelope. Then another. She wouldn't look back up at me. Now Rose couldn't talk, a rarity I'd asked for a *billion* times was happening right in front of me. Rose held the opened envelope and was studying the check with her name on it, speechless. She was trying to gather herself, which I'll say again, I *love* about her.

And believe me, it wasn't just her, I was still in ecstatic shock. My check was much, much bigger. My Big Deal actually *closed*. I had allowed myself to *dabble* in the excitement of the dream, of selling everything and starting my own group, but I could never really let myself *own* the dream. It was more like a dream leased from a distant relative, kind enough to let you use it on the weekends, providing you didn't stretch it out, or fart in it.

Only now it wasn't a dream. It was *the best fucking day of my life.*

"You need a minute?" I asked. She nodded yes. I watched her, feeling really proud to have done this for such a wonderful person. I waited while she stared at the check.

"I can't accept..." She was choked up, "What did I do to deserve this Parker?"

That's exactly why she deserved it. She never asked for anything and worked her ass off, for 10 years, without complaining. "Are you joking? When I talk to folks and I reference 'our' deals, I think of you and me as the 'our,' not me and the Penis Penis's! All they do is provide money, you and I do the work. Just like I got a percentage, I felt like you always deserved a percentage. I thought 6% was appropriate."

"Stop it Parker," she hated it when I referred to the Doucherie by their penis penis names.

"Sorry, I'm fired up though. You should be too. This is six percent of my share and I want you to have it. Like you said earlier, it's too late now."

"This is three hundred seventy-five thousand dollars!" she half-screamed, catching her own volume, "Nobody's ever done anything like this for me. I'll have to ask Rog if I can keep the money."

"Oh no you don't, you earned this! This is yours to share with him if you choose. Consider this payment for work you've performed. That's your name on the check."

"Don't you worry, it makes him feel better if I do; he's not turning down this kind of dough."

I never understood how some older ladies continued to wait hand and foot on their husbands, without complaining, and wished my wife Margot would pay closer attention. "I hope there's enough money in that account, you might want to cash it quick. It would certainly give me comfort."

"Oh, plenty of money to cover this in 88007," she said, reciting the partnership account number, one of three trillion she had committed to memory.

"Yes, so again, really quick, not to belabor the point, but in your analysis, when you add the three hundred and seventy-five thousand to my proceeds, we didn't get *that* bad of a deal did we? Total value?"

"Nope, ya done good kid, like you said, I also didn't consider what an unattractive recap deal this would be because of those turkeys. You're right, nobody would want them as a partner, Heck, I'm surprised they let you out. You and I are the only ones who do any work around here. What did you fight about? You never told me."

"Tommy was upset when they found out you were Investor One, and then we fought over how you'd get paid, that's when I yelled."

"Why did you yell?"

"They wanted to pay you themselves, at a later date," she nodded; she knew what that meant. She sat in silence.

"Rose?"

"Just... excuse my French, but I don't like those gosh darn turkeys." In the ten years we'd worked together she had never uttered a single swear word. Ever. Not once. The depth of her goodness was amazing.

"Neither do I, do you want to know something else?"

"Do I really have a choice? I think I've had enough already."

"I'm not quitting real estate to become a writer. That was a ruse."

"Oh thank goodness, you'd go broke!" she said, genuinely relieved. "That was a stretch by the way, but you had me going with that story about the bear. Why go through the ruse?"

"Hicks thought, and I agreed, that convincing them I was leaving the business was the best way to get the deal done. It took their eye off the ball, which allowed me to steal their most valuable asset."

"Parker Duque!" she whispered looking like she was about to faint, "Don't you dare. That's not your style Bubb, don't you dare tell me, I don't want to know what you took, I don't want any part of it," she thrust the envelopes toward me to take back.

"Relax Rose, I didn't *steal* anything." I watched the concern on her face turn into confusion.

"Well, what are you stealing?"

"While they were concentrating on pricing and not worrying about me competing against them, they left a giant hole in another part of the settlement."

"*What?*" she was genuinely confused. I could see her big brain reconciling the deal points I'm sure she had inadvertently memorized.

"You. You're the most valuable asset this company has."

"Me? Ha!" she cackled, genuinely amused, "That's nice kiddo, but you can't take me with you. Have you read the contract?"

"I've read it several times now actually, and Hicks wrote it. I know I can't ask you to come with me, but if you quit your job here, after six months you can come work with me. Hicks says the language in the contract is non-binding, and Georgia is a right to work state anyway."

"Oh Parker," tears were forming in her eyes, "are you—"

"Oh Rose." I interrupted, "I'm not asking you to marry me. I'm also not asking you to work for me. I want to make sure you know I'm asking you to come work *with* me, as a partner, in six months. You're not a secretary. I mean, you are, *technically*, but only because those guys are idiots. Who would let a talent like yours file leases, pay bills and answer phones? You have a real nose for the deal, you're honest, people like you, and you're fucking brilliant."

"Parker!" Rose shot me a grandmother's look of unbending disapproval at my swearing.

"Well excuse *my* French, but how many times have I told you, you could run this company yourself? I mean, you pretty much do."

"What are you going to do then, for six months? You have no hobbies," she hated talking about herself, which I loved about her.

Since being hassled by my wife and trivia night aren't really hobbies, she had a valid point, which was annoying. I decided to be annoying back, for sport, "Well, maybe I *will* write my story about the bear."

"Ohh," it had worked, she seemed disproportionately horrified, "you said that was a ruse."

"It was, but I've been meaning to do it since college." It was mildly entertaining, Rose looked at me like I was announcing an unlikely new career in porn.

"Yeah, now I get it. You know I'm a big reader don't yah?" I did, but felt her question was rhetorical. "It just drives me crazy when they put a snappy cover on a dud."

"You really have no confidence in my writing?"

"Very little. I read your writing every day, dear. Don't get your feathers ruffled, you do have good design taste, and I'm sure you'll sell some copies based on a snappy cover. I just hate it when people that can't write trick you into buying their book with a snappy cover."

"Well then, I appreciate your confidence in my snappy cover abilities."

"I hope you aren't thinking of me editing it. The swearing will be too much for me."

"We've already talked about this too much. It was the only plausible ruse we could think of. Listen, I'm not going to lose any sleep if I don't write it. Real estate pays the bills— have you met my wife?" Rose's brow furled; she had already shared her thoughts on that subject. "I'll tell you one thing though, I'm not writing anything or doing jack squat for a couple of weeks, except maybe get a new car."

"Oh golly Parker, I'll never forget your kindness, you've been so patient and taught me so much. Don't get me wrong— my kids are my proudest achievement, but I never knew I could be good at anything other than secretarial work. You've given my life a second wind, and please don't make one of your fart jokes; I'm trying not to cry here."

"But you can't quit. You want to, but you can't because even though you just received three hundred and seventy-five thousand dollars, you consider it principal and you would never spend principal on living expenses, so you can't afford to take six months off."

"Would you?" She was right, she held back the tears.

I shook my head, "No." and looked at the unopened envelope marked, "2."

"What's this?" She asked.

"I can't remember. Open it, let's see." Never had a shit eating grin felt so good.

"Oh Parker! This is—"

"Six months' pay at your current rate plus twenty-two thousand dollars."

"Too much. I was going to say this is too much Parker! Are you asking me to quit and come work for you now?"

"Nope, I'm telling you that you should quit this hell-hole and take six months off. Then come work *with* me as a partner, not *for* me. You're smarter than me, so I know you understand what I'm saying."

"I... don't know... what to say. What is the twenty-two thousand for?" She said in between muffled tears.

"Well, thirty minutes from now you'll realize if you quit today you won't be fully vested in your profit sharing. This is to make up for that." The hug I never had a chance to stop was here again, except this time I didn't fight it. Hell, I'd probably hug back if I could've freed my arms. As goofy as she was, this was my new partner, she was going to make life easier for me, and I was going to make life easier for her.

"This is too much, another forty-two thousand dollars?" she sobbed, releasing me from her grip. "This is all too much. I'm sorry Parker, I can't take this. Plus, who's going to get anything done around here if I leave?"

I smiled, "Isn't that a glorious thought? 'Owner's risk.'" Rose scoffed, recognizing the term. "That's for the owners to worry about, isn't it? That's what they love to say that when they hoard the money, 'Owner's risk.'

Employees leaving for better opportunities is an owner's risk, right?" She looked like a deer in the headlights. "Give it back then if this is too much for you." I said, holding my hand out.

She gave both checks straight back to me, zero hesitation. "NO!" I laughed, "Only you! I was just kidding. It's too late, the deal is done, I can't take it back."

She looked at me in disbelief, "They'll sue you."

"Bring it on. I'm flush with cash and my best friend's an attorney. I'll enjoy every minute of it, they don't have leverage over me anymore." *I felt like saying that a hundred times.*

"Quit joking. If I come work for you, those turkeys will sue you."

"Maybe. Hicks Krugler has assured me they'll fall short if they do and I trust him like I trust you. What do you always tell me? Don't borrow worry?"

"What will I do for six months."

"Did you really just ask me that?"

"I'm sixty-two."

"You're a late bloomer."

"I'm just saying I'm not going to be working forever, I'd like to retire in three years," she shook the checks, "I could retire now if I wanted, but I don't want to, I also don't want to work past sixty-five Parker."

Only Rose would be this honest at this moment. "Understood. Then join me for three years and retire better, think about it. You know we'll have fun. I need to get going though. Let's have a celebratory dinner at Hal's when Dick's in town. It's on me, what do you think?"

She seemed to hesitate, "Well, Dick wouldn't—"

"I won't bring Margot."

"We would love that." She stood up, her newfound wealth clenched in the fist of her throwing arm, "I'm going to go tell those turkeys—"

"Why don't you wait a day or two," I interrupted her, "and wrap everything up nice and tidy for them. Even though they don't deserve it, you need to leave on good terms. Then we'll both get to watch them implode naturally, of their own incompetency. Remember what I taught you." I was being facetious, as this secretary had taught me, "Never—"

18

"Burn a bridge," She finished the lesson.

"Exactly. If I can hold back, you can. Besides, the less they know, the better."

"You don't want to show our hand. I get it." She looked at the checks again and held them up, "But this is too much money."

I held up the wire transfer confirmations Hicks had brought me, "Have you seen these? We did this together Rose. I can understand if you don't want to leave Thomas Properties. This is a progressive company and you have a bright future here, all these phones to answer, and bills to file." I motioned to the endless row of putty colored Steelcase file cabinets.

There was silence between us, it was our moment and we deserved it, we did it together. I could have made my money without her, but if we're being honest, probably not as much, with half the fun and considerably less Dick talk. I appreciated her; she earned the money.

"The money is yours to keep either way. You've earned it and I wanted to share it with you, it was the right thing to do. If you do choose to partner with me in six months, we'll find a place to invest all of this." I waived my wire transfer confirmations.

"And most of this!" She smiled her own shit eating grin as she held up her checks. I was so proud of her; she was finally getting her due. Rose stood there, stalling, and I knew what she was doing— she was deciding whether to come in for a *third* hug. Usually, when the number of hugs is already at two, I'm OK with a handshake or even a *Good luck Parker* with a stunted wave goodbye, but I knew it wouldn't be that easy. "Parker, I know you don't like hugs, but gosh darn it, all you've done for me!" She came at me like a midwestern mother would; fast and deliberate, delivering a strong hug, pregnant with warmth, tailed by an unexpected peck on the cheek, and a fast exit signaling the moment was over. Rose stopped at the door and turned back to me, "Oh my gosh, your call is still on line two, should I ditch it?"

"Yes!"

"OK. He asked for you though. A guy named Phillip; he sounds like he might be a tenant. Can I take it and ask?"

"Phillip?" I asked, my euphoria slammed its brakes, "Did Phillip sound gay?"

"Oh golly Parker," She paused, remembering, "not at all, he sounded sad. He sounded like a nice fellow though."

"Not happy gay, gay as in your cousin Herman."

"Oh. *Homo sexual gay* gay, yes, he sounded very homo sexual gay. He sounded like a nice, sad, homo sexual." For some reason, Rose had the tendency to annunciate extra syllables when pronouncing concepts that eluded her, "He asked for you specifically."

I knew who Phillip was. *Really? Today? Now?*

"Whaddya want me to do Bubb?"

"I'll take the call; I think he might be my old house cleaner." I looked at Rose. This was it, our end here in Thomas Thomas town. I waited until she was looking me in the eyes, "Rose, thank you, for everything, this is the best fucking day of my life."

"The swearing already, sheesh!" She shook her head as she looked down and away from me. She was gathering herself together but stalling which, like I said, I loved about Rose, but this was new. She couldn't look at me, she was emotional, she positioned herself in the doorway, half in, half out, and spoke to the floor, "Thank *you* Parker. And yeah, I know..." her unshakable Midwestern voice cracked as she wrestled against her puckered crying face, "best *fucking* day of my life too." And she was out the door.

4

CLUTCH THE PEARLS

I had imagined that earning a great amount of wealth, as my grandfather had, would be a very satisfying event. I had even faux-lamented, on more than one occasion, that my grandfather's success had essentially robbed me of that very satisfying achievement. Naturally, I was careful to lament this only in the company of others in my same situation, where there was an unspoken agreement barring unsolicited, practical solutions like, "Don't use your trust fund, go do it on your own!"

I was a million miles away from that kid, sitting with my new friends, pride, and satisfaction, in my "old" office as I had just *earned*, by myself, a great amount of wealth. Chances are I wouldn't have considered six million dollars a great amount of wealth as a kid, but then again, my head was also three feet up my ass. And just so you know, its hard to keep things in perspective with your head three feet up your ass. In the real world, to real people, six million dollars was a tremendous amount of money, especially when you actually had to *earn* it yourself.

I picked up the receiver and punched the flashing line for the last time, "This is Parker Duque."

"Parker?" a sad sounding voice broke the silence.

"Yes?" It was definitely my Phillip. I instantly regretted taking the call. Good moods always had a tendency of getting me in trouble.

"It's Phillip; I used to clean your house."

"Phillip!" I hesitated, probably too long. "How are you? How is Benny?" *Is your combined weight still over six hundred pounds?* "Hey, I'm glad you called, I swear I was going to call you guys about the necklace—"

"We broke up," he interrupted; I could hear his voice crack. Phillip and Benny cleaned our house until my wife's favorite pearl necklace went missing.

"Listen," he said, "I was wondering if I could come over and get some weed from you?"

"Phillip?"

"Yes?"

I instinctively looked to make sure my office door was closed, but smiled when I realized it no longer mattered, "I buy my weed *from you,* or at least I used to."

"DUH, that's why I'm calling you."

"Phillip, I don't sell pot, I buy pot. I haven't smoked it for months now, remember? We started drug testing at work?"

"You own the company! Why are you taking drug tests? That's the dumbest thing I've ever heard of," he giggled, "*drug testing yourself.* I don't have the money to *buy* it, silly goose, I was hoping you would *give* me just a little bit. I don't need much; just enough to get me through the weekend, like, a half ounce."

I couldn't help but laugh. "A *half-ounce?* Are you sure a *half-ounce* is going to be enough to get you through the weekend?" There was no response and I can't stand silence in a conversation; it's a weakness of mine. "I was just kidding Phillip, that's a shitload of weed for two days, I'm not sure I've ever had that much at one time." No reply, nothing at all. I waited. The silence was killing me, "Phillip, a half-ounce would last me a year."

Still no response, only the audible sound of what I'd guess was a quivering lower lip. More silence, I couldn't take it, "I actually have no idea how much I have left, but I'm sure I've got enough to get you through lunch. Listen, I'm sorry about you and Benny. Are you—"

"Yaaaaay! Can I come over now?" He asked before I could even show faux concern for his break-up.

I looked at my watch; it was 4:05. I really didn't want him coming to our house, "I'm at work but I could—"

"Wonderful, I'll meet you at your house," he interrupted and hung up.

I called him back, "Phillip! You hung up on—"

He interrupted me again, "How did *you* get *my* number? Did Benny give it to you? That insufferable little nipple tweaker!"

"Phillip, I can meet you, I just wanted to tell you it's very important we meet in the alley. Margot is home and she'll go nuts if she sees you, and by the way—"

"That cunt."

"Phillip! That's *my wife!* If I remember correctly, *you* were the one asking *me* for a favor." It didn't surprise me; I knew he wasn't fond of Margot. As long as I'd known Phillip, he'd never been scared to burn a bridge, *or a six-unit apartment building* if you got him mad enough. "I was going to say, I know you didn't take Margot's necklace."

"Well," Phillip paused, "Benny took it. But I have it, I took it from him, you don't want it back though, trust me."

Are you kidding me? Unbelievable! I was convinced they were innocent, and my wife was just really dumb. Margot was right the whole time, but unfortunately, still really dumb.

Benny my ass. I'd bet my last dollar it was big gross Phillip with his dirty, stubby, little fingers. What kind of cleaning person has dirty hands anyway?

"*What?*" I shouted into the phone, collecting myself as Rose gave me a concerned look through the glass wall of my office, "Oh, I want it back, bring it or I'm calling the police."

"Easy tiger. Trust me, you don't want it back. You don't know where that thing's been if you know what I mean. Don't be a dick, Parker. I'll see you at your house," and hung up, again.

"*Son of a bitch!*" I gasped as I punched the redial button. No answer.

On the way home I had to pull over to regain my composure after I realized what Phillip and Benny had done with my wife's expensive pearl necklace. After the necklace had gone missing, I'd had a conversation with Margot about *why* she thought they would take it, because it made no sense to me.

"What would two old, dirty, hippies want with a pearl necklace?"

"They put them up their rear."

"*What?*"

"you heard me."

"When you say 'rear,' do you mean their *butthole?*"

"Do you have to make everything gross?"

"*I'm* making *this* gross? I'm just trying to understand."

"They put them up their rear end and when they're about to orgasm, they yank them out." Margot threw her hands up, "My pearls are probably up Phillip's rear end this very minute."

"Hold on. Gay guys do this?"

"Anal beads? Gay *and* straight people use them. It's not as big of a deal as you're making it, how square *are* you? Do you really want to talk about this? You look like you're going to throw up, honey," She said, wisely stepping out of my known vomit range.

"I'm sorry!" I apologized as I hurled.

After a little clean-up, there was a mutual understanding about both our back doors being off-limits, but we disagreed on how to treat the disappearing necklace. The next day, without telling me, Margot fired my weed dealer(s).

Now we have a cleaning service that cost twice as much as Phillip and Benny, and I have yet to find a new source for weed. The worst part was Margot was right all along, about the theft and probably about the purpose. Phillip was right too. *I really didn't want the pearl necklace back.*

My house has a garage in the back that's accessed from a narrow alley shared with neighbors. There's an office above the garage and my friends and I call it, "The Barn." Any time there's a guy's night, we usually end up smoking bongs and shooting the shit in The Barn.

As I drove up, I could see Phillip's beater in the driveway next to my wife's car, *in my spot.* Needless to say, in any alley situation parking is at a premium and Phillip knew this alley and this dynamic. I pulled up behind him and whisper-shouted, "Hey, Phillip." I waited, my engine still running. *"HEY! PHILLIP!"* Still no answer, not even slight movement. *"PHILLIP! PHILLIP!!"*

I couldn't honk because I didn't want Margot to hear me and see Phillip—she'd go apeshit.

"PHILLIP!" I screamed one more time under my breath. I could see the giant, hairy, klepto hippy sleeping in his front seat. A piece of burning incense was scotch taped to his sun damaged dashboard, sending up a rope of dirty grey smoke that disappeared as it rose through the air. *Doesn't he know that when you go to someone's house you don't park in their spot?*

Halfway through the unenviable task of parallel parking my car in the narrow alley, I heard the sickening crunch of a telephone pole going coital with my passenger side door. Normally, I'd lose my mind over something like this, but this was the *best fucking day of my life.* This was a good excuse to treat myself to a new car, although now I was confident I'd get screwed on my trade in value. Optimism was new to me and fit like a pair of tight pants I was anxious to take off.

"Phillip!" Phillip and his ponytail jumped awake as I poked him in his shoulder. It felt and shook like Jell-O, "You're in my spot."

"I'm your guest!" he said, rubbing his massive shoulder, "That hurt! I bruise easily, see?" He pulled up a leg of his cutoff sweat shorts to expose a purple, yellow, and brown bruise the size of a basketball on his hairy inner thigh. The bruise was pretty gross but looked like a flower compared to the big hairy nutsack that dropped into the picture as he was letting his shorts back down. *Did he have eczema on his balls? Is that a thing?* As the thought grabbed me, I hurled all over the driveway.

I have a vomiting problem. I throw up when I'm grossed out. It happens to me more than I'd like, although these days if properly warned, I can control it for the most part, or at least reduce it to dry heaves. Dry heaves are still unpleasant and terribly anti-social, but they're quite a bit better than having barf come out your nose.

The problem is exacerbated by my vivid imagination. If you tell me a story where Phillip's twin sister is feeling sexy in a hidden location far away while several dozen unicorns frolicked in the mist all around me; I will, without fail, have Phillip's twin sister in my mind, right in front of me, flicking her minnow. No frolicking unicorns, no mist, just the least desirable part of the story, right there in front of me, in high definition. I looked at Phillip again after I wiped my mouth and thought, *this is the guy that used to fold the end of our toilet paper rolls into little triangles?*

"Oh my, I see you're still throwing up?" he laughed as he got out of the car and pushed the throw up off the driveway into the grass with his flip-flopped foot.

"Please don't." I begged him to stop.

"You've been so *aggro* towards me Parker, I don't appreciate it, not one bit. I'm trying to help you. Geez, what did you have for lunch?" Phillip inspected another barf chunk before he pushed it off the driveway.

I begged him again, "Please stop, I'm going to throw up again if you keep doing that."

"I told you Benny took the necklace, not me, don't be a dick to *me*. Or could it be Margot? She isn't putting out, is she?"

No, not really, I thought. "Phillip—"

"*I knew it!* I knew she was that high-maintenance-no-reward type the moment I met her, just like Benny, that insufferable little sausage smuggler."

This was the first good news I'd heard from Phillip, that he and Benny didn't have a lot of sex.

"Listen," I snapped, "this *dick* is giving you weed, so stop with the talk about my wife, do you understand me?" He recoiled and at once I felt terrible, because Phillip really was all bark and no bite. "Look, I'm trying not to lose my temper but you're the one being the jerk. *That's my wife.* You just can't call her names like that. You can't be pissed because she fired you. You stole her necklace!"

"That's beside the point" Hands on his hips, tears forming in both his eyes. "She took you away from us."

"What?" I didn't like where this was heading and I really didn't want to have to touch Phillip, whether it was a hug or even a pat on the shoulder. "OK, that's kind of creepy Phillip. We never hung out, ever. How did she take me away from you?"

"You were our best customer, our favorite. Both Benny and I agreed on

26

that." The tears in his eyes were real and getting more pronounced. He sniffled dramatically, "That little pig faced, fuck toy."

"I'm sorry you and Benny broke up, I really am Phillip, let's go ahead and get you taken care of." I circled well around the big man, careful not to touch him, and walked up the steps to the upstairs portion of my garage, unlocking the door.

Phillip was right behind me as I went over to the bookshelf and pulled a faded shoe box off the top shelf. Before I could open it, Phillip sobbed, "Benny just loved your bong, he said it was perfect, that horse-dicked, donkey-fluffer."

"Thanks, I got it in Berkeley from a sidewalk vendor—" and then it struck me, "Wait, how did you know I had a bong in here?"

"Sugar booger, that cum belching road whore and I have been smoking out of that bong, once a week, for the past five years."

"Here?" I felt violated.

"That's one of the reasons we liked you so much, you have a great setup and the nicest bong in town." While he spoke, he was half exploring, half picking, remnants of a gigantic cold sore scab, partially hidden by his sparsely whiskered goatee.

I looked at his gigantic cold sore and then at the rim of the bong, *my* bong, which we had apparently been sharing the last five years. I thought I could see little herpes germs dancing like whirling dervishes around the glass orifice. *I'm never touching that bong again.*

I pulled the Tupperware container of weed out of the box, "How did you get in here?" I asked, exasperated but still curious.

"Silly boy, I have a key. We made one from the set you keep in the kitchen. Well, I mean, Benny made one, that ass munching Muppet fucker."

"Phillip! I referred you to my friends, are you doing this to them?"

"Benny did it, not me!" he said, indignantly. "Is this it?" He held up what was left of the bag I'd bought from him three months ago.

"It's even less." I said as I put half of it into a folded piece of paper, "Give me the key Phillip, I know you have it, I'm not buying this Benny crap."

He looked at me half amused, like I'd just come up short on a math problem he'd already solved. He shook his head like a petulant, unkempt three-hundred-pound older brother would, "If I give you the key back, then how am I going to smoke this?" He made an exaggerated game show gesture toward the weed he'd once sold me that I was giving back to him, *for free.*

I didn't say anything, I looked down at the bong and felt a phantom tingle in the corner of my mouth. I turned around, put the lid on the shoe box and handed it to him.

"Are you serious? You can't possibly be serious!"

"It's yours to keep Phillip." I said, staring hard at his gigantic cold sore to solidify the resolve it takes to give away, arguably, the nicest bong in town.

He was genuinely moved, and why not? It was a hell of a run. Phillip had trespassed my home office, soiled my bong, burgled my wife's expensive jewelry to stick up his or Benny's rear end, and I was giving him most of my weed and my only bong. It looked like he was going to cry, and I was paralyzed with fear he was going to give me a hug. I don't like to hug or touch regular people, let alone strangers, or gross people, and Phillip was both very strange and very gross.

Phillip put the shoe box down, pulled the bong out, kissed it, and carefully set it back in, "Well, I can tell you one thing," tears were forming in both eyes as he violently pulled me into his mass without warning, hugging me tight, "that's the nicest gift I've ever been given."

Horrified I was being swallowed up, I let my body go limp. I didn't want to touch any more of Phillip's back than I had to and certainly didn't want to communicate any desire for the hug to continue. Midway through the squeeze part of the hug, I winced and patted what felt to be several rows of side-fat. Every guy knows this pat signifies, *OK, the hug's over, let's release.* But Phillip didn't let go, he just squeezed me harder, round two. To be fair, it *was* a great bong.

I was not, however, going to touch those fat rolls again to perform a follow-up pat, because, you know, I can't imagine those rolls ever get a thorough washing. People like me who have vivid imaginations and throw up easily live in a dangerous place because we can't always control what we're thinking about. This situation was no different.

28

Any pragmatist will tell you there's no way Phillip's getting his arms back there to lift and scrub in-between those fat rolls, even if he wanted to. As I was trapped in this post breakup, bong gifting hug, my mind wandered. I wondered if Benny ever washed under Phillip's back fat rolls in the shower. It seemed practical, but then again, it also seemed disgusting, and I wondered if that was the reason Benny left Phillip. I could be completely wrong though, Benny was fat too, so there must have been some kind of awkward back fat roll washing reciprocity, that if anything, might have served to keep them *together*.

It occurred to me I had little understanding of what Phillip must be going through. When he looked at potential new boyfriends, in addition to the regular attributes he sought out, he had the difficult question of, *Will they be OK washing my hard-to-reach regions?*

Even though it sounds mean, I'm not trying to be mean, and I think if you saw Phillip, you wouldn't want to touch him either, let alone be held in an extended embrace.

Please let me go, please let me go. I felt grateful I was wearing a long sleeve button-down shirt, so our skin never touched. I could smell Phillip's body odor and perhaps a hint of patchouli, that or the incense he was burning in his car.

After he released me, Phillip said, "Hold on" and raced, like only a larger hippy could, out the door. I heard my wooden stairs cry under his weight and enthusiasm. *What was he doing now?* Within a minute, the stairs cried out again and he was back in the doorway, holding a small Tiffany & Co. box like someone scared of afterbirth might deliver a baby. He threw the familiar little baby blue box on the table, took a familiar shaped key off his key chain, and set it next to the box.

He pointed to the box, "I rinsed it off, but you should probably clean it yourself or have it cleaned professionally. Personally, knowing what it's been through and how many times it's been through it, I would have it cleaned *professionally*. I would pay them to clean it really, really, well too. How funny is that? I'm a cleaning professional and I'm telling you to have it cleaned professionally!" He shrieked an impossibly happy laugh, "Any who,

I wasn't going to give it to you, but since you're being so nice!" He looked at my bong, and I looked at my bong. I felt sad at first, but then I looked at the gigantic cold sore peeking out from under a dry scab in his goatee, and I was happy to never touch it again.

"Well, thank *you* for giving us our pearls back. Grab that bong and go do your thing, everything else will fall into place, you're going to be great, trust me." I didn't mean any of it, I just wanted him to leave.

"Oh Parker Duque, you *are* a sweet man." Phillip said as he packed my bong and my weed back in the box with the same enthusiasm and passion I was using to avoid touching his back fat again. "Goodbye. And thank you, sweetie, thank you!" he said again as he tucked the box under his meaty arm and walked out without looking back.

"Goodbye Phillip." I said as much to myself as to him. I looked at the baby blue Tiffany & Co. box sitting on the table. I didn't know what to do. *I rinsed it off?* My first instinct was to smell it to confirm my worst fears but then I thought better of it. It was the equivalent of touching high voltage wires to see if the power was on. I had a pretty good feeling "rinsing off" the necklace might not be enough to take the smell *or* the *e-coli* off. I sure as hell wasn't going to touch it. If I had a nuclear hazard warning sticker, I would have sealed the box with it.

I took a piece of paper out of my printer and used it as a buffer to open the box, the necklace looked fine, I could get it professionally cleaned seven or eight times and then place it in a strategic place where Margot could find it herself. Regardless, I'd deal with it later.

You know what you can't stop? Progress.

5

"BEAU" DUQUE

I settled into the couch, looking in awe at the light blue box as I dialed my older brother, Beau.

"Hah row?" It was my five-year-old nephew, Landon.

"Landon, this is your Uncle Parker, how are you?"

"Ahh, I am good Runcle Parker-san." Landon said

A quick explanation and/or warning— Beau's wife left when Landon was three months old. From that day on, Landon had been raised, almost exclusively, in a cliché bubble by a Chinese nanny named, and I wish I was kidding, Ms. Livingston. Because of this, he has taken on Ms. Livingston's Chinese accent and speech cadence.

If you can't tell by now, my brother Beau is quite a character, so it's entirely possible this Chinese woman's *real* last name isn't "*Livingston.*" No one in my family had ever seen any documentation on Ms. Livingston, and she seems generally confused if I ask her how Bill or Eddie are doing. The only thing I knew for sure about Ms. Livingston was that I didn't like her.

"Is your father home?" I asked

"Hold on, I have a rook." I could hear the phone drop and cute little feet scamper.

"Haroooo, this Ms. Rivingston"

"I was calling for Beau Ms. Livingston, is he—"

"I'm right here silly! I have it Ms. Livingston, thank you! How are you

Parker?

I waited; I didn't hear the click from Ms. Livingston hanging up the phone.

"Parker?"

"I'm waiting for her to hang up."

"What do you mean? Ms. Livingston, are you on the phone sweetie?"

"She's still on— She *was* still on. Did you hear the click just then?"

"She's a curious soul, that's for sure. How are you?"

"That's unacceptable Beau, do you care that she listens to your phone conversations?"

"Boor-ring. Can we talk about something else? Did you close today? Are congratulations in order? Talk to me."

Over the years I had become convinced my older brother and best friend, William Andrew Duque, was gay, yet for some reason beyond me, he wouldn't admit to it or act on it. Beau made Liberace look like a hardened lumberjack.

He went by the name "Billy" growing up but started introducing himself as "Beau" while attending dental school in Atlanta. There's no "Beau" in *any* part of his name or his upbringing, no cute childhood anecdote, nothing. After I initially questioned the name change, he confessed to wanting a "fresh start," then didn't speak to me or answer my calls for two weeks.

I'm sure Beau *did* want a fresh start, but the name change was, unequivocally, because he fancies himself a doppelganger of the "Bo Duke" character from the old TV show, *"The Dukes of Hazard."* When someone makes the connection and says he resembles the *"real"* Bo Duke, he absolutely loves it. He's not delusional, he does look *exactly* like the real Bo Duke, probably because he's grown his hair out and styles it *exactly* like the actor John Schneider did on TV a hundred years ago. Sometimes, for shits and giggles, before I introduce people to Beau I note the resemblance and suggest they mention it to him. It's tremendously entertaining because he lights up like a fucking Christmas tree.

Beau is one of those dentists that introduce themselves as a doctor because *technically*, they are. If someone questions whether he's really a doctor, he'll calmly explain that he *is* a doctor, but not a *medical* doctor in a dismissive way, then never speak to or look at them again, ever.

"Yes, it closed a couple hours ago, finally!" I said.

"Well, that is one big damn deal! Congratulations Parker, I'm so proud of you! Remember when you came down here and cried yourself to sleep on my couch night after night? You lost all your money and the love of your life? You told me you wanted to die." This was true, it made me smile thinking about it. "Now you're rich with your own money and married to a stone-cold stunner!"

"I remember. Are you—"

"And I bankrolled your lazy ass for months and months..."

"I paid you back."

"Because I made you pay me back, with interest. Another proud day for me and Dad. You've come a long way Parker!"

"Thanks Beau, I'm not gonna lie, this is the *best fucking day of my life*. Let's celebrate with a beer at trivia tonight, are you in or what?"

"No, I'd love to, but I'm wrecked. I'm so sorry, had I known it was really going to close this time, I would've made arrangements to celebrate. I'll have to take a rain check. I played twenty-seven holes today, the last nine without a cart," he released a stress filled sigh, "and I have 2 crown replacements tomorrow, I have to be on my 'A' game. They're depending on me."

"OK, this will be two weeks in a row you've missed it." I was disappointed. Like I said, my brother's pretty much my best friend. Given proper notice, he's always been there for me and outside of the fresh mani-pedi, his habitual sweater cape, perfectly coifed hair, and an overly feminine gait, he was the quintessential big brother that *any* guy would be lucky to have. "Listen," I said, "you need to fire Phillip and Benny."

"Who are Phillip and Benny?" he asked, genuinely confused but supremely interested given my use of the wording, *you need to fire.*

"They clean your house, I referred them to you."

"Oh, the big gentlemen, Ms. Livingston released them a while back, she thought the hairy one was stealing her cucumbers, and besides, I don't want unattractive people like that in my house, it was affecting the energy. Don't you laugh at me, I could feel it, I really could."

I stopped laughing and gulped.

"Why do you ask?" he asked.

"I'll tell you Sunday, I'm trying to take Piper to the park before I go, I've got to hustle. Give my love to Landon."

"Toodles!" he said cheerily and hung up.

6

THE TRUTH ABOUT MARGOT

My other best friend is a yellow Labrador Retriever named Piper who pretty much does four things; eat, play fetch, look for a place to sleep, and sleep. Her athleticism is misleading for a dog that sleeps constantly, she reminds me of Barry Sanders the way she jukes other dogs at the park.

Piper probably thinks I do something dangerous, like a professional javelin catcher or something and might never come back, because when I get home, she's so happy to see me, she shakes like a fistfight inside a fur coat. It's the highlight of my day. Other than that, she sleeps, and for a Labrador, sleeping is total and complete.

After walking through the back yard like a ninja I snuck into my house as quietly as I could. Piper was nowhere to be found so I knew she hadn't heard me come in. Apparently, Margot, my wife of three years, hadn't heard me either, because I could hear her talking on the phone to her friend. Ninety-nine times out of a hundred I won't eavesdrop on Margot, because honestly, the less I hear her speak the better, but this conversation had me intrigued from the get-go.

"Oh yeah, I'm already rich gurl. Parker's selling all of his apartments to his boss and starting his own company." I smiled; she was bragging about me. "He told me it was over six million dollars! And half of it's mine! That's right beotch, you're talking to a millionaire."

My wife is beautiful, but dumb, and some of the stuff she says and does embarrasses me to no end. I was conflicted, I wanted her to be proud of me, but it was also horrifying she was talking about actual numbers. Doesn't she know that when you talk about money, you're supposed to be vague enough for people to think you have way *more* than you actually have? What in the world was she doing telling people such private information and why wasn't she inflating the number like everybody else does? I leaned on the doorway toward her direction and listened more, wondering if I should stop her.

"Well, I don't know. I should probably go ahead and get pregnant now. Now that I know there's enough money."

Umm, I thought we'd been trying for over a year.

"I know, I know," she continued, "the thought of giving birth scares the hell out of me too. He wants kids so badly. I'm not even sure I want kids to tell you the truth, but all I have to do is have one and he has to take care of us for the rest of our lives."

My heart dropped to the floor.

"Hell no girl, I'm on the pill. He believes anything I tell him. I make those decisions. I wear the pants in this marriage."

The other person must have been talking because in the silence I could hear and feel my heart beating in my face.

"He's nice, he's smart, funny, and obviously he's a good provider, but there's just not an attraction, a spark, you know? There's no biology between us, he's ugly and I just can't get past it. I thought I could with the money and all, but I can't. I mean, he's not *ugly*, ugly, he's just not my type."

Are you serious? I couldn't believe it. More silence. The door trim felt cold against my face as I stared at granite countertops and the end of my marriage. *Should I just go kick her out? Should I call Hicks?* No, I'll see him at trivia tonight, he can give me the name of a good divorce attorney. I was surprised at how quickly I was ready to quit our marriage, but then it didn't seem like much of a marriage after she said those things.

I thought of the six million dollars I had wired into our *joint* investment account that afternoon. I made every last penny of it and half of it was *hers?* Probably. After we got married, Margot worked at the Gap for maybe four or five weeks before she quit, vowing never to return to "retail hell" after she

36

was "rescued." Apparently by an ugly rich guy.

"I can't even look him in the face when we have sex," she continued, sounding *amused,* "I know, I know, I'm bad, but you know me gurl, I keep it real, I call it like it is."

I was crushed. I was white hot, sick to my stomach. I mean, I'm not *that* ugly but I'd never felt uglier.

Piper walked around the corner, saw me, and stopped. She didn't shake violently; I must have looked as sick as I felt because she looked nervous like I might throw up on her. She had reason to, I'd thrown up on her before. She stopped in her tracks and stared at me like I was an object set out of place. I could hear Margot laughing in the background, I couldn't make out what she was saying, but frankly, I didn't want to hear anything more. I wanted to sit down but I couldn't move. I felt waves and waves of horrible washing over me as I connected the dots and more and more answers, laced with embarrassment and anger, continued to bludgeon *the best fucking day of my life.*

This sucked balls, if we're being honest, I had suspected it here and there, but now I knew my marriage was a sham. I felt like I was hearing the punch line to a joke that I desperately wanted to bomb, but in my mind, I could see everybody laughing, *"Oh, you thought she married you for your personality?"* Who else knew I was the clown in this circus? My dad used to make fun of rich guys that married hot bimbos, *"Sure, she can suck the chrome off a trailer hitch, but you got a 50/50 shot at having a dumb-ass kid."* Whether my dad ever saw irony in that humor, I'll never know.

The house I grew up in was a full-blown mansion, and on the third story you could step outside the billiards room window onto the roof. I know, right? A *billiards* room? At the tender age of nine, I was screwing around on the roof like I'd done a thousand times before but hadn't noticed a new plastic tarp, hastily installed to cover a leak. I ended up slipping on the tarp and sliding down the roof until I fell off.

As bad as that sounds, it was even *worse.* The roof wasn't steep, so there was roughly two full hours of torturous stop and go sliding down the tarp before I fell off. I was horrified the entire time about the fall because I knew there was a wrought iron fence with sharp pickets directly below me. *Would the pickets go through me if I landed on them?* I went hoarse calling out to anybody who might hear me. I was only nine years old. I tried to lay flat, digging my fingers in for a grip that wasn't there, but whenever I tried to move I'd slide further down, five feet at a time, slowly toward the edge before making a miraculous stop.

With about ten feet left to go, I accepted I was going to fall. I decided to roll over to my right as much as I could, *as fast as I could*, to try and avoid falling on the picket fence below. I gathered up all my courage and on the seventeenth count of three, I went for it. Nothing from my plan worked, I slid like a rocket down the roof. I remember falling end over end, horrified the whole time I was about to be impaled on a picket fence, only to miss it by inches. I snapped my collar bone, sprained my wrist, and broke my nose very badly. Blood from my nose was everywhere. I ran all the way to our neighbor's house, screaming obscenities because my "brains" were coming out of my nose.

I felt like I was sliding down that roof again, in my own kitchen. Only now there wasn't a way to avoid the picket fence. *She thinks I'm ugly?* I thought she loved me? She wasn't lying; she never looked me in the face when we were knocking boots. *Who was she talking to? Her girlfriend? A man?*

This was supposed to be the best fucking day of my life. *The best fucking day of my life,* God damn it.

It didn't take long for the rejection to turn into anger. I agonized over how much of her shit I'd put up with, and for what? We don't have kids and Piper sleeps all day, she didn't have a God damn thing to do and she lived the life of leisure, *on my tab.* I'd gently encouraged her over the past year to at least volunteer somewhere, maybe get herself some structure, some purpose. But instead of organizing charity events, she's *going* to charity events, insisting I go with her, and prancing around like we have more money than we do in front of people that know we don't.

Who knew charity events were really marriage fairs for well-connected women, looking for their next stop on the gravy train? I had no idea when I met Margot at a fundraiser my boss made me attend. My boss's wife introduced me to Margot as her husband's "rich, eligible, VP of Acquisitions." This young woman, Margot, was a *rising star* at The GAP. Before I knew it, we were married, and she quit her job.

I remember the conversation we had after she quit The Gap, "Retail is so *humiliating.*"

"Then get a different job," I told her, "I'd like to quit working too, but we don't have enough money."

"Boomer's wife doesn't work."

"They have two kids, she works! Just not in an office. Besides, Boomer has twice the money we have, and he sells fake boobs in Atlanta. He's recession proof, we aren't."

"Great, so you want me to start pumping out kids? Is that what I am to you, a big sperm donor?" she said indignantly

"A sperm donor?" I knew what she meant, she was so earnestly dumb, she mangled sayings all the time but I was still getting used to it, "No, I'm not saying that, I'm telling you that you need to work." There'd be no response and like I said, I can't stand silence in a conversation, "Why don't you go back into modeling?"

"Modeling is so *humiliating.*"

Piper was sitting in the middle of the kitchen, still looking at me. She must have been trying to figure out what was different about my entrance tonight. I used my sleeve to wipe off the tears running down my face and smelled Phillip's body odor laced with patchouli. I turned around to leave the house, I wanted to think it through before I confronted her. *Do I even want to talk to her, ever again?* I was surprised again by how easy it was to let our marriage go. I needed to speak to a lawyer; maybe I could hide some of my assets?

As soon as I turned around to walk out, Piper went crazy and I heard Margot say, "He's here, shit. He's home early, I can see his car, gotta go."

Piper jumped on me as I opened the door again. I shut it loudly to fake my arrival. I went over to the refrigerator, opened it, and stared at all the expensive gourmet food she'd never eat. The expensive food that I'd eventually throw out because I was the only person interested in cleaning out the gigantic Sub-Zero refrigerator she just *had* to have. Margot came into the kitchen, but I didn't turn to face her, I couldn't. Instead, I gathered my strength staring at the jar of dill pickles that despite my repeated protests, she *always* ate, giving her breath a distinct, ass-like smell.

"How was work?" She startled me, I could hear from her voice that she was sitting behind me on the counter, probably in a great mood. I knew she looked effortlessly beautiful because she always did, and I hated her for it. "When do you close your big deal? How much do we get afterwards?"

How much do *we* get? "They pushed it back a couple weeks." I said, lying to an unopened container of ridiculously expensive stuffed olives.

"*Again*? Why? Are they trying to take advantage of you?"

"Nope, just some title issues. I hope it's not a big deal, it could take a couple months."

"You should sue them, this is ridiculous. Anyway, I was thinking, can we go ahead and get new furniture for the living room? I spend all day in there and I want it to be nice."

This is too rich. With my composure back, I shut the refrigerator door, turned to her and said "Nope. And I've been going over our finances, and we can't swing it anymore without you working, especially if I'm starting a new business. My salary is going away, so you need to get a job." She was speechless, which I knew would quickly turn into indignity, then devolve into a hissy fit, which I wasn't about to stick around for. I enjoyed the moment for a split second, shrugged my shoulders, and went up the back stairs so I could change clothes and walk Piper. *And get the fuck out of this house.*

Margot called up to me, "You can't go to trivia at Moe's and Joe's tonight. We have the Buckhead Arts Auction!" She knew it was bad news and I could tell she was taking pleasure delivering it, *fuck me running.* I put on jeans and slipped into my flip flops. I sat down on the bench at the end of our bed, dejected, staring at the tennis ball Piper was holding in her mouth. Then it hit me, and when I say "it" hit me, I meant the absolute, most beautiful, most fantastic idea I'd had in *years*.

"What are you smiling about?" She asked me, looking gorgeous as I bounced past her through the kitchen.

I stopped at the back door, "Just wait," I said, full of devious energy, "I'm going to make your day!"

Two minutes later I was back, smiling ear to ear, "I'm going to look like a fool here, but..." I tossed the light blue Tiffany & Co. box on the counter next to her, trying to hide my hygienic panic as I made a bee line to the sink to wash my hands, vigorously.

"*Oh. My. Gawd!* You found them!" She screamed like a little girl. "You found my pearls! Where were they? Do I have to give my new ones back?"

"I found them under my bathroom sink last week, totally random. You must have put them there by mistake. I wanted to surprise you, but I had them cleaned first and it took longer than I expected. Margot was holding the necklace up to the light, unknowingly inspecting Phillip's rinse job. "Did you miss them? I thought you could wear them tonight! And yes unfortunately, we do need to give the replacement pearls back, it'd be insurance fraud otherwise." I smiled. *You can't stop progress.* I couldn't help myself, "Don't just stand there, put them on!"

"Yes!" she said as she put Phillip and Benny's anal beads around her neck. Within seconds Margot had part of the strand in her mouth. "You went cheap on the replacement necklace; they weren't long enough," she admonished, "You see, these are the perfect length." Margot put them back in her mouth, then took them out again to explain, "I love putting them in my mouth, I feel smarter, it helps me think."

"You should wear three at a time then."

She missed my insult completely, "Weird taste."

"Probably the cleaning solution the jeweler used," I lied as I walked out the door with Piper, "he said it was nontoxic so you should be safe. I'm sure the taste will go away eventually."

"That's Gah-wate, I don't mind a wittle queenah," she said, unable to speak with Phillip's butthole dipped pearls in her mouth.

7

HERE WE GO

Two weeks earlier, 10:55 PM. Madison County, Iowa.

Connie felt like she was prettier than all the other girls in her friend group and given her willingness to accept promiscuity as a full-time endeavor, her nonexistent sex life was as disappointing as it was puzzling. Sexually, you could say she had complete ownership of her body and was willing to give it to anyone, free, with no strings attached. If you passed her extensive criteria (an engorged member) and wanted to play "hide the sausage," you didn't have to ask; she was ready before you were even *thinking* about hiding it.

You probably know someone like her, spending what seemed to be a lifetime of abstinence with only the finest intentions, until one day their steely discipline lapses and they get a taste of what they've been missing. After the waves finish pounding the beach and the volcano's done erupting, they can't believe what they've been missing, and panic-fuck anything that moves in an attempt to "catch up."

The impetus of Connie's crazed condition, her lone sexual encounter, was one part incredible, ninety-nine parts disappointing. It started abruptly with little talk and ended almost before it began with, if you can imagine, even *less* talk. All she remembered of the experience was the awkwardness and discomfort of the act being whisked away by a mind-numbing pleasure that lasted just long enough for her to think, "*Good Todd. I'm getting laid,*

I'm actually having sex!"

She had considered the experience her "sexual awakening" and even though it was less than ideal, it mattered not. She had tasted it; it was on her lips, beating in her chest, and her pelvic region tingled whenever she thought about it. From that point on she discretely hoped, longed, *ached* for sex in any way, shape, or form. She didn't dwell on her lack of success, she was hooked, she would put herself in the position, *no pun intended*, and when it happened, she would be ready to take advantage.

Cheap, semi-anonymous sex fit within her criteria of any way, shape, or form, so she didn't mind standing out in the middle of this field, awkwardly avoiding eye contact with several other ladies her age. Connie's friend Clara had told her the owner of the farm's middle son, Erik Schneider, would meet Lu Anne, Connie's older arch nemesis, out here after Friday night football games to "make the sex." Clara also told Connie her friend Bessie walked up on them by mistake and Erik ended up giving Bessie the business too. *Did he really?* Connie asked herself, her wheels turning. Why else would these other ladies be out here in a hay field, late on a Friday night?

Erik was hung like a horse and half as smart, or, as some would say, the perfect man. Connie had known who Erik was, and had heard several people make fun of him, but she'd also seen him one afternoon in tight pants, with his shirt off; that was enough for her: she wanted to ride that train. All week she had wondered what she could do to make Erik notice her, to differentiate herself from Lu Anne. She developed more and more swagger as she realized she was not only younger than Lu Anne, she had way better tits.

Connie felt a troubling presence and sure enough, it was Lu Anne. *Damn it.* What the hell did he see in her? Her tits were saggy as hell for her age, National Geographic saggy, dragging on the ground, saggy. Poor Lu Anne, tonight was Connie's night, she could feel it in her hips, and she knew her tits looked fantastic. She was willing, and *Oh*, was she ready.

Connie was ripped from her fantasy. She sensed movement, a panicked tension amongst the rest of the ladies. Connie looked excitedly toward the farmhouse. The moon was romantic, she hoped to see the silhouette of Erik's muscular frame against the shit crammed chicken coups, but alas, no Erik. Connie looked back at the ladies, who were looking skyward in the opposite direction. Connie joined in and immediately saw what they were looking at, it seemed like a star was falling. Wow, it was falling *fast*, towards them, right *at* them!

Connie began to panic. She couldn't move though; she was paralyzed with fear. The object came at them with impossible speed and then, in a silent and uneventful *"Pop"* it stopped on a dime, five feet in front of Connie. The object, an orb of some kind, levitated inches off the ground in front of her. The orb made a pulsating sound and appeared white hot as it hovered peacefully, like it was awaiting something.

Connie looked at the other ladies, breathing hard and sweating, and like them, she couldn't believe she was still alive. Awash in a wave of relief, she screamed, *"Fuck!"* Well, she tried to scream *"fuck!"* which was always her go-to mental cuss word, but verbally, all that came out was *"Moooo!"*

It came out as *"Moooo!"* because Connie wasn't a young woman, Connie was a cow. Or if you prefer, you could call her a heifer, a dairy queen, a moo cow, cowimus maximus in Latin. Have you ever seen a cow's tongue? Having an 18-inch tongue and no lower lip pretty much means you're probably super popular with the ladies, or if you're a cow, you can't say shit, literally or figuratively. I don't know if you've ever noticed, but cows can't vocalize anything outside of "moo" or some variation of "moo," which is limiting as far as communication. Yes, Todd had picked on Connie and her bovine brethren to perform his cruelest *non-religious* form of punishment.

And who is this *Todd?* If Connie and her crew could speak, I'd bet one of the first things they'd tell us is that we'd been calling the "Big Guy" by the wrong name, forever. Well, from the moment he made himself known unto them. Only cows know this, but Moses was the dude that screwed up Todd's name. Yes, *that* Moses. Don't blame Todd, he corrected Moses like, three or four times before giving up. *"No, no, Moses- it's TODD not GOD, with a "T" and two "D's." Would you please stop writing? Moses? Don't you have some paper you can use instead of that stone tablet? Seriously, this is going to take forever."*

The next time you need a favor or miracle, try asking for *Todd* instead or if you use his full name, *Theodore Burven Fuct*, you might have better luck, but only if you get the pronunciation right. If cows could speak, they'd also be the first to tell you Todd's not *nearly* as chill as people think. Can you even imagine how annoying it would get, being called the wrong name for thousands of years?

Anyway, Todd talks to Connie, Lu Anne, Clara, Bessie and Co. on regular occasion, part of the time to chit chat, but mostly to catch them up on juicy gossip. By the time the average cow is four years old, Todd's already shared the answers to every interesting unknown fact on Earth. He does this knowing full well they can't tell anybody.

They can give us knowing glances, but that's about it. In one stroke of quasi-vengeance, Todd told the cows *everything* and said, "But don't tell anyone, OK?" and then made sure they couldn't, ever. Every cow you see is a know-it-all without a license to boast... All the world's mysteries; Stonehenge, JFK's Assassination, the secret formula for Coke, Tom Cruise's sexuality, who's so vain in Carly Simon's song, everything! You name it, cows know it, they know *everything*.

Why this cruel torture? This severe punishment? It's a long story for another day, but what a lot of people don't know is before Todd punished them, cows were easily the biggest assholes going, I mean, *major league* assholes.

But this was something Todd hadn't informed the bovine nation about. Connie tried, "Todd? Oh Todd? Connie here, 3rd place in the 4H milk-off last week, remember me? Thanks, by the way, for clearing that milk duct blockage, that hurt like a bitch, but I guess you know that already! Where are you Todd? What the hell is this thing Todd? If we lick it, will it taste like salt? 'Cause I could use a nice salt lick right now. When's the last time we had a friggin' lick of salt? Todd? Can you at least stir the farmer into putting out a couple of measly salt blocks?"

Connie was getting frustrated, still no Todd. Pissed off, she struggled to remember why she was even out in this field until, adding insult to injury, she turned around to see a shirtless Erik Schneider, standing on a footstool enthusiastically pounding his horse cock into none other than Lu Anne herself. And if she hadn't known better, Connie was sure she saw that saggy titted bitch wink at her. Erik was muttering something to Lu Anne about, "Someone earning herself a nice salt lick" until he looked toward Connie and saw the orb, hovering and pulsating in front of her. He stopped mid coitus and gasped, "what the...

And then it happened.

8

A DISCERNIBLE GESTALT

Atlanta, Georgia

"Would you like another drink Mr. Duque?" it was the cute cocktail waitress who'd cleverly interpreted the cash I was slipping her meant, *please bring me unnaturally strong drinks.*

"Is there alcohol in these?" I joked.

"Yes sir," she said with a knowing smile.

"This auction is excruciating, don't you think?" The cocktail waitress smiled, unwilling to offend the octogenarians seated at our table. "That's a good word for this isn't it? Excruciating. It's a big word too," I turned to Margot, "I just learned it last week and think it's a good fit for this occasion, don't you?"

We were in one of the oldest country clubs in Atlanta, attending an art auction for a charity I'd never heard of. It was five hundred dollars just for the tickets to get in, and the room was as big as the bank accounts of our fellow travelers aboard the SS Fullofshit. All night I'd been wondering how I ended up in this room, with this woman, thinking my next drink might unlock the mystery. It didn't work, but at least I was shit-faced, this was *supposed* to be the best fucking day of my life.

"Parker Duque, you are embarrassing me. Please stop drinking, all my friends are here."

"Bullshit. You don't have a single friend here. We're sitting with geezers I don't even know. Sorry Geezers." I apologized, "Where are your friends? I don't see any of them. Do you really have friends here? Have you gone to a club with anyone in here? Did they get carded?" I said, looking at the old birds across the table from me. Scar tissue was fighting a war against itself all around the table, as surgically frozen faces attempted to show their condescending disgust. It only egged me on, "Aren't we too poor to be in a place like this?"

"Parker!"

"Margot!"

"Stop!" She looked serious.

"You stop. *You're* embarrassing *me*. Get a job. How do you think we're ever going to be able to buy one of these pieces of shit if you don't work?" I made a gesture to point out the impressionistic (I think) paintings that lined the stage in front of us. As I shrugged off the surgically strained looks of disgust, the art dealer had stopped, and was waiting for the commotion to stop. He was annoyed I interrupted the "education" he was providing; how these mosaic globs of paint in front of us were actually art, more specifically, why we shouldn't have a problem paying a lot of money for globs of paint.

Margot put her face in her hands, and I looked toward the stage only to get an "Eat shit asshole" look from the con artist, I mean art dealer. He was waiting for me. *And fuck you too, Phony.*

He cleared his throat, channeling his best Thurston Howell the III impression, and resumed his talk, "Though exceptionally diverse in pictorial terms, the collection we are offering tonight has a discernible gestalt to it." He looked back at me, I nodded my head in agreement, his newest fan. "The curators share a passion for work with neuro-aesthetic, psychological and morality that is articulated in imagery that is lyrical, whimsical, fantastical and highly metaphysical. Their passionate love of color coupled with mastery of juxtaposition has allowed the assemblage of an 'Alternative Philanthropic Universe' in which we can relish living."

"*What?*" I couldn't take it, "Time out." I stood up and looked from side to side, "Who got that? Seriously, what did that mean in English?" There was dead silence.

The art dealer started to speak up, "Sir—"

"No, no. You got your turn. That was absolute rubbish, and I'm not even British." There was quiet laughter from the cheap seats and Margot, pearls locked in her mouth, was staring daggers at me. "I'm going to need another drink. Quickly please" I added as I made eye contact with our cute server. I could hear some clucking coming from the ladies at our table and smiled, I knew they'd ostracize Margot for my behavior.

"Seriously, look at these paintings. This isn't skill! I can paint this. The emperor has no clothes, right? Have any of you even read that story? All these rich people here, I know there must be at least a couple smart ones, you couldn't all have trust funds. Somebody please, help me, what did he mean?"

"We didn't lose two hundred million making faulty toilets!" Came from the back of the room. I didn't really have an answer for that, nor did I expect it.

"My Dad is twice the man any of you will ever be." I was slurring, which might have affected my credibility, but that's never stopped me, "You're all phonies, bid high for this fine art, you fucking phonies." In a series of uncoordinated movements, I fumbled for my wallet, pulled out the valet ticket, and threw it into Margot's Salad. I actually meant to throw it next to her plate but after I saw it land in her salad, it seemed perfect right where it was.

"Oops." I said as I slammed the last of my drink. Normally I keep a couple ice cubes in my mouth to chew on the way out, but perhaps lost in my showmanship, I had managed to fill my entire mouth. I didn't care, I was done talking anyways.

Margot's pearls fell out of her flabbergasted mouth, she was speechless. I turned around and walked out through a cacophony of trust fund indignance from a sea of tight-assed motherfuckers. Two club staffers were smiling ear to ear, holding the double doors open for me, as if I were visiting royalty, it was a fantastic way to leave an event.

"*Asshole!*" Margot yelled after me.

I returned a fist bump from a pony tailed staffer, turned around calmly at the door, and looked directly at Margot, then the art dealer, and then everyone else. I regretted my mouthful of ice, but I had one last thing to say and I wasn't about to miss my moment, "All of you can thuck a dick."

9

TOO LATE

From the street Atlanta looks like any other big city but go to the top floor of any high rise and you'll see treetops, miles and miles of treetops. I'm not saying you won't see any buildings or roads, but for the most part it's canopy. Most of my family lives within the city limits amongst some of the oldest and most beautiful of those trees, in a neighborhood called *Virginia Highland.* Despite its intown location, Virginia Highland has an American small-town feel. The neighborhood sits on top of a hill, east of downtown Atlanta and during the winter you can see the city's skyline from almost anywhere in the neighborhood.

In a typical sought-after neighborhood, the diversity of its residents disappears as fast as the home prices go up, but in the Highlands the diversity remains intact. It's a very popular area for all walks of life in all colors; college kids, yuppies, families of all stages, and of course, the hippies. From almost anywhere in the neighborhood you can walk to a restaurant, bar, or boutique and its charm is what drew my family to it like third graders to recess.

My brother Beau attended dental school in Atlanta and was the first Duque to make Atlanta home. The rest of my family followed after our family company, Duque Industrial Fixtures, went down the toilet. *Pun intended.*

Moe's and Joe's is a small, smoky, neighborhood bar that peddles Pabst Blue Ribbon (PBR) without shame and almost always has an open booth.

There are a shitload of bars in Atlanta and quite a few in the Highlands, but for me, it's Moe's and Joe's or nothing.

On Wednesday nights, Moe's and Joe's had trivia. "Torpedo Trivia," for me, was every bit about hanging out with my closest friends, but for a couple of the guys, winning the trivia event was everything. We never won. I think sometimes certain teammates might have resented me for not caring, or enjoying the team name announcements so much. I didn't care, literally.

Our little trivia night hosted teams with fantastic names, some were stolen from porn films like, *Indiana Bone and the Temple of Poon,* or some of the younger groups spawned creative originals like, *it's only small when it's this cold* or classy crowd favorites like, *my couch pulls out, but I don't,* or *Lap dances are always better when the stripper is crying.*

Getting out of the cab I was worried I'd missed the night altogether but was relieved to see three of my good friends still holding court at our usual booth, towards the back of the bar. I was also relieved to see there was a fresh pitcher of PBR waiting for me.

Hicks Krugler poured me a beer as I walked up. With him at the table were my tall and lanky neighbor, Rusty Winkle and our mutual friend, Boomer Spence. Rusty lived across the street from me and was the principal at Grady, the local high school. It was Rusty and I that started coming to trivia night at Moe's and Joe's with regularity, adding my brother Beau, then Hicks, and then Boomer after that.

Despite my insistence on keeping the group small and exclusive, it had added randomly attending satellite members organically over time. These members could sometimes ruin the chemistry, stressing me out at the beginning of each outing, scared one of them might walk through the door, the same way you worry the large, smelly looking fellow walking down the aisle of an airplane is destined for the empty seat next to you.

"Wow, where have you been?" Rusty asked, sliding over to make room for me.

"Getting into trouble at an art auction" I said as I slid into the vinyl booth, "I forgot about it, and Margot wouldn't let me out of it."

"No sweat!" said Hicks, "We were wondering where you and Beau were.

You have to pay tonight."

"Oh, I'm going to pay for tonight, that's for sure." I wasn't kidding.

"Boomer, tell Parker what you just told us." Rusty looked short of breath like he had been laughing hard, which he did a lot.

"I was just telling the guys that I had to have 'the talk' with my son about jerking off."

"Umm, what talk is that?" I had to ask

"You know, lock the door, don't get caught, do it in the shower, like everybody else," he said, shoulders shrugged.

"That's not the funny part. Jesus Boomer! Tell him how you knew it was time to have that talk."

Boomer was drunk, "Oh yeah, we were having dinner as a family with both sets of grandparents and my wife asked him, 'Neal honey, please stop blowing your nose into your t-shirts. It's disgusting, sometimes I can't pull them apart, your snot is like glue!'

"At the dinner table?"

"In front of everybody!"

The laugh was exactly what I needed, and the reason I found my way back to my buddies. I knew Boomer's kid Neal and in my mind, I could see him shitting his pants at that dinner table, "Oh man, that's fantastic. How did you guys do without me?"

"Seventh. Out of Nine. The Cleveland Steamers won again." Hicks said as he topped off my Pabst Blue Ribbon, "Let's not dwell on opportunities lost, let's celebrate your capital event instead, although it looks like you might have started without us at the auction. You had a big day today Mr. Duque." He raised his glass and Rusty, Boomer and I followed with the inaudible clinking of plastic cups.

"Well, it's not that much if you want to buy a bunch of apartments, but it's a start, right?" They nodded and looked to me for a little speech, which I really didn't feel like giving, so I just said, "I couldn't have done it without you Hicks Krugler." I drank half my beer it tasted so good, "Rose flipped when I gave her the money."

"It looked to me like you both flipped out."

"Because I love Dick? You should know we were talking about Rose's brother Dick." Hicks laughed uncomfortably, not sure whether to believe me, which made me laugh harder, "Where is everybody, did anybody else make it?" I asked the table.

"I haven't talked to your brother," Hicks said, "and you just missed Kujawa, he left after trivia was over, Brock is MIA."

"Well, Beau Duque is beat up from playing too much golf, poor kid. I talked to him this afternoon. I'm glad Brock didn't show up, I hate it when he's here. We need to tell Kujawa he's not allowed to invite people. He's way too nice, I can't stand Brock, inviting him was unfortunate, telling him we come every Wednesday was catastrophic."

"Agreed. He's an ass. I can't stand him either," Said Boomer.

"I think we all agree, he really is MIA though" said Hicks, "I wasn't kidding. His wife called me looking for him. He never came home from Iowa. He's been missing for two days."

"Good," Said Rusty, without looking the least bit concerned, probably because Brock Martin was a *dick*, in fact, he was a *professional dick*. If you've ever had a sneaking suspicion there were people within the insurance industry, tasked with finding ways to deny or reduce insurance claims, you were right. Brock Martin was *that* guy. There were thousands of "Brock Martins" across the country, but none with his misanthropic zeal.

"Who was he denying in Iowa?" I asked.

"I was waiting for you to get here before I told it." Hicks laughed, pointing to me.

"Why?" I asked.

"I'd have to tell it twice if I didn't. You won't believe it, it's a very strange story. I have no idea where he is or why he hasn't come back although I think he may be having a genuine health crisis."

"He's losing his marbles. End of the story." Rusty beamed, he hated Brock the most.

"I think so yes, you can decide for yourselves. Do you want to hear the story or what?"

Rusty, Boomer, and I all begged together, "Please."

"Brock was working on a claim filed in Iowa to replace some dairy cows. The farmer who filed the claim literally wrote in the claim his son was, 'just being a teenager' with a cow, in a hay field on a Friday night and witnessed the 'supernatural' accident firsthand."

"It's believable so far." Boomer laughed.

"Please," Hicks said, he hated to be interrupted, "there was an explosion of a military-like orb-bomb, that blew up without making a sound, and blew off the bottom four inches of the cows legs. The cows were still alive and well, because the 'explosion' cauterized the wounds. The cows can limp around on their little cow nubs if they need too, but most of them just lie down on their sides, with no interest in being milked."

"What?" Rusty, Boomer and I asked in unison.

"It gets stranger. The farmer wanted to slaughter the cows and filed a claim before doing it. Brock denied the claim because they were still able to produce milk, despite their mobility issues. So instead, the insurance company would pay for new little wooden shoes to be made for the cows."

"Little wooden shoes? For cows? Rusty asked.

"Were they Dutch cows?" I couldn't resist.

Hicks ignored us, "The difference between supplying the little wooden shoes and replacing the cows was $25,000, so Brock's boss sent him out with a bunch of wooden shoes to see if they could make it work. I told him it was ridiculous, but he said the ends of the cow's legs were perfectly cauterized so the little wood boots should work for a while. I'm not making this up."

"I don't deal with many cows in real estate, but I don't think they can walk around on nubs, even with little wooden shoes on."

"That's part of the insurance company's plan, that's the kind of guy Brock is. They just want to keep the cows alive long enough to prevent the farmer from re-filing the claim."

"Scumbag." Rusty couldn't believe it either, "He's probably in a proctologist's office. I bet that farmer shoved those wooden shoes up his ass."

"We need to un-invite Brock," I said, "even Leslie doesn't like him. Have you noticed she doesn't talk to us when he's here?" There was general agreement at the table. Something would have to be done. Something awkward, something I would rather pay someone else to do, like cleaning a port-a-potty.

"Can you believe we drink with that guy?" Boomer said to Hicks as he emptied his beer. "I've got to split."

Rusty slid out of the booth, "Well gentlemen, and I use that term loosely, I've got to go too. Boomer I'll walk with you." He looked at me directly, "Are we all set for tomorrow Mr. Duque? You should pack it in too."

"For what?" Hicks Krugler asked.

"I'm speaking to his student body tomorrow. You know, just something a tremendously successful big shot like myself does, speak at the Grady Last Day of School Assembly."

"I asked him to talk about the 'tuning forks' thing." Rusty explained dismissively.

"Duque, I think you're confused. Tremendously successful big shots speak at graduation ceremonies." Boomer said, then looked at Rusty, "So in other words, you couldn't find anybody else?"

"Not a soul. Hicks was next on the list, and *he's a lawyer.* I just needed a warm body to kill time. The state requires us to keep students until 12:30 to get an extra day of funding. If it were up to me, I'd have them leave after homeroom roll call."

"You didn't tell me that!" I said, feigning disappointment, "I'm just *filler?* I'm just the rice and beans of the burrito?"

"You're the meat Parker! You're the main dish, and what you've got to say is very important. Especially to kids who've been waiting forever to get the heck out of that auditorium." Boomer, Hicks, and Rusty all started laughing and I couldn't help but join.

"Whatever. Just wait. Did you get me the tuning forks?" I asked Rusty, "It sounds like I need all the magic I can get."

"Yes, and we have microphones set up too, so you don't have to worry about everyone being able to hear them. It's a better setup than you deserve." Rusty smiled, "Here's a silly question, did you bring me a copy of your speech?"

"I'm winging it brother. You know me, I'll be fine."

"I do know you. That's why I asked for a copy of the speech and that's why I'm worried. All kidding aside Parker, please behave yourself. We won't be in a smoky bar on a hall pass from our wives. No cuss words and nothing racy, OK? These are high school kids, but they're still kids and their parents go ape shit over the smallest things. You slip once and *boom*, we're all on the nightly news."

"You're fucked Rusty." Hicks confirmed what I could tell Principal Rusty Winkle was already worrying about.

Despite my sophisticated new attitude of *fuck everything*, I loved Rusty Winkle and didn't want to cause him any trouble. I appreciated and understood the heads up. I also loved giving Rusty a hard time, "Always a principal. My little brother Chuy is going to be there, I'll behave myself. I've got to or he'll tell my Dad and the shit will really hit the fan. Don't you worry Dr. Winkle, you can depend on me, Ok?"

"Ok, that doesn't help me at all. I'm still very worried. At least stop drinking, I need you in my office by 11:00 at the latest. You look like a hot mess already."

You have no idea.

"Thanks for the beer," Rusty continued, "see you tomorrow. Don't be late!"

"You can count on me sweetheart." I told him as he and Boomer walked away.

"Are *you* really speaking to a gym full of high schoolers?" Hicks laughed incredulously.

"An *auditorium* full of high schoolers. Rusty's full of shit with this 'I'm worried' routine. He asked me, hell, he *seduced* me into doing this, I'm not a public speaker."

It was probably a good time to talk to Hicks about Margot, but it could wait. Honestly, I'd be happy never saying her name again.

"Unbelievable. I guess you do have a good riches-to-rags-to-riches-again story." He picked up his beer for another toast, "Here's to a fresh start. Have you settled on a company name? Do you have office space picked out?"

"No and no. Not yet. I may take a break."

"*You* are going to take a break? That should be interesting. You can't sit still for five minutes, what are you going to do?"

That was a good question. For starters I might just throw up. I felt sick thinking about my unplanned need to change plans. *What the fuck am I going to do?* "I don't know what I'm going to do." I said, telling the truth.

"What's that supposed to mean? You don't know what you're going to do? I thought you were going to keep buying apartments?"

"Of course I am, sorry. I was thinking of something else, but we can talk about it later." I was embarrassed with myself. Real estate was the only thing I'd ever really done, and I'm good at it. *It's the one thing I'd done successfully.* I was determined to keep my situation with Margot from sidetracking my life. I lost *everything* and worked so hard, for so long to get it back. Thankfully, we didn't have kids.

"OK good because I'm about to turn into a pumpkin. Are you ready to leave?"

Where would I even go? "No, I'm going to stay and finish the beer I'm apparently paying for."

"OK. Again, congratulations on your deal. You've earned this success."

"Thanks Hicks. For everything, I mean it. You did a great job."

"Wait 'til you get my bill! Good luck tomorrow, don't get carried away."

"Please."

"Oh man Parker, you could get Rusty in trouble, remember, these are kids, not adults, control yourself."

"Et tu Brute?"

Hicks slid out of the booth with the awkward coordination of a lifelong attorney and leaned in with a smile on his face, "Yes, and thanks for the beer."

Hicks was right, I did earn this success. It brought a smile to my face thinking I had, by my own hard work, made more money at the age of thirty-six than most people would make in their lifetimes. I honestly never had the confidence in myself to think that I could do it. Unlike most people, I grew up thinking I'd never have to hold a real job. I assumed I'd end up like most of my friends' older brothers and take a fancy titled bullshit job in the family business, faking like I was working. Families like mine hired *real* people to come in and do the hard work.

It embarrassed me thinking back to those days. My family was ridiculously wealthy, and I was ridiculously lazy. I was so lazy, I even had a plan to weasel out of *fake* working. It was actually genius, I started telling people in college I was going to be a writer.

I fell into the idea, I had taken a creative writing class in college because I'd heard it was the easiest English elective available and also because it didn't start until 2:00, which meant I could sleep in until 1:45.

The grad student that helped our professor run the class was a less than average guy, like myself, except all my classmates thought he was a God. I couldn't understand it, he was so full of shit and nobody ever called him out for it! He never shared *anything* he'd ever written with us. *Nothing, not a single god damn thing.* He'd criticize what we did, but I never read a single thing he wrote. It absolutely floored me that someone could get so much credit for doing *nothing* at all.

That was a *eureka* moment for me. Becoming a writer seemed like a very impressive and artsy way to "fake" work. My plan was to tell everyone I was a writer working on a novel. I'd keep giving optimistic updates if people asked and if they volunteered to read it I'd say, "I'd love that" and never send them anything. If they continued to press me I'd reiterate that yes, I'd let them read it, but not until I was happy with it. Do you see the genius in that? Independently wealthy writers can get credit for working without ever having to prove it, or more importantly, *without ever having to work.*

Unfortunately, or fortunately depending how you look at it, when my trust fund imploded, my fake writing career imploded with it. Using writing as a distraction in getting my big deal closed was probably as much as I'd get out of my short lived "writing career" at this point, something Rose would agree with as well.

I did meet Sarah in my creative writing class though. She was a beautiful girl who would eventually become my girlfriend. She was fantastic because she found writers particularly sexy, and I particularly wasn't. In fact, if I wrote something clever for an assignment, she'd get so amorous she'd pursue *me* for sex, which is something I can assure you had never happened before.

Going through my current situation with Margot and thinking of Sarah hurt more than it usually did, as she was *the one*. Everybody has that former flame, way in the background, helping them doubt current and future decisions, co-authoring the "What if…" thoughts. Sarah was mine.

10

BROCK MARTIN

"Dukey," I was startled out of my daydreaming to see Brock Martin, the douche bag, slide into the booth opposite me, "where is everybody? Is Krugler here?" He looked like he just fell out of a tree and hit every branch on the way down. He wasn't dressed in his usual semi preppy attire; his clothes looked like they were stolen from the clothesline of a 1990's weightlifter. There was something different about him, he looked strung out. It looked like his neck hurt the way he held his head low, but then his neck couldn't have been a problem the way he kept checking the front door over his shoulder.

"No, Hicks left ten minutes ago. What happened to you?" I instantly regretted asking. It was time for me to go before he got there, and after he showed up, it was *really* time for me to go. Leslie the waitress saw me, and I signaled for the bill.

"Dude, we're fucked. You won't believe what happened to me. They're going to blow up the Earth."

"Who is?"

"Aliens," he said, seemingly more panicked, still looking around. "They're boring through the earth and they're going to blow it in two. I was just in Iowa and saw the whole fucking thing."

Great. He *was* strung out on something. "Are you ok? I'm not sure your elevator is going to the top floor."

"Please Dukey, you have to listen to me. We can't talk here; let's go to your house. The CIA is after me."

"*No.* Is this a joke?" I looked around for more pranksters, "I don't know about Iowa, but in Georgia, you can't say 'Aliens are going to blow up the Earth' and 'the CIA is after me' in one conversation without being committed."

"God damn it!" He grabbed my arm and looked me in the eyes. He was unshaven, and his breath stank like hell, "I know this sounds crazy but I'm *not* crazy, I'm telling you the truth. We need to get out of here. We need to go to your house. I'm serious."

"You know what Brock? Fuck you. Get your hand off me." This was not the day to mess with me.

"I understand completely; but hear me out and then we really need to get out of here." He started rambling off his story, "I went to Iowa to settle a claim for a dairy farmer, but when I went out there, the whole farm had been fenced off. I had a brilliant settlement idea, and didn't want to give up, so I went into town to see why the farm had been fenced off."

"I mean it was like Waco or something, a full-on military presence. I found the farmer's son in town, or rather, he found me and told me all about it, he saw everything. Right after we talked, I watched him cross the street thinking he was a lunatic too; but seconds later I see him being taken away in a big black suburban, just like in the movies. Twenty minutes later, they quarantined the whole town. Legionnaires' disease."

"What's that?"

"It's bullshit, that's what it is, aliens are trying to blow the earth in two."

"But you're here?"

"I got out. Nobody can contain me."

"Of course not. When you say quarantine, this Legion air disease, I'm assuming it's an infectious disease or something?" I said, moving further away, he didn't look healthy.

"No, it's bullshit. Haven't you been listening to me? Aliens! We're being attacked by Aliens!"

"We aren't," I looked around the bar for aliens, "I only heard you say Iowans are being attacked. By Aliens. Or are we being attacked by Iowans?"

"The Earth is. I'm not joking Dukey. The kid saw *everything*."

"What else did the kid tell you?" I wondered if I had ever talked to a legitimately insane person before. Plenty of crazy people through the apartment world but Brock seemed insane.

"That this orb came down from the sky, hovered just off the ground, then pop! out comes a ring, he said it looked like Saturn. The ring cuts anything in its path, that's how the cows lost their feet. The ring then starts going towards the ground and turning the dirt below it into metal. Now it's this huge metal cylinder boring into the Earth. It's still going, they can't stop it. The military is out there and had the entire town surrounded."

"I got out, that's why they're after me, they don't want me to tell anybody and start a panic. This is it; this is the alien invasion we all knew would come. This could be the end of the world Dukey, this isn't the movies."

"And the cow jumped over the moon. That's just great Brock, and don't call me Dukey again. I don't have the patience for you tonight." I meant it.

"The farmer's kid told me the about the cylinder. It's about 100 feet across and made of a metal he's never seen. It hums. The farmer started digging on the side of it with his backhoe. When they got down about ten feet, they watched it get deeper and deeper. Then the thing turned into a magnet and pulled the backhoe right into it, crushing it flat. The magnet action fucks up everything around it. When I got close to the farm, my cell phone got all scrambled up. Something big is going on and it's not from this earth. Like I said, we have to get out of this bar."

"I'm trying to and it's not going to be with you. You need to go home now." I was slurring my words, "Your wife is worried sick about you. She called Hicks looking for you. You should go home and get some rest. This isn't funny. You can quit now, I'm not buying it and I've had a shitty day, so don't push it."

"There are black Suburbans all around my house, asshole. Do you really think I'm crazy? Come see for yourself. Do you think I'm doing this for fun? Do you think I have cow shit all over me for effect?" *I knew I smelled cow shit.* "You know what, Dukey? You're a dick. Fuck you, I've never liked you anyway."

"Well then, we finally have something in common."

"You think you're so high and mighty, being nice to everyone, including the fucking waitress. Let me tell you something, she gets paid to bring us beer! You make me sick."

He took off abruptly, bumping into people on his way out without apologizing, like a dick would. It was the second time in one day I was called a dick. I wished I would have remembered to kick him out of our trivia group, but that would turn out to be moot as well.

11

THE WALK HOME

Walking out the door of Moe's & Joe's, I was blasted by the warm, smoke free air of an Atlanta summer night. Beautiful college girls and their mop haired boyfriends walked the bar scene hand in hand. My thoughts returned to my college sweetheart, Sarah. I had always considered her, before today, as my "other" true love. But now by process of elimination, she was my clichéd one and only.

I'm sure she has three or four kids now and married to a better man than me. She was a better person than me in every measure and it just made me sick with longing to even think of her. Still, I wondered if she ever saw college kids in love and thought of me. The answer was most likely *no, she never thought of me.* The truth made my heart ache more if that was even possible, kind of like getting a big painful zit on an already excruciating boil.

"Excuse me sir." It was a very short man with tightly cropped blonde hair. He was strikingly handsome and dressed in dark clothes, wearing a windbreaker like the FBI wears, except there weren't any letters.

"Can I help you?" I asked him.

"I was wondering, have you seen this man?" It was a photo of Brock Martin carrying a bag I'd bet had little wooden cow shoes in it.

I was shocked to see Brock's picture there in front of me and probably waited too long before I replied, "No. I haven't."

Everything that Brock had just said to me started flowing through my mind. *Aliens blowing up the world? The CIA out to get him, so he doesn't start a panic?*

"You know him though?" The little scary guy grabbed my arm and held me by my elbow. I instinctively tried to pull my arm out, but it was immovable, stuck in his grasp like it was bolted to a telephone pole or something. His grip was like a python, the harder I pulled, the tighter he held me. The disturbing part was he seemed to exude no additional effort. I looked little blonde scary guy in the eye and understood very quickly, this little man could twist me into a pretzel at a moment's notice.

"I have no idea who that man is, please let me go." I struggled to no avail and then when I stopped, he smiled at me.

"Why did you pause?"

"I was giving it some thought, I thought it might help if I could tell what was in the bag. It's just how I work. What is he wanted for?"

"This man unfortunately, has had a mental breakdown and is threatening to harm his family. That's why we're taking it so seriously, Mr. Duque."

"How did you know my— Hey, that's my..." I struggled again but he tightened his viselike grip. He had somehow taken my wallet out of my back pocket without me knowing and was studying my driver's license under the streetlight with his other hand. I was scared speechless. What the hell was going on and who was this guy?

When little scary guy was done, he looked me in the eyes and didn't say anything. It was like he was performing a lie detector test, I hoped he was terrible at it, because I was lying through my teeth. He looked at the people walking down the street towards us, then back at me, then back at the people still coming, then across the street at another group of college students. He seemed apprehensive and disappointed.

Without warning, little scary guy jerked his head in the opposite direction and put up his finger to tell me, without words, to be quiet or my arm would be violently yanked out of its socket. I didn't see or hear a thing, when all of a sudden, a large vehicle's headlights appeared down the street in the direction he was looking. A group of black Suburbans rushed past us going twice the speed limit and little scary guy's phone chirped inside his coat. *He had heard them before we could even see them.*

"Have a nice night Parker," he handed me my wallet and ran like a gazelle, albeit a tiny gazelle, in the same direction the Suburbans were going. I stood there, scared out of my mind, watching this little man in black taking care to run in the shadows, disappearing down the sidewalk.

"You too..." I whispered and took off at the fastest clip I could without looking like a scared little girl. If there weren't so many people on the street I would have run, screaming like a motherfucker, arms flailing and all. I was secretly hoping Brock would come out of the bushes so I could smash his face in and be the hero. I knew he'd come unhinged; he just didn't seem right. Brock Martin was the psycho you read about in the newspaper that goes nuts and kills his family to spare them death by alien forces. Now *that* sounded believable. *Aliens* my ass.

12

HIGHER EDUCATION

My head was ringing as I sat in Rusty's office. I'd woken up only 40 minutes earlier in my carriage house, with Piper breathing in my face, smiling as much as a dog could. She wasn't mocking me because my world had fallen apart, she just had to pee.

Even with a pounding hangover, I felt the last day of school excitement coursing through the building. I watched throngs of smiling students bounce past the big windows of Rusty's office. I was flipped the bird by several students, which I thought was fantastic.

"You could have showered." Rusty walked into the office like a gust of wind. I could tell he was concerned.

"You could tell I haven't showered?" I stretched as I answered, like limberness might somehow help my situation. "I slept in the carriage house last night. Margot and I are fighting." I was wearing the Thomas Properties golf shirt I kept in my car for emergencies like this. I also kept a stick of deodorant in there, so between that and changing my shirt I figured I was good. Oops. The last thing I wanted was for Rusty to be concerned I couldn't do this. After all, I did tell him he could depend on me.

"Can you do this? You look terrible. You told me last night I could depend on you."

I took the coffee from him and set it on the table next to me, "Thanks, but you know I don't drink coffee. I've got to get out of here."

"I know you don't drink coffee, that was *mine*." He grabbed his coffee back and looked at me, "No sweat. This is probably for the best. I'll cover."

"No, I'm giving the speech, I told you I'd do it. I mean I have to get out of Atlanta. Margot and I are done."

"That's pretty heavy. Are you sure you can do this?"

"Oh yeah, I'm looking forward to the speech. It wasn't easy for me to get here if you can believe it." Rusty's confidence in me had waned but I knew he was too polite to boot me, "I wish someone would have given us a heads-up speech when we were in high school."

"What?" Rusty seemed confused, "Nobody gave your class a heads-up speech about tuning forks?"

"Well, not that I remember listening to. I wonder if anyone will listen."

"You'd be surprised. That's why I asked you. I think they'll listen to you. You're not so bad."

"Thanks, Rusty. I needed that." I hugged him. I am not a hugger. *What the fuck was happening to me?* Rusty was such a wonderful guy he hugged me back. He knew I needed it too.

"Are you ready to do some good?"

"No. Please don't do that Rusty. You ruin it for me when you say things like that."

"Sorry, I'm a motivator, I can't help myself. Are you ready to fill twenty minutes of stage time?"

"Wait, twenty minutes?" I coughed back, clearing my throat. "I need to speak for twenty minutes? That seems like a long time."

"Oh God." Rusty lowered his head.

"Just kidding. Can I get more time if I need it?" My lying didn't make it better, "Is Jesus here?" Rusty laughed, I knew he got a kick out of that.

"If you mean your brother Chuy, yes he's here. He stopped by before homeroom looking for you. Everyone's in the auditorium by now. We'd better go. It's that bad with Margot?"

"It's over. She doesn't love me. I'm not sure she ever has. She was after my money; I should have known. Other than that, I thought we had a lot going for us."

"She's a bitch, dude. I know you're not supposed to say things like that in case you two get back together, but I'll risk it, she sucks, I never liked her."

"You are 100% correct. I overheard her talking to her friend on the phone when I got home from... Listen, do you still have Phillip and Benny clean your house?"

"Hell no! The big guy that wore the cut off sweatpants grossed me out. My wife caught them trying to steal Charlie's whiffle ball bat, so we lied and told them we couldn't afford a cleaning service anymore. Why?"

I gulped, "Just checking. I'll probably go to Beau's lake house after this to figure things out. Tuning forks?"

"Umm, we should be good, there are two sets on stage. They're color coded for frequency whatever that means. I sucked at science.

"Great."

"I can hear the band playing now, we should get after it. No cussing, OK?"

I smiled, "Sure. Let's go set these fuckers straight."

13

TIME TRAVEL

The Grady High School Auditorium was overrun by pimple faced students and body odor. As a group, the students looked smelly with unimpressive hygiene, so the BO didn't surprise me nearly as much as the lack of energy did. This was the last day of school, what was wrong with these kids?

I spotted a fabulous burst of blonde hair in the audience and smiled. It was my little brother Chuy, strategically hidden in the back, near an exit. Even from a distance, I could see he was horrified. Horrified, but still beautiful. When I told him I was doing this, he flipped out and begged me not to. I thought he'd be excited about me speaking to his school, but I was completely wrong. After a lengthy negotiation, we agreed I would give my speech, but with zero references to him, specifically or in a familial manner. Whatever.

Rusty spoke himself before introducing me, long enough for my mind to start wandering. I loved that he and Boomer still refused to admit I was faster than them on skis, even though our entire trivia group witnessed it first-hand last winter. Rusty and Boomer were athletes, and athletic looking, I was neither. You can imagine their displeasure as I'd pass them, effortlessly, on the slopes, over and over again. Maybe I should add another nugget of wisdom to my speech and tell his students, *never try to out-ski a rich kid.*

Looking behind Rusty, I saw the tuning forks setup on stage and remembered I was hungover, and about to speak to four billion smelly kids. Panic set in. *Why am I doing this? I'm not a public speaker, I don't even have kids.*

What was I going to talk about? Why didn't I write something down? I'm about to disappoint one of my best friends...

Wait. I gathered myself as I remembered the "stress reversion mantra" my brother Beau had pioneered and taught me years ago. Whenever you're freaking out about something, take your fear, i.e., *why am I doing this*, reverse it and add, "Why the fuck" in front of it. Then you have to say it in a confident manor. Why the fuck *wouldn't* I do this? From there you can freestyle, What the fuck *wouldn't* I say to these kids who desperately need my nuggets of wisdom? You get it.

I was mouthing my stress reversion mantras, getting pumped up and feeling like I had something to say to these horrible smelling kids when I redirected my focus back to Rusty. His concern was palpable as he stared back at me through the silence of the auditorium.

"Am I on?" I asked Rusty's assistant, whose incredulous reaction I took as a yes. *Why the fuck aren't I on?* I said to myself as I walked a fuck-you-strut to center stage. The room was enormous and the idea of this much attention got me so excited I made the mistake of breathing through my nose and damn near passed out from the smell. In the apartment business, when you get into a strong odor situation, you learn to breathe through your mouth, which I'd been doing since I entered the Auditorium.

It may have been me almost passing out, but I'm pretty sure it was my fuck-you-strut that scared Rusty, because I didn't even know a fuck-you-strut existed until just then, but when I was close enough, I could see fear in the eyes of my favorite principal. He looked afraid and pained at the same time, like he'd just blown a huge purchase and I was planning on using the microphone he was holding to tell his wife. He instinctively moved it behind his back.

"I'm coming in, son, you best give me that mic." I whispered in a low, excited tone. I had a tendency to speak southern when I attempted macho. Rusty handed me the microphone like he'd just made a career ending mistake. It was a little dramatic if you ask me.

"Hello everyone! I'm Parker Duque and I want to say right now, I am in no way related to anybody here at Grady. I am especially not related to my little brother Chuy Duque, there in the back." I proudly pointed at my little Mexican brother, paralyzed by fear in the audience. Paralyzed by fear, but still beautiful.

"Now that we have that out of the way, I'll start with a question, *do you know what you can't stop?*"

Nothing. Not even a smart-ass answer, nothing at all.

"Progress!" shouted an overeager Rusty, stage right.

"Thank you, Dr. Winkle." This was a horrible start, but I guess it didn't matter, I wasn't sure I believed in progress anymore myself. *Why did I think this would be fun?* Had I just thought this out beforehand, I would have totally reconsidered. We weren't in a smoky bar, drunk, goofing off. I didn't know Rusty was going to be super-serious about "being an adult" and not swearing. This was *not* fun and honestly, I was disappointed they weren't filming it.

If I'm ever a dad, one of the first things I'll tell my kids is, if you're going to do something crazy, film it. That way, you can either capture greatness, laugh at the mistakes, or show the emergency room doctor exactly what happened.

I didn't want to disappoint Rusty though, "When Dr. Winkle invited me to speak at the Last Day of School Assembly, I thought he was drunk. Not because we'd been drinking for three hours playing trivia, but because I didn't think any of you would want to hear what I had to say."

I smiled and looked over at Rusty, I was proud to have him as my friend and drinking buddy. I thought it might be a special moment, but he'd turned white as a ghost. He was staring at me, exasperated, and mouthed the word, "*please.*" And then I think he mouthed "*for the love of God*" but I wasn't completely sure because he's not religious at all. Oops.

"Just kidding! We drink Sprite at trivia! And even if he was drunk, on Sprite, he was adamant the next day, he thought you guys might benefit from my story, and what *I'd* tell my high school self if I had the opportunity, so here I am." Crickets from the audience. Sheesh. This and my head hurt like a motherfucker, *there's no way I can fill twenty minutes.*

"I know you're probably thinking, what wisdom could *this* guy share?

73

Young, impossibly handsome, he looks like he doesn't have a care in the world." Finally, some laughter from the zombies, all at my expense, but I didn't care, that was the joke, it's easy to see I'm not that great looking. "But for someone as young and handsome as I am, I've been through a lot. I'll give you the *Cliff's Notes* version of my life, and you can decide for your yourself."

"For me it started at birth, I won the genetic lottery. I was born into the Duque family, spelled D-U-Q-U-E, not D-U-K-E like the University. We weren't a wealthy family, we were a *ridiculously* wealthy family from up north in Elgin, Illinois. Elgin's about fifty minutes west of Chicago. My grandfather started what we preferred to call an 'industrial' company that became a leader in porcelain toilets and lavatories."

There was life in the auditorium with mention of the toilet business. Several small voices in the crowd could be heard making my family's infamous connection to popular culture. *The Shitter Albatross*, as my mother used to call it, *We're one rung above a funeral home empire.*

"That's right, let's go ahead and get this over with. If you've ever heard a classy person announce on their way to the bathroom, 'I've got to take a Duque,' That's my family, the Duques. That's my heritage, toilets, Duque Industrial Fixtures. *Aren't we proud?*

"For me, the notoriety and the money were short lived though. The downward spiral in my story starts when Congress decided Americans were using too much water and reduced the amount new toilets could use per flush. My well-meaning father, Lucas Duque, bankrupted the company trying to develop a water saving toilet that eliminated buckshot and feces in one flush, which we now know is *impossible.*

"I remember Dad ranting after a couple drinks, 'No person should have to eyeball their own buckshot, and they sure as hell shouldn't have to deal with a remnant on holiday, just because tree huggers are concerned about water conservation.' That's what my dad called floaters, 'remnants on holiday.'

The students were howling and finally getting into it. I was hoping they would, I knew we had *one* thing in common. Just like me, most kids think bathroom humor is hilarious. Poor old Rusty looked like his butt was

74

puckered, but I'm sorry, you can't tell my family story without bathroom humor, and he knew that. This was becoming too stressful, so I decided to avoid looking at him for the rest of the speech.

"Anyway, Dad would lose his mind over it, 'Have they seen Lake Michigan? That's a lot of water! We aren't running out anytime soon! Where's the decency? Just give me two gallons, *two gallons!*' Like any man, the more he drank, the more he'd ask for, 'Just give me five gallons, ohhhhhhh, you wouldn't *believe* what we could move with *five* gallons! I could get it all the way to Washington with five gallons!'" I knew not to look Rusty's way, but I felt despair coming from his general direction, like maybe a clipboard had been dropped or thrown.

"Well, enough with the glamour. I was throwing a house party a month before I graduated, the first Duque to graduate from Purdue *without* an engineering degree, and my father shows up. He was there to tell me the twenty-seven-million-dollar trust fund he'd set aside for me was 'revocable,' and that 'revocable' means, 'can be taken away.'

"Our company had released a line of toilets with a new design that didn't work, and the Duque Industrial Fixture Company was no more. My company stock was worthless and what little was left of my trust was being transferred into my mother's name. Our estate in Elgin was foreclosed upon and sold for pennies on the dollar to a country club nemesis of my father's. Good times.

"OK, I've probably gone too far down this road," I fought the urge to look as a chorus of murmured agreement came from Rusty's direction, "but you can imagine the impact it had on a kid who grew up as wealthy as I did. I mean, until then, there wasn't an itch that hadn't been scratched. My wealth had become a big part of my identity, and probably the main thing I was known for, 'The heir to a toilet fortune.' And let's be honest here, when you're not the best-looking guy in the room, having a truckload of money goes a long, long way. I was the guy who picked up the tab for the entire bar at Harry's after Purdue won its big football game, *both times*. I was the guy who'd buy late-night pizza after the bars, for twenty people. Everybody wanted me around because I never minded footing the bill.

"Obviously, when my dad left that night, I was devastated. It didn't take long for my world to start falling apart. I was such a self-centered asshole, even my girlfriend left me, and she was probably the only person who *might* have liked me for who I was, instead of what I could pay for.

I didn't give up though. I still had advantages, unlike most, I was lucky enough to have a college degree and no student loans. I went into real estate, humbled myself and worked really hard. It was a slow start, but eventually I was allowed to invest my own money into the deals we were buying. After a while, the projects started adding up, and before I knew it, I had significant capital holdings. I was a success.

"Had you asked me as a trust fund kid if I could get a job and be successful on my own, I would have told you I could, maybe even convincingly. But on the inside, I wouldn't have believed a single word of it. Now, I don't have twenty-seven million dollars, but the money I have, I made myself and people, that's a great feeling. Not everyone can say they're self-made. I surprised myself. It's a little embarrassing I was *forced* to do it, but who cares? The important thing is I did it. Maybe you can surprise yourself too?

"With that out of the way, let's get started, who here believes in time travel?" Every geek in the auditorium raised their hand. Some felt strongly enough to *stand* and raise their hand. "That's kind of a Star Trek question, I know, but don't be worried, I'm talking about *pretend* time travel."

Any geeks left on their feet fell to their seats, disillusioned. The enthusiasm of the entire geek student body had left the building, "*Pretend* I travelled back in time to be here today with information from the future. Several great nuggets of wisdom you wanted to send back, to give yourself a heads-up. Is that too confusing?" I could see right away it was.

"Ok, scratch that. Let's say you have Mr. Sheehan for History this year and your good friend had Mr. Sheehan for History last year. A good friend would let you know that ol' man Sheehan makes his tests, *including the mid-term and the final,* out of the study guide questions at the end of each chapter. Well, with that scoop, History's going to be a whole lot easier, isn't it? That good friend is performing the same sort of time travel I'm doing for you here today. I mean, I'm not giving out specific answers, but hopefully some thoughtful insight to make it easier for you to figure out your own answers.

76

"Think about it, what if your friend told you this after you got a crappy grade in History? You'd wish you could go back in time and tell yourself everything was *right there,* in the study guide that nobody ever looks at, *because it's a study guide.* But you can't do that, can you? You have to rely on a friend who has already learned the lesson and been thoughtful enough to 'send it back,' like me.

"Honestly, I went to my last high school reunion and if I could do legit time travel, I'd love to go back and tell myself who turned into what, because I'd been giving a lot of people, *way* too much credit. The most popular kid from my high school, the Homecoming King, sells cologne at a kiosk inside the worst mall in town. I could give you other examples, although I'm not sure you guys would appreciate how crazy it is that Sean Calligan, the tough as nails transfer student from Virginia, ended up as Chief Creative Officer of the vaunted Miami fashion house, Marc Fischer Couture.

"Hopefully today we can put things into a little bit better perspective, that's the first nugget of wisdom I'd like to share with you. It's super important because life is all about perspective, how you choose to look at things. Remember to keep things in perspective and life will be easier, for you and probably the people around you.

Let me give you an example, think of somebody who had just been told they had three months left to live. That's a horrible situation. Could you think of anybody who'd jump at the chance to trade places with them? No? What about a political prisoner in Siberia, wrongly jailed in a Gulag, starving on mush, forced to eat cockroaches in the dark, with no human contact, sleeping on concrete, knowing this would be their routine until death, however long that took.

"Do you think that person would want to trade places? Three months to go outside, visit loved ones, blow the rest of your dough on great food? Three months to live sounds fantastic to someone locked away in a Siberian prison! Who do think would get the most out of their last three months of life? Someone angry they were robbed of a longer life, or someone grateful they weren't locked away in a Siberian prison? Perspective.

"Sure, that's extreme, but just remember this, as bad as you have it, someone else has it worse, so buck up little ponies! That's the truth. My mom always says, *'life is what you make it,'* and it drives me crazy because she's always right. Now I say it all the time. Sometimes you don't want to hear it, mostly because it's always true. If you don't like something, do something about it, life is what you make it."

"I doubt high schools have changed much from my days and I suspect there's a giant group of you here at Grady that feels like you don't fit in. I get it." Several pockets of nerds in the auditorium raised unsolicited hands, signaling they were beyond help. I ignored them, "Nerds, geeks, stoners, awkward people; whoever doesn't seem to fit in here, my heart goes out to you and I mean that, like I said, you're the reason I came here today. And now that I've explained perspective, I'd like to help you use it with this next nugget of wisdom from the future."

I went to the very front of the stage, mostly because I'm pretty sure I made a judgey face when the nerds raised their hands about not fitting in, I wanted everyone to know, despite that short lapse of control, this was being delivered with nothing but good intentions.

"So here's the thing, I didn't come here to tell you I feel sorry for you, and what you've gone through. I won't waste either of our time with that because that's not gonna do a fuh... That's not going to do anything for you."

Out of the corner of my eye I could see vigorous movement from Rusty. I did almost drop an f-bomb, so despite my previous resolve to avoid looking in his direction, I caved. His arms were spread wide in disbelief. He broke into a filming mime and stage whispered, "For the love of God, cut the swearing!"

Wait. *I'm on camera?* This is being *filmed?* I turned to the other side of the stage, which looked identical, except instead of an upset Principal, there were a pair of greasy haired A/V geeks, manning the oldest camera I'd ever seen. *Game on.*

"Like I said, I didn't come here to tell you I felt sorry for you, not at all. I came here to give you *great* news. *Fantastic* news. Ready? *High school doesn't last forever.*" I let the obvious soak in, "Seriously, that's what you need to know. *High school is such an incredibly small part of your life.* It might seem like it'll go on forever, but only because you don't know any better. If you hear anything I say here today, hear this, *high school doesn't go on forever and it will be over before you know it, good or bad.*

High school has its moments of greatness. It's the first time in your life you have a little bit of freedom and you feel like an adult, which is exciting, I get it. That's why high school can feel like *everything* for someone in the middle of it, especially if they've lost perspective. But I'm here to give you perspective and tell you that High school is *nothing* in the big picture.

"This is your life, at the end of the day it's up to you guys. Remember, *life is what you make it.* High school is what you make it. High school can seem like forever if you let it. It can give you insecurities, invisible scars you'll wear for the rest of your life if you let it. The four short years of high school can impact *your entire adult life* if you let it. Please, what I'm telling you today is, don't let it. *Don't let such a small, inconsequential period of your life, have such a disproportionate impact on who you become as an adult.* Don't let it. High school is nothing in the big picture, trust me.

"Think of it this way; if you're eighteen when you graduate from here and you live to be eighty, you'll have sixty-two more years left to live. Sixty-two years is a helluva long time! Some of you will spend those sixty-two years clinging to four years of high school, but hopefully, the rest of you will be moving onward and upward, while the homecoming king squirts cologne on your wrist at the mall and the homecoming queen cleans your teenager's toilet four times a month.

"The world is so much bigger than this high school and these four walls. You can run as far away from here as you want, because you'll never hit a wall that says you can't go any further. You might have to jump into a boat or get a passport, but where you stop is up to you and not the walls around this place.

"Dr. Winkle told me half of you won't go to college after high school. You should reconsider. College is different now, it's not elitist, college is for everyone. Don't worry about college being too hard, it's not, trust me. Most of my friends are dim bulbs and they made it through. They had to put in the work, but they made it through. Even if you have to flip burgers while you go to community college, you should do it. It shouldn't be a question of *whether* to go, it should be a question of *where* to go.

"Why is it so important? I'm oversimplifying it, but college is more than getting a degree, it's where you'll find out who you are, and what you want to be. It's tough to get anything right at eighteen, let alone a career path. College is better than high school because you can expect to be left alone. There are very few meatheads in college and most of them are easily avoidable. This gives you time to learn independence and explore your interests while you figure out who you are and what you want to do. You only get one life; if you are smart, you'll make the most of it. You might even be able to go to a party or two while you're in college. Hell, you might figure out who you are at a party there. Once—"

I caught myself late, I regretted both the swearing and the party references instantly, and I knew not to look back at Rusty. "So that was my second point, college is for everybody now, you should use it to figure out what you want to do with your life. If you have a chance or a desire to go to college, do it or find a way to do it, period.

"The next nugget I would tell you is a favorite of mine, it's a concept proven all around us, every day. *There is somebody for everybody.* In a sappy romantic way? Sure, absolutely. But you should know that it's just as relevant, if not more, for friendships. You'll make countless, lifelong friendships *after* high school, trust me. You haven't met them yet, maybe they're in a different auditorium right now, but I'm going to go out on a limb and say they're probably feeling the same way about a lot of the same things you are.

"I say it to myself all the time, *there is somebody for everybody.* It makes me happy, and it brings me comfort, it should bring you comfort too. It's one of the things that makes the world go round, people loving people. Even if you feel alone sometimes, you are anything but alone.

"Let me put it in a way you can understand. In my high school there were twelve hundred students; at Purdue University there were thirty-five thousand! If I found three friends out of twelve hundred students at my high school, then theoretically, I could expect *eighty-seven* friends from the thirty-five thousand students at Purdue... Those are fantastic odds.

"And listen, if it turns out college isn't for you, don't sweat it, because these days you don't have to go to college to meet people with similar interests, you guys have the internet. Consider this, if you're a person who loves parading around, belting out the *Sound of Music* in German, while playing an accordion and wearing nothing below the waist, you're probably one in a million. The good news is the earth's population is almost *seven billion* people. That means there's probably forty-three members in the Osaka, Japan chapter of the 'Parading around, belting out the *Sound of Music* in German, while playing an accordion and wearing nothing below the waist' fan club. Trust me, *there is someone for everyone and it's a wonderful thing.*

"Another nugget I would pass on to you is a saying from Eleanor Roosevelt, '*Nobody can make you feel inferior without your consent.*' If some meathead calls me a midget, I'm not going to sweat it, because I know I'm five-foot-ten, I'm not a midget. The point is, people can't make you feel bad about yourself unless *you* let them. Don't let them. Embrace who you are. Keep this in perspective; it's easier to embrace who you are if you remember there are thousands of people out there whom you've never met, cheering you on in spirit. Why? *Because they're just like you*, you aren't alone. If you feel alone, go find your people, they're out there, trust me, it's a numbers thing. Seven *billion* people.

"The next nugget from the future I'd share with you is really, really simple and I wish someone would have told me this earlier; *be nice and treat everyone with respect. It*'s just like college, *it's not hard.* My thing is, treat people with respect at first, and if they show over time they don't deserve it, you can stop— let's not go overboard, right? But until then, 'be nice and treat people with respect.' Your life will be so much better for it. And being nice doesn't mean doing nice things for people or stuff like that, sometimes being nice is *not* doing things to people.

"You can tell a lot about people by how they treat the people around them. When we make fun of someone it makes us feel better about ourselves. Everybody wants to feel better about themselves, no matter how good they have it. Don't fall into that trap. If you need to make fun of somebody in a mean way, try not doing it, put your effort into something more productive.

It might seem hard at first, but just like everything else, it gets easier with practice.

"I'm not saying you should become Gandhi or anything, if something happens that needs to be made fun of, you know, that's too funny to ignore, by all means, let loose, but do it in confidence to a friend, don't do it in class or in a situation where it will get back to the person. Treat people with kindness and respect, be nice, and you'll go far, it's another proven, winning combination."

"OK, that's all I can think of from the future right now. I gave Rusty, I mean Dr. Winkle, a copy of my speech and he lost it, so I've been winging it up here the whole time. The last invaluable nugget I want to share with you involves props." As I walked over to the tuning forks, I spied Rusty shaking his head, mouthing a relieved, "*finally*" to his assistant.

"At some point during your freshman year, your physical science teacher probably showed you this experiment. Watch what happens when I strike this tuning fork and set it next to this group of tuning forks."

I struck the fork hard and set it in its stand next to the bigger group of tuning forks.

"Who knows what's going to happen when I stop this from ringing?" Three or four geeks had recovered enough from the disappointment of "pretend" time travel to raise their hands. Naturally, I ignored them.

I touched the fork to stop it from vibrating, "Can you still hear it?" I put the microphone up to the group of tuning forks, the same sound was ringing. I could hear a reaction from the crowd as I pulled out the ringing tuning fork from the larger group and put my microphone next to it. The ringing was the same as the fork I had struck initially.

"Did you see that? I didn't even strike this tuning fork but it's ringing like a—" I caught myself, "None of the other tuning forks are ringing though. All I did was strike that fork and set it next to this group. This tuning fork started vibrating along, but only this one, none of the others. Did anybody see me strike this fork?"

About a hundred smartasses screamed, "*Yeah!*" from the crowd, happy with their super witty outbursts. I was just happy they were listening.

"No, nobody saw me strike this fork because I didn't. This is called *resonance*. When one tuning fork is struck in the vicinity of another with the same natural frequency, they both vibrate. The other tuning forks have different natural frequencies, so nothing happened with them."

"That's what I want to convey to you. This is how life works, this same thing happens inside us. Everybody has their own tuning forks, there is nothing you can do about it. When some fancy pants says something 'resonates' with them, this is what they mean. You've got 'tuning forks' for everything, music, recreational activities, friends, life partners, careers, pets; you name it.

"Take music as an example. I'm lucky, I have multiple tuning forks, one for almost every genre, so I can listen to a bunch of different kinds of music and enjoy myself. Not everyone's so lucky, a couple weeks ago I had a coworker tell me I listened to 'bad music.' That was her opinion of my tuning fork. It's kind of rude when you think about it, like telling me I have a big nose. I can't change what my tuning forks ring to, just like I can't change my big nose. Why would I listen to someone tell me it's bad? My only concern in life should be to keep those tuning forks ringing, and ring the shit out of 'em, right?" I saw Rusty shaking out of the corner of my eye.

"Telling someone their tuning fork is 'bad' is such a self-centered act it should be embarrassing, but most people have no idea and do it anyway. Don't try to run someone else's life, respect people's individuality, and they'll respect yours, that's another proven, winning combination.

"Remember what Eleanor Roosevelt said? *No one can make you feel inferior without your consent.* When my coworker said I listened to 'bad' music, I was unmoved because I knew my tuning forks loved that music, how could they be wrong?

"I hope that makes sense to some of you and you enjoyed this talk. Maybe, hopefully, it's changed your perspective. I'd hate for you to look back and think, "I should have listened to that Parker Duque dude, he was right."

Binggggg! The period bell pierced the air with a singular, obnoxious ring and students started rustling in their seats. I was pretty much done and Rusty was already speed walking to me, grabbing the microphone as everyone in the gym started howling, probably glad my speech, and their day, was over. I was glad too.

About a minute later a second bell interrupted Rusty's final announcements and the entire student body finally went apeshit. A flood of students gave me high fives and other truly original compliments on their way out of the auditorium. Rusty was right, some of them actually listened... *Did I help any of them?* I was basking in this unnatural feeling, thinking, *holy shit, is this what it feels like to do good?*

And then I saw him again.

14

AGAIN?

Little scary guy was dressed in the same outfit he'd been wearing the night before. He was every bit as good looking as he was short, and he'd replaced his vacant countenance with a genuine smile. He was staring at me, clapping. I looked at Rusty and then looked back, but little scary guy was gone. It must have been my mind playing tricks on me because there's no way someone could disappear so quickly. I looked back again and all that was left were some rich kids talking by the same door, smirking at me and laughing, probably because they could.

My little brother Chuy was predictably nowhere to be found so I said goodbye to Rusty who was officiating the mass exodus of students out the auditorium exits. I walked out the way I came in and laughed, probably too hard, as misfits right and left hollered through the crowd about their need to take a Duque.

I was deep into the high school parking lot, twenty feet from my car when I heard him again, "That was great Parker!" My elbow felt little scary guy's iron grip on it. Again.

"Can I help you?" I pleaded.

"You have, you really already have. Gosh Parker, I wish you would have given that speech to my high school. It's probably impossible to see it now, but I didn't fit in, I wasn't one of the popular kids. Everything you said in there was prophetic! You might not realize this, but you just saved lives in there. Maybe even your own!" He was genuinely excited.

"*What did you say?*" I was terrified, little scary guy was freaking me the fuck out.

"Now, don't hold me to this because I still have to talk to Peaches." he looked troubled, but in a good way. "This is a new wrinkle now isn't it?" He laughed and slapped his thigh. I could see that he had *my* car keys in his thigh slapping hand. *How does he do that?* He was genuinely tickled by something, maybe because he'd extracted my keys so easily, without me noticing. *From my front pocket.*

He was so fast I hardly even saw him move, but all the sudden I was dizzy like I'd just had my bell rung by Mike Tyson.

"What the..."

He held me up and I heard my car beep twice as he unlocked it. "Wow you are a tough cookie! I usually knock people out with a punch like that, and you're still here aren't you? But that's great. Listen, don't get your hopes up because like I said, I still have to talk to Peaches about it, but I think we're going to take you with us instead of killing you." I tried my best to look back at him in a manner a real man might look at his assailant, but I passed out.

"Mr. Duque. Parker! Oh dear, you're not nearly as tough as I thought." I looked up to see little scary guy slapping me in the face lightly and found myself sitting in the passenger's seat of my own car.

"Did you just say you were going to kill me?" I asked. I was probably ten inches taller than him and at least fifteen pounds heavier but I was in absolute fear of little scary guy. He just seemed... superhuman?

"My, this is an awkward situation! Yes, I've been ordered to suppress operational leakage by any means necessary," he was glowing, "it's the first time we've had red level clearance and Peaches and I are having a ball! An absolute ball! If this isn't the way to go out, mmm, Lord help me!" I wasn't quite sure how to take this excitable little man. "Please don't get upset Parker" he continued, happy as a lark, "As you may or may not know already, you only had another week or so to live anyway."

"What? What do you mean I only have another week to live? What in the fuck is going on? Who are you?" I started to get testy, and the smile disappeared from his face like I had pooped in his soup.

"Listen Parker, while I do appreciate your inquisitive nature, you need to let me ask the questions. If you don't, I'll kill you right now and toss you in a car trunk with Brock Martin's dick in your mouth."

Brock Martin? I thought to myself, *what the—*

He grabbed me by the arm and pulled me closer to him, "You'd be dead right now had you not moved me with your speech back there. But you need to understand this, so I'll be perfectly clear, you give me one fucking ounce of trouble or try to run from me and so help me God I will kill you on the spot. I can shoot you in front of the Chief of Police if I want to. That's how far my clearance goes on this. So, do not, fucking, test me. Do you understand? I don't want to kill you, I really don't, *but I will.* It would actually be much easier if I just killed you." He stopped and appeared to be thinking.

Oh my God. This guy is completely insane. He's nuts, and he's going to kill me, "I'm sorry. I'm sure you can understand, this is just a shock to me. I honestly don't even know what's going on."

Little scary guy put his hand back down on the seat. "Brock Martin didn't tell you anything? Really? Weren't you at the bar with him?"

"Yes, but I thought he was crazy. He told me aliens were blowing the earth in two with magnets."

"He's right."

"Come on!"

"Well, without going too far into it, he was right for the most part. He told me everything he knew, and he didn't know shit, but he knew enough. So do you now I'm afraid."

"What do I know?" I was confused.

Little scary guy sighed, "There are identical cylinders all around the world, perfectly aligned, that when blown up will cut the Earth in half. They're self-coring electromagnetic metal cylinders. Our scientists don't know what type of metal it is because they can't remove a sample to study. The cylinders are indestructible. We can't stop them; they're slowly digging themselves down into the Earth. That's actually what self-coring means, I didn't know that."

"Do we know it's aliens?"

"Not confirmed, but I've laid eyes on the cylinder in Iowa, and it's unlike anything I've ever seen. It's definitely the real deal, I'm sorry. I hoped it was a joke too, but this isn't a movie, it's as real as real gets. That's why I have clearance to kill anybody I even *think* knows about it, to keep the world from panicking."

"I understand that concept. I think we can work out a deal. You don't have to kill me. I won't tell anybody, and if I do, nobody will believe me. Please. I don't even know your name. Let me go. I promise I won't tell anyone."

"Negative Parker Duque, absolutely not. I'm not going out as a soldier who neglected his last order. World panic would be worse than getting blown up. Let's talk about this though, it must be horrible having your family name used as a common bathroom phrase."

"Apparently it won't be an issue for too much longer."

"Well, that's a good way to look at it!" He seemed amused, "I probably shouldn't have told you! It's a big bummer, but Peaches and I have made our peace with it. Oh Gawd, Peaches just cried for hours when I told her. But Parker Duque, here's what I've found in life; You always have to look at the bright side! Peaches and I are going to be together until the end of time!"

I wished he wasn't so excited about the world blowing up, "Where are we going? Do you mind me asking?"

"Well, we are waiting here for my little peachy pooh first!" He said as he pulled my car over to the curb on N. Highland Ave.

"This is a nice car for something so old. In fact, I think we'll drive your car because ours is starting to smell like your friend." He took my keys out of the ignition and got out of the car, giggling at the apparent joke he'd just cracked. The Ford Crown Victoria in front of us had government plates and when little scary guy opened the trunk, I saw it also had a dead Brock Martin. The cause of death was probably related to the bullet hole in his face, which I was alarmingly OK with.

I'm sorry, but dicks like Brock Martin deserved to get shot in the face. Everyone thought Brock went to Dartmouth because he always wore Dartmouth gear around the neighborhood. He went to *chiropractic school.* If someone asked if or when he'd attended the school, he'd answer, "I wouldn't if they begged me, I'm just a fan of their sports program." *C'mon.*

When Little Scary Guy grabbed a black backpack from underneath the dead Dartmouth fan's body, Brock's lifeless arm popped out of the car's trunk opening. Little Scary Guy balanced the backpack on one shoulder while using his free hand to tuck Brock's lifeless arm back in while slamming the trunk door down. It didn't work. Brock's arm had fallen back into the opening and the trunk door bounced off the dead dick's arm, springing back open. In the fastest move I'd ever witnessed; little scary guy steadied the trunk door with one hand and pumped bullets two and three in Brock's face.

Little scary guy looked to me, "Oops, I thought he was still alive." He shrugged with an embarrassed smile like maybe he got caught taking the wrong umbrella out of a PTA meeting or something.

I was trying not to look and even though I missed it completely, I could tell his second attempt didn't work either, because the trunk door bounced back into view. Little Scary Guy disappeared from view, then sprang up, facing me again, pretend jamming Brock's freshly severed finger up his own nose. He was thrilled with this improvisation, looking to me for my approval, which I was happy to give since he might kill me, but also because Brock was a dick and it was kind of funny even though the severed finger was gross.

With the lifeless, nine fingered body of Brock Martin in the trunk of the car in front of us it was clear I was in deep shit. Any doubt this might be some elaborate hoax was out the door. I was either going to die at the hands of some crazy midget-ish superhuman or have the world disappear underneath my feet. Little scary guy came over to the car and opened my door.

For some reason I wasn't scared, "Are you really telling me the truth? This is really happening? *Aliens* are blowing up the Earth?"

"Parker, I'm so sorry to tell you, but it is true. As outlandish as it sounds, especially after you made such a difference to those kids today, it's all for nothing." He opened his wallet to show me his badge, "You can call me Dusty." He was a CIA agent with a fancy rank and title, but what stood out to me was his name wasn't Dusty. It was Denis and it only had one "N" in it, like the way you spell penis.

Denis took me by the elbow again, opened my rear door and gingerly helped me slide into my own backseat, then slid in himself. He was so small we both fit on the passenger side, but before I could slide over to make room, I asked him, "Denis, what are you—"

He struck me like a mongoose, square on my thigh. I was dumbfounded, I barely saw him move and the pain was completely out of proportion to the strike. It was so intensely excruciating I might have, if given the option, elected to hack my entire leg off with a dull axe, because I guarantee you it would have hurt less.

"If you call me that name again, you're fucking toast. Do you understand me Parker Duque? Last warning." He was pissed, big time, "I will gut you so fast you'll be able to watch yourself die." I shut my eyes to avoid his gaze and started thinking about being gutted. It would probably hurt less than the charley horse he just gave me. When I opened my eyes again, Denis was back behind the wheel of my car. I was crying now. I felt so much pain. I felt so hopeless. I knew I should probably say sorry to the little psycho, but it felt better and less dangerous to continue sobbing and holding my leg. Clearly, Denis had taught the CIA course in charley horses.

"Parker, I'm so sorry. I must work on my temper; it gets the best of me from time to time. Actually, I guess it's useless to work on it now!" He laughed his scary little big laugh. "That's one of the great things Parker, we don't have to work on improving ourselves anymore. We don't have to watch what we eat, obey any laws. We don't have to do shit. And please Parker, please call me Dusty. As you can imagine, I got made fun of quite a bit for my name. My father was illiterate."

Through the haze of my pain, my attention was drawn to the apartment building across the street, where a massive black object spilled quickly out the side door. To my amazement, the largest woman I'd ever seen in comfort shoes, began an impossibly graceful sprint the entire length of the building, then disappeared quickly behind it.

I've got no problem with big people, if you know the science of obesity you know they can't help it, and you should feel lucky you're not in their shoes. I just try to always remember, *there's somebody for everybody*, and leave them alone.

It's harder to ignore big folks like this woman though, she was a giant. I'm talking about what my brother Beau calls, "I gave up" obese. Seriously obese like, "take the door frame out to get them to the hospital before they die" obese.

Moments later this massive giant appeared around the far side of the apartment building, walked at a brisk pace toward us and dropped, like a cat, off a five foot tall retaining wall onto the sidewalk. I watched, unable to speak, her athleticism was remarkable, she was easily six and a half feet tall, maybe taller. She continued nonchalantly, straight towards us, she was *gigantic*, larger than I had originally thought possible.

"Here's my Peachy Pooh!" Dusty squealed. There was no mistaking this little man's affection towards this incredibly large woman.

The giant crossed the street diagonally in a mind-blowingly athletic jog and slowed to a walk as she approached us. She smiled directly at Dusty as she squeezed herself through a six-foot opening between my car and the government owned Crown Victoria in front of us.

After nearly ripping the door off its hinges she poured her massive body into the front seat of my car, ass first. After she settled in, she tilted her meaty head to the side and awaited an eager smooch from her little Denis, who was just as eager to climb her mass and give her a teeny smooch on her giant, sweat glistened cheek. *There is somebody for everybody.*

15

PEACHES

"Who's this asshole?" She tried to turn towards me, but it was physically impossible because she was so incredibly obese, "Did you save him for me?"

I felt like I should move to the driver's side to distribute the weight as my poor car seemed like it was at a 45-degree angle to the street, which couldn't be good for the suspension. Peachy Pooh had no visible neck, just a blocky nub set atop a huge ball. I heard the power seat controls strain under her weight as she tried in vain to give herself more room. I lifted my injured leg over and slid to the driver's side behind Dusty, pleased I hadn't been shot in the process. She grabbed the rearview mirror and used it to get a good look at me. Clearly, she had adapted to her lack of mobility.

"Peaches, this is Parker Duque, her husband." Dusty said as he motioned towards the apartments. I think Peaches shrugged, but it was hard to tell because she had no neck. She looked amused as she looked at me in the rearview mirror and said, "Oops."

"Oops what?" I asked.

"Parker, I have some more bad news for you." Dusty delivered the news slowly like a good friend might deliver salacious gossip, "Your wife was having an affair."

I was stunned. I guess after yesterday it shouldn't have come as a surprise, but the information coming from these two killers could only mean one thing.

"Emphasis on *was!*" Peaches laughed. "Murder- suicide. It happened about a half hour ago."

Dusty looked at Peaches with a smile and screwed himself sideways, somehow getting past her massive body to deliver another kiss on her cheek, "I just love how good you are at your job. Do you know that? You know you didn't have to bother with that anymore, didn't you?" Peaches could hardly contain her smile as Dusty gushed, "Your professionalism knocks me out. Wait, you did it for sport, didn't you?"

Peaches was so proud of herself; it was almost as though she had pulled forty orphans from a blazing house fire and was ready to go back in for the gerbils.

"Did they both write notes?" Dusty asked coyly. I still had a hard time believing any of this could be true, including the cheating. I wondered if Peachy Pooh killed an innocent couple by mistake. I just couldn't see Margot cheating with someone in *that* building, she would have thought it was way too gross. When I reasoned Peaches had probably killed the wrong woman, I was surprised, and alarmed by my disappointment.

"No, I got the lady to write one, he wouldn't buy it, I made it work with just one note though, she was dumb as hell, she could hardly write a sentence."

Maybe it *was* Margot.

"Hey Asshole, if it helps you at all, he was an unemployed loser."

"Thanks, they must have been perfect for each other." I said.

"She was beautiful though; I'll give you that. I don't know how *you* landed a piece of ass like that. You rich or something?"

I looked at the fat blob in front of me and thought with strange indifference about Margot cheating on me with another man. I could rationalize how she thought I was ugly and didn't want to have sex with me, but I never thought she'd *cheat* on me, it seemed so cold. I wondered how many people knew? I wondered if the people that knew thought about it while they talked to me. The thought was incredibly embarrassing.

You know you're having a pretty tough day if your wife being murdered is one of the bright spots. I thought about it more and couldn't help crying. On top of my hangover and the incredible pain still throbbing in my thigh, this had to be a new record for the longest, continuous string of bad news ever delivered to one person.

Good morning Mr. Duque, you're going to die today, your whole family is going to die within the week, and your wife has been cheating on you but actually that's moot, because we just killed her, and you'll probably be dead soon too.

"Parker, sweetie, you're going to have to pull it together. I'm not going to listen to a grown man cry for very long. If you don't stop, I'm just going to go ahead and kill you. I'm sorry, I understand, I really do, but I'm no longer working on my patience because like I told you, I no longer have to." Peaches high fived Dusty surprisingly high considering the strength it must take to get that ham hock of an arm up in the air. She grabbed the rearview mirror and looked back at me, "Do you want to shoot her a couple times?"

"We don't have time dear." Dusty said testily.

"Oops, sorry Asshole. Don't say I didn't try to help!"

I stopped sobbing and sat back against the seat and looked out the window of the car at the row of cute craftsmen bungalows the Virginia Highlands are known for. They'd be space dust in a week.

"You know what, Asshole? It doesn't even matter she was banging a really hot guy with a huge dick." Dusty shot a look over at Peaches. "What?" she said back to him. "You know I always look; it was huuuuuge." Dusty shook his head laughing, looked back at the road and pulled out into traffic. "Hey asshole, don't you want to know why it doesn't matter she was banging a really hot guy with a huuuge dick?"

I didn't answer.

"Awe shit! Did you already tell him?" She seemed mad at Dusty, "How come you don't ever let me tell nobody?"

"I do! Peaches, sweety, you get to tell everybody!"

"You told that dick last night! I wanted to tell him, and you just had to steal the spotlight!"

"He knew already! I just filled him in on the stuff he didn't know!"

"Exactly" Peaches was upset. She was so fat I could hear her breathe.

"Peaches, I let you shoot him in the face! It would have been so easy for me to kill him right there on the street, but I knew you always wanted to shoot a

94

dick in the face. I brought him back for you, didn't I?" Like any boyfriend, Dusty was upset he wasn't getting credit for being thoughtful. He grabbed her sausage fingered paw, "Just so you could shoot him in the face."

I never knew that divvying up murders and breaking horrible news could put such a wedge in between a couple so in love. You never hear about that on Oprah.

"Oh, butter biscuit, that was special, you know how I love trying new ways of killing people." Peaches tried to turn her massive body towards Dusty in an effort to give him a "Thanks for letting me shoot that guy in the face last night" smooch. She gave up as quick as she started though, probably because she remembered she couldn't turn her massive body anywhere except a wheat field or something.

"I know you told this asshole, so I'm killing him, right? I think that's only fair."

"He's not an asshole Peaches. He's a wonderful, understanding man and that's what I wanted to talk to you about."

"Help me take this jacket off first; I'm sweating like a cute little piggy." Dusty and Peaches giggled and wrestled panels of nylon for two or three minutes until they had somehow extricated her from her windbreaker. I helped Dusty wrestle the windbreaker into the back seat like a troublesome parachute and I couldn't help but notice it would double nicely as a four-person tent if you were in a pinch. Peaches was wearing a black sleeveless shirt and looked like ten pounds of fat stuffed into a five pound bag.

Naked or exposed fat people almost always make me throw up if I look at them too long. And here I found myself in the unenviable position of being less than two feet away from Peaches and the cottage cheese factory she had working on her arm. My mouth started to fill up with saliva, I knew I was close to hurling. I also knew after I threw up, Dusty would probably have had enough of me, good speech or not. Would he snap my neck without me even seeing him move or would he let Peachy Pooh shoot me in the face to get himself out of the doghouse? I had to get myself back under control.

Miraculously, I was able to calm down. I just looked out the window while reminding myself how much it will suck to die right now, regardless of the fact I would die in another week or so. I wanted that week. I'm single again and I have six million dollars in the bank!

I had fought and clawed my way back into money for almost a decade and a half and finally reached a point where I could relax a little, and now some fucking aliens want to go ahead and blow us up. I remember when I was little, I used to "melt" ants on the sidewalk with a magnifying glass. I wondered if the aliens were going to have fun with us before they blew us up. I felt like I'd just climbed a mountain and Peaches, Dusty, and some little green men were waiting for me at the top with baseball bats. I needed to start thinking about how I would get away from Dusty and Peaches; I had nothing to lose.

With her jacket off, Dusty turned again to Peaches, "I almost missed him, did I tell you that? After you left to follow her, he came stumbling out of the carriage house. That would have sucked."

"Who?" Peaches asked

"Peaches, were you even listening to me?" Dusty shrugged it off and shot a thumb my direction, "Mr. Duque here. I followed him to the high school where he gave a wonderful speech that would've really made a difference to those kids if the Earth weren't about to be blown in two. I wish when I was in high school someone would've told me the things he said to those smelly kids today. I recorded the speech with my Fanny Pack Camera; let's take him to the Nest and I'll play the speech for you. If you watch it and still want to kill him afterwards, I'll clean up the mess."

"Do you mean it?" she asked.

"Heck, I'll hold him for you, if you promise to aim better than Nashville." Dusty laughed, "He seems like a decent man; I'd rather you kill him anyway."

"Dusty, you're such a softy. I'll watch it for you because I love you," she grabbed the rear view mirror to look at me again, "and then I'm going to kill him."

I was trying to keep looking out the window, away from Peaches, when I saw something move out of the corner of my eye. When I looked over, I knew I was a goner. Dusty was gently rubbing Peach's gigantic arm. As he was moving over the different regions of her gigantic appendage, his hand sunk into her flesh like he was trying to flatten a fitted sheet on a waterbed.

Each pass of Dusty's tiny hand revealed endless cottage cheese. I projectile vomited instantly.

It happened like a hiccup. I knew it was coming but there was nothing I could do. I heard a strange noise as I was unloading what was left of my stomach into the back seat of my own car. It wasn't a gun trigger clicking like I thought it might be, it was something less expected. Peaches and Dusty were laughing so hard that I started laughing too, even before I was done hurling.

That's when I *really* knew I was a goner, because that's how psychotic people kill innocent people. They laugh and get the innocent person to start laughing too, nervously at first, and then when the innocent person starts laughing in earnest, the psychotic person stops cold, pulls out their weapon, says something crazy, and kills them on the spot.

But nothing, we all just kind of quit laughing together, no killing. I wiped my mouth and looked out the window to see the sign for the Peachtree Dekalb Airport wave like a flag in the breeze, only I knew from experience it was a huge metal billboard and shouldn't be waving in the breeze.

"What the?" I looked down at my leg and saw Dusty, laughing again, holding my knee steady so he could finish unloading whatever the giant syringe *sticking out of my thigh* had in it.

16

ROOM WITH A VIEW

It was ironic how bad I felt when I woke up because I might have been in the world's most comfortable, luxurious bed, in a room that was just as fancy and impressive. The bedroom's oversized double doors were left open, and I could see I was in an ultra-exotic supervillain type hideaway, straight out of James Bond-ville.

Floor to ceiling plate glass windows framed an incredible ocean view, but it wasn't nearly as incredible as the pain I was feeling. I couldn't move at all and I assumed it was my worst fear, total paralysis, although I didn't actually bother checking because I was afraid it would hurt too much. A few minutes later I started weeping when I realized I wasn't paralyzed, and it might still be possible to crawl to a car and drive it into a tree or a wall or something. You know it's bad when you feel like only death can stop your pain.

Considering all I had just gone through, it was only fitting that I woke up in an exotic, clifftop lair. I had been kidnapped by a tiny, violent, unnaturally strong government assassin whose portly girlfriend was inclined to kill me for shits and giggles. What did the tiny killer do to me? It was so hard to move. Whatever drug he injected me with must have come with a label that said, "Large animals only, DO NOT use on humans." I wanted to cry out of frustration but crying felt like it might hurt more than help.

Thinking was the only thing that didn't hurt, so naturally I thought about the end of the world, and soon my heart ached as much as my actual body. The end of the Duques, the end of Piper, the end of all my favorite places; Virginia Highlands, Moe's and Joe's, Lake Rabun, Purdue. What a bummer, I haven't gone back to Purdue since I graduated. When I lost my trust fund, I felt like I'd died, and nobody showed up at my funeral because I couldn't pay for the beer anymore.

Even in my very crowded pity party, the person that kept popping up was Sarah Campbell, my college girlfriend. I'd thought about her almost every day for fifteen years, which I know seems pathetic and creepy, I couldn't help it. It's also not lost on me that it's embarrassingly one-sided, because I can assure you, she didn't *ever* think of me.

And if I'm being completely honest, I'm sure Sarah *avoided* thinking about me, because our last memories were so painful, I'm sure they easily overshadowed all the fun we had together. What I conveniently left out is that I was still reeling from my father's trust fund revocation tour when Sarah told me she was pregnant but ending the pregnancy. I begged her not to, not because of the baby, but because I selfishly knew if we had a kid, she'd be stuck with me. She was the only good thing I had left. She wouldn't listen to anything I said.

I was also dumb enough to accuse her of getting pregnant to trap me, then ending the pregnancy after finding out I was broke. Looking back, I recognize that as a major fail, but like I said, I'm not the best-looking guy and Sarah was beautiful, she could've dated anybody she wanted. She had a fit telling me how wrong I was, but she still broke up with me, left school and ended her pregnancy. *Was I that wrong?* It was the last time I saw her.

Nobody ever talks about abortions, but they happen, and it happened to us. It's my biggest failure, start to finish. The pain I caused her, I felt so bad. She had the procedure alone, without me because she hated me, and I couldn't blame her. I was desperate to be there with her and for her, but I had no leverage, this was just another horrible situation my selfishness had put her in. I wrote her a check, made out to the clinic to cover the procedure and when I saw it was cashed, I cried every time I was alone for a month. I hadn't spoken to her since she coldly gave me the name of the clinic over the phone.

I wondered what Sarah was doing right now, was she in tremendous pain like me? I wondered what she looked like; was she still beautiful? Probably. Beau had heard she was married with a couple kids, living in Saugatuck, the same small town in Michigan she grew up in. The thought of her made me ache inside. She was going to die too, and I'd never get to see her again. I used to fantasize about going to Saugatuck. I could have answered all my creepy questions by *accidentally* running into her at her hardware store, but I could never think of a *reasonably* legitimate excuse to go. After I got married, I gave up on the idea because it seemed like cheating on top of the creepy, but I remained deathly curious. I guess it didn't matter now anyway.

After torturing myself over Sarah for too long, I decided to exert just enough energy to throw back the covers and quickly added it to my list of the year's most regretted decisions. I was nude and my penis was ultra-flaccid with alarming shrinkage, like I was dying from the flu. My thigh was already covered with a remarkable bruise and my leg felt like it had been re-attached with rusty barbed wire. I was relieved to spot my clothes in a pile by the open doors, although the relief evaporated almost instantly as my head continued its rhythmic throbbing. Nothing was spared, even my face hurt, and both my eyeballs felt dangerously close to popping out, which would be completely unacceptable.

Everybody's got things they try to avoid at absolutely all costs; situations where the mercy of a quick death is preferrable, I call them "game overs." If you ever see me with an eyeball popped out, go ahead and shoot me. If you don't have a gun, I'll probably be looking for one myself. Having your eyeball popped out or getting *anything* stuck in your eyeball are game overs for me, I'm sorry.

I sat upright and cautiously slid my legs over the side of the bed. A door next to the bed led to an extravagant bathroom where my steady weeping turned into crying when I held my ultra-flaccid, shadow of a former penis. I knew I couldn't afford to lose the fluids I was peeing into the toilet my family didn't make. I willed myself to stop peeing the entire time, but it didn't work. I put my clothes back on and drank out of the bathroom faucet for damn near twenty minutes before I came up for air. The water helped, I was no longer looking for an easy way to die as I ventured beyond the bedroom, out into the modern and spacious supervillain lair.

I realized why Dusty referred to it as "The Nest." Judging from the dramatic views, we were perched far above a stunning blue ocean. As I scanned the horizon through the endless wall of glass, I saw Dusty and Peaches at the edge of the cliff, doing yoga or tai chi or something.

Dusty was wearing tightey whiteys and Peaches donned a painted-on set of black spandex workout gear that left no fold to the imagination. As you might've expected, I violently hurled about four gallons of water and a decent amount of Pabst Blue Ribbon all over the window. I used a People magazine to squeegee the hurl further down the window, hoping to make it less noticeable. It didn't really work. Giving them less reasons to kill me seemed savvy, but I felt so bad I half welcomed death at the hands of Peaches.

Searching around the kitchen I found no food in any of the cabinets. What kind of nest didn't have food? Were they going to eat *me?* I could easily see Peaches eating anything, *and a lot of it.* I felt like I was going to throw up again if I didn't eat something quickly. I opened the refrigerator and there were several carafes of Orange juice and nothing else. I grabbed the carafe closest to me. The orange juice was so incredibly delicious after I started, my body took over and I couldn't stop until I'd drained the entire carafe. Oops.

I felt like making a run for it, but I had just thrown up violently and drank a shitload of *orange juice*, so any escape requiring strenuous movement was definitely out of the question unless it involved more hurling. I also had no idea where I was, and I likely had only one shot to pull off any escape. I probably didn't have long to escape; I had a feeling Dusty had already done as much as he could to protect me from his girlfriend's passion for killing assholes.

I looked at them through the window again, both were remarkable athletes, although it appeared Dusty had demonstrably better balance. They also had a table with stuff on it that resembled food, so I decided to look death in the eye and headed out towards them. I walked over a long, bluestone patio and up several stone steps to the perch-like rock formation Dusty and Peaches were balancing on.

Dusty's body was specimen-like and on the absolute opposite end of the spectrum was the rotund athletic killing machine, Peaches. *Did they have sex?* I had to change mental course immediately or I'd have thrown up again, and my disappearing penis was my body's way of telling me I needed to keep that orange juice inside me.

Dusty was balanced perfectly in some Yoga stance on the very edge of the cliff; his arms and legs were ripped and bulging, with veins weaving in and out of muscles I didn't even know existed. I stopped less than two feet away from both of them, but their concentration was so intense they didn't hear me, or if they did hear me, they chose not to acknowledge my presence.

I looked at the table behind us and my heart did somersaults when I saw a bag of off-brand powdered sugar donuts sitting innocently next to a fruit dish and yet another carafe of orange juice. I looked at the off-brand powdered sugar donuts, then back at Dusty balanced on the cliff's edge on one foot with his arms held out to the side. I had to hand it to him, I about shit my pants just watching him. I wondered why he felt the need to do yoga *on the edge of a cliff.* He should be filming it; I would.

Dusty slowly moved his arms up until his palms came together in a pointed position straight above his head while still balancing on one foot. Once he locked into position, he began more rhythmic breathing. He had to be superhuman, one wrong move and he'd fall hundreds of feet down a rocky cliff. Peaches clearly didn't trust her balance as much because she was about three feet back from the edge and doing the same pose except with two feet on the ground. I bet if she tried to put all that weight on one leg it would break.

I felt weird like maybe I should announce myself because they still hadn't noticed me standing behind them. I was their captive, so I expected there was some form of etiquette to follow but it wasn't as though I'd snuck up there like a *ninja*, did I really need to announce my obvious presence? Again, I felt like less is more, especially coming from an asshole. The bag of donuts looked so delicious. For some reason I was less afraid of Peaches than Dusty, but I knew any donut I took would be a donut taken from her, by an *asshole.*

I looked at the moody giant again and decided it wasn't worth the risk. The disappointment was crushing.

Was Dusty watching me from a yoga induced higher plane? Had I made a move, was he waiting to tell me the donuts were earmarked for the sumo girl of his dreams, Peachy Pooh? I looked at the donuts again, they were off-brand but like I said, they looked *delicious*. I looked back at Dusty, balanced perfectly, literally on the edge of a *cliff*, which made me nervous, so I looked back at the donuts. I wondered if they were made by Hostess but didn't pass muster, then sold to a reseller who slapped their label on the bag. Honestly, I didn't care, I loved all powdered sugar donuts.

Then I pushed Dusty as hard as I could off the cliff.

17

CLIFF DIVING

Dusty didn't say, "You fucking dick Parker" or anything like I would've, had I been pushed off a cliff. He didn't fight the push or try to turn, instead, he jumped gracefully off the cliff like a platform diver, arms spread, doing a graceful slow-motion flip, and landing like a cat would, twenty feet below on an outcropping of rocks I didn't even know was there.

Now, when I say, "landing like a cat would," that's *wildly* misleading, because although he did land on all fours like a cat would, he didn't land *softly* like a cat would. By the time Dusty hit that outcropping, he was falling so fast he smashed down pretty much like the Coyote does in the roadrunner cartoons, just not as flat. Peaches and I were both in shock; the fleshy "thump" Dusty's body made landing on the rock was sickening.

"You little asshole!" she said and dropped to her knees at the edge of the cliff, attempting to get a better view of where Dusty had crash-landed. "Baby! Baby! Are you alright? Oh, Baby your arm!" I ran behind the breakfast table seeking protection, but the big woman didn't come after me. That's when I came up with another genius idea.

Peaches was kneeling at the edge of the cliff looking at her little guy when I shouted, "Peaches!" and threw the bag of off-brand powdered sugar donuts perfectly, in a slow arc *just* beyond her reach and over the edge of the cliff.

If I didn't know better, I'd say she seemed confused as to why I'd waste a whole bag of off brand powdered sugar donuts, "What in the..." she barked in disgust as she stretched for the donuts. She seemed more pissed at *this* injustice than me pushing Denis off a cliff. To her credit, she almost got a hand on that bag of off brand powdered sugar goodness before she lost her balance, and honestly, it would have been one hell of a grab for anyone that big. She started a slow-motion roll over the edge. She fought her momentum, but it was like watching her try to turn her massive body in the car, it wasn't happening. In an incredible display of athleticism for a large woman still in her comfort shoes, Peaches sprang from the cliff. From what I could gather after the fact, it wasn't to land on another outcropping, she was going after those off-brand powdered sugar donuts.

"Peaches!" I heard from under the cliff, it was Dusty, "Peaches, No, NO, NOOOO!"

I looked over the edge to see Peaches' body violently tumbling down the rock face of the cliff. There was no outcropping of rock to land on and if there were, who's to say the outcropping could even take that kind of impact? It was incredible to see her bounce the way she did. She looked like a gigantic, jelly filled weather balloon, smashing rocks from their billion-year perches with each cliffside impact. Peaches finally slammed into the ocean below creating a mushroom cloud splash that could probably be seen by fishermen five miles out. I looked down and over at Dusty who was bleeding from his forehead and had a sharp bone protruding from his bloodied left arm.

"You killed her! You killed my Peachy Pooh."

Did I though? I'd like to think I just *contributed* to her death. Regardless, I was flying high. What I thought was certain death two minutes ago was now euphoria beyond anything I had ever experienced. I drank as much orange juice as I could before answering Dusty, "No Dusty, you can relax, I didn't kill Peaches. I just threw the donuts. It was her love for off-brand powdered sugar donuts that did her in."

"I'M GOING TO KILL YOU PARKER DUQUE. I AM GOING TO KILL YOU AND IT'S GOING TO TAKE SO LONG, YOU WILL BEG ME TO END YOUR LIFE."

I walked back to the edge, "Dusty, I'm not saying that you can't kill me or that it doesn't scare the hell out of me, but it's hard to take you serious right now, you just don't seem to be in the best position to do it anymore. I mean just look at your arm. You're losing a lot of blood and you still have to climb up this cliff with one arm. Frankly, it seems pretty unlikely, even for you." I had extreme confidence because the wall of rock between Dusty's outcropping and my perch seemed impossible for anyone, even for a healthy Dusty to climb. Even so, given my experience with him so far, if Dusty didn't have a jagged bone protruding from his left arm, I would be shitting my drawers.

Dusty took off his tightey whiteys and used them as a tourniquet on his broken arm.

"Dude." I said, "That is the smallest penis I have ever seen, and you wouldn't believe how small mine is right now."

Dusty didn't say a thing but turned away.

"Oh my gosh, I'm sorry Dusty. I wasn't making fun of you for that. It just came out. I was just surprised, that's all. Your balls seem pretty big though. I bet you're very fertile. Is that why you were so sensitive about your name being spelled like Penis? Because your Denis is so small?"

Poor Dusty. And I mean that. I know he's going to kill me and all, but that's a tough thing to live with. The saying "size doesn't matter" or "It's not the size of the wave but the motion of the ocean" are just to placate those poor dudes with tiny ding dings. Think about it, if you are the biggest, smartest, best looking guy in the room but you had a dick the size of a pinky finger, nine out of ten people wouldn't take you seriously. No matter what you do, you might as well have a little asterisk following you around.

"*Didn't he climb K2 without an air tank and no Sherpa to guide him?*"

"*Yeah, he did, but I heard his dick is the size of a minnow.*"

"*Really, that's probably why he climbs mountains.*"

Dusty growled from below, "*BY THE TIME YOU FIND YOUR WAY INTO TOWN I WILL HAVE CLIMBED UP THIS CLIFF. I WILL NOT STOP UNTIL I FIND YOU AND I AM GOING TO KILL YOU IN THE MOST PAINFUL WAY YOU COULD EVER IMAGINE. IF YOU CAN IMAGINE, MR. DUQUE, PAIN IS SOMETHING THAT I'M VERY GOOD AT.*"

"What, do you think this is a James Bond movie? I'm not leaving you here until I know you're dead. I always wondered why they didn't just shoot

James Bond when they had him instead of leaving him to die by a really slow-moving laser or something. You're a secret agent, wouldn't you want to know your arch nemesis is dead? I would. I'm not letting you climb up and I'm not leaving until you jump off. Game's over Dusty. Go ahead and join Peaches"

"I'm not jumping off." Dusty was still turned away, hiding his small penis and large testes from my sight.

"Dusty, the world is ending anyway, just jump and be with Peaches again. I can't kill you, it's not in my nature, pushing you was hard enough. I'd really appreciate it if you'd just do an assessment of your situation and jump." I laid down to look over the cliff's edge, it made me nervous to stand there. Dusty bent down and turned around with a rock in his hand. I wasn't trying to be mean, but I couldn't help it, "Wow, that's a small penis."

Dusty launched the rock at me and it seemed way off. I intended to say something witty about his missed toss, but all I got out was, "Ha!" because it wasn't a miss. The rock knocked me out cold as it nailed me on the back of my head on its way down.

When I came to, I panicked and looked back over the edge of the cliff to see Dusty climbing, one handed, with only six or seven feet left to go.

"*Fuck!*" I jumped to my feet and got a whole pineapple and a pitcher of orange juice from the table. Even in the middle of a crisis I couldn't resist pounding more fresh squeezed orange juice, I chugged half the carafe and felt the cells in my body gasp in relief as they rehydrated.

"I'm going to enjoy killing you Mr. Duque! You might want to reconsider your situation and jump, because I'm going to make you wish you were dead."

"Dusty, if there's anyone that can do it, it's certainly you. Take a break and let's talk this over."

"Fuck you Duque" He grunted and pulled himself up another foot closer to me. I poured the orange juice all over him and the rocks he was climbing on in an attempt to make them harder to grasp. Dusty screamed as the fresh squeezed orange juice hit his bloody forehead and went into his eyes.

"Do you like pineapple?" I said as I dropped it on him, hitting him squarely in the face. Dusty growled like a bear and continued to look for another handhold.

I grabbed a chair and said, "Hey Dusty, you look tired, take a seat." The chair hit him squarely in the forehead and stopped. He pushed it off and smiled. The climb looked easier; he was going to kill me, slowly. I ran to get another chair.

"Parker, Parker, Parker." As he got closer, this small, tiny penised man with a compound fracture was getting his confidence back, "This is going to be the most fun I've had in quite some time. I'm going to bring you to the brink of death and then pull back. And then I'm going to fuck you in the ass."

I had a second chair waiting and looked over the edge to see him smiling at me.

"Dusty, I don't believe in hitting a man while he is down so don't take this the wrong way, but just out of curiosity, how could that even be possible when your penis is so small? I mean, you don't have the length to get it past my butt cheeks?" I threw the chair at him but completely missed.

Dusty watched the chair sail past him while he hung from one arm, "Oh, Parker boy, don't you worry about my penis, I'm going to use the same giant dildo I used on Peaches' sweet ass last night."

I quickly visualized the act Dusty just alluded to in my mind with Peaches gargantuan white ass front and center. No unicorns frolicking in the mist, just Peaches and her giant dildo.

I threw up acid, bile, and gallons and gallons of delicious, fresh squeezed orange juice all over Dusty in four or five powerful hurls. He would lean one way or the other and try to duck the hurl, but my aim was deadly accurate. I couldn't throw a chair, but I could put hurl anywhere I wanted within a ten-foot radius. With each face shot, Dusty screamed in pain and at one point even tried to use the broken arm to wipe my hurl from his face and eyes, but he couldn't raise it high enough. He looked like a marionette with one missing string. I could see his grip weakening and saw he was slipping off the stone. Within two seconds he was falling again, missing the outcropping by at least a foot, and bouncing down the cliff face, very much like Peaches did, but Peaches, as far as I could tell, never had a leg come off. That must have hurt.

Holy shit. Dusty and Peaches were gone. I wiped my mouth, took in the view and sat in silence, in shock. After a couple minutes my heart stopped racing. Turning around I saw a helicopter parked on the roof. I walked back into the house wondering how CIA operatives have the money to afford this kind of set up?

This all sucked so incredibly much. I guess you could say I'd gotten used to bad shit happening to me, but in this instance, *everybody* shared my bad luck. Even my buddy Tom "Kid" Maxwell, a professional sperm donor and the luckiest son of a bitch I'd ever known, was going to die soon.

I went back into the house and noticed Dusty's black backpack by the fireplace, there was money piled next to it. Upon closer inspection I saw Dusty and Peaches had used stacks of hundred-dollar bills to start a fire. More depressing proof it was the end of the world. I wandered around the house and found my car keys in the trash can, along with Denis and Peaches' CIA badges. If you can believe it, Peaches was her real name, and by judging from her title, Peaches Ancreem Wengerd was Dusty's boss. I also found and managed to avoid her gigantic Dildo even though I felt like it should be thrown over the cliff, for safety reasons.

Through a door that was just off the kitchen I found Dusty's office. There, on the middle of the desk was a folder with a clichéd "TOP SECRET" red stripe printed on it. It was labeled "Operation Icarus," which I couldn't help but envy because that would have been such a cool name for my Big Deal. I opened the file up and read the whole thing, which confirmed everything Brock, Dusty, and Peaches had told me. I had somehow managed to hold on to a little hope that all this might be too crazy to be true but there it was, right in front of me. Pictures of a huge metallic thing, buried in the ground. One of them with two backhoes magnetically crushed to the sides like steamrolled Muppet dolls.

There was a summary of the other "self-coring electro-magnetic" cylinders and their locations around the Earth. Probably the most disturbing was the red page detailing Dusty's orders with a "terminate if necessary" directive that must have sent shivers of joy down Peaches fatigued spine.

I walked outside, torn apart, and sat on the safer part of the cliff where Peaches was exercising. I bawled like a small child, not for the looming destruction of our planet, but for my current situation.

Motherfucker. I lost all my money, and the minute I made it back, *the fucking world's toast.* I thought about all the people in my life and whether I'd even be able to get back to them, or even get to say goodbye. With my luck, when the earth splits in two I'll probably be getting ass raped as part of a violent gang ritual in a train car traveling across the underbelly of South America. *Perfect.*

After a good ten or fifteen minutes of pessimistic bawling and helplessness, I realized that this was *my* world that was about to be destroyed and it was up to *me* to save it.

18

A NEW PLAN

"Fuck that." There was no one around to hear me say it, but it didn't matter, the relief from turning my back on the world was instantaneous. *I'm the wrong guy for that job.* I work in real estate, I can hardly make my own breakfast, let alone do something incredible like stopping aliens from blowing up a planet. Besides, I hate working under deadlines. If Dusty couldn't save the world with his superhuman strength and minuscule penis, *why should I even try?* That's something that only happens in movies and this wasn't a movie, and it wasn't a dream that I could wake up from. My only hope was to make the most of it.

Making the most of it meant I needed to get back to the States to see my family again. If I could get back in time and stay alive in the process, who knows, maybe I could go to Saugatuck to see Sarah? If this were a movie, she'd be conveniently single after having an unexplainable run of bad luck with men. She'd admit she was wrong to leave me, I'd tell her I didn't care, and we'd spend two or three days doing "we're so in love" montage stuff, until the world blew up under our feet.

But this was real life, and she was married to another dude who could probably beat me up. They had kids, and I bet the oldest kid was probably getting close to being able to beat me up too. Regardless of the physical harm they could cause me, they were a family, and although I'd proven adept at being a selfish dick, I would never try to interfere with a happy family, even if it was the end of the world.

I carefully got up from the cliff and walked back to Dusty's backpack full of money. I put a thousand dollars in my wallet and slung the backpack over my shoulder. About a quarter mile down a winding driveway with thick foliage on either side, I came upon what appeared to be a coastal highway. The asphalt was faded and in need of restriping, but other than that, it seemed to be in decent shape.

I was betting I was in Mexico or somewhere in South America and began following the road down. Sure enough, after twenty minutes or so, a small Latino looking man in a beat-up jalopy of a pickup truck came winding down the hill behind me. He pulled over after seeing the money I was waving in my hand. *You know what you can't stop? Progress.*

"Gracias." I said, "Me llamo Parker." He looked at me confused. "Aeropuerto, por favor. Can you tell me what country we're in? Que es Ciudad?" My Spanish had pretty much been exhausted, between Aeropuerto and Ciudad.

He answered in perfect English, "Southern California, *Asshole.*"

19

WHAT A RIDE

I looked at my watch. Even with time changes it had been less than ten hours since I shoved Dusty off a cliff. I wasn't lamenting killing Dusty, I was patting myself on the back for making such unbelievable time. I regretted not showering before leaving the Nest, but enjoyed chit chatting with Waleed, who had his own smell going on and didn't seem bothered by mine. The small, chain smoking driver was sunny and quick to laugh. We feasted at an In-N-Out burger, Dusty's treat. We had such a good time he refused the stack of money I offered him, even after driving me to a small private airport, forty-five minutes away. I jammed it in his seat.

First class accommodations were to follow. I was in the lobby less than fifteen minutes when I overheard a worker say *Atlanta* while talking on his radio. Twenty minutes later I'd convinced an elderly lady traveling to Atlanta with her full-size poodle, Moose, to add me to her flight. She was a plucky old broad by the name of Rosemary Cowl, and when I asked her to wait a couple days before spending the fifteen thousand dollars I'd given her to help 'grease' her decision, she didn't skip a beat.

"Why don't I wait three weeks and throw this at some young men in Paris?" She replied, "The girls and I have a big trip planned. Will that work?"

I grabbed another five-thousand-dollar bundle from my bag and handed it to her, "For you and the girls then."

20

THROWIN' SOME DOUGH

As I was sliding into the worn leather driver's seat of my old Lexus, I couldn't help but admire Rosemary's sleek Gulfstream sitting like a piece of sculpture across the tarmac. The difference between the two machines was laughable. It's funny how flying cross country in a sleek Gulfstream and sunbaked vomit can change how you feel about your car. I looked at the backpack full of Dusty's money in the seat next to me and decided, while fighting off a gagging reflex, it might be time to treat myself to a new rig.

Thirty minutes later I was driving the nicest car I'd ever owned in my life and the first brand new car I'd ever bought. Too bad I'd only have it for a week or so.

There was a familiar pounding in the air, and it was coming from the direction of the service department entrance. I pulled the car around and asked the kid sweeping the floor, "Is that a CD?"

"No, it's Metallica, *Ride the Lightning*." He turned down the volume.

I laughed, "I know, is this playing off a CD and is it yours? I'd like to buy it."

"It's my CD. How much?"

"If you can load it for me, I'll give you five thousand dollars." The car was German and fancy, and I had no idea where the CDs even went. The sales guy said it had a six-disc changer, but I couldn't remember where and I was too exhausted to try. I was also fine using Dusty's money to ease my burden.

"Serious?" he said as he pulled a boombox out from under his service podium and removed the CD.

"As a heart attack." I pulled a packet of money from Dusty's bag and showed him, "What's your name?"

You should have seen him jump, "Balton Warren, Sir." Within seconds he had the CD in the changer cassette and the cassette back in the glove compartment.

"Here you go." I handed him the money.

"You were serious?" he asked, holding the money like he'd have to give it right back. Tears started rolling down his cheeks, but he wasn't crying or making an ugly cry face.

"Balton, what are you—"

"You can call me BA," he said, still staring at the thick stack of bills in his hands. "You really giving me this?"

"It's yours. I love Metallica, *Ride the Lightning* is an all-time favorite, one of my first records. I just bought this rig and that's *exactly* what I needed to break this beast in with. There's like, four million speakers in here." I was pointing to the stereo and the speaker arrays, but he wasn't looking at anything but the money. Crocodile tears were coming out, but no ugly face, no bawling, *how did he do that?* He was stoked and I felt great. The money in the bag meant nothing to me. I'm not even sure I could spend it in a week if I wanted to. "What are you going to do with the money BA?"

"Buy my family food Sir. Real food, times been tough, my little girl is skin and bones."

My heart broke into pieces without warning. *Hungry?* I wasn't expecting *that* answer, he didn't look old enough to be a father. In my mind I could see his hungry daughter. I started tearing up myself and grabbed four more packs of Dusty's money, "Do you have any more CD's?"

21

GET BACK, PARKER

It felt great making BA's last week on earth kick-ass and I felt great doing it with someone else's money. I blasted Metallica as loud as my fancy new stereo would let me. With every window open the beautiful day pounded through the hand sewn leather interior, I felt lucky to be alive. I played the air drums and sang my heart out the whole way home. It was an incredible car and I wished I could enjoy it for more than a week.

I pulled into my driveway and remembered Piper. I shifted into DEFCON ONE level panic and ran as fast as I could to the back door. In my mind I could see Peaches looking at Piper, calling her "asshole," and shooting her dead. I cried, "No, no, no!" in a panic as I ran up the back stairs to the house, feeling helpless again. If Peaches killed Piper I would crawl until I found a low spot and lay in it until I died. What did it say about me that I was relatively unaffected by my wife's murder, but would be devastated if Piper had met her maker?

Piper was waiting for me as I ran to the door. "Baby!" I shrieked and held my arms out. Instead of her usual vibrating welcome, she raced past me into the yard and gave me a *"What the fuck?"* look as she urinated for about five minutes straight. "Baby!" I cried again holding my arms out to embrace her. She ignored me yet again and went from her peeing posture straight into an arched position, violently dropping a deuce any horse would be proud of. She'd been locked up in the house forever. "Don't worry sweetie," I said, the relief overwhelming, "I'm never going to leave you again, ever." I meant it.

I took a long, hot shower even though it felt super creepy knowing Margot, the woman I'd shared this shower with, was probably still lying dead in some dipshit's apartment. I grabbed some clothes, shoved them in a duffle and walked around the house, taking one last look at all the work I lovingly put into it. Like my new rig, *and everything else*, it was a shame this house and all my hard work would soon be space dust. When I opened my front door to collect the mail, my brother Beau was standing on our stoop.

"Why aren't you answering your phone?" He was in running clothes, probably in the middle of a run although there were no visible signs of sweating. Behind him, an APD patrol car pulled up slowly to the curb. I was stunned— I had a feeling I knew what was coming. Beau noticed the look on my face and turned around to see a lard ass Atlanta police officer squeeze himself out of the patrol car. Beau looked back at me; I couldn't speak. The cop waddled up, his belt probably hadn't touched his waist in twenty years; instead it divided his huge belly into upper and lower regions.

He identified himself as sergeant *something* Roland, but I didn't get the first name because I was too distracted by the whole belt around the belly thing, his faux waist, I guess you would call it. I wondered, when did he decide to move his belt from his actual waist to his belly? Was that a sad day or did he think, *Wow, I can see my belt again. This looks fantastic.*

"Is one of you Parker Duque?" he asked.

I snapped out of my faux waist thoughts, "I am, how can I help you officer?"

"Can you tell me where you've been for the last 48 hours?"

Beau snapped out of the blue, "At my lake house."

"I didn't ask you sir."

"Well, why are you asking?" Beau continued aggressively. I could always count on my big brother to save me and he was always prepared to.

"Actually," I interrupted, "I don't mind telling you, it's probably an entertaining story if you aren't me. To answer your question, like my brother was saying, I was at the lake yesterday, but it starts earlier than that. I got into a huge fight with my wife after I made an ass out of myself at a charitable art auction. I then left her at the auction and proceeded to get even drunker at Moe's and Joe's, to the point where she made me sleep on the sofa in my carriage house. And, in the typical male fashion, or so I've been told, I made a bad situation worse by going to my brother's lake house instead of coming home to 'talk about what I've done.'"

"Mr. Duque, I have some really bad news for you. Do you want to go inside and sit down?"

"No, tell us now!" Beau blurted out, he loved bad news. The cop looked confused, but I nodded for him to go ahead.

"I'm sorry to tell you this, Mr. Duque, but we found your wife dead last night." I feigned shock, which wasn't hard, because I was already scared out of my mind. "With her lover. It was a murder-suicide. If it helps you sir, it looked like she was trying to leave him. I know it's hardly a consolation, but she wrote him a note saying she was choosing her husband." The cop seem moved, "Then he shot her in the face and killed himself."

"Why did you ask him where he was if it was a murder-suicide?" Beau asked indignantly.

"I had too, it's what we do, he's the husband. The husband is always involved."

"But you said it was a murder-suicide."

"Habit, I guess. I knew you didn't do it; forensics listed the time of death as happening during your speech. I was there for your speech, that's how I knew you didn't do it."

"OK. So, do you need anything else officer?" Beau asked, bothered.

"Well, I hate to break it to you Mr. Duque, but you got a lot wrong in your speech there. I was the homecoming king and look at me now. I just made sergeant!" He put one hand on his gun and tugged at his vinyl name tag with the other.

"Seriously?" Beau was incredulous.

"Yeah, my partner and I were assigned to the assembly at Grady. I'm also a Grady cop." He looked like a cat that had just swallowed the canary, "Just saying." He looked at a visibly upset Beau and then back at me, "And I'm sorry for your loss."

Fittingly, I was in shock. Not that there was a lard ass cop critiquing my speech while telling me about the demise of my wife, but about what I had just narrowly avoided. I felt so thankful for the work ethic and cold efficiency of my former captor. I could see Peaches bossing them around, her purpose driven by an excitement that only comes from doing something you love. To her credit, she did it well enough to snow the cops. Had she been lazy and shot both of them in the face, I would've been spending my last days on Earth in the slammer.

"Jesus." I said.

"Sir, are you going to be all right?" The cop placed his sausage fingered hand on my shoulder. Beau's face was whiter than mine.

"I don't know. I don't know how to react." I felt Oscar level skills coming on but thought it best to pull back. "Sir, what are my obligations?"

"Excuse me?" lard ass cop was surprised.

"As her husband, what do I have to do now, what are my obligations? Because I don't ever want to see her again. Both her parents are still alive. Can they take care of the body and the funeral arrangements? I don't want anything to do with her. If you need to bury her with the indigents that would be fine with me too."

"Parker, you don't mean that!" Beau said with his trademark *clutch the pearls* move.

I looked to Beau, and then I looked to lard ass cop and said, "Yep, I'm afraid I do. I would like to... Are you writing this down sir? I would like to volunteer to pay the costs to have her and her lover buried where they bury the homeless people. I'll pay extra for it.

"Buried with homeless, husband to pay..." lard ass cop murmured as he took the notes.

"If her parents don't agree to it, they can pay for it." I added, as Beau looked at me in stunned silence.

"Contact parents for payment..." After the newly minted sergeant finished writing his last note, he looked up, more amused than he should have been, "I don't blame you Mr. Duque, that guy had a huge dick."

22

BEAU KNOWS

Beau looked through the window to ensure the officer had driven off, "You weren't answering your phone because you killed Margot and her well hung lover?"

"No. But Beau, it's several billion times worse. We should sit down for this."

I told him about shot-in-the-face Brock and what he'd told me about aliens blowing up the Earth. Beau seemed to be taking me seriously until I told him about how huge Peaches was, and how fast she could run and jump.

"Parker, are you OK? Did you kill Margot and her lover? You know I love your creativity, but I don't think this is the time or the place. You can tell me anything and I'll help you. I'll even help you bury the body, but you have to tell me the truth. I think you're under a tremendous amount of stress right now, selling your business and finding out about Margot's infidelity."

"I couldn't give a fuck about Margot!" I meant it too, mad that he would even give her cheating a dignified label like *infidelity.* "I understand you think I'm crazy, because the story is so unbelievable, but I saw the top-secret government file. It was legit. I read the whole thing! There was a farm boy out in a field having his way with an older cow named Lu Anne and a silver orb came down and stopped a foot off the ground. The kid said a laser came out of the center like the rings around Saturn and cut through anything in its way. That's how the cows had their legs cut off and that's why Brock was out there. He was trying to dick the farmer on an insurance claim."

"This laser began burrowing into the ground without displacing the dirt. The laser was turning the dirt into metal, creating a cylinder. Now the metal cylinder is five hundred feet wide and going deeper and deeper as we speak. The army corps of engineers say they can't stop it, let alone figure out what it is. The metal has electromagnetic qualities and every time they try to dig around the cylinder the thing turns magnetic! I saw a picture of 2 huge backhoes crushed flat against the surface. There are cylinders like this encircling the Earth, the GPS coordinates of their placement are perfectly aligned. Perfect as in not one of them is off by an inch, perfect.

The report said the metallurgic qualities and the precision of the cylinder placement indicate the origin is most likely, *extra-terrestrial*. Based on the current growth rate of the cylinders, it said we had two weeks left. That was a week ago. We're fucked and I'm not crazy, I'm telling you the truth."

"The farmer kid was having sex with a cow named Lu Anne? It actually said that in the report?" Beau was stuck in the minutia.

"I didn't think stuff like that really happened either."

"Do they name all the cows in Iowa?"

"That's an interesting question and I wish I knew the answer, I do, but can we get back to the point here?"

"Did the farmer kid get his legs cut off?"

"He was on a stool. The stool was cut in half, there was even a picture of it. The kid and his entire town are being held in a 'Designated Secured Location' so as not to spread panic and chaos."

"What was the kid's name?"

"Are you kidding? Because I just told you the world's about to be blown in two, and you're only asking me about the kid banging a cow part?"

"I'm sorry, Parker, I'm really, really sorry." He started toward me to give me a, *sorry you've gone crazy* hug, but I stopped him. "We need to get you some help. You're telling me Margot and her lover died in a murder-suicide orchestrated by a poorly endowed government assassin and his four-hundred-pound lover, and that you thought you pushed them off a cliff in South America, but it was really Southern California?"

"Hold on. Peaches killed Margot and her lover, she also fell off the cliff trying to grab a bag of off-brand powdered sugar donuts, I didn't push her. I *did* push Dusty off the cliff, but he landed on an outcropping and only broke his arm, although it was a pretty bad break. It wasn't until I expertly threw up on him that he lost his grip and fell to his death. Everyone knows one armed climbing is dangerous."

"And her name was Peaches?"

"Yes. Feel this lump on the back of my head, I wouldn't do this to myself. Dusty hit me with a rock."

Beau felt the lump, "Fair enough, but I want you to know that I love you and I'm here for you and we're going to get you help."

"I'm not crazy."

"OK. You are under a lot of stress, deny that.

"Beau."

"It's too much Parker."

"How do I prove it to you then? I can take you to the car with Brock's body in it."

"Gross. No thanks. You said you were in California yesterday; can you prove that?"

"Yes!" I announced triumphantly. I pulled the "In-N-Out" burger restaurant receipt from my wallet like a winning lottery ticket and handed it to Beau. He went white and sat down in shock, staring at the receipt.

"Look at the date."

"It's a lot of food."

"I also bought lunch for the little guy who gave me a ride to the airport. In-N-Out burger is so good."

"Is this a joke? Please tell me this is a joke. Let me off the hook." Beau looked up at me.

I had tears in my eyes. It felt so good to tell someone, especially someone I could trust to believe me, like Beau. He had bailed me out of so many situations, but there was nothing he could do this time, and that's what made me lose my shit, that and thinking of all Beau was about to lose. We cried together, which I couldn't see myself enjoying on a regular basis, but it felt good to share my end of the world grief with someone else.

"What are we going to do?" He looked at me, "We've got to do something!"

I didn't say anything. I could tell Beau was going through the "It's up to me and my kid brother to save the world" options in his head and I was afraid he might think one of them was viable.

"Well, we've got to do something..." He trailed off like he'd just stopped short of a mistake.

"Save the world?" I said, in fear.

"Yeah, fuck that." He said, coming to his senses after a moment of contemplation, "I guess we just make the most of it, right? Do you think we could do something to save the world?"

"Hell no, I put too much milk in my cereal on a daily basis, I can't save shit."

"Thank God, I have no interest in trying either. Can you believe we live 20 minutes away from Six Flags and I've never been? What does it say about me that I have to wait until the end of the world to go to Six Flags?"

"A lot actually." I laughed, "I'm going to say goodbye to everybody around here and go to Saugatuck."

"Michigan? Why?"

"Sarah Campbell."

"Oh. Sarah Campbell from Purdue, Sarah Campbell? She's married, with kids."

"You told me. Who told you that?"

"I can't remember. I think Dina Bockos."

"Well, Dina would know. I don't care though, I'm not going to profess my love or anything, I just want to see her again and see what she's done with her life. I know it sounds creepy, but even before the world was ending, I would think about her almost every day. Have you ever felt like there was one that got away?

"I've never wanted anyone to stay."

"Well, Sarah is mine. I'd just like to be near her when the world blows up, is that too corny? Plus, if I can't be with my family, where else am I going to go?"

"It's not corny at all Parker, she was your first love. She was wonderful, but why wouldn't you stay here with us? That ship has sailed, she's married with kids. Stay here with us, we're your family."

"This is the last place I want to be. Outside of you guys, why would I want to be here? To bask in the afterglow of Margot's exploits? That's a pretty sucky last week of life, don't you think? And even if I wanted to, I couldn't stay here. I *have* to leave in case they come back for me; just knowing about this has me marked for death."

"*Jesus. Why did you tell me then?* Now I'm a marked man! I have a child!"

"I needed to tell someone, and you thought I killed my wife! I couldn't let you think that! Plus, you're my best friend, who else am I going to tell?"

"You're right, I'm glad you told me. I'm your big bro, I love you unconditionally and I don't care if you committed womanslaughter. Seriously though, tell me the truth, you didn't kill her, did you?"

"Beau. I didn't kill her!"

"OK, OK. We can't tell another soul— for once the government's right. There'd be mass hysteria if everybody knew, and that would harsh my mellow, big time. Stay here with us, we'll take the risk together. I'll tell you one thing, the first thing I'm doing is getting Gramps out of that disgusting home. I hate the thought of him in there. He told me he just sits in his bed, waiting to die. I was there last week and he asked me to unplug the humidifier."

"What?"

"He thought it was his life support machine." Beau laughed.

"I can't stay Beau, I'll help you with Gramps, but I have to leave Atlanta."

"I understand, I guess. Well, you can't fly. You can't buy a plane ticket with cash and the government might be watching your credit cards for activity."

Shit sauce. I didn't think about any of that. I just financed 100% my new car, tickled I'd never pay them back. Oops. There was nothing I could do now, but I knew they'd could come looking for me in Atlanta, so my time here had to be quick. I pointed to my new car parked in front, "No sweat, I'll drive."

Beau was already looking through the window at my new rig, a massive, midnight blue BMW 750Li. I joined him. It was the most beautiful car I'd ever seen, and in my mind, the finest road machine man could build. "Holy shit, is that your new car? That. Is. Gorgeous! I belong in that car!" He looked at me, deathly serious, "Parker, are you sure you haven't lost your marbles?"

"I'm not crazy Beau, the situation is." I remembered Dusty's bag of money, "Let me show you something else." I opened the black backpack. Beau was speechless as I handed him stacks of money. I felt sick with regret, "Here Beau, this is for being a great big brother and the best friend anyone could ask for. Dusty and Peaches were using it to light their gas fireplace."

"They should be shot." He flipped through the stacks of bills in lust.

"Well, how about falling down a cliff and bouncing off jagged rocks? What's it called when you break your arm, and the bone comes out of your skin?"

"A compound fracture."

"Well, after I pushed him off the cliff, Dusty's arm broke like a twig, it was a compound fracture, and it was disgusting."

Beau didn't seem to think it was as great as I thought it was, "You're serious. This is really happening isn't it? You couldn't possibly be making this up and playing a trick on me."

"I'm sorry Beau."

"Well then why on Earth are we sitting around here talking about this? Let's go get Gramps while Landon's with Ms. Livingston."

"Perfect." I asked Beau, "You know what I'm the most pissed about?"

"What?"

"Look at me, I haven't eaten junk food or smoked weed forever, I run 12 miles a week to stay skinny like this and it was all for that cheating whore. I wish I had been eating like that cop has for the last five years."

"Well, I'm going to have to call *bullshit* on that one. You haven't smoked *as much* weed and you still eat garbage. Remember getting torqued out of our minds two weeks ago and watching an entire movie in those shitty, uncomfortable 3D glasses?"

"Then we found out the movie wasn't shot in 3D!" I laughed.

"I got lost going to the bathroom and you ate, like, five or six of those foot-long rice crispy bars?"

"OK, well not as much weed as I *would* have smoked, and those rice crispy bars don't count, they're mostly air."

"Right, but you look great, and you feel better about yourself. I can tell."

"Well, all bets are off now. I'm going to eat like a pig and smoke like a fucking chimney."

"No Sir, that's a bad plan. You get way too paranoid when you smoke as it is. You should be asking yourself if you want to be baked with the CIA after you and the Earth about to be blown in two. *That* would be great for you."

He was right. "OK, great points, I'll skip the weed but I'm going to eat garbage food exclusively."

"You know what I think sucks, Parker? You'll never write the story you told me about at Christmas. The one about you and me except we're all country and we fish? I thought you were going to write that during your break. I just think that's a travesty." I made the mistake of telling Beau the older brother from The Bear was based on him. "Every time you send me a funny email, I always think to myself, *when is he going to write that story about his big brother?* If I can remember correctly, somebody else wanted you to write that story too, what was her name?"

Beau's narcissism was clouding the picture. He was bummed I wasn't writing about *him*, not because I wasn't writing; Beau was always in the market for a tribute. Unlike Rose, he encouraged and embraced every tribute, compliment, or accolade pointed in his direction. He was a narcissistic genius, quickly using Sarah as leverage to get what he wants. He was right— she wanted me to write the story too, we came up with it together.

"It's a moot point now, isn't it?" Saying it made me feel weird until it hit me, Beau's narcissism clouded the picture but illuminated another genius idea. *What if I wrote it now?* How long could it take? It didn't matter, I didn't have to finish it! As long as I'd started writing, it would give me a sliver of credibility I might need in Saugatuck.

I'd stay with my plan to waltz innocently into Sarah's hardware store and feign shock at the coincidence, "Oh my gosh Sarah, you're not going to believe this coincidence, but I've just started writing The Bear!"

"You have?" she would say, filled with curiosity.

"Yes, and I'm not a loser anymore and I've been super-successful in real estate." I would probably do it smoother than that, but you get the drift. I wonder if I could actually finish the short story. . . Would she read it and look back fondly about us, or think, *that's the asshole that made me get an abortion?*

I liked the idea of writing it for her *AND* Beau, it seemed less creepy than writing something for a married woman as an excuse to see if she was still hot. It *was* a tribute to Beau after all, and he deserved it. It couldn't take me that long to write and, If we're being honest, I doubted I'd ever see Sarah again. With my luck, she'll probably be away with her family on summer vacation. For some reason though, I still found myself wanting to write it and go see Sarah. Fuck it, that's my new plan.

"Why don't you and Landon come with me to Saugatuck? I'm going to ask Chuy to come too. I'll write this tribute to you if you drive." I said to Beau, trying to leverage his narcissism for my benefit.

"I love the thought of me driving that car but there's no way I'm spending three of my last days driving you across the country."

"It's a twelve-hour drive." I realized after I said it, it wasn't a fit. Beau didn't have the patience nor the attention span. If I had someone to drive me, I knew I could finish it before we got to Saugatuck. It was a short story and I'd long since worked it out in my head.

"Not wasting twelve of my last hours on the highway, no way Jay."

"What if I drive and you fly, will you come with me to Michigan? I'll buy a kick ass house for us to live out our last days in style. You know how beautiful Saugatuck is during the summer! We can take the whole crew- Landon, Chuy, Grampa, Ms. Livingston, everybody!"

"You're inviting Ms. Livingston?" Beau was amazed.

"I don't give a fuck anymore Beau, Ms. Livingston can drive me!"

"That's funny, we could tape 2x4s to her legs to reach the pedals! '*I no can see, Pahkur Duque! I no can shift! Pahkur Duque!*'" His imitation was pitch perfect.

"Yes! Let's do it!"

"Parker, I'm sorry, I can't. My life is here in Atlanta and I can't leave it. I understand why you have to leave, and I want you to scratch your itch." His conviction was visibly fading, "Do they have a Six Flags up there?" He paused, "No, actually, we'll stay here with Mom, Dad, Gramps and Chuy, you go. Follow your heart."

There was a knock at the door. Beau froze and I jumped into the hall closet. I felt like a ridiculous coward until the massive bruise on my thigh started aching, reminding me of why I was hiding. Even though I saw him fall to his painful death, I had a weird feeling Dusty wasn't done with me yet.

"Jesus! Am I glad to see you!" Beau laughed, "Ohhh Parker, you can come out of the closet now!" The joy at which he used this joke was telling. I wondered if it was finally time for him to come out, I mean, now that the world's ending and all. He's got to be bumming about that. I wondered if that's why he wanted to stay back in Atlanta. If you're gay, Atlanta is a pretty spectacular place to be.

"Please don't call me that. You know I prefer Chuy." It was my adopted younger brother Jesus, a Mexican youth who just happens to share his name with a famous carpenter you might have heard of. Chuy, pronounced "chewy," is a common nickname for folks named Jesus, which I hear there are a lot of, but I only knew one.

Seeing Chuy brought a smile to my face. He was dressed in what has come to be his uniform, a knit polo shirt with the collar upturned, navy shorts, and flip flops. His shorts were shorter than the usual shorts you might see on a 15-year-old boy and you couldn't blame him for wearing them. Jesus "Chuy" Duque, by all accounts was a beautiful young man, a Mexican Adonis with sun kissed blonde hair, long legs, and a year-round tan. His blonde hair certainly stood out, but Chuy's legs were breathtaking.

I envied Chuy for his legs, I didn't own shorts. My legs are so white they reflect sunlight onto nearby objects like a mirror would— a conversation starter, sure, but also a distraction I didn't want any part of. I'm sure my legs could be tan with the help of a nuclear-powered tanning salon, but the only time I ever care is when Chuy is over, and understandably, he never wants to go tanning.

Both my parents smoke weed, but my father smokes a *lot* of weed. Chuy is a wonderful part of the Duque family as a result of my father's voracious weed habit.

One night, Dad was walking off a giant Atkin's Park BBQ sandwich. As was the practice before he went on walks, he torqued up beforehand. Twenty minutes into the walk he freaked out and mistook a simple case of indigestion for a four-alarm heart attack. He called mom like his hair was on fire and screamed for her to call an ambulance. She of course started freaking out and screamed like *her* hair was on fire as well, *"Tell me where you are! I'm calling you an ambulance!"*

It looked like they might have been racing toward a speedy resolution until Dad shared his location, "Two doors down from the incredibly hot woman who lives in the white house in back of Murphy's Restaurant." Mom did what every wife who had been pushed over the edge one too many times would do; she hung up. It was Chuy that found Dad that night, lying on the ground, faking death, or as most people call it, sleeping.

After Dad realized he wasn't dying, Chuy introduced him to his mother, the incredibly hot woman who lives in the white house in back of Murphy's Restaurant. She would later become his girlfriend and roommate after mom kicked him out of the house.

The incredibly hot woman who lives in the white house in back of Murphy's Restaurant was named Debra. Debra worked as a hairdresser and was a couple cards short of a full deck. She was proof that if you're good looking enough, nobody cares about any of your shortcomings, and certainly not my old man. A year earlier, Debra had "adopted" Chuy on the beach while on vacation in Mexico.

It soon became clear, Debra's desire for a personal hair model and billboard was her primary reason for adopting Chuy. She was already well-known for her skill in dying hair blonde and creating natural blonde highlights, but having Chuy walking around looking like a young, Mexican Brad Pitt put her business over the top. I remember her speaking for twenty minutes at dinner about Brad Pitt's hair in *A river runs through it*. Debra was a skillful practitioner; she had both Beau and Dad's naturally Lion-like manes glowing like I'd never seen, and I know it hasn't been easy for Chuy to keep his hair as beautiful and blonde since she left. I asked Mom why she spent money keeping Chuy golden and she told me without hesitation, *what Jesus wants, Jesus gets.* A handsome Mexican kid with Blonde hair in short shorts doesn't happen in every room, so Chuy was used to the attention and most times, welcomed it.

Dad had expertly applied his natural blonde hair and the money *illusion* to get into Debra's pants and they'd dated a while until Mom and Dad split their assets. When Dad wasn't able to pay for everything like he used to, it wasn't good. It turns out, after the illusion of money dried up, so did Debra's passion for fucking way older men.

Somehow, some way, my father got my mother to take him *and* Chuy back and they've been together, unmarried, ever since. Now Chuy's a Duque, the adopted Mexican son of Dad's weed induced dalliance. He's basically been on his own since the age of eight as both of my parents have grown weary of parenting. I spend a lot of time with him as a result and you couldn't ask for a nicer kid, funny and odd with too much swearing perhaps, but a great kid.

"Umm, what's with the hug?" He asked after I let him go. Poor Chuy was going to be devastated about Margot.

"Margot died yesterday Chuy." Beau couldn't wait to share the bad news. I was ready for Chuy to start bawling.

"Dead?" he looked confused, not upset, "As in six feet under dead?"

"Yes." Beau and I said together, Beau with more enthusiasm.

"Are you OK?" Chuy said to me.

"I'm going to be fine Chuy."

"OK. Bummer, Right?"

"Meh," I shrugged, "not really, she was cheating on me and her lover shot her."

"Whooaaaaa, what a fucking ho!" Chuy exploded, "Good riddance, right? She was hot though bro. You were hitting that, weren't you?"

"We were married."

"That's cool. So you got yours then, don't sweat it." He high fived me,

"Did you ever take dirty pics or anything like that?"

"Chuy!" Beau stopped him cold. I started laughing.

"No such luck Chuy." I looked over and Beau was laughing too.

"Great speech bro, but I thought I asked you not to mention me."

"Whatever. I'm proud you're my little bro, no way I'm not shouting you out."

"Really?"

"I said that wrong."

"Yeah." He said, smiling. He wasn't upset, I knew he'd get a kick out of it.

"Am I the only one who hasn't heard about this speech?" Beau asked.

I turned to Beau to explain, "Rusty asked me to speak at Grady's Last Day of School Assembly?"

"Somebody named Dustypeaches69 posted it on YouTube bro, there are, like, a gazillion views. You're a star now."

I looked at Beau and he looked at me. His usual George Hamilton tan was two shades whiter.

"Chuy, I know you're an accomplished driver already, but how's your Driver's Ed coming along?" I asked, intrigued by the possibilities.

"Terrible, Pops won't let me drive his car and you know I'm a great driver. Mom says she doesn't have time."

"Let's practice, you can drive my new car."

"We're about to spring Gramps from the old folks home." Beau said, excited.

Chuy didn't hesitate, "Fuck it, I'm in."

23

FOR THE LOVE OF SHOES

We piled into my new car. Chuy was smitten with the luxurious interior and eager to get behind the wheel. I was sitting shotgun, ignoring how beautiful Chuy's legs looked against the ivory leather upholstery, and Beau sat in the middle of the back seat, buckled tight for safety reasons, although he wouldn't admit to being terrified.

"Holmes, this is the 750i, the flagship."

"Nope, it's the 750Li, the long version. The back seat has an extra foot, like a limo." I corrected him.

"Is it safe?" Beau asked

"Very." I said, "You'll be fine, the Germans are good at cars."

"Holmes, have you told Parker what Landon did at Osteria?"

"Chuy, I wish you'd quit using '*Holmes,*' it's so cliché." Beau protested.

"What, because I'm Mexican?"

We both answered in unison, "*Yes.*"

"Are you telling me to ignore my heritage?"

"I would venture to guess that 'Holmes' is not part of your Mexican heritage." I intervened.

"Parker, 'Holmes' is part of *my* Mexican gangster heritage."

"He's got a point Parker, it is." Beau had lost the absolute confidence he normally wears, "Have you seen *Colors*- with Sean Penn and Robert Duvall?"

"See?" Chuy was looking at me instead of the road.

"The road!" I pointed spastically ahead as Chuy nonchalantly looked back towards the road.

Beau was trying to incorporate the other two seatbelts into his safety program when he continued, "Anyway, listen to this; we were having a wonderful dinner on the patio at Osteria and afterward Landon was playing with the cutest little boy."

"Uh oh." I said, "What did he do now?"

"If you'd stop interrupting me, I would tell you. So, I'm watching Landon play with this adorable little boy, and it looked to me like he was laying the groundwork for something. You know Landon's mother had gypsy in her blood, so I kept watching and I was right. It was spectacular, it was like he was leading the cute little boy into a trap. He would drop his Barbie in front of a chair and then run behind it. The cute little boy would go pick it up and bring it around to Landon, who would hold the chair and look over at the little boy's parents to see if they were watching. I said to myself, 'what on earth could he be doing?' He's like a little performance artist, you know? So, after a couple times, the little boy bends over to pick up Landon's Barbie and wham! He slams the chair forward and knocks this kid out cold, I mean flat on his back. It was hilarious!"

"That's terrible!" I screamed.

Chuy was laughing his ass off, "Right?"

"Will you two *puh-lease* stop interrupting me? I'm coming up on the best part! So, he runs around the chair, he's so *fast!* You should have seen him scurry, like a cute little chipmunk! He rips the kid's shoes off, grabs his Barbie and runs inside. The little boy's parents didn't even notice him lying on the patio for like three or four minutes! *Can you believe that?"*

"Is this a joke? Because this is too horrible, even for you guys." I looked at Chuy.

"I got nothing to do with it Holmes, but I knew you'd freak. They are fucking loco!" Chuy was laughing so hard he was snorting.

"Chuy!" Beau yelled like a father would. "Clean your language up. Have some dignity for Christ's sake."

I didn't turn around, I knew Beau was looking at me, assigning the blame for Chuy's potty mouth, which is only *partially* true. To exclude his parents from that blame would be an egregious mistake; he lives with them, they swear more than I do, and there's *two* of them. The truth is, Chuy's an accomplished swearer, he used *"fuck"* too much, but that's a rookie mistake. As far as I was concerned, he could swear as much as his little heart desired, I'll enjoy every minute of it, I mean, it's the end of the world and we were all about to die. *Fuck it.*

"Let me get this straight, you're beaming because your child shoe-jacked an innocent little boy?" I couldn't believe it myself.

"I just thought it was cute it was all over *shoes*. Do you see the connection? Seriously, he *loves* shoes, just like his old man." He continued, beaming with pride, "The parents weren't even watching their boy." Beau fashioned his hands like he was in a gay hold up, "Stuff like this happens when you don't watch your children. When the parents finally took notice, all hell broke loose. I just slipped out in the chaos."

"It sounds to me like Landon was checking to see if the parents were watching and waiting, until they weren't, *like a predator*. Does that not concern you, what do you mean you just slipped out? What did you do?" I asked, I was genuinely appalled.

"Nothing. That's what I pay Ms. Livingston for!"

"Good lord, did she give the poor kid his shoes back? Was he *OK*?"

"Well, she tried to keep them. She had them stuffed in her bag, but they were *hideous*, so I made her march right out there and leave them in a place where someone would eventually find them.

"Where were you?"

"I hid in the women's bathroom with Landon."

"What in the... why the women's bathroom?" I asked, afraid now.

"Duh? They wouldn't think to look for us in *there*."

134

24

SOUP OR NUTS?

Our grandpa, or Gramps, lived voluntarily in an upscale nursing home called Lenox Garden Estates, a luxurious, one-story facility in Buckhead. Gramps, like my father, had just enough money to last the rest of his life, provided he never did anything reckless like helping family members or donating to charities. Even though it was his choice, it bothered me that Gramps was in a nursing home, but not enough to have him move in with me, so I was thrilled Beau would try to get him out. I'm sure Gramps and Ms. Livingston would get along wonderfully, kind of like the Middle East does, except with more firepower and less manners.

Gramps' mental acuity was slipping a bit with age, and about a year ago, he and Chuy were driving home from Chuy's wrestling practice when Gramps had a stroke and took the wrong ramp onto the highway. Accidents happen but this was an *exit* ramp and cars were now coming towards them at eighty miles per hour. As if things couldn't get worse, Gramps is a big guy, nearly impossible to move and his leg was jammed on the accelerator, blocking the brakes.

Chuy, the Mexican gangster boy wonder, steered the car through incoming traffic from the passenger seat and drove around I-285 (which is the highway that runs in a circle around Atlanta) *two* times before the gas ran out. He never hit a single car, although he had a police escort for the last lap. The doctors said the extraordinary amount of adrenaline produced during the event must have heightened his coordination and that the resulting "*super-coordination,*" their term, not mine, would eventually wear off. It hasn't.

After the incident, Chuy came over to show me his new super-coordination by bouncing a quarter into a shot glass, *fifty* times in a row. He took my twenty dollars and wondered out loud if there was a faster way to make money using his new gift. The challenge was most well-paying, super-coordinated athletic sports require a measure of physical power, something Chuy did not have. It was Gramps who pointed out the solution at a family dinner; Chuy could get an above average NBA contract straight out of high school if he could just make *half* his three-point shots. Easy peasy, all he had to do was run around until he was open and shoot the ball. At the very least, his legs looked fantastic in basketball shorts.

He couldn't make a single shot. Although he can literally grab a fly with chopsticks, that super-coordinated little Mexican couldn't make a three-point shot to save his life. Chuy remains bitter to this day, convinced Mexicans have a basketball suppressing gene. "Look at the data," he said, throwing an NBA roster at me.

"Gramps!" Chuy shouted as he jogged in and gave a big hug to Gramps, who was watching TV from his bed. It was nice to see a high school kid still be affectionate and not self-conscious. Chuy was one of the sweetest, most genuine human beings I'd ever met. He swore entirely too much, but he made up for it with his fun, infectious personality.

"Who's the Mexican?" Gramps said flatly to me and Beau.

"It's me, Grandpa, *Chuy.*" Chuy laughed, patient with Gramps' memory loss.

"Oh, you." Gramps looked at me with a puzzled face as Chuy was hugging him and I nodded affirmatively.

Gramps wasted no time, "Boys, they took my Super-Nut. They still haven't put it back! Beau, you told me they were going to put it back in! I want my nuts back. Both of them! My regular nut and my Super-Nut!"

"Excuse me one second Gramps. Beau, can we have a quick chat?" I pulled Beau away where I could whisper, "You told him he'd get it *back?*"

"I wanted to leave," he whispered back, "I caved."

136

"By telling him *he'd get his 'Super-Nut' back?*"

"You weren't there. He was crying for it, I got emotional. I wanted him to have it back too."

"It doesn't exist. How are you getting out of this one?" I recited Gramps favorite line, "You mess with the bull, you get the horns."

Gramps real name was Crawford Duque and he was the most talented person I'd ever met. He was the reason my family had money; he might have lost his edge with age, but I wouldn't mess with him; Gramps was a force of nature and the physical embodiment of clever. Beau's troubled countenance told me he hadn't thought things through.

"Gramps, you still have your regular nut. It's in there somewhere." Beau said patiently, which was unlike him. He was scared, "The other one was not a super testicle; it was a benign tumor. You had a seminoma, that's a type of testicular cancer, the good kind, so you were very lucky."

"Lucky my ass. I've got no balls. I can't live like this, without my balls. Hey Muchacho, pull that plug there, I've had it with this world." Chuy pulled the plug as commanded, and the TV went black. Gramps seemed frustrated, "See if you can find another plug to pull, amigo."

After Gramps was taken to the hospital for his stroke, the nurse charged with bathing him discovered the huge tumor on Gramps' left testicle. The nurse also discovered, unfortunately, that some seventy-eight-year-old men can still get persistent boners. Grandpa had had it for years— the tumor, not the boner, and was convinced it was a gift from God, so he kept it a secret. The tumor stretched out his ball sack quite a bit so now that his "Super-Nut" had been removed, he has this outsized ball sack, just hanging there with a singular, I would think lonely, nut that he was hesitant to even acknowledge.

"Gramps, how would you like to get out of this place and come live with me and Landon?" Beau asked nervously, like it was a first date.

"You get me my Super-Nut back and I'll move into a refrigerator box under an I-20 overpass." His answer was crisp and deliberate, "Otherwise, I'm staying put. Both of you know why I'm here." For the first time, Gramps irresistible smile surfaced through the doom and gloom. This was the Gramps I knew, the sex fiend.

"Why are you here Gramps?" Chuy asked, curious.

"Please don't tell him." I asked Gramps, knowing it was no use.

"Well, Panchito, there's a ton of broads here and I'm the only guy with a working member. It's like shootin' fish in a barrel. The security guys here couldn't pour piss out of a boot if the directions were written on the heel. I can do whatever I want, whenever I want." He gathered himself and looked at me again, "Parker, can you take me to the bathroom?"

My answer was swift and resolute, "No way. I've seen you go by yourself a hundred times." His stern eyes were intimidating, but I didn't care, "Are you really not feeling good? Why are you laying in your bed like you're in the hospital? What's wrong with your couch?"

"I told you, I'm dying without my Super-nut. I'm also trying to watch TV in my underwear for a little bit, there's nothing wrong with that. I was going to pull on this," he motioned with both hands to his privates, "before dinner to get warmed up. There's a big party downstairs tonight. At least that's what I was trying to do, until you clowns showed up."

"OK. C'mon, let's go." I conceded to Gramps, anything to stop him from talking about nailing GILF's in front of Chuy. Everybody has an inner goalie that stops our improper thoughts from entering the real world but Gramps goalie had been knocked unconscious by his stroke and showed no signs of improving anytime soon. His honesty could be terrifying in public.

Gramps got out of his bed and I followed him through his sterile quarters into the bathroom and closed the door behind us. Gramps sat down and started to pee like a lady.

"I read about you in the Business Chronicle. I'm very proud of you Parker, I knew you had it in you."

"Thanks Gramps, that means a lot to me." It was all I could say. Ordinarily I would be emotional because I'm an emotional person and Gramps was a personal hero, except the bathroom was so small I couldn't help noticing my hero's ball sack was dangling in toilet water. Gramps hated it when I cried, so maybe this powerful distraction wasn't all so bad. Nope. "Gramps... Pull up your..." I paused, not sure of guy protocol, "Your scrotum is in the toilet water. You're getting pee on it."

His head was in his hands though, he looked like he might be crying, which wasn't Gramps at all. He was genuinely distressed. How could such a smart, capable man think he had a Super-Nut from God? It was hard to see my hero slip. Gramps was a star to me. I remember growing up it seemed like everyone in Chicago knew him or knew of him. I bent down so I could console him, but mostly to avoid seeing his junk again.

I hoped he was crying about letting his ball sack fall in the toilet water again, "Gramps, just pee standing up and that won't happen, or maybe just hold it on your thigh or something."

"Don't you understand Parker? I just want my nuts back. Can you have your brother put my nuts back in?"

"Beau is a dentist, Gramps, he doesn't—"

"Boy, look at me." His eyes were wet, blue, beautiful, and serious, "I need my Super-Nut back. I don't care about the little guy, keep him in a museum for all I care. I'm dying, I can feel it every day, life is slipping through my fingers, Parker. I'll die if I don't get my Super-Nut back, soon." He put his head back in his hands.

I almost started crying too, but nothing emotional, Gramps let a fart while he was peeing, and it was beyond thick. Old people are sneaky like that. He started shaking, an innocent bystander would think it was the inescapably horrific odor, but I knew Gramps was crying because he was mourning the death of his Super-Nut. Gramps' crying really affected me, but so did the thick stench of a sexually active, seventy-eight-year old's inner bowels. Then another genius idea hit me.

"Gramps, we're going to get you your Super-Nut back, the little guy too."

25

MOM AND POP

My parents, Lucas and Felicia Duque had both spent *lifetimes* being naturally beautiful. When they woke up, after they got out of a pool, it didn't matter, effortless chic followed them wherever they went. An honest assessment would put me at less than average looking with little to no chic, which had to be a constant source of shock for my parents. Despite this genetic setback, they loved me, but also had my intelligence tested several times, just in case my good looks had been sacrificed for some other extraordinary trait, differentiating me from the other children.

There had to be *something* that would warrant a snappy introduction like, "This is our son Parker, he's off the charts in reading comprehension," instead of, "this is Parker, our youngest."

Beau had inherited my parent's fabulous looks, so no further testing was required, he was set for life. It sucked I had to take all those tests, but it was totally worth it. After my parents were told I wasn't a genius, repeatedly, they pretty much stopped expecting anything from me, and low expectations fit my stress tolerance perfectly.

Any visit with my parents started at the Chevron gas station in the heart of our neighborhood. Dad's *secretary*, Ms. Dee, was a wonderful woman who worked behind the counter full time as her real job. My father had never *not* had a secretary, so he worked out a deal with Ms. Dee and her boss, Nure, for her to keep his calendar and take his calls. In exchange for a nominal monthly fee, Ms. Dee would book his appointments if he ever had any, and he would check every morning when he picked up his paper.

"How are you Miss Dee?"

"Well, well, well. Hello Mr. Parker, I'm doing fine, just fine, thanks for asking. Is this all or do you need to see your Daddy?"

"I do. Does he have anything available this afternoon, I was hoping to go over there right now?"

"You can't. Mr. Parker, what are you planning on doing with all this?" Ms. Dee was looking at the counter, it was an obscene aggregation of powerful gas station medicine; Vivarin, Monster Energy drinks, several Little Debbie Cosmic Brownies and all the Andy Capp Hot Fries they had left.

"I'm not planning on sleeping anytime soon, that's for sure."

Ms. Dee harumphed, "Mr. Parker, your daddy told me you sold your company. He told me you were rich now, a self-made man. He was walking on air."

It was nice to hear, "Well, I didn't sell a company, but close to that. I'm going to be a writer." I had no idea where it came from, but it felt fun to say. Nothing really mattered anymore, why not?

The smile left Ms. Dee's face, "Have you told your Daddy that?"

"No, why?"

"It sounds like a mistake."

I smiled, "Did you say he had anything open today, Ms. Dee?"

"I told you, you can't, Mr. Parker. He has the rest of the day cleared for your mother."

I knew what that meant and what I'd have to do. My mouth started a pre-vomit watering, I quickly handed her a hundred-dollar bill, "Thanks Ms. Dee, keep the change."

My Mom and Dad, both in their late fifties, were stealth sex fiends. Perfectly normal on the outside, sexy dirty on the inside. There is a cabinet in my father's office that contains over thirty years of them bumping uglies on video. Innocent titles tell of the locations, but not necessarily the content; Grand Canyon '76, Bahamas '82, Lake Tahoe '84. God help anyone that mistakes those tapes for family movies. Beau and I have an unwritten rule to never discuss the cabinet or its contents, but we both know it's there. I won't go into my father's office, and Beau won't go into their house.

I climbed the steps up to their front door and knocked. I was excited I'd get to see them again and say goodbye. Something I thought impossible while sitting on Dusty and Peaches' cliff.

"Parker boy! Did you make an appointment?" My father opened the front door in his bathrobe. I could tell they'd been smoking up a storm from the dank smelling, bluish cloud of pot smoke that floated out the open door, past me, and down to the street. If Lucas Duque were an animal, he'd be a lion. He was a perpetual magazine ad, his tan was fresh, and his blonde hair sparkled in the sun. He looked more and more like a younger version of Gramps, just as beautiful although not as smart, which I always thought was the weed.

"I did, she told me you were busy, but I have some bad news and I wanted to talk to you and Mom really quick."

"I'm sorry son; we aren't available right this minute, although I hear a celebration is in order! Would you like to book dinner tonight? Did you ask Ms. Dee for my availability?"

It was then I noticed the bulge in his robe, he had a boner. My father had somehow, unfortunately, come under the false notion that boners were *natural* and shouldn't be discouraged, or hidden, when they show up. Instead of giving him hell, Mom thinks it's hilarious, which doesn't help anything. I took a step back and pointed to Dad's angry little soldier.

"I swear, this isn't sex related, I just woke up, it's morning wood, I have to pee" he said, pointing to his boner, "Your mother and I haven't even started up yet."

I dove towards the nearest railing and hurled in the bushes.

"You need to see a shrink about that, Parker. You can't keep throwing up every time you see a boner, it's natural."

"I'm not sure I have a choice, Dad. I think I might be allergic to something around here." *Overt parental sex maybe?* "Dad, Margot is dead."

"Oh, son—"

"*Dad!*" I jumped back. Like a good Dad, he had come in for a hug. He looked confused until I pointed, again, to his morning wood, "She was cheating on me and her lover shot her."

"That skanky bitch."

"Yeah, I pretty much feel the same way. Listen, I'm leaving Atlanta tonight, I don't want to be around here after everyone finds out. I'd like to avoid the embarrassment."

"You're leaving? Parker, you didn't? I would understand I guess, if—"

"Jesus, Dad, no." I would have loved to tell him the *entire* truth but knew I couldn't, "I didn't kill her, nor would I want to for *cheating* on me. Would you understand it if mom killed you for cheating on her?"

"Oh yeah, sure. Honestly, there were *several* times when I thought your mother was going to kill me." There was an awkward silence as we both replayed a couple of those near-death experiences in our minds. Dad seemed happy to move on, "So where are you going?"

"Michigan."

"Michigan, where? Saugatuck?"

"Yes." I didn't want to offer more information.

"Going to the beach, huh?" Just like his boner, he knew something was up, I wasn't one to go to the beach.

I pointed to Dad's boner and said, "Do you need to pee? I can wait. Seriously."

"Parker, Parker, Parker. Don't be immature, this is natural, it can wait. You don't get these?"

"I do get them, but after I pee, they go down. That's the goal I'm after here. To talk to you without a boner."

"I remember Sarah, she was lovely. Is she single?" How in the world did he make that connection?

"She's married with kids."

"So you *are* going to see her? I knew it."

I hated that I was so annoyed with Dad the last time I would see him. Instead of cat and mouse games, I decided to tell him the truth, why not? "Yes, but no. I need to get away from Atlanta. Saugatuck is a beautiful place, far away from here, and while I'm there, I can check up on Sarah and see what she's done with her life, in the least creepy way possible. Something I've wanted to do for a while."

"She was the one that got away, wasn't she?" It looked like he understood.

"Yes." It felt cathartic to tell him.

"Sounds like a little girl rebound move to me; but my philandering wife didn't just get shot dead by her lover. That's got to be tough. Listen, don't freak out. Margot was beautiful, but let me tell you something, Parker, and you've probably heard this from me a hundred times before, for every beautiful woman you see, there's a guy out there that's tired of fucking her."

"Hi Mom." I said. Dad's eyes became the size of pancakes. She was standing behind him.

"What did you just say?" She asked.

"Margot is dead mom." I said abruptly, saving my old man's ass.

"Oh honey!" she launched herself on me and I was thankful for the hug and thankful that women didn't get boners.

"She was cheating on him and her psycho lover killed her." Dad added from the background, a real empath.

Mom was crying, she held me at arm's length, "I knew she was a whore."

"Yep." I shrugged, by that point I wasn't upset about Margot's death anymore. I had almost died at the hands of Dusty and Peaches; funny how that'll change your outlook.

Piper had disappeared into the house after my dad opened the door. I thought nothing of it until she came back out with a dildo in her mouth. She sat eagerly in front of me, waiting for me to grab the huge vein covered penis and chuck it. I would have too, for fun, except it was my parent's vein covered penis. I threw up over the other side of the porch.

"Oh Piper! Bad girl! She's worse than Landon, did you hear what that boy did?" Mom grabbed the sex toy from Piper's mouth and hid it behind her back. Piper, realizing a game of large, veined dildo fetch was not in the cards, found a spot in the ivy next to their porch and went to sleep.

"Beau told me this morning." Dad started cracking up, his boner still going strong, "I love that little guy, I've always been a big shoe guy myself, so I don't know that his Dad can take *all* the credit."

"Lucas, watch yourself," Mom started cracking up, having finally noticed dad's boner, "I've got plans for that."

I hurled yet again, nearly missing Piper.

"Please stop you two." I begged from over the railing.

"It's *natural* Parker." Dad insisted, "Hey, guess what? Parker is leaving tonight to go see his old girlfriend from Purdue?"

"Oh Parker, I loved her! Sarah? That sounds rash. Have you thought it over?"

"That's what I said." My father announced, proud of his rare parenting involvement.

It *would* be rash if we weren't about to die, but I couldn't tell mom either, "Dad's making it into a bigger deal than it is." It wasn't worth correcting or even answering more than that. I looked at them both, understanding this would be the last time I saw them. I knew they wouldn't come to Michigan.

Professions of love weren't exactly commonplace among the Duques, this was unknown territory, "I think you guys have been the best parents a guy could ask for and I love you both, very much."

My mother gave me a big hug, successfully shielding me from Dad's boner, "Oh sweetie, we love you too Parker." Both she and Dad were tearing up.

"Would it be OK if Chuy came with me for a couple days? I'll keep him out of trouble?"

They looked at each other with wild eyes and said in unison, "Yes."

I started tearing up as my mother hugged me again. I could feel the dildo on my back, but I didn't care. Dad came in for a group hug, but we were both able to hold him and his little soldier at a safe distance.

I walked back down the stairs to the street and let Piper in the car. After I closed the door behind her, I looked up again. Mom and Dad were still standing there, smiling.

"Parker, I'm proud of you son. You earned that car!"

I didn't know what to say, how do you say goodbye to your parents for the last time? "Thanks Pop!" was all I could muster, hoping they hadn't heard my voice crack. Tears filled my eyes as I watched my parents take their penises inside.

26

MY NEPHEW'S KEEPER

My brother Beau lived in Druid Hills, a neighborhood next to mine filled with stately mansions, set far back from the street on one to two acre lots. Beau had wisely diversified his trust fund, well before the demise of Duque Industrial Fixtures and he, Dad, and Gramps had split what was left of it. Beau was self-made too; he had built a thriving dental practice on his own and was rolling in cash.

Beau's marriage was atypical and brief; his wife had left him shortly after Landon was born, never to be heard from again. They seemed happy enough at first, other than the fact she liked to dance with husky women at bars and he liked to fill cavities. Beau never told us why she left, and we never asked, probably because none of us liked her.

Shortly after his wife's mysterious departure, the only nanny that could handle Landon turned out to be Ms. Livingston. Ms. Livingston couldn't have been more than four and a half feet tall. The tiny Chinese woman was anywhere from fifty to two hundred years old and would be mildly pretty if her face weren't stuck in a continual state of disgust.

For someone who couldn't stand Americans, she sure picked a peculiar place to live. Of that disgust for Americans, I seemed to be at the top of her list and I didn't like her either. She seemed intent on raising Landon as her own little Chinese disciple and Beau didn't seem to mind as long as his participation was in a limited role. Ms. Livingston wasn't that much taller than Landon, they had the same accent, and spoke about the same amount of broken English.

"Ahhh, Haroo Pawker-san, we have been expecting you. So sorry to hear of Mrs. Margot. She of clazy bitch for sure."

We finally agreed on something, "Thank you, Ms. Livingston."

"Beau Duque in study with Mexican boy and Grandpa no balls."

"That's Chuy, Ms. Livingston. You've known him for five years. His name is Chuy."

"Me no care, me no like Parker Duque and me no like Mexicans."

"What did you say?" I turned around, upset at her comment, only to see she had gotten into some sort of defensive posture.

"I say, me no like Mexicans, or what you say? Wetbacks?" She thumbed her nose like Bruce Lee would.

"Seriously, if you call him or Gramps another name, I'll kick your fucking geriatric ass right here. Do you understand me? I don't care that you're a woman or how old you are." I lied.

"Wetback, droopy sack" she said immediately, taunting me. She wasn't afraid at all. She was in a full-on defensive pose now, like in the movie, *The Karate Kid.* I'd like to be able to say I didn't let it escalate because she's a woman, but the truth is, I'm no streetfighter and I was afraid of getting my arm broken by a midget/racist/geriatric Chinese woman.

"Ms. Livingston! Put away the praying mantis darling. Parker, we're all in the study." Beau had breezed into the foyer where Ms. Livingston and I had been squaring up. He grabbed my arm and led me to safety, towards his office.

"I hear rover boy had huge election! So sowry!" came from the hallway in back of us.

I looked at Beau, still holding my arm, "Did you tell Ms. Livingston Margot's lover had a huge dick?"

Beau looked at me and shrugged sheepishly, "She must have read it in the paper." I stopped dead in my tracks and looked at him, disgusted. He broke, "OK I told her. It was too juicy! Admit it, it's *juicy!*"

"Please quit telling people about Margot's lover and his big dick. Can you do that for me? Summon all your strength and discipline, let's just try to keep it a secret, OK? For me?"

"For you, my dear brother, I will do it. Or at least I'll try. Sometimes I get swept up in the moment, you know me."

"You need to fire her Beau, I'm serious this time. She's a racist. She called Chuy a *wetback*. How does she even know that term?"

"You're wrong, she loves Chuy. She makes tacos especially for him, every time he comes over."

"Chuy hates tacos."

"Maybe she hates you? Have you ever thought about your role in this, Parker?"

"No, I haven't, why on Earth would she hate me? You should fire her; she's messing up Landon, he's not speaking English correctly and doing horrible stuff. The shoe-jacking thing was alarming, not cute."

"He would be devastated, Parker; he loves her like a Chinese Grandmother. I don't know what she has against you. Maybe she's threatened by how much Landon loves you, or maybe because you keep telling me I should fire her. I should think that would be unnerving."

"You think she's jealous of how much Landon loves me?"

"No, not really, I just thought it sounded good and might get you off my back. We've only got a few days left, right? Why rock the boat?" He was right.

We walked into Beau's cherry paneled office, which was immaculate, stylish, and *very* gay. Gramps was sitting behind the desk like he owned the place and Chuy was across the room looking at nitrous oxide tanks in a dental supply catalog.

Chuy and Gramps had been laughing pretty hard about something before we came into the room and seemed pleased at my arrival.

"Holmes! Bummer, right? About the huge cock?"

27

BYE BYE BIG BROTHER

"Did you find Gramps Super-Nut? Did you call the government?" I asked Beau directly once we were in the office.

Beau was the worst actor ever. He began his rehearsed response, which included awkward body language that stopped just short of winking at me, "I did. I called the department of—"

"I'm getting them back tomorrow!" Gramps interrupted, "Sorry to hear about the giant schlong, Parker, I feel for you, that's the only way this whole situation could have been worse. Tough break kid."

"I'll be OK Gramps, thanks." I stared daggers as best I could over at Beau. He shrugged his shoulders and mouthed, "*Juicy.*"

I was distracted by something out the window that appeared to be rising and falling in the distance. Upon closer inspection I saw Landon balancing on the top of his play set, then jumping off, belly flopping into a tiny kiddy pool below. Then running back up to do it again.

"Holy shit! Is that safe? Is he going to hurt himself?" I erupted, pointing out the window to the unsupervised little guy laughing his way through what looked like ten-foot drops into six inches of water.

"Ms. Livingston's family worked in the circus. She taught him that. Isn't it impressive? That's a fifteen-foot drop." Beau said, hardly containing his pride.

"That's quite a boy you got there, Billy." Gramps beamed.

"Gramps, I go by Beau now."

"What? Your name is Billy, and you want to be called Beau? That doesn't make a lick of sense. Do either of you have any singles?" Gramps had pulled out his wallet.

"Why?" Beau asked.

"To tip the Mexican kid that brought my bags in, you dumbass. He's just been sitting around, waiting on us, and all I have is a twenty." Chuy, unnerved, held out his hand for the twenty.

"Did you get me a laptop?" I asked Beau, ignoring Gramps confusion.

"Yes, and I got you some snacks for your trip." Beau hoisted two bags full of Hot Fries and a bag of off-brand powdered sugar donuts from behind his desk, "I also got a power converter for your car."

"Thanks, it already has a plug built in, if you can believe it? I couldn't believe I drove my old car around for so long."

"Seriously Holmes, your old car sucked." Chuy laughed, "Did you ask Mom and Dad if I could go?" Chuy asked.

"Yeah, we're good to go. Beau, this is a weird request, but can I take your cell phone? Everybody and their brother are going to be calling me when this hits the paper, and I don't want to talk to any of them." I took the battery out of my phone and threw it and my phone in Beau's garbage.

"Good point. You can't take mine though, I use it for work. You can take Landon's, just don't let him know you're taking it, he'll freak." He pulled a Hello-Kitty phone from his desk drawer and handed it to me.

"Seriously?" I couldn't believe he gave a five-year-old a cell phone.

"I give it to him after dinner, when it's not peak minutes."

"You gave a five-year-old a cell phone?"

"Of course. Why not?"

"I guess I'm just old fashioned. Who does a five-year-old call?"

"He calls mainland China a lot, but mostly me or Ms. Livingston. He's starting to read and calls when he gets stuck on a word."

"I heard Margot was getting calls on the bone phone, *long distance!*" Gramps said, giving a high five to Chuy only to stop and look at him again, confused. He looked back to me and Beau, "Hey, seriously, who's going tip the Mexican? He's waiting."

"That's your grandson Gramps, his name is Chuy." Beau chided Gramps as Chuy laughed and shook his head.

Gramps still looked confused. "We aren't Mexican, are we?"

Beau and I answered in unison, "We are."

"That explains a lot, although you don't look Mexican." Gramps pointed to Beau.

"Muy bien." I said, "Chuy, hand me that pen and a piece of stationary. Beau, you're the only guy I know that has stationary. I'll be right back; I want to say goodbye to Landon first."

28

NOT TOO SMART

"Runcle Pawker-san!" Landon yelled from atop his play set, "Watch theeth!" Balanced high atop a monstrous playset, Landon launched himself into a graceful swan dive, never pulling out of the swan, and belly flopping into a tiny kiddy pool below. It was an impressive belly flop considering he had splashed out all but two or three inches of water from the kiddy pool.

I knelt down, arms outstretched for a hug as he came running to me. I was so glad to see him one more time. What a sweet boy. He ran at me, full speed but instead of launching into a hug where we both laughed as we tumbled over, he soccer kicked me right square in the nuts. It was even more excruciating than you could've imagined, because his cute little foot bounced off my bruised thigh before his soccer-style kick found its mark. I rolled over into a fetal position. I couldn't breathe or make a sound. My eyes were closed, and I saw stars. I felt Piper lick my face, then watched her curl into a ball next to me and fall asleep. I closed my eyes again; the stars were still there, floating around in black. I could feel tiny hands on me, searching my pockets. I forced my eyes open again to see Landon yanking his Hello Kitty cell phone out of my front pocket.

"Ohhh, rooky heeyah. What theeth? Not too smart tlying to takey Randon's cell phone Runcle Pawker-san, not too smart!"

Had I been able to speak I would have said, "How on earth did you know?" but my left nut was screaming in pain like a chainsaw cranked at full throttle.

Landon placed his hands behind his back and started an evil back and forth pace in front of his me, his powerless victim. "Randon know tings Runcle-san, no test Randon."

I had an idea where the leak might have originated from. I looked over toward the house and saw Ms. Livingston disappear behind the drapes inside, "Oh sweet Jesus. Landon, don't ever do that again."

He nodded yes and smiled a Cheshire grin, "Me no kick Runcle Pawker-san, if Runcle Pawker-san no takey Kitty."

"No," I handed Landon the stationary, "I wasn't talking about kicking me in the nuts, although that definitely has to stop; I was talking about referring to yourself in the third person. It's creepy, don't ever do that again."

"Are you going to cly Runcle-san? Ms. Rivingston say you soft, say you cly rike baby."

"Of course! There are many occasions Landon, where it's OK for a guy to cry."

"Daddy says you cly rike baby because you have big heart, does big heart hurt? Why you clying Runcle-san?"

"Do you guys talk about me clying— crying a lot?"

"Only when Ms. Rivingston bring it up Runcle Pawker-san, it prenty funny. She do imitation of Runcle-san. Randon and Daddy have big, big, funny raff." And with that Landon started giggling uncontrollably and I started too, despite my leg aching and my nuts feeling like they were on fire and someone was trying to put them out with a sharp rake. It's impossible not to laugh when Landon starts his little cackle.

"Come here buddy. Your dad told me you're starting to read; you're turning into a big boy! You're smart just like your dad. I want you to read what I wrote on your paper." I pointed to the stationary he was holding.

"I ruh, I ruh ah, I ruhve you Randon. I ruhve you Randon!" He was so it excited it made the aching in my nut seem almost distant. Almost.

Ohhh Buddy!" I gave him a big hug and started tearing up thinking how special this little guy was, and how it was all for nothing. I'd never get to see what Landon turned into. "I'm going to go on a trip with Runcle— Uncle Chuy and I just wanted to tell you how much I love you. I'll be gone for a while."

"Rokay Runcle Pawker-san, Randon roves you too. Can I go now?"

"Yes, Landon, you can go."

I watched him run back toward his play set. He stopped, turned around, and came running back to me. I instinctively covered my nuts. He stopped short, stood silent in front of me and stared me in the face for a minute, like he was trying to memorize it and then he gave me another sweet little bear hug. I kept protecting what was left of my left nut throughout the entire sweet little bear hug because I was scared.

I was trying my best to hold back the "clying" lest I become dinner theatre for them again tonight. When he released me, he dug into his swimsuit pocket and handed me his wet Hello Kitty cell phone back.

"You takey. Goodbye Runcle Pawker-san."

29

ROAD TRIP

"You've driven with me at least five times, you know I can drive, mother-fucker." Chuy was looking at me, smiling. If you weren't careful, his blonde highlights could hypnotize you.

"I don't care if you swear, but could you not call me motherfucker? You sound angry. You can drive when we get to the highway, which I'm still nervous about. You don't have your license yet."

"Yeah, I know, I can't believe you're letting me drive either, I'm stoked. I bet you this motherfucking motherfucker goes a hundred and fifty miles per hour. Dad said you sold your business. Is this all you bought? Not that this isn't a bad-ass motherfucking ride, I just thought you'd get more for all your shit."

"Just out of curiosity, are you trying to set a record for saying mother-fucker? *Motherfucker* is like a fine wine, you don't bring it out often, you save it for the right occasion, and you don't gulp it down, you sip and enjoy it."

"If you like the motherfucking wine, why can't you gulp it down, Mother-fucker?"

"OK, I think you might be having a 'motherfucking' seizure. Can you stop please?

"I'm just excited to drive this beast!"

"I understand completely, this is the nicest car I've ever been in. THe funny thing is, *technically*, a friend bought this car for me." I used five thousand dollars from Dusty's backpack and financed the rest. I was tickled about the financing part, because I knew I'd never have to pay them back.

"I'd like to meet that motherfucker; did you blow him or something? What kind of a dude buys a badass rig like this for another dude?"

"Actually," I said, "he passed away and left me some money. He was a guy I met through a friend and we took a road trip together, with his girlfriend. It's a long story."

"We've got time Motherfucker, I'm picking up what you're putting down; lay it on me."

"Actually," I said pulling into neighborhood Chevron to fill up, "you're gonna start driving, stop saying motherfucker, and I'm going to start writing."

"What? When are we— you want to leave now?"

I'd always been the guy to fart around when it's time to do something, clean out the closet, load the dishwasher, whatever, I'd never been in a hurry. Now though, I felt an urgency like never before, like I was walking on thin ice, one crack away from being swallowed up. I'd never thought about dying until now, and now it was imminent. I had to see Sarah before it was too late.

"Yes! Of course we're leaving now. We can go get your stuff, but we need to hit the road."

"No can-do Holmes, I have a party to go to tonight."

"Seriously?"

"School's over Motherfucker, there are a ton of parties. I might be getting *laid* tonight! I can't go then. I want to go with you, and I want to drive this motherfucking spaceship until the wheels fall off, but action means satisfaction Holmes, especially when you're trying to break the curse. It's my last night!"

"What's breaking the curse?" I asked.

"Losing my virginity Holmes!"

Holy crap. I was speechless. I don't know why he said, *it's my last night,* but it really hit me hard that it *might* be, "We can go after your party tonight; I'll wait as long as you need."

156

30

ALWAYS CHECK THE LOCK

Landon's pink "Hello Kitty" phone started vibrating and meowing across my coffee table. I grabbed it; "Jesus" was calling. It had only been two hours since I dropped him off at home, "Chuy?"

"Come pick me up and we can go. Bring me some of those energy drinks and I'll drive straight through." I looked at the cooler of energy drinks I had just packed with ice and then at Piper sleeping like an angel in front of my bags.

"I'll be right there." As I hung up the phone, I heard him say "WAIT!" but it was too late. The *Hello Kitty* phone shook again, and I punched the talk button, "What?"

"Where were you going to pick me up?"

"That's a good question. Where are you?"

"I'm in Druid Hills, on Lullwater. Towards North Decatur if you come from The By Way. Hurry the fuck up, please." He hung up.

Lullwater was one of the prettiest and wealthiest residential streets in Atlanta and the end of school meant parties. Someone on Lullwater must have been having a blow-out because there were cars as far as the eye could see, lining both sides of the street. I drove slowly until I spotted Chuy sitting on the side of the road, in front of the house where they shot the film, *Driving Miss Daisy*. Piper barked out the window when she saw Chuy and then laid back down to sleep.

"Are you OK? What happened? It's only 9:00."

He slinked into the front passenger seat, "It's embarrassing, keep driving please."

That was fine with me, although I was curious, "Did you pack already? Are you ready to go?"

"Yep, swing by the house and I'll grab my shit."

"Gotcha." I didn't press, it was clear he didn't feel like talking.

"Do you want to talk about it?" I asked, just in case. He was silent, I would wait.

Chuy eventually broke his silence, "I got caught punching the clown."

I could never keep up with his sayings, and this confused me, but the way he said it felt like he was confessing to something, like he'd forgotten the parachutes after we'd just jumped out of a plane.

"Interesting. Why was there a clown at a graduation party and what did he do to you? I can't stand clowns either. Who are those people anyway? Is that their full-time job or are they just part-time creepy?"

"Not literally. Didn't Mom teach you what a *saying* is? Holmes, do you think I actually punched a clown?"

I was at a loss. "Yeah, I'm pretty sure somebody eventually taught me what sayings were but apparently they didn't cover the circus topics."

"I got caught doing the five-knuckle shuffle."

"Beating off? Jerking off? Masturbating?"

"Hey now! Easy Motherfucker!" He had both hands up like a panicked crossing guard. I suspect it had something to do with me entering the "parent zone" using the word *masturbating*. It made the situation awkwardly formal, like how you'd tell a doctor your *penis* hurts but you'd tell a buddy your dick hurts. As I said earlier, the parenting of Chuy was done by committee. I took the liberty of assigning myself the fun job, the older brother he could talk to and swear in front of. I loved that he trusted me, and I was often the first one to know if there was trouble with Chuy, like maybe a poorly punched clown.

"At a party?" I almost drove off the road, not so much because Chuy got caught whipping up a handmade protein shake at a party, but because

"punching the clown" was just about the most genius thing I'd ever heard.

This is where brothers, genetic or adopted, are different than sisters. A sister would say, *"Oh... My... Gawd! Why were you masturbating?"* A *brother* would ask the same thing I did, *"Why didn't you lock the door?"*

"I thought I did!" Chuy said incredulously, "The lock didn't work. It's probably a three-million-dollar house and the motherfucking bathroom lock doesn't work. It turns like it works but nothing holds the God damn door shut. She saw everything."

"Who caught you?" I asked, very interested.

"There were probably seventy people there, and the one person who decides to use the out of the way bathroom is Jessica."

"And who is Jessica?"

"Motherfucker, don't you listen? Jessica is the girl I've been after since grade school!"

"My bad, I remember now, the one with the 'adult size' rack. I should've known that. What'd she do?"

"What the fuck do you think she did? She screamed and ran!"

"Did you finish?" I asked, having fun. He didn't think it was funny though, he just looked out the window. "What'd you do?" I asked again, this time more seriously.

"I called *you* motherfucker. I got the hell out of there. What in the fuck do you think I did? They're probably coming up with nicknames for me right now, I have to go to a new high school."

I looked over at him and smiled, "Cool hand Duque?" He didn't seem to appreciate my quick wit *half* as much as I did. "Listen Chuy, don't sweat it. Every guy you know does it. A lot. I don't want to pile on when you're down, but don't you think you should be unloading your gun somewhere safer? She probably came looking for you after you disappeared for twenty minutes."

"That wasn't an issue. I can do the whole thing in under two minutes. I went up there to empty out my nuts. I wasn't even enjoying it; it was all business."

"What?"

"Rittenhose told me you last longer during sex if you jerk off beforehand."

"No, I meant what do you mean you can do the whole thing in under two minutes?"

"I can jerk off in less than 2 minutes." He seemed kind of proud about it. I tried to reconcile this awkward, unsolicited information with my own experience, only to end up more confused and depressed with each attempt. I couldn't cook a Patio brand frozen burrito in two minutes. *Jesus.* If there were ever a race, my little brother could relieve himself faster than it takes to cook a 55-cent microwave burrito. Now *that* was a convenient, super-coordinated talent/gift.

"After the accident with Gramps, my super-coordination thing is so good that I can just..." He was grinning now.

"Jesus." It was all I could say, again.

He stopped smiling and said, "Can I ask a question without you making fun of me?"

"I can't promise that right now buddy."

"Are you a screamer? Do you scream when you release? Does it make you feel better?" The way he was asking me it seemed like he was serious, like he actually wanted an answer.

"What? What do you mean a screamer? When I play Yahtzee?"

"Either. Having sex or jerking off, when you climax, do you scream?"

Climax? Is that what kids are calling it? I was disappointed. "Nope. I never scream. Never felt like it was important. Well, I screamed once when a girl licked my taint, but that's it."

"What's a taint?"

"It's the area between your balls and your asshole, *it taint your balls and it taint your asshole.*"

"But you wanted to scream because it felt so good?"

"No, I screamed because I thought she was going to lick my butthole."

"Did she?"

"No! Never let anyone mess with your BH, nothing good can come of it. It's got a super important day job, it's dirty, and it doesn't need any more traffic than it already gets, trust me. Get some paper out of the glove box and

make a note. Keep it in your wallet if you need to, that's an important rule."
Like I said, I'd always been the brother he could talk to, I figured since it was the end of the world, all bets were off and we could talk about whatever the fuck we wanted to, or at least the fun parts.

"Sex feels better for me if I scream when I release."

"When you climax?" I chuckled, "I thought you said you're a virgin?"

"Sorry, I am. I meant blowing a load." He was serious.

I pulled to the curb in front of my parents' house when it hit me, "Wait a minute. Did you rub one out at dinner last Sunday? When you said you bumped your elbow in the bathroom?"

He smiled a beautiful, sheepish grin as he shrugged his skinny shoulders. He grabbed the rear-view mirror, mangling it like Peaches had in my old car, and ran his hand through his thick, artificially golden, mane. He smiled back at himself, did a fresh pop of the collar and turned to me, "I'll be right back, feel free to be out of my seat by then. You know I was born to drive this motherfucker."

I watched him spring up the front stairs to my parent's house, looking like a jelly fish swimming up to the surface of the water. *Jesus.*

31

MICHIGAN OR BUST

With his bags in the trunk and his mood clearly elevated, Chuy settled into the driver's seat opposite me, "Pass me an energy drink, Motherfucker."

"Are you calling me motherfucker because I asked you not to?"

"What do you think, *Motherfucker*? I'm very excited to drive this beautiful beast." He looked at my laptop, "What are you going to write again?"

I handed him an energy drink. I had amassed a cooler of them and four packs of Vivarin to keep me awake for the rest of time, however long that might be. "I'm going to finish a short story I started a long ass time ago." I laughed; I was starting to talk like him. I looked at my caffeine supply in the back seat and smiled. It felt like I was back in school, with a term paper due tomorrow and I was just about to start a heroic all-nighter.

"How long will it take you?" He seemed unsure of me.

"Five or six hours, tops. I've worked the story out in my head over the years so it's really just a bunch of typing at this point. It should be easy."

"Cool. Where in Michigan are we going again?"

"Saugatuck. It's paradise, you'll love it."

"Who are we going to see?"

"No one. Although we may see my old girlfriend, that's part of the reason I'm writing this."

"I don't know her, right? What's her name?"

"Correct. She's from way back, pre-Chuy. Her name is Sarah."

"Do you think she's going to leave her husband for you?" He wasn't interested in the writing anymore.

"No, I don't think she'll leave her husband for me, but that's not why we're going up there. We're going up there to leave Atlanta."

"And why are we leaving Atlanta?"

"Margot and her friend—"

"Monster Cock?"

"Margot and Monster Cock will be in the news and I don't want to be around for the aftermath."

"Gotcha. But you just said you're writing this story for Sarah?"

"Well..."

"What if she got hot? Would you try to bang her then?"

"No. Chuy, stop. She's married, she has kids, get the love angle out of your mind. I'm not writing this to look impressive so I can get in her pants, I'm writing this so if we do run into her I won't feel like a disappointment. I'm writing this for myself, even though I'm writing it for her. Does that make any sense?"

"No."

"We came up with the story together at Purdue, I needed an idea for a creative writing class. She and I stayed up all night coming up with the story and the characters. I never used it, but we kept developing it for fun... It felt like we lived with the characters. She called it, 'The Bear,' and she made me promise I'd finish it, and I promised her I would. Then we broke up. I don't want to show up without it. I want to be able to say I kept my promise. I was such a different person then compared to now."

"What do you mean?"

"I was an annoying, spoiled, super-rich kid in college who didn't care about keeping promises. I'm no longer spoiled or super-rich, and keeping promises is important to me."

"It sounds to me like you still want to get in her pants."

"Chuy, I'm not even sure we'll even see her on this trip— you're making a mountain out of a mole hill."

"Beau told me she'd be in her hardware store."

163

I looked at Chuy. He knew he screwed up, "You little dick." Chuy's face erupted into a giant, dazzling smile. "You've known everything this entire time. What else did Beau tell you?"

"That she's your, 'one true love.' And that I should help you break up her marriage if she's still hot."

"Disregard *everything* Beau told you."

"What if she looks like a big brown turd? Will you be pissed you wrote your short story?"

"I worry about you sometimes, Chuy, but it's times like this that I don't. Let's take it one step at a time. Like I said, we may not even see her. I won't lie, I'm deathly curious, I do have an itch that needs scratching, I just don't know how itchy I am."

"Well, that's just great, Motherfucker. Do you think she has a promiscuous daughter? How hard was it to get down her pants?"

"Don't you *ever* give it a break? I hope she has all boys, and actually, even if she had girls, they'd be way too young; we've been out of school for less than fifteen years."

"Bummer. Whatever. This motherfucking rig is the bomb." Chuy commanded the 750Li through the Atlanta connector to I-75 North and we were on our way. His super-coordination made him the smoothest driver I'd ever ridden with.

I looked down at my laptop. The title was done, and the opening line was finished. Sarah and I came up with it together, I thought about the fun we had that night and told myself it's now or never. Literally.

32

THE BEAR

THE BEAR (First Draft), A SHORT STORY BY PARKER DUQUE

CHAPTER ONE

BOOTS AND ALL

I couldn't sleep. I wanted to, but I couldn't. I guess part of the reason was I had *all* of my clothes on, including my new boots. I went to bed like that. And let me tell you right now, if you want to get a good night's sleep, take off your boots.

Still, I wanted to be ready in case we hit the road early like my dad talked about the night before. "Jack, Sam" he said, "We've got to get to bed early tonight, we have a big day tomorrow. Grandpa's going fishing in the morning and said he'd wait for us if we get there early enough. Sam, I bought some new bait that we can try to catch Big Frank with." Dad must have been excited to go too, because he said it about fifty times over dinner, even though I'm pretty sure we agreed to it the first time.

What I couldn't figure out is why Mom seemed excited for us to go too. Didn't she know that all three of us were going to be gone starting tomorrow for a *whole week*? With us gone she isn't going to have anyone to cook for, nobody to play catch with, and she sure as hell won't be able to figure out any of the sports games on TV without us there to answer her questions. What was she doing smiling like that? Just like Dad said after I found him sleeping on the couch one morning, "Sometimes Sammy boy, women can be hard to understand."

Just in case you are confused, Big Frank is a huge catfish that lives at the bottom of the fishing hole in the back of my grandpa's farm. My grandpa named him Big Frank because the catfish kind of reminded him of a huge dumb kid in his class that was named Big Frank. Grandpa also said Big Frank the kid was "touched" and that he died a long time ago after the tractor he was driving ran over him. Now I can figure out a lot of things, but I have yet to figure out how you can run over yourself with a tractor that you are driving. Jack said that if there were pigs around, they would have eaten Big Frank's guts. He said that if you get run over by a tractor, your guts will probably be hanging out all over the place and that pigs will eat some gross shit if there's nobody around to stop them. I haven't ever seen any pigs in a cornfield though, so I imagine Big Frank's guts were safe and Jack just likes making up gross stuff about guts being eaten.

I sat up in bed and looked over at my alarm clock; it said 5:17 and the little red dot was next to the "AM." Just in case you were wondering, I figured it out myself one morning, the "AM" means "after midnight." I could tell my brother Jack was up too because his room is right next to mine and I could hear him moving around in there. I looked at my tackle box by the door and wondered whether I could do anything with it that I hadn't done the night before. I decided I probably shouldn't start messing with it though, just like I shouldn't take my boots off, because I wanted to be ready to go.

I shut my eyes and pictured how it would go in my head. My dad would walk down our hallway, knock on my door and say, "Sam, time to go. Let's get this train moving!" Then he'd knock on Jack's door but before he could say anything he would look over and see me step out of my room, completely

166

dressed and ready to go, boots on and all. He'd nod to me and I'd give him the cool nod I've been practicing right back, without looking too excited to go fishing because that ruins the "cool" part. Dad would then turn back to knock on Jack's door, but the door would open before he could knock, and Jack would be standing there completely dressed and ready to go too. Dad wouldn't say anything. He would smile and give us both a nod and we would all three walk down the stairs, straight through the kitchen where Mom would say, "You boys have to eat breakfast before you go!" And Dad would say, "Courtney, these young men were ready to go the minute I knocked on their doors. Sam was so ready, he even slept in his boots, didn't you Sam?" and I wouldn't say anything, I would just look at her and when she looked at me, I would nod my head just a little bit, as to mean, *"Yeah, I slept in my boots."* Then Mom would nod her head just a little bit back at me and say, "you guys better go, this healthy breakfast would only slow you down. Take these candy bars and eat them on your way." She wouldn't even cry and tell us how much she's going to miss us like she always does before we go to Grandpa's for the week. Then we would jump into Dad's truck and burn rubber the whole way out the driveway. You are probably thinking, *Wow, that would be awesome!* And I'd have to agree with you because it *would* be awesome.

I looked at my bedside clock and only ten minutes had gone by. You are probably saying to yourself, *why doesn't he just go ahead and see if his Dad's ready?* Well, I would if my dad hadn't told me just last week that if I came into their bedroom again before six, the "you know what" would hit the fan.

I know he meant that *"shit"* would hit the fan because I'd heard him say it a hundred times. Not in front of me mind you, only when he thought I couldn't hear him. He gets in trouble if he cusses in front of me just like I get in trouble if I cuss in front of him. We both cuss quite a bit even though I'm just a little kid. I figure I got good at cussing from being around the guys that work for my dad. They are *great* at cussing, especially a super tough little angry guy named Arthur, who everybody calls "Shorty." When you are a kid though, you can't cuss out loud. You have to cuss in your head or else you'll get in a shitload of trouble.

Just in case you are confused like I used to be, when he says "the shit will hit the fan" he is using a *saying*. Sayings, until my mom explained them to me, really confused the hell out of me. Shit won't really hit a fan if "the shit hits the fan."

I found out about sayings over a year ago. I was in the hallway outside my dad's office waiting for him to play catch when I heard him say the shit was *definitely* going to hit the fan, and it was definitely happening *today*. Well, who wouldn't want to see *that*? I ran into the living room and was surprised to see my Mom reading a book in front of the only fan we own. It was a fan we had in the living room window in front of my dad's chair. Well, I started thinking about the whole thing and couldn't help laughing. When Mom asked me what I was laughing about there was *no way* I was going to tell her. I couldn't stop laughing and then she started laughing too and I bet we both laughed together for at least an hour straight, even though she didn't know what we were laughing about. Well, after I stopped laughing, I started feeling guilty my Mom was *definitely* going to get shit all over her if I didn't tell her to move out of the way, but I got over that pretty quick. Like my dad says, one of the great things about Mom is she enjoys a joke just as much as the next guy. After another ten minutes of nothing, I ran out to the porch to see if there wasn't a cow or one of Mr. Bugna's dogs in front of the window. I closed my eyes and pictured it in my head, and it made me laugh even harder. If my teacher could see the sight that I could see in my head she would say, "WOW Sam, that is SPECTACULAR!" She uses the word "spectacular" quite a bit and in this instance, I would have to agree with her. After about another 20 minutes I pretty much gave up and asked Mom if we had any other fans around that I might not know about. She wanted to know why, and I told her because I wanted to see what it looked like when shit hit it. I mean, who wouldn't, right? Well, turns out, "the shit is going to hit the fan" is a *saying* which means there is going to be a whole lot of trouble, trouble as in I end up with soap in my mouth and dinner in my room while my dad gets yelled at in the kitchen. If you were to ask me for advice on what to do if you hear the shit is *definitely* going to hit the fan, I'd go ahead and start running.

I bet you are probably thinking; *sayings are confusing for me too.* I don't blame you. It turns out I was using sayings even before I knew they were sayings. Like when I say the thought of shit actually hitting a fan "cracks me up." I don't get *cracked* up; I'm just laughing.

Jack and I made up a saying too; "*staring icicles*" which is totally cool, and it might be my favorite. Another saying my dad uses is, "all bets are off." You would think that when the boss or the person in charge, such as my dad, says, "All bets are off" that the bet you currently had with your brother was automatically off. And you would also feel pretty good if you knew you were going to lose that bet. Especially if you wouldn't have to clear the table AND wash the dishes AND dry them off AND put them away. But that's just not the case. Just in case you are confused, the only person that can call off a bet is the person who's winning or the person who is tougher, which in most cases is going to be my dad. My dad once stared down a real live bear and that's the honest truth. So when my dad says, "all bets are off" I think he means, as far as I can tell, that the rules no longer apply and that what the tougher person says, goes. If not, the shit is *definitely* going to hit the fan.

CHAPTER TWO

GRANDPA'S FARM

Going to my grandpa's farm with "the men" (my dad and my brother) is my favorite part of the summer and we do it every year. My dad doesn't work that week, which is great. Dad has to work all summer, *every* summer. Can you believe that?

My mom says it's a vacation for her too, but I figure that must be a saying because like I told you already, what in the world is she going to do for a week without *us*? When she comes up at the end of the week, she always says she missed us terribly and cries even though she's happy. Even though I don't miss her when I'm fishing or chucking apples against the big oak in back of the barn, as soon as I see her, I remember that I missed her terribly too, without even knowing it.

My brother Jack says it is silly of me to be so excited to go to Grandpa's farm because we already live on a farm. It doesn't bother me though because I could tell just by talking to him last night that he was just as silly as me. Grandpa's farm is way, way better than ours, it has actual farm animals, two ponds to fish in, and it's where Jack and I were born. My dad was born there too. Apparently before Jack was born my mom put up a big fuss about giving birth to him on a farm instead of a doctor's office or a big hospital but after Dad talked her into it, she said she wouldn't have it any other way.

The lady that delivered us still lives down the road and when we see her, she acts as if she could care less. Can you believe that? I would think that it's a pretty big deal to deliver babies and that if you delivered me and Jack both you would want to ask us questions about how we are doing in school, were we catching any fish and if we play sports and all. I heard Grandpa whisper to Dad after we saw her once that she has something stuck up in her butt, which would explain why she keeps getting fatter.

Grandpa's farm is a lot smaller than ours, and Grandpa is the one that does all the chores. On our farm, my dad works mostly in a building at the front of the property and pays a bunch of men to do the actual farm work, which is mostly in the fields. We don't have animals and Mom doesn't want us to even get close to the tractors because they are HUGE. What fun is *that?*

One time, one of Dad's workers got his arm pulled clear off by a tractor, which is one of those things you'd rather see happen than have happen to you. Grandpa's tractors are big but aren't so big that you need a ladder to get up to the cab and as far as I can tell, there's nothing on them that'll pull one of your arms off. They are all bright green John Deere's because, my grandpa says, "Nothing runs like deer."

My older brother Jack has already driven one of Grandpa's tractors, and he's just two- and three-quarter years older than me! I figure I'm going to be allowed to drive a tractor either this trip or next, and I'll have to sit in Dad's lap just like when Jack started.

Jack also told me Grandpa said he can drive the Honda by himself this trip, which would be a really big deal. In case you are confused, we call the four-wheeler the "Honda" because it is made by a company called Honda and it's a lot easier to say Honda than it is to say four-wheeler. A four-wheeler is like a motorcycle except it has four thick tires, so it doesn't fall over when you get off it. My grandpa says the Honda belongs to my dad and that he would NEVER buy *anything* for his farm that was made by foreigners. I asked my dad, "If the Honda *is* ours why can't we take it home?" He just laughed and told me that the Honda is Grandpa's and that he gave it to him for his birthday a while back. He also told me that it drives Grandpa crazy because it's the only thing on his farm that doesn't break down. As far as I can tell, Grandpa doesn't have any problems *driving* something made by foreigners, because he drives that thing everywhere.

Grandpa is retired and doesn't grow but one field of corn and one field of hay and he only does that so he can feed the animals he has left. Dad says that other farmers pay Grandpa money to grow corn on the rest of his land, which sounds like a hell of a good deal to me. That would be like someone paying me to eat grape flavored Big League Chew bubble gum, which is my favorite. I asked him once why he didn't just stop all together and he said that if he did, he would be bored to death and that a man can't just fish every day. I wonder if that is a saying too because I know for a fact that I could fish every day if I had a fishing hole like Grandpa's.

Like I told you before, my Grandpa has two fishing holes. The fishing hole I'm talking about takes a while to get to if you have short legs like mine, but I can make it there pretty quick if I run, which I almost always do. If Grandpa lets Jack drive the Honda, I bet we could make it there in five minutes! Well, I actually don't know how long it would take us, but it would be a lot quicker, and I wouldn't get so out of breath. One time Grandpa let Jack drive the John Deere lawn tractor to the hole and I wound up getting off and running because the dang thing was so slow.

There's also a woodshop on Grandpa's farm with tools where Dad teaches us how to make things out of wood. A lot of times we fix things for Mom but one time we made baseball bats and even though it's too heavy for me to swing right now, it's my favorite bat. Right next to the wood shop there are apple trees that you can sit under and either eat the apples or chuck them into the big oak tree out back. In case you are confused, when you chuck a fresh apple hard enough into an oak tree, it explodes.

Grandma doesn't like us to pick apples off the tree to throw because it's a waste of a perfectly good apple. "Use the apples on the ground!" She would yell at us. I always wondered how she knew we were taking them off the tree because you can't see us from the house. I've thought about it and even asked my Mom and all she said was, "Mothers know when their children are up to something! It's a magical power we have." I can tell you right now though, that is a total load of crap. I didn't tell her I knew it was a total load of crap though. If she really had a "magical power" of knowing some of the things that Jack and I have done and gotten away with, we would both be goners by now, especially Jack.

There are probably thousands and thousands of other little reasons why Grandpa's farm is much better than ours, but it would take me thousands and thousands of minutes to tell you about them. The biggest reason his farm is better than ours is because Grandpa's farm is where our roots are. My dad says it's important to remember where you come from and a man needs to make time to get back to his roots. I haven't seen my mom's roots; in fact, I don't know where my mom's roots are because she doesn't have any brothers or sisters and both her parents died when she was in college. I can't imagine not having a mom or a dad anymore; I guess that's why she calls Grandma and Grandpa "Mom" and "Dad" even though they are really my dad's parents.

It feels good to be at Grandpa's and I figure it's because the three of us are all getting back to our roots. In case you are confused, "getting back to your roots" is a saying too. As far as I can tell, "getting back to your roots" means going back to the place where you were born, or where you can do some really great fishing, or both in our case.

CHAPTER THREE

JACK, DAD, AND MY BIG HEART

My brother Jack is two school grades and almost three years older than me and for the most part I would say he is my best friend. We don't do everything together like *real* best friends do on account that he is two grades older than me, and he *is* my brother, but out of all my friends, Jack is my favorite. He takes care of me when Mom or Dad aren't around and pretty much anytime I need taking care of.

The only time we don't get along is when we are in fights. We argue about who gets to do what first and stuff like that. Just because he's the oldest and he's pretty much a lot stronger than me Jack thinks he should get the first shot at everything and that I should respect my elders. Just in case you are confused, "respect your elders" is another saying that I figured out. It means old people get the first shot at *everything*. Obviously, old people make up sayings and rules like that. But even when we are in big fights, he's my best friend which sounds awfully confusing but it's true.

For instance, one time Jack and I were in a huge fight because I had lost his baseball glove after he asked me not to use it. He said there was nothing wrong with mine and he was right, but I knew I could catch fly balls better with his glove and he wasn't even using it, so I borrowed it for a game. I probably dropped 20 fly balls and then lost it somewhere between the baseball field and home. I didn't mean to lose it, but I did.

That very next day after school I was getting beat up by the school bully named Kenny Johnson for no good reason, or at least no reason good enough that I can remember right now. Actually, now that I think about it, I might have said something to him about showering more often, but why would a kid who was going to be in *high school* next year be hanging around the jungle gym with 5th *graders* in the first place? Jack says that sometimes when I say things; it comes out sounding like I'm a wise ass. Just in case you are confused, a "wise ass" is someone who's right about something and knows they are right but acts like an ass when they tell you you're wrong. I swear I wasn't *trying* to be a wise ass; he really did need to take a shower because you could smell him from ten feet away. For real.

Anyway, he was sitting on top of me making me eat dirt and I was crying and trying to spit the dirt out when who shows up out of nowhere and personally delivers a big old can of whup-ass to Kenny? It was Jack. Even though he cussed me out for probably ten hours that morning after I told him I lost his glove, he still came to my rescue, which is probably something he is used to by now. When Jack heard that I was getting beat up, he ran clear across the entire school grounds, from the baseball fields to the jungle gym, and just so you know, that's a hell of a long way. Jack gave it to Kenny pretty good too and made him cry even though Kenny was a grade older than him. Jack asked me if I wanted to feed Kenny dirt like he did to me, but I couldn't because I was still crying and wanted to go home and also, I just didn't want to do that to anybody, even Kenny. Jack told me on our way home that he understood, and it was just an option he was giving me and that it's good that I didn't feed Kenny dirt. After that we laughed because Jack smelled terrible, pretty much just like Kenny

Let me set this straight right here though. I didn't just lay down, eat dirt and cry. I put up a fight before Jack got there. Who knows? I might have even softened Kenny up a little bit for Jack to come in and whup-ass. I think Jack knew I put up a hell of a fight too, because he never even made fun of me for getting beat up or crying or eating dirt, ever. And I know you are probably thinking, *OK kid, that's what a big brother is supposed do, right?* But here's the thing; Kenny has a big brother in high school named Mark, who is 3 grades older than Jack and Jack knew full well he was probably going to get a large can of whup-ass from him, delivered personally.

I learned about whup-ass from Shorty, the tough little guy that helped run our farm. He was the first person to tell me and Jack about Dad and the bear and that Dad was a hell of a wrestler and could deliver a truckload of whup-ass in his day. I felt horrible because not only had I lost my best friend's baseball glove, he was also going to get a large can of personally delivered whup-ass just for protecting me from a bully. I swore that day I'd sooner eat a cornfield full of dirt than to do that to him again.

So now that I've come this far, I might as well go ahead and tell you the rest because it gets real good. The next day Kenny's older brother Mark shows up with two of his buddies and Kenny at the baseball field. I wasn't there yet, but my friend told me that Jack tried to talk to him about how I didn't do anything to Kenny, and he didn't do anything to Kenny that Kenny hadn't already done to me, but that didn't work. Well, by the time I got to the baseball field from the jungle gym, which is a hell of a long way, Jack was sitting on Mark's chest, feeding him dirt. No kidding! Jack had probably 6 or 7 friends just standing around Mark's two buddies and Kenny, who just stood there watching with their mouths open, like they had just seen a chicken give birth to a cow. I looked at Jack and although he wasn't the one eating dirt, it looked like he got it pretty good too. I felt bad about Jack getting hit in the face, which is a big deal in a fight, but he said it didn't hurt one bit and I believe him. In case you haven't figured it out by now, my brother Jack is a really tough kid and probably the toughest kid in our school. I'm proud that he is my brother and almost best friend.

That night, their dad, Mr. Johnson, who is a real tough looking guy himself and probably five or six grades older than my dad, came tearing up our driveway and walked to the house real mad, cussing at the ground, rubbing his fists. Jack and I ran to my bedroom where we watched him from my window. We both got a real good laugh out of it too because he obviously hadn't ever met our dad. After we heard Dad raise his voice about Mr. Johnson tearing up our driveway, we ran like hell to the front door and saw Mr. Johnson standing there with a surprised look on his face like maybe he had just walked into the girl's bathroom by mistake and the principal was in there.

Dad saw us and told us to wait for him in his study and then I felt sick to my stomach. We were sitting on the couch in my dad's study and Jack put his arm around me and said, "Sammy, let me do the talking and we'll be OK. Don't you worry. You didn't do anything wrong." After they talked for a couple of minutes, Dad asked Mr. Johnson to wait on the front porch and my mom brought him an iced tea, because she was a classy lady. If it were up to me, I would have had our dog Olive pee in a cup and tell him it's delicious country lemonade.

Dad came into the study and looked at Jack like he was really going to give it to him until Jack told him our side and how the Johnson kids were tough bullies at school. Jack did all the talking and pretty much told him everything except for the part about me telling Kenny he might consider showering more often. Dad was obviously very upset that I got beat up for no reason and upset that there was fighting at all. I knew he was as proud of Jack as I was though, because even though his mouth was regular, the entire time he told us all that stuff a grownup is supposed to say about fighting he had a smile in his eyes, especially when we told him that Mark Johnson was *three* grades older than Jack.

Anyway, Dad sent us back upstairs and we ran like hell to my window to hear Dad promise Mr. Johnson that nobody from our family would beat up anybody from his family as long as his boys minded themselves. Mr. Johnson looked confused at first, but then seemed to agree it was as good a plan as any and politely told him to thank my mother for the iced tea. He walked back to his car real fast and drove his truck down the driveway slower than my grandma does. I remember that night perfectly, like it was last night even. When Jack and I saw how slow Mr. Johnson drove out of the driveway, we started laughing for probably a good hour or so until Mom came up to tell us the same stuff Dad had about fighting although I think she really meant it. She was pretty much talking to Jack the whole time because he was doing most of the fighting.

Mom doesn't ever want us to fight, *even if we win.* She ended up making us both go to bed early. Even though we got punished, I can remember how proud I was of Jack and Dad that they were so big and tough. I am tough for my size, *I think*, but I'll never be big like Dad where even tough guys like Mr. Johnson will look at me and think, "Gadzooks! I'm not going to start anything with *that* guy."

My dad is a big guy, and everyone knows him, especially around my grandpa's place because that's where he grew up. It seems like everywhere we go around there; they know him and slap him on the back and say stuff like, "Big John! You look great! How long has it been? Too long! What a nice surprise!" I'm not kidding; even the ladies act all nervous, like maybe they were wondering if he was ever going to pick them for his kick ball team or something. When Dad comes to our school, all the kids, even my friends who have seen him a thousand times, say, "Whoa Sam! Your dad is hee-uuuge!" Most of the time I felt proud because he's my dad, but other times I'd just end up thinking, *"are they wondering what happened to me?"*

My mom is a little woman. Don't get me wrong, she is not little like those people you see riding tiny bikes around at the Circus, but she's full grown and still shorter than Jack. When she's standing next to my dad it looks like if Dad were in a hurry to get to a movie or something, he could just go ahead and tuck her under his arm like a newspaper and run out the door. I got my mom's genes, so I look a lot like her and I'm pretty much the smallest boy in my grade. The good part is that just like her, even though I'm not big, I'm pretty smart. I'm probably the smartest kid in my grade, although if you met some of the kids in my grade, you'd see it's not like I'm the smartest kid at NASA or anything like that. The good part about being smart is that you don't have to study as much, so you have more time to play sports.

You can tell that Jack got Dad's genes because he looks just like him, and for his age he is hee-uuuge. When people meet us and they ask how old we are they nod and smile when I say, "ten" and when Jack tells them his age, it's always something like, "*Twelve! YOU* are *twelve? You can't be twelve?* Aren't you a chip off the old block?" Nothing against my mom because she is great, but sometimes like when someone is feeding me dirt, I want to be more like a chip off of my dad's old block.

In case you are confused, having someone's genes is not a saying but an actual thing. A gene is a book of instructions that God writes on how to grow and you can get some pages out of your mom's book and some out of your dad's. Last summer I was upset about getting all of Mom's genes on being little and I told Dad that I wished I had gotten his genes on being big. I'm glad I did too because he made me feel a lot better. Dad told me that we all, including Grandpa, have Williams' blood running through our veins and that I had something that none of them had, even him.

Dad said that I had a big heart and that's the thing that he loves the most about me and that heart is what you measure a man by. Well, I'm not even a man yet and Dad said that my heart was probably the biggest in the whole Williams family. At first, I was confused, because like I told you before, my dad is "hee-uuuge" and he must have one hell of a big heart himself. Dad told me that having a "big heart" was just a "saying" too, and that it meant I'm smart enough to care about the right things and that I care more than most people. Dad says that a big heart like mine is super rare and that he wished more people were like me. He also told me that my big heart is why I cry easier than some people and that's what makes me special, because having a big heart is just like being tall, you have to be born with it. You can't just *want* to be tall and then you get tall, believe me, I know.

Let me go ahead and set this straight right here though, I never cry like a wussy, like when you get stung by a wasp or get hit by a baseball. When I get stung by a wasp (seven times now) or hit by a baseball (twice) I say, "Dannnnnnng!" as much as I need too but I never cry. I suppose you're asking yourself, *well what does he cry about?* Because those are two things that make most people cry. Well, to give you an example, when our dog Herbie got hit by a train and died last summer I cried for a full week and a half longer than anyone else. When Dad brought Herbie back home in one of our old living room drapes Mom and Jack cried, but probably only for a day. Me, I couldn't stop, I would take breaks from crying but then I'd remember something like I wasn't going to be able to take him fishing again and the crying would just come back like a case of the hiccups. I *might* have cried a lot more than them about Herbie dying because he and I were best friends but looking back I'd say it's mostly on account of my really big heart.

33

A PROUD HERITAGE

"What are we doing?" We were exiting the highway about an hour past Chattanooga, or Chatta-Vegas as my friends call it.

"We need gas Hemingway."

"OK. I'll pump. What's wrong with this station?" I asked, pointing to the gas station we just passed.

"No can do. That place is a wreck. I've got to drop a brown trout into the live well." He pointed to my wallet, "Is that for me?"

I laughed and handed him two, twenty-dollar bills as he was getting out of the car, "Go nuts."

Just as I had suspected, Chuy's super-coordination made him an incredible driver. He was a great driver and a great companion. Even though my head had been in a laptop the entire trip, I loved having him with me, he had turned into such a funny kid. The first time I met him he was just a kid, your average Mexican orphan with magnificent blonde highlights. We had a big sit-down dinner with the entire family and my mom, being the culturally sensitive woman she is, made *tacos*.

Between the obvious cliché of tacos, the flatulence they produced, and the revelation that Chuy's real name is Jesus, his welcome into the family was a warm, funny one, with many a tear shed, although the tear shed part might make it seem warmer than it actually was. Most of the tears shed owed their providence to Gramps' farts, which were like a baseball bat to the face.

I paid cash for the gas and got myself some candy inside the station. It might've been all the energy drinks I'd consumed, but I was feeling great. In the short time we'd been driving, I'd actually written a decent amount of stuff. I couldn't help thinking about Sarah reading it, recognizing little Sammy and laughing, it made me happy. Happy and embarrassed because I knew it was absolutely and completely one sided. I was probably a blip on her boyfriend screen, and a bad blip at that.

What was I thinking? Was I making a mistake? Fuck it, it's the end of the world. I knew it was creepy but I couldn't help myself, there was some creepy inner drive within me, pushing me further. I knew what I was doing with the rest of my life; I wanted to see Sarah Campbell one last time. Even if it was from behind a parked car or from a distance with the aid of binoculars.

"Are you still good to drive, Chuy?" I asked, handing him a Monster. "Are you hungry?" I handed him a bag of Hot Fries.

He took both, "I feel fucking great! I just took a shit that came out of the water!"

I laughed so hard I choked on the sweet tart I'd just popped in my mouth, "You know Chuy, all the shit jokes, I think they're hilarious, but not everybody thinks they're funny like I do. You have to know your audience. You don't talk about taking a shit so big it breaks the surface of the water to girls, do you? Because if you do, you're going to have to wait for someone pretty special to break the curse."

"No can do, Motherfucker," he said earnestly, "It's my heritage, I'm a Duque. I'll be more than happy to wait for a girl I can joke with about turds. I don't want to date a girl you can't fart around, like Margot. I want a girl that thinks it's funny I saw a monkey at the zoo throw shit at a wall, spread it around, and pick the corn out of it. I mean, I want her to think it's gross, but I want her to say to me, 'God damn Chuy, that's fucking funny.'"

You could make an argument that everything shit related wasn't his heritage since Chuy was adopted, but if you did it in front of my family you'd get punched in the face. Why am I even giving Chuy long term advice right now? Like Dusty said, we don't have to work on bettering ourselves anymore.

"Chuy, you're right. It's your heritage. I won't say another—"

"Look at that!" He said and pointed to a couple that was jogging past us on the sidewalk, "You know that dude hasn't jogged for two or three years. That's just his pussy way of trying to get her back in shape instead of saying, "Baby, your ass is getting huge!"

"Would you say that to your girlfriend?" I said, pissed. Even if it's the end of the world, there's never a reason for a Duque to talk to a woman disrespectfully, unless it's Ms. Livingston.

"Nah, I was just making a joke Holmes, lighten up. I would never say that to a girl, I would just break up with her. Besides, I'll NEVER date a girl with a jiggly butt like that. You don't have to worry about Chuy, Chuy can handle his shit"

"I worry about you when you talk about yourself in the third person."

"Margot had a great ass. She might have been a bitch but she walked around naked all the time didn't she? She was slamming Bro—"

"Hah! Fuck Margot." I instantly regretted the wording because the minute I said it, I saw Chuy's eyes lost in thought, and I knew *mentally*, in that hyperactive teenage imagination of his, he *was* fucking Margot.

I didn't know what else to say other than to express my concern, "Where are you going?" because he was turning left across two lanes of traffic into the disgusting gas station we had passed up fifteen minutes earlier.

The car horns faded behind us as we flew over the bumpy entrance and through the lot, skidding *perfectly* into an empty spot. He put the car in park, looked at me and said, "I have to piss again. Sorry Bro, Chuy has tiny tanks."

I looked at the clock and waited, knowing this probably wouldn't take long. I was letting all this crazy behavior go because it was the end of the world, and Chuy was taking every inch he could, he was a Duque after all. I wondered if I should reel it in a bit with Chuy...

Fuck it, we're going to die soon anyway. Sure enough, after two or three minutes I heard a muffled scream and Chuy popped out thirty seconds later. *Jesus*.

34

THE BEAR (CONTINUED)

CHAPTER FOUR

A NEW PLAN

"Hey." It was Jack, he had opened the door to my bedroom and I'm not trying to be gross, but I nearly pooped in my pants. I looked back at my alarm clock— 5:47 after midnight.

"Jack, the shit is *definitely* going to hit the fan if you don't go back to your room. It's not 6:00 yet!"

Jack didn't care, he looked serious, "Sam, something's wrong. Grandpa's here and Mom's up, they're sitting in the kitchen right now. Did you *sleep* in your boots?" he lifted up the covers and looked to see if I was really wearing my boots or, I suppose, to check if my feet grew like crazy overnight. He got into bed next to me and rolled over so we could talk. We were both already fully dressed and ready to go, boots and all.

"Where's *Dad*? Grandpa is *here*? We're supposed to be going to Grandpa's!" I was so confused. I could feel my body heat up and my stomach turn like when you sneak into the kitchen at church and eat four or five donuts and then have three glasses of Jesus' blood, which, in case you are confused, is really just delicious fruit punch with ten percent real juice.

"I don't know, let's go ask them," he said as he threw my covers back and slid off the bed. I couldn't move, I didn't *want* to move. Why was Grandpa here when we were going to *his* farm and where was Dad? Dad sure as hell wasn't in our house. If he was, he would be sitting with Grandpa and Mom drinking coffee, he loves drinking coffee and telling stories.

I figured I'd better go check it out even if it wasn't 6:00 yet. I got up as quick as I could and raced after Jack who was stalled at the bottom of the stairs, spying on something in the kitchen. I couldn't see around Jack into the kitchen, but I could hear my grandpa ask Mom what she was going to do with no kids to chase around (she never chases us). "Oh, I'll think of something," she laughed. I was terrified to see Jack walking away from me and towards them.

"Hello Jack."

"Hi Grandpa, what are you doing *here?* We were coming to see *you*" said Jack. I watched my Mom get up and put her hands through Jack's hair as she went to the sink to pour out the coffee she'd been drinking. Figuring no shit was going to hit the fan I came running out to see Grandpa too. "Grandpa!" I ran toward him and jumped into his lap, "Where's Dad? Mom, where is Dad?"

"Sammy!" he smiled and gave me a big hug. I love my grandpa.

"Dad is upstairs sleeping; Grandpa is here to pick you up. You are riding with him," Mom said as she came over to plant a big wet one on my cheek like she always does. Jack doesn't like her to do that because he's older, but I still like it because Mom's great.

My heart sank and every ounce of excitement I had trapped in my little body just up and left. This was not a good option. *"Where is Dad? We were all going together! Grandpa, we were going to come see you, you didn't have to come get us."* My Mom looked me right in the face and I was afraid she could see I might cry.

"Mr. Bugna had a terrible fire last night and your Dad went to help. He called Grandpa and your grandpa was very nice to get up early and come get you"

"Is Dad coming? I don't want to go if he's not."

"Why is Dad helping Mr. Bugna?" Jack asked, "he's the competition. *Did any animals get burned alive?*"

"All the animals are safe- it was his hay barn that burned down. When a neighbor needs help Jack, you help your neighbor, and when your Daddy needs help, Mr Bugna will help him. That's the way I raised your Daddy and that's the way he'll raise you." Grandpa said sternly.

"Mr. Bugna won't ever help Dad. *Nothing died? Just the hay barn?*" said Jack, seeming bothered.

"Louis (Mr. Bugna) will help him now," Grandpa said, smiling once again. "Jack, did you *want* something to die?"

"No. Just checking" He said. I knew Jack though and I knew if the answer was, "yes, there are dead animals everywhere Jack" all we would have seen was his back as he was running for the door. He gets a kick out of dead stuff and I imagine burnt cows would have been a pretty big hit with him. I like looking at dead stuff too I guess but I was more concerned about driving with Grandpa.

I looked at my Mom and she put both of her hands on my face and said, "Your Dad is very excited to go to Grandpa's with you. He'll be there tonight before you go to bed, but he needs to get some rest before he goes. He's been up all-night honey."

"He can sleep in the car!" I said.

"Who's going to drive then?" Jack said, looking at me like I had three eyeballs.

Oh yeah, I thought to myself and then slid off Grandpa's lap and went to get my stuff. As soon as I got halfway up the stairs my big heart kicked in and I started crying as quietly as I could.

Just in case you are confused, riding with my grandpa 15 minutes in his truck is no big deal. Driving an hour and a half with grandpa can be just terrible and depending on how big your heart is you might cry too. I'm not trying to be gross but when you ride with grandpa you aren't allowed to fart, or he will cuss you out. "What kind of manners did your mother teach you, boy!" he would shout, "Did you grow up in a barn? Have respect for your elders and hold it until you get outside!" It's dangerous too, because when he cusses you out, he looks at you instead of looking at the road. Jack farted a doozy once and Grandpa nearly ran off the road *twice* while cussing him out. Jack's fart almost cost the three of us our lives, which is scary for a little kid.

I bet you are thinking, *big deal, just don't fart then, right?* Well, *we* don't anymore or at least we die trying not to. The worst part though, is like most rules; they don't apply to old people. Like I said before, I'm not trying to be gross, but Grandpa lets farts that are so thick you can almost feel them in the truck with you. Grandpa drove us home last summer and I prayed it would be the last time because he was letting them rip the *entire* way back. That night we were watching TV and I smelled Jack's shirt and it smelled like Grandpa's farts. The smell was in our clothes like smoke is the day after you sit around a campfire.

Does Grandpa get mad and yell when he rips them? Hell no. He just looks straight ahead and keeps driving. You can never tell when he farts either, because when old people fart, they don't make a sound. No matter where you are when an old person farts, you're not going to get any kind of early warning to get the hell out of there. Jack says old people's butt holes must just be too tired to make a good, loud sound. What fun is *that?* I don't ever want to get old. When you smell one of Grandpa's farts it's like getting slapped in the face really hard by a mean teacher, with no warning.

It's torture because if you say anything about his fart you are going to get cussed out and if you make a fuss trying to hold your nose you are going to get cussed out. Don't even *think* about opening the window if it isn't already opened. If you don't want to get cussed out when my grandpa farts, just look straight ahead and think about something really great like reeling in Big Frank. Jack once just *looked* at me wrong after Grandpa let one and he got cussed out.

I always sit in the middle and Grandpa's farts naturally hit me first, so I always try to make the most of it, like Mom says, and turn to watch the fart hit Jack. Well one time when he finally smelled it Jack looked back at me and he was *cross-eyed.* He said he wasn't even trying to be cross-eyed, that's just how bad they are. Once Grandpa lets one rip, everyone knows it, and there is pretty much no more talking until *he* starts the next conversation. Don't get me wrong, I love my grandpa. He is the greatest, but I love him a whole lot more when we are doing stuff outside.

I was so disappointed I was laying face down on my bed not even wanting to go when I felt Jack lay down on the mattress beside me. I had stopped crying by then even though I still wanted to cry some more but I didn't. Sometimes I can control my big heart and right then I was glad that I could, because I especially don't like to cry in front of Jack or Dad. You could cry in front of my Mom about anything and not even think about it because she's a mom and moms, as far as I can tell, will use any excuse to get hugs from their kids. Jack and Dad wouldn't ever tease me or anything for crying, but they never cry so I would rather not cry in front of them. It's hard to explain. I looked up and Jack was smiling at me.

"Hey Sammy, what's wrong? Dad is still coming; he just won't get there until tonight." Jack grabbed me, spun me over and sat on my stomach holding my arms back by the wrists so it looked like I was surrendering during a gunfight.

"I'm waiting to go with Dad," I told him.

The smile left his face, "*What*? Don't you want to go fishing today in the back pond? What if we catch Big Frank today? Dad bought this new kind of catfish bait. I've got it in my tackle box, it's got real blood in it Sam! We won't even have to walk! Grandpa said he is going to let me drive the Honda."

I knew all about the new bait, I saw it in a magazine at the grocery store and asked Dad to get it. "I don't want to catch Big Frank (*I was lying*), and I don't want to sit through Grandpa's farts (*I couldn't have meant it more*), I'm waiting to go with Dad."

The smile came back to Jack's face as he let go of my wrists, rolled over next to me, and started to laugh. Jack always seemed to know when to let up. You could say it was one of Jack's hobbies to manhandle me and throw me around, but he would almost always lay off me before I got hurt. I've never done it myself, but it *has* to be fun to be able to pick someone up and throw them.

He breathed in a deep breath and we both stared at the ceiling, "They are *terrible,* aren't they?"

"Spectacular," I said.

He looked at me confused, "Spectacular means great Sam, but I think I know what you're saying. Do you remember last summer when he drove us home? It was so bad it made my eyes water."

"It made you cross-eyed! Our clothes smelled like poop." I added and we were both laughing now. Jack could always cheer me up.

"What is Grandma feeding him? Tar? It wouldn't be so bad if he would let us roll down the window or at least laugh about it like we do with Dad. There's no women around, why in the hell can't we fart like men and laugh about it or *at least* roll down the window. Maybe I'll say something about it to him this time." If you haven't noticed by now, Jack is great at cussing too.

I looked at Jack, "You will get cussed out."

"You're probably right" he said, "but maybe not, if you come with us, I promise I'll roll down the window, even if he cusses at me. I'll even try to talk to him about it." I couldn't believe it, but Jack always keeps his promises, even if he's going to get in trouble.

"OK, but only if you promise, and only if you leave me out of it," I said as I jumped up on him, trying to pin him down like he did to me moments before. I almost had him too because I'm real fast, but right as I was on top, he threw me off and I bounced like a skipped rock clear off the bed and into my dresser.

"Sorry buddy," he said as he lifted me off the ground effortlessly, "I've got it! I've got it!" He said, dropping me right back on the ground and ran out of the room. I got up and ran behind to find him in his room looking through his dresser drawer.

"Here, Sammy Wammels, is the answer to all our problems. We'll be fishing by noon," he threw me a bottle of something called "BEAN-O."

"What is this?" I asked.

"It's magic, that's what it is. If you drink it, you don't fart"

"Spectacular! Does this really work?" I said. I mean, how could there be something as incredible as this and I didn't know about it? It would be like someone really smart walking into your living room and picking up your TV remote and saying, "*what does this do? I haven't seen one of these before. How does it work?*"

"How did you get this?" I asked, still amazed at what was in my hands.

"Remember when I got a detention for farting in English? Mrs. Hood gave it to me after I told her I couldn't help it. She said now that I have this stuff, I don't have an excuse."

"That detention was for *farting?*"

Jack smiled like a proud father, "Yep, me, Stump, Win, Neal, and Mills were all letting them rip and *I* got busted. Too much power." I could *definitely* believe that.

"Have you tried this stuff; does it really work?" I was skeptical, it did seem like magic and I'm sure pretty much most magic is fake.

"It's supposed to, but I haven't tried it, I sure as hell don't need it, I *like* farting. I guess we'll find out today, we'll put it into Grandpa's coffee."

All the BEAN-O air left my sails. Jack was right, why would you want to take something that stopped you from farting? That would be like inventing something that made candy taste exactly like spinach. Impressive, sure, but what good would *that* do? I remembered that *I* wasn't going to be the one taking it and then I remembered the thick smell of Grandpa's farts and I looked back down at the tiny bottle again, "*Spectacular.*"

I didn't know how he intended to do it, but with Jack, if he tells you he's going to do something, like making milk come out his nose, he'll do it.

"Get your stuff and let's go" he said as he grabbed the tiny bottle of magic out of my hands, grabbed his pack with his sleeping bag attached perfectly and walked out into the hallway. Jack turned and looked at me still standing at the foot of my bed. I was wondering why I can't roll up my sleeping bag like his and he said with a patient smile, "Let's go buddy." As always, he gave the command and I followed without worry. My brother Jack could fix anything.

I watched Jack like a hawk at breakfast to see him make his move and he never did. I was getting real worried as I got into Grandpa's truck.

"Here, hold this" Jack said as he climbed in beside me and started digging deep into his front pocket. *Spectacular!* I thought as I held onto the coffee Jack had brought for Grandpa.

"It says here to add one drop for every 8 ounces of water. We'd better go with five drops."

"Are you sure? Grandpa is old. He could die if you give him too much."

"Don't you worry Sam, the person that wrote these directions never smelled one of Grandpa's farts, he'll be fine," Jack said, dropping the last of the five drops into the coffee. I put it into the cup holder, and we waited for what seemed to be like ten days.

When Grandpa got into the truck, he looked at us and said, "Who wants to go fishing?"

"I do! I'm going to catch Big Frank this time." I meant it too.

"Hey you two! Were you in such a big hurry you didn't intend on saying goodbye to your mother?" It was Mom at the window of the truck. "Mom!" I shouted; I was so nervous I *was* going to leave without telling her goodbye! Jack and I got out and she gave us both hugs and kisses, but she gave me an extra big hug. I love my mom.

"Rog, do you want another cup of coffee? I don't want you falling asleep at the wheel with my precious cargo." If he was here, this is where Dad would say, "Courtney, you're going to suffocate these boys." And she would say, "With love? Impossible!"

"I already thought of that, Mom, thanks though. Here you go Grandpa" Jack thrust the coffee at Grandpa, and he laughed.

"Well thank you Jack, that was very nice of you. Let's go boys. Grandma's anxious to see you."

"Give her my love and tell her I'm excited to see her on Saturday," Mom said.

Grandpa took a sip and said, "Ahh, you make a mean pot of coffee Courtney, tell my son we're waiting for him and his new bait, I've got a feeling Sam here is going to catch Big Frank this week and he won't want to miss it."

"I've got it, Grandpa" Jack hurried, "it's in my tackle box, the new bait. Mom, tell Dad to hurry up, we've got fish to catch." Mom shut the door for Jack and just stood there smiling and watched us go until we turned out of the driveway.

CHAPTER FIVE

ON THE ROAD

For the first ten minutes, we talked a while about Big Frank and who was going to catch him and how big Grandpa thought he was by now. I asked Grandpa if I caught Big Frank could I get him stuffed and hang him on the wall in my room. He just smiled and said I'd have to ask my dad but thought it'd be better if I let him go so someone else could catch him.

"Like who?" I asked, "We're the only people that fish that hole." If I was allowed to cuss in front of Grandpa I'd have said "*Hell no, that son of a bitch is going on my wall where he belongs!*" Let him go? If you would have said something that crazy in front of Grandma, she would have said, "well, I *never*" and left the room. In case you haven't figured it out by now, "Hell" anything and "son of a bitch" are my favorite cuss words.

Grandpa took another sip of his coffee and I smiled and looked over at Jack and he was rolling his window down even though it was cold this early in the morning. Genius!

"You know what Jack, I appreciate the coffee, but I've had two cups already and you know how your grandma feels about me drinking too much coffee" he reached in front of me to give Jack his BEAN-O coffee. "Throw this out your window and roll it up tight, it's a little chilly out there." I turned, panicked, to Jack who was already staring icicles at my grandpa. As soon as I saw Jack's face, I felt a lot better about things.

"I thought you said this coffee was good? Does Grandma tell you not to fish too much? When we have wives are they going to make all our decisions for us too? I'm confused because Dad makes all his own decisions. Besides, who here would tell her if you had another cup of coffee? Would you Sam? I wouldn't."

I shook my head "no" in Grandpa's direction and saw that he was laughing but not making a sound like a lot of old people do. I suppose laughing is just like running fast for old people. The older you get the worse you are at it. I bet Grandpa can't even run anymore he's so old. Don't get me wrong, Grandpa is still strong as an ox and can probably push a tractor out of a ditch by himself, but if he tried to run fast, I could just see parts of his body falling off or something.

Just in case you are confused, "staring icicles" is the saying that Jack and I came up with that I told you about earlier. "Staring icicles" is when you look at your opponent in such a way that you are telling them (with your eyes) that they are going to lose even before they start and that it's useless to try too hard. Jack does it in baseball games when he goes up to bat. In baseball when you go up to bat, the pitcher can't pitch to you until both of your feet are in the batter's box. Jack puts one foot in the box and waits until the pitcher looks at him and then gives them the old icicle treatment until the umpire says something to Jack like, "Let's get moving kid." It works too; Jack hits home runs all the time.

Jack gave Grandpa back the coffee and he probably drank it in under ten minutes. I felt safer after it was gone but was still worried until I decided to let it go. Dad had told me a long time ago (last year I think) that if you worry about the things you can't control you will miss out on life. He was right too, I had no control over Grandpa's farts and besides, if he did fart, Jack was going to say something. He promised he would, and that would be a good show too.

Like I told you earlier, when we are riding with Grandpa and we have to fart real bad, we have to hold it in until we stop to go to the bathroom or get gas, which is no big deal right? Except Grandpa doesn't do either. Most people just pull over and get gas but not Grandpa. He has a big red plastic tank of gas in the bed of his truck and if he ever runs out, he goes back and pours more in, but not before he slams his fist on the dashboard and says, "Damn it!" like something absolutely horrible has happened to him. One time we never stopped, and I held a hell of a fart in for probably half the trip. My sides hurt so bad I almost cried by the time we got out of his truck. It made for a spectacular fart because I had to hold it for so long, but it wasn't worth the pain. Actually, looking back it was a great enough fart where it probably *was* worth it, but I wouldn't try it again unless I had to.

The other thing that can make it a tough trip with Grandpa, as if fart attacks weren't enough, is getting stuck behind a slow-moving car. Unfortunately, the only way to get to back to our roots is by two lane country roads. Grandpa will see a car way up ahead and say, "Good Lord, what do we have here?" Then he lays on the gas until he catches up to them where he'll say, "Would you look at... aww ... C'mon... would you... Get moving! aww, for the love of..." and then he'll slap the steering wheel and just kind of hold his breath. Grandpa will then continue to cuss at the poor people even though they couldn't possibly hear him.

He'll then pound his dashboard every 2 minutes and say, "COME ON" as he drives five feet off their bumper, and he will drive five feet off their bumper until he's able to pass them. You want to see fireworks? You don't have to wait for the Fourth of July, try giving Grandpa the bird when he is five feet off your bumper.

The country roads we take to Grandpa's farm wind and turn all over the place so there are very few spots you can pass another car *safely*. With Dad you hardly even notice, he just slows down and waits for a chance to pass them without even cussing or anything. With Grandpa, he gets up on the wheel and the first chance he gets, he hits the gas and passes them. When we do eventually pass them, he has us sit back so that the people in the slow car can see him cussing at them as he passes. He shakes his fist at them and says, "Learn how to drive, would you!"

He says the same thing every time and one time we said it and shook our fists too and oh, did he cuss *us* out. "*I don't care who's doing what. You two need to be respectful to your elders.*" I can't wait until I'm an elder.

Depending on how long we have been behind someone and how angry Grandpa has become will determine how much risk he will take in passing them. You would think that he would be extra careful with Mom's "precious cargo." If Mom could see how we have passed some of these cars she would hang Grandpa by his pinky toes! Sometimes when Grandpa passes a car it's fun like being on a rollercoaster but most times it will, like Shorty says, "make you butt hole pucker up so tight you could squeeze a quarter in two." Like I said before, Shorty was the best cusser on the Farm.

Most of the times the other car will slow down as Grandpa passes, probably thankful he isn't on their back bumper anymore. If it is old women in the car, I bet you they're probably saying something like, "*Oh dear! Those poor children,*" as we pass them.

After an hour of no farts, I actually began to enjoy the ride. "Grandpa, is it really true that Dad stared down a real live bear?" I asked. My uncle Gary told us the whole story last summer at Grandpa's and I wanted to hear it again.

"Yep, he did, and your Uncle Gary was there too," he replied.

"Did Uncle Gary really poop in his pants?" Jack asked, laughing.

"You would too, young man. He shouldn't have told you that. I just don't understand your fascination with bathroom humor..." He paused and looked at us both. I was about to shit in *my* pants as I looked to Jack. He quit laughing too, realizing he might just have opened up a can of whup-ass.

"Listen to me, the both of you;" he continued, as I wished for a car of slow driving old ladies around the corner to distract him from delivering what I expected would be another bathroom humor speech that we weren't allowed to laugh during.

"You don't mess with bears." He had my attention back. "Your father got lucky. He was a foolish, *foolish*, young man, full of piss and vinegar, and he could have been killed. Bears are very dangerous; they are wild animals and when they have young ones around, they will *kill* to protect them. They can outrun the fastest human and climb the tallest tree. If a bear wants to make lunch out of you it's his decision and his decision only."

"Grandpa, stop. You're scaring me," I said, *he really was*. "What if we get eaten when we're going fishing? How could you let us go fishing when you know we could get eaten by a *bear*?" Uncle Gary never said anything like that when he told us the story. I started to think maybe if you are old, and you drink too much BEAN-O it might make you want to scare little kids just for the hell of it. Can this really be true? Jack put his arm around me to comfort me, but it was too late, I was crying a little bit again, mostly because I didn't know what I was going to do now this entire week.

I was never going to go fishing on Grandpa's farm again. Are you kidding me? In my head I could just see a bear ripping my arm off and going ahead and eating it like we eat fried chicken on Monday nights. As much as I wanted to catch him, Big Frank was safe, and if that fried chicken didn't taste so delicious, I'd stop eating it too. I wonder if the chickens knew I was going to eventually eat their arms, would they be as afraid of me as I am of bears?

Grandpa pulled over to the side of the road and put me on his lap, so I was leaning against the driver's wheel. I was trying so hard not to cry but I was devastated, it had been such a disappointing morning and now this. I didn't look at Jack because for some reason I felt like he wouldn't see me scared and crying if I didn't look at him.

"Samuel," Grandpa said in a calm voice, "I'm sorry, I didn't mean to scare you; I just wanted you two to take bears seriously. We haven't seen a bear on our farm in over twenty years. I would never let anything happen to you. If I thought there were bears on my land you would not be allowed to go past the lower barn."

"How do you know?" I asked.

"The bears have moved up north, mostly because of the land being cleared for farming and also because of all the neighborhoods they have built, like the ones that were built on Mr. Politte's land. Bears don't like to be around people any more than people like to be around them. Also bears leave signs they're around, like scratches on trees, footprints and yes, Jack, they leave big piles of scat in the woods."

I was so relieved that there weren't any bears and then when *Grandpa* joked about a bear shitting in the woods, I couldn't hold it back and just started cracking up. Grandpa started laughing and Jack joined in too and we all just laughed for a good two or three minutes. It was great. Mostly it's because I realized Grandpa would fish with us today and Dad would be with us the rest of the week and honestly, with Dad or Grandpa around, I'm not afraid of anything.

"Grandpa, maybe I should carry a gun to make Sam feel safe." Jack added after we all stopped laughing. Jack and I had been trying to take a gun out by ourselves for the longest time. You don't get to shoot at anything fun when there are grownups around and you wouldn't believe how many things there are to shoot at out back.

"I *would* feel safer, Grandpa" I added.

He looked at me and then Jack and then into the side mirror and drove back onto the road. "When you boys are ready, I will let you take a gun out."

"When will that be?" asked Jack, "just curious." Grandpa just smiled.

"Grandpa, what would you do if you came upon a bear like Dad did, would you stare him down too? You are just as big as Dad" I asked.

Jack interrupted, "Dad told me that if it came to it, he was prepared to wrestle the bear because in this world you can either fight or lay down, and the Williams family fights. I asked him if he was ever scared and he said, "NO" and I believe him,"

I turned to Jack and asked, "When did he tell you that?" I couldn't believe I missed Dad talking about staring down that bear.

"He told you he wasn't scared?" Grandpa asked, kind of shaking his head like maybe Dad might have been scared, but I knew that Dad wasn't scared of anything except Mom sometimes, and I can understand that.

Before Jack could say, "Yep," Grandpa smiled and said, "If I came across the bear it would depend; if I were on Piper (his horse) or the Honda I would get the hell out of there, but if I were on foot, I would play dead."

"Huh?" we both said together, it seemed like the least tough thing a guy could do. Play dead?

"If you two ever come across a bear, you need to play dead, just drop down and lay real still. If the bear doesn't see you as a threat, he'll lose interest and just keep going. Most people make the mistake and run, and they pay dearly for it."

"Grandpa, if the bear was hungry and you played dead and just laid there, he would eat you for sure." Jack laughed, shaking his head, obviously not buying the play dead strategy.

"Jack, sometimes brains are better than brawn. Like my daddy used to say, it takes a coward to bury a hero." Grandpa could probably see the fear creeping back into my eyes because he put his hand on my leg and shook it, "There are no bears on our farm Sam."

"Do you think Dad was scared, Grandpa?" Jack asked.

Grandpa smiled and said, "Well, I don't know a man alive that wouldn't be, but if he told you he wasn't, I'd believe him. Come to think of it, I think that outside of your uncle Gary, that bear was probably the most scared. That was the year your Dad went undefeated in the Big Ten."

When we pulled in the driveway Grandma was waiting for us. She came out to the car and kissed Jack as he got out and gave me a big hug as she took me out of the truck. For an old broad (Grandpa calls her that sometimes), she sure is strong. I'm not as big as Jack or Dad, but I'm not exactly a lightweight either. My grandpa's dog Buddy ran up to us and was more excited to see me than I was to see him. I like him a lot, but I wouldn't lick him in the face for five minutes just because I was excited to see him.

Buddy is great to go hunting with, but not fishing because more often than not he'll jump in the water right where we're fishing. When a big dog like Buddy jumps in the water it scares the fish away, so you have to move to another spot, which is a pain in the ass, especially if you are catching fish. Buddy is a Labrador and that dog just can't stay out of the water, even when it's cold outside and the water is freezing. Dogs must be like women because sometimes they are hard to understand.

I put my stuff in the house, poured myself a glass of the cherry Kool Aide that grandma always makes for me and then ran out to the back of the wood shop to see if there were any new wasp nests and there were a ton of them! Even if you don't get stung too much it could take a good couple of hours to knock them all off. I looked around for a long stick but couldn't find one, so I took my slingshot out of my back pocket and was about to load it but decided I'd go ahead and wait for Jack. I couldn't start without Jack because he's the one who came up with the idea of knocking down wasp nests as a game in the first place.

Just in case you are confused, one of the great thrills in life is knocking down a wasp nest. All you need is a long stick or pole, or a slingshot if you've got good enough aim, which I do because I practice all the time, and some wasp nests. To play, you just take the stick or whatever and knock down the nest and run like hell. Jack started letting me do it with him when he thought I was ready because if you can't run like hell you will get the shit stung out of you. I have gotten stung seven times already and I'm only 10. When Jack started letting me play, he made sure I had a good head start since my legs are shorter and any wasp worth his salt would go after me because I was the easier target. Now we take turns knocking them down and we run in opposite directions, so the wasps have to decide which one of us to go after. At first, I kept following Jack after he knocked down a nest and he would laugh and say that I should trust him and run in another direction because more than likely they would come after the two of us and get me because I was slower. I didn't listen to him until two wasps stung the shit out of me at the same time. Once that happened, I've been going in a different direction and neither of us hardly ever gets stung. Grandma likes us to knock down the nests because she has raspberry bushes behind the wood shop, and she doesn't like wasps around when she is picking raspberries and who could blame her?

When you run from a wasp it's important to zigzag and keep waving your arms around your head. Grandpa says wasps go for your eyeballs. I once had a wasp come so close to my eyeballs that I had to close my eyes while I was running, which is never a good idea. Running into a tree hurts more than getting stung, believe me. I came up with the waving your arms around your head idea right after I ran into that tree.

I counted 14 wasp nests which is four more than there were last year. I decided to go find Jack so we could get ready to go fishing but not before I had thrown an apple or two. Speaking of apples, there were plenty on the ground to chuck. I picked one up and chucked it at the big oak, aiming it right at dead center and BAM! It hit right where I had aimed it and exploded perfectly. 14 wasp nests, plenty of apples to chuck, and perfect aim, this was shaping up to be a great trip. Maybe I really will catch Big Frank this time!

I grabbed a fresh apple from the tree and ran back to the house where Jack was already sorting out Grandpa's fishing poles. His tackle box was open, and I could see the new bait Dad bought. I dream all year long about catching

Big Frank and I'll tell you what, we are having a devil of a time catching that son of a bitch. Grandpa is the only one who has seen him, and Dad says we have to take his word for it, because a man of character like Grandpa doesn't lie and that we ought to grow up to be just like him.

I wish I had scuba equipment so that I could just go after him with my own two hands or at least just to *see* him. I figure I should be big enough next summer to try it. You see, you don't want to go after a fish that is bigger than you because you could get eaten yourself. Grandpa said he was probably bigger than me but smaller than Jack by now, and it was Jack who told me you never want to fight someone on their own turf, like *underwater.*

Jack looked at me and said, "Grandpa said we can take the Honda!"

"*Spectacular!* I just went behind the barn and there are 14 wasp nests and probably more apples than we can throw in a month!" I spit out an apple seed in between breaths. "My very first try I hit dead center!"

"How far away were you?"

"I was in back of the line, I swear." I was too. It was a near perfect throw.

"Well, we'll have to have a game tonight after dinner and Dad will keep score"

"I'll get the Honda." I said as I ran towards the barn. Jack and I can both drive it but neither of us, up until now, has been allowed to drive it around back on our own.

"Wait for me if you can't get it out." Jack shouted after me, "*Put some gas in it, Grandpa said it needs gas!*"

The barn where Grandpa keeps the Honda was open and the Honda was pulled in perfectly for me to get it out. Grandpa's barns smelled different than ours, better than ours, probably because they were made out of wood instead of metal. Even though I knew a barn might not smell good to a lot of people, it smelled good to me like maybe a favorite meal that you only get once in a while, or like when Mom cooks cinnamon rolls for us as a treat when it's raining on a weekend. I looked where Grandpa keeps the gas and the only gas can that was there said in all capital letters, "MIX — NOT FOR THE HONDA." In case you are confused, some gas has oil mixed in with it and you are not supposed to put it into tractors or four wheelers. Jack and I found that out the hard way and I expect that Grandpa added that writing, as he says of a lot of things, "for our benefit."

I couldn't find the regular gas so I figured we could get some out of Grandpa's truck later. The Honda started right up, and I drove it perfectly the whole way except that I popped the clutch when I went for the brake as I came to the porch and killed the engine. I went ahead and acted like I meant to do that though, it had to look pretty impressive for a ten-year-old. Jack was watching me pull up with both our poles already outfitted in one hand and the tackle box in the other.

"Sam, you are getting pretty good, but driving in first gear the entire way is going to kill the transmission. I think you'd do better to try shifting gears. We'll have to have a driving lesson this week."

"Why don't I just drive to the hole? You can give me a lesson on the way" I already knew the answer. I didn't move though. Jack handed me the poles, tied the tackle box to the rear rack, pulled it tight and said, "Sam, you can drive it when we get back, after I teach you how to get it out of first gear. But first, we've got fish to catch." He climbed on in front of me and started the engine.

"I didn't put gas in it. All I could find was the mix gas." Jack wrenched his neck back around, killed the engine, and asked, "You didn't put any of that in did you?" He was very serious like maybe I'd told him I just pulled the pin out of a grenade.

"No" I said, "the can said not to put it into the Honda."

The smile came back to Jack's face and he started up the engine again, "Good, well let's go then. If we run out, we'll just walk back."

"Should we get Grandpa?" I asked

"Nope, Grandma is giving him hell for drinking too much coffee, he'll meet us there."

"How did she know?"

"It's Gram, she knows everything. Do you want to go catch Big Frank?"

I was going to yell, "Yee Hawww!" like a serious cowboy would, but Jack popped the clutch, and we were off. Just for the record, I actually don't know what popping the clutch means, but it happens before everything cool on the four-wheeler or when you make it die. I grabbed around Jack's stomach with one arm and held the fishing rods behind me with the other and we took off towards the fishing hole.

CHAPTER SIX

THE BEAR

We rode pretty slow on the Honda until we crossed the railroad tracks that ran through the farm because Grandpa could still see us, but after that, Jack took off like he was racing a cheetah (which is the fastest animal on the planet). We were going so fast I turned around to see Buddy slowing to a walk and then becoming a little brown dot as we raced ahead. I hoped he wouldn't follow but I knew he would find us, he always does.

Grandpa's corn was bright green and growing way over our heads. It grew thick on both sides of the two-track drive that led to the back of Grandpa's farm and kind of felt like we were zooming down a hallway in my school, except we were outdoors. The sun was starting to get hot and ordinarily if I had slept in my boots and gotten up so early, I would have been pretty tuckered out by now, but I was so excited I didn't feel the least bit tired.

We started slowing down and Jack turned to me and said something that I now know was, "hold on to the rods!" Well, he whipped the Honda off the road right into the cornfield! I screamed, *"Nooo!"* but I didn't mean it. I held on for dear life and just started cracking up. If you've never driven through a full-grown cornfield on a four-wheeler, you really ought to. That's all I'm going to say about that though, that and if you do drive through a cornfield make sure it's not your Grandpa's and make sure you get away without being caught.

Stalks of corn slapped us on our arms and legs as we bounced up and down over the rows in the field. The farther we went in, the harder I held on to Jack and the harder I laughed. I had dropped the rods a long way back after I started having trouble holding on. I was having so much fun I wasn't even thinking about how we needed them to go fishing.

Sometimes I wonder why Jack does stuff like driving the Honda through the cornfield because everyone knows the shit is going to hit the fan when Grandpa finds out. Maybe he thinks Grandpa won't notice, but how could he not? There were going to be two trails about four feet wide going into the corn and coming out, maybe about thirty feet apart from one another. I guess shit hitting the fan doesn't bother Jack as much as it bothers me or maybe he's just like a wild animal. You can't make a wild animal follow the rules like a dog or a cat. That's why you can't have a lion or a bear as a pet. I remember my dad explaining that to me when I was little. If you can't train an animal to live inside your house and not tear it up and not eat you, it's called a wild animal. Wild animals just don't have it in them to follow the rules.

I remember when Jack tried to jump a ditch with our neighbors riding lawn mower once. It was the craziest thing I'd ever seen. Not the jump really, I thought he had a pretty good shot at making it when I saw the ramp they built and he had a pretty decent hill to pick up some good speed, but what I couldn't figure out for the life of me, is why Jack would try it. I also couldn't figure out why our neighbor Lance would let Jack try the jump on his Dad's *brand-new* lawn tractor. Didn't they know they would both get in trouble? He did manage to jump the ditch, but the tractor stuck into the far side of the ditch like an arrow gets stuck in a target and both of the front wheels busted off and rolled down to the bottom of the ditch. Jack was thrown farther off the tractor than the actual tractor had jumped. If you had seen the way he and Lance were jumping around afterward though, you would have thought it was a perfect jump with a smooth landing and there wasn't going to be hell to pay. Oh, did the shit hit the fan that night. I guess Jack is pretty much just a wild brother.

After we came out of the cornfield and stopped on the road my side hurt from laughing so hard. I had little cuts all over my legs and my eyes were crying but I wasn't *crying* crying, my eyes were crying because I was laughing so hard. I just felt great. I was so excited to be here and have Jack and Dad and

Grandpa and Buddy all to myself. I took a deep breath and stopped laughing but didn't stop holding on to Jack, I never wanted to let go. He had been laughing too. "Where are the poles, Sam?" He got off the Honda and pulled out an ear of corn that had stuck between the engine and the frame.

"Back there" I pointed, still laughing, to the field of corn with the two newly plowed paths.

"Sam!" He looked at me, shook his head, smiled, and said, "all right then, let's go and get them." The Honda stuttered and then the engine went out, smoke coming from underneath where fresh green corn husks were hanging down. Jack looked at me and then back at the Honda. "We'll tell Grandpa after we go fishing." I was stunned. Were we out of gas or did we get corn in the engine somewhere? The shit was *definitely* going to hit the fan now. Waiting to tell Grandpa until after we were done fishing was just fine with me though. We back tracked the entire path only to find the fishing rods were about ten feet from where we had started in. I thought I held on to them for much longer, but it looks like I'd let go as soon as the corn started hitting us. Jack had said that it was probably smart of me to go ahead and drop them, but I knew it wasn't smart, I was just having fun and those poles were in the way.

We were both running back to the Honda when I ran into Jack who had stopped 10 yards short of it. I laughed, thinking he was playing around again and then I saw the bear.

It was the biggest bear I had ever seen, actually the only bear I've ever seen but he was as big as our dad. He saw us too. He stood up on two feet and I could see that he was skinny, dirty, and tall. He was way taller than our dad. He had been eating the corn that Jack had pulled from the Honda. He swayed like he was off balance and let out a huge roar. I was white hot in my chest and I could feel my heart beating in my face. The bear's teeth were brown and long and he had spit all over his mouth. I was frozen in place.

Jack spun around on me and grabbed my shoulders, hard. "Sam, I want you to listen to me and do what I say." I thought I saw terror in Jack's eyes too and that is when I threw up, all over the both of us. It was red from the *cherry Kool Aid* I drank back at the house and had pieces of the beef jerky in it from the car ride earlier. That was the difference between me and Jack. He was trying to save us both from getting eaten and I had pretty much just coated the both of us with delicious gravy.

"Just like the wasp nest game Sam, we are going to run in two separate directions, and he can only chase one of us, and I'm going to make sure he chases me. I'm going to make sure nothing happens to you, and nothing will, as long as you do exactly what I say." The fear had left Jack's eyes. "Run straight into that cornfield and go ten rows in and head straight towards the farm. Go get Grandpa."

"Which direction are you going to run?" I pleaded, as he turned me around and pushed me towards tall rows of corn in front of me, "GO SAM!" He shouted and I did. I ran as fast as I could and I tore right into the corn, afraid of what was to become of Jack, screaming and then starting to cry after hearing another ferocious roar.

Is this really happening? Dad. If only Dad were here this wouldn't be happening or maybe Grandpa would show up with his big gun, the one with all the etching on the side. Then I thought of what Grandpa had said about outrunning a bear and the absolute terror hit me. If I kept running, Jack would die. That big ugly son of a bitch would be eating Jack.

It was at that point I realized *I* would rather be dead than have Jack die saving me. I stopped in my tracks, turned around and started running back toward Jack and the bear as fast as I could. I wasn't crying because I wasn't scared anymore. I really didn't know what I was going to do at that point to tell you the truth, but I wasn't running back to become a bear's lunch. I was running back to help my brother and best friend.

Dad always tells us that we are family and that the bond that we have is special and forever and when someone in your family needs help, you help them. When Dad would say things like that to us, I had always just assumed that it meant Jack needed to make sure I didn't get beat up and I wouldn't snitch on Jack when he did something wrong. This, as far as I could remember, was the first time Jack actually needed *my* help outside me not snitching on something crazy he had done, like peeing in Mr. Leonard's gas tank. As I was running, I felt for my slingshot, it was still there, I took it out.

About ten feet in front of the opening I stopped to pull the ammo out of my front pocket and heard another horrible roar. Could I really kill a bear with a slingshot? Could I scare it away if I hit it in the eye maybe? Blind it? Even though every bit of fear I had in me before was back, I didn't stop. I made my way out of the corn slowly and was horrified to see that Jack was just standing in front of the bear, staring at it without moving. The bear was on all fours now, maybe five or six feet away from Jack.

The bear stood up again in front of Jack and time seemed to stop. I screamed, *"Go Jack GO!"* but Jack just stood there. He was tiny compared to the bear and then I realized he was trying to stare down that bear just like Dad did when he was young.

I laid down on the ground because that's how my aim is the best. I pulled back my slingshot as far as I could but couldn't figure out what to aim it at. I can hit anything with my slingshot, serious, I just didn't know what to hit. The pellet in the leather holder felt so small now compared to the bear but there was nothing else I could do.

In my mind I could hear Grandpa telling us again this morning how dumb Dad was to try to stare down a bear and now I realized how right he was. And in that moment, it hit me, and I knew exactly what I had to do. It was like someone turned the volume down and I couldn't hear the bear's growling anymore as I pulled the slingshot back again. I found my target just perfect in the middle and without even waiting, I let it fly. If you've ever fired a slingshot with a pellet in it you would know that once you fire it you can't see the pellet until it hits something, but I swear I watched it sail all the way until it hit Jack square on the back of his head. I watched my brother Jack fall to the ground. I laid my head down and watched in complete terror as the bear came down and looked, confused, at Jack lying still in front of him.

I couldn't have moved if I wanted to. I wasn't making a sound, but I was crying like hell on the inside wondering if *I* had just killed my brother. The bear walked forward and swatted Jack so hard with his front paw that Jack's limp body moved probably two or three feet. He rolled Jack, back and forth and, spit flew out of his mouth as he ROARED down at him. I was laying on the ground playing dead (with one eye open) twenty feet away and I could see Jack's shirt was now soaked in blood. I can tell you that in that moment I was prepared to die and if he was going to start eating Jack I was going to run over there and kick that son of a bitch square in the nuts. I'm not kidding either. If he was going to eat Jack, I wanted him to eat me too. I guess that's what being a brother is all about.

The last thing I can remember is seeing that bear roaring down at Jack's blood covered, unmoving body as I tried to get up but couldn't, feeling dizzy and hearing what I thought was a bark...

35

BACK IN THE HEARTLAND

I saved my work and shut the laptop. I had been staring at the same screen for over fifteen hours. The various stimulants were doing their job admirably, I was wired out of my gourd but felt goofy and alive. The expanse of parking lot asphalt in front of me was baking under the late morning sun. Thankfully, Mother Earth was able to carry on another day.

We'd parked at a truck stop when Chuy got too tired to continue. Both he and Piper were snoring away in the back, Piper laying her head on Chuy's chest. I was having way more fun than I'd expected, writing as fast as the words would come, laughing to myself as I wrote. It was great, but man, oh man, *it's a lot harder than I thought it would be.* I wasn't even close to finished. The minute I started thinking about how great I was feeling I made a terrible mistake. The armies of sugar and caffeine in my stomach became nervous and started fighting each other, enough to warrant opening my door.

The mistake I made was looking at the navigation system. We were thirty minutes south of the mapped destination of Saugatuck, Michigan. We were also thirty minutes away from Sarah Campbell or whatever her name was now. Who knows how many minutes away we were from the end of the world? I threw up a mixture of caffeine, junk food, and any confidence or direction I might've had.

"God damn!" Chuy laughed from the backseat, "You sick bro, or just in the fish aisle?" My family had labeled my vomiting quirk as being *"in the fish aisle"* because I can't go anywhere near the seafood section of a grocery store without hurling.

"I'm OK. Probably too much caffeine."

"Did you finish your story Holmes?"

"Not even close. It's so much harder than I thought. Do you want to read it for me?"

"Motherfucker, school is out!" He laughed and shook his head, "I'm not reading jack shit until it starts back up either. Sorry."

"Let's get some showers here and I'll drive."

"Showers? Here? Gross."

"Yep, they have showers inside, you rent them. Or I'll get us the best room in Saugatuck if you start proofreading my story. I can't look at it anymore."

"What if I don't want to?"

"Then we shower here. It's your choice. I know of a really nice bed and breakfast in Saugatuck if that sounds better; all you'd have to do is read it while I drive and mark the parts that don't make sense."

"They have showers here?" He asked, his face contorted, weighing his options.

I nodded yes thinking I'd just bagged a proofreader.

Chuy smiled and opened his door, "Let's go get cleaned up Motherfucker, you stink."

36

HARPER'S HONEY

There was silence in the car as we headed towards Saugatuck (and Sarah) and I welcomed it. I decided in the truck stop shower my plan to go to Saugatuck was reckless. I also decided I was a big, big pussy who was scared as shit, but seeing it was the end of the world I was OK with it.

Nothing feels better than having the bar for success lowered, and you could imagine how great it felt when I no longer burdened myself with the pressure of finishing my story or making contact once more with my one true love. Instead, I cleared any semblance of a plan and resolved to take things as they came, which meant I would more than likely quit writing and just spy on her like a creep. At the very least I just wanted to see what she looked like since we'd come this far and then we'd probably get the hell out of Dodge. Basically, I had decided that this coward was more than happy to bury the hero.

Maybe we could creep outside her store until we saw her and get dinner at Wick's. I'd let Chuy get a good night's rest and we'd drive back to Atlanta in the morning. Then we could spend our last days with family, including Gramps, who probably had his Super-Nut back already, which I knew would be tremendously entertaining.

As luck would have it, our buddy Boomer sold breast implants to real doctors and Beau had convinced him to let us *borrow* a "double D" sample. Another good thing about the world ending was you didn't have to worry about returning anything you borrowed or dentists losing licensure over ill-advised scrotal procedures.

"I wasn't beating off in the shower" Chuy announced out of the blue. This was fine, because according to my calculations, we'd talked enough about his sex life to last a lifetime, or four. Come to think of it, between Dusty, Gramps, Dad, and Chuy, I was OK with never seeing or talking about another man's privates for *one hundred* lifetimes, which meant a lot less these days, but still...

"I thought I saw a huge spider, that's why I screamed, that place was disgusting."

"That's good Chuy, because if you'd punched your clown guy in the face in there, you'd *definitely* get an STD." His head shot towards me so fast the only thing missing was the "crack!" you'd hear from a whip. My shower room was spotless and I'm sure his was too but aren't big brothers supposed to torture their little brothers with misinformation?

"It's *punch the clown*," his level of concern was obvious, "not punch a clown in his face."

"It's fantastic, is what it is. I knew that, I was just testing you. I was also just kidding about the STD." I said, laughing and pounding the steering wheel. I heard Chuy murmur another *motherfucker* under his breath.

Saugatuck, Michigan ha always been one of my favorite places in the world. It's a dreamy little beach town on the Eastern coast of Lake Michigan. The shoreline is picturesque, with shallow beaches that lead up to giant dunes crested with hardwoods and evergreens. Downtown Saugatuck is a charming little town, minutes from the beaches, nestled into Lake Kalamazoo. In the summertime wealthy people dock their boats and mingle with the multitudes of Midwesterners that flock there. They all come to beat the heat at the local beaches or shop in the fun stores that line Butler Street.

My family had vacationed in Saugatuck often, but I really got to know and love the place while visiting Sarah and her family over school breaks. Saugatuck was the reason why Sarah and I connected in college. She loved what a small world it was, where I'd vacationed in her hometown and both of us chose Purdue in Indiana rather than the in-state Big Ten choices most of our friends had made. I didn't think it was a big deal at all actually, I just went with it because I thought she was beautiful.

In my many visits to Saugatuck I'd experienced two very different towns. In the winter it's desolate and beautiful and in the summer, it's congested and beautiful. Sarah's family ran a hardware store in the tourist section of town and every time I visited, I wondered how they managed to stay in business and put Sarah through school because they didn't sell much.

In case you were wondering, they didn't carry the Duque toilet line. Sarah's father Pat always seemed happy to tell me why. It would start with a tour. "Let me show you something," he'd say, then walk me over to the plumbing section to point out the obviously non-Duque toilet he carried, "it's not a Duque, because they don't work worth a shit. No pun intended. People would tell me it took three flushes and want their money back. I can't be selling three flush toilets to my customers young man, I'm sorry."

I had no problem with that, except he told me *every time* I walked into that hardware store. At that point in my life, I was only concerned about the stock price of Duque Industrial Fixtures, not the actual products. I was too naïve to know the two were interconnected.

Driving through the bustling downtown brought so many memories back, mostly how hard it was to find a parking spot during the summer. It's possible a third of my swearing catalog was developed while my parents searched for a parking spot in Saugatuck.

Sun burnt shoppers lined both sides of the streets, snacking on ice cream cones and moving in and out of the quaint brick stores. Tiny birds risked their lives eating scraps off the sidewalks while dodging the elephant-sized feet of midwestern tourists. Being back in Saugatuck was exhilarating and terrifying at the same time. The more I recognized, the more memories came back. My heart felt like a lump in my throat.

We were going slow enough where I noticed the three cars ahead of me were waiting on a car pulling out of an *incredible* parking space. I was crushed, because I *never* get those spots, I knew one of the three cars ahead of us would take it. My disappointment vaporized as soon as I realized the incredible parking spot was thirty feet away from Sarah's hardware store. Way, way,

way out of my comfort zone. The downside of having Chuy with me was I couldn't do anything with the anonymity I desired, like hiding in my car and spying on Sarah's store for the entire day. I didn't want him to know what a creepy wussy his older brother had turned into, so all my instinctual, go-to options were off the table.

The first car that stopped short to let this person out of their coveted spot kept going. *Are you fucking kidding me? Did they not see that spot?* I wasn't kidding when I said this was a premium, *premium* spot, right in the middle of all the action, they must have been going home.

The second car passed the open spot and didn't even tap their brakes. *What the fuck? Did they not see this fucking spot open up?* It was killing me, I can't drive by that spot if it's still open, but I can't park in that spot because it's way, way too close to Sarah's store. The car in front of me tapped its brakes and started their turn signal, they were taking the spot. It was now a moot point. *Thank, fucking, God.* I had never been so relieved to lose an incredible parking spot.

Then without warning, they sped off, leaving me with fifty feet of pavement, a premium parking space, and a mind-crushing decision.

"Motherfucker. Look at that spot. Park there Holmes!" Even Chuy was excited about it.

Yes Chuy, I see it. Practical Parker was screaming into my left ear, *oh my God, oh my God, oh my God, you can't pass up that parking spot. Are you kidding me? During tourist season? You can't."* Then the Big Pussy Parker would say calmly into my right ear, "*You have to drive past this spot Parker, it's way too close to Sarah's building, this is too much, too fast. What did we decide coming here? Let's take it slow, find another parking spot that isn't so dangerous.* Big Pussy Parker's calm words didn't help, just like it didn't help when I noticed the parking space was really *a space and a half,* mostly shaded... *Must... Keep... Moving...*

"Fuck me running," I announced as I turned into the spot too good to pass up. I picked a fight with a thousand years of human evolution and lost; I didn't stand a chance. *At least Chuy doesn't know we're this close to Sarah's store.*

"Holmes, there's Saugatuck Hardware, is that her store?" Chuy asked, undoing his seatbelt.

There was nothing I could do; he was too smart to fool. "Yes, her family owns it. Hold up Chuy."

"Those poor people. I betcha Home Depot is killing them, are they broke?"

"I don't think so, they own the building. This is pricey real estate around here. It's probably worth a million bucks."

"Holy crap, for that building? Aren't we going in?"

My stomach was turning in knots... Sarah Campbell could be in the building right in front of me.

"No. Let's just do a walk by first and see if she's in there, why don't you wait here." I felt like a fifth grader about to drop off a note that said, *do you like me? Check the yes or no box.* Piper got up and stretched in the back seat, made eye contact with me, curled herself back into a ball and went back to sleep. I rolled down the windows halfway so she wouldn't get hot in the car.

"You're kidding right? I drove this whole way and you're pussing out?"

"No. I'm not pussing out," *Of course I was,* "I just want to start slow, OK? Cool your jets and do what I say, and no matter what, don't go into that store unless you are following me. Got it?"

Chuy shrugged dismissively, shut his door, and started walking, fast. I sped up, panicked to catch him. The nervousness and exhilaration I'd been feeling in the sanctity of my own car tripled when I saw her. I froze in my tracks.

Sarah Campbell was 25 feet away from me, setting up a display in the front window of her store. She was exactly how I remembered her; except she was more beautiful than ever. She was dressed in a hardware store apron over a white shirt, red shorts, and flip flops. Her brown hair was pushed back in a ponytail and her olive skin was already tan from the summer sun. I forgot how graceful her hands were, her long fingers adjusted the jars stacked within the display she looked close to finishing.

The front door was propped open and Chuy had already gone into the store. If I could've yelled at him without making a sound I would have screamed, *"Get back here! Now! Please! Please! Please!"* because I had never been so afraid in my life. Chuy stopped in front of Sarah and I could see the display contained several humongous jars of honey. With a jar of honey balanced in each beautiful hand, she stopped what she was doing and smiled at him. She asked him something, and he started talking which I knew meant certain disaster. *Fuck it, it's the end of the world, why the fuck wouldn't I go in there?*

I took a deep breath and put one foot in front of the other until I broke the store's threshold. Sarah's attention was naturally drawn to the next customer. When she saw me, she dropped both jars of honey, shattering one. She didn't say anything, and I didn't say anything. Chuy hustled over, picked up the jar that wasn't broken, and tried to hand it back to her but she was still staring at me with her hand on her chest. Her wedding ring sparkled against her tan skin and it hit me with a dull thud that I was just a customer standing there and that's all I'd ever be.

"Parker?" She asked, her voice cracking, clearly surprised by my sudden appearance.

I searched for something witty but was interrupted by a perky little thing carrying four more jars of Honey, "Nice work Mom!" She looked at me and I recognized her although I'd never seen her before.

I turned to Sarah, "Is she, is this, is she your daughter?" I asked excitedly, I hadn't even thought it was possible. My head felt like it was going to explode.

"No!" Sarah said sternly.

"MOM!" The girl said, half smiling.

"What's your name?" I asked the girl.

"Harper."

"How old are you, Harper?"

"How creepy are you stranger?" She snapped back, looking exactly like her mother. I never thought I could love anyone as much as I loved Sarah Campbell, but I was wrong.

"Is she?" I stopped. I could see Sarah tearing up. This child named Harper had my eyes. How could I handle this tactfully? My mom would always say, "There's a time and a place for everything" and I was glad I'd taken that philosophy to heart because I realized this was a very sensitive situation which called for a certain degree of finesse.

"I'm your father, Harper!" There was silence as Harper looked at me, alarmed. She dropped the four jars of honey *she* was carrying. More silence. I expected the ground was covered in a deadly delicious mixture of Honey and glass shards, but it was hard to take my eyes off the daughter I never knew I had. "Why didn't you tell me?" I pleaded to Sarah, *my* eyes tearing up now.

Sarah looked incredibly upset, "You're not her father!" she sounded like she meant it. She was convincing enough, I immediately looked back to Harper, embarrassed, thinking maybe I got her age wrong? But as soon as I looked at Harper again, I knew Sarah was lying. I could see myself in Harper and best thing was her mother's beautiful genes had hidden every bit of awkwardness my DNA might have brought with it. It was wonderful and I was her father, I knew I was.

"Mom? He's my father, isn't he?"

"No!" And without warning, Sarah Campbell jumped over the shards of glass and honey, disappearing through a side door labeled, "Private."

"Wow." Harper said, "This answers some questions." I could see her mind working, "This, is a doozy!"

"Hi," I held my hand out, I'm Parker Duque and this is my little brother Chuy Duque."

Chuy held his free hand out, "You can call me Uncle Chuy."

Harper did a double take at Chuy's beautiful blonde hair and his long legs and smiled, "OK, Cool."

"I'm not sure what to say next. Your mother was my girlfriend in college, we broke up. I didn't know..." It sounded empty and hollow, so I stopped. I was overwhelmed by joy, and I was exerting every effort I could to not cry. I was pretty sure crying might take this into the creepy zone with a teenage girl. I was a dad for ten seconds and I was already scared of blowing it.

"Yep, I'm putting it together, you're the guy from the scrapbook," She had an amused delivery, cool as a cucumber.

"Scrapbook?"

"I've found Mom asleep on the couch with a scrapbook three separate times. No biggy right? But most of the pictures are of you and her, which at the time I thought was messed up because, obviously you're not Dad. Like I said, this is a doozy!" she emphasized doozy, stretching it out, it killed me, she was so funny! "Don't cry!" she reached out and held my arm.

I lost it at doozy. Who says that? She was so cute, and she was my daughter with Sarah Campbell. I was doing a silent, ugly cry with my head down to hide the ugly as much as I could. I couldn't help crying though, it was the best fucking moment of my life.

"Are you mad at her?" she asked.

I couldn't respond right away; my ugly cry was paralyzing. I was able to shake my head no and then blubber, "Nope. Happy."

Harper hugged me, "You're sweet Parker Duque. You should go talk to Mom."

"She needs time, don't you think?" I asked, feeling like the wussy I was.

"No, she's had time, I think she owes us an explanation, don't you? I bet she never told you she was pregnant and got trapped under her secret."

I smiled, "And this one's a doozy!" I stretched it out like Harper did. I walked nervously towards the door marked "Private" until I heard another jar of honey break. I looked back to see a frozen Chuy, mouth agape, standing over a fresh mass of broken glass and Honey.

"It slipped," he said sheepishly. Harper was laughing hysterically.

"I'll pay for all this," I said, gesturing to the piles of gooey danger.

"Yes you will!" Harper rang back confidently.

"What's going on out here!" Sarah burst out of her hiding spot, almost hitting me with the door.

"Chuy dropped another jar. I'll pay for all this mess Sarah, I'm sorry to just show up here."

"You can't just waltz back into my life and start staking claims!"

"I'm not staking claims! I didn't even know." My head was spinning.

"Harper, we obviously need to have a talk, a long one. What you need to know right now is this doesn't change anything. This is Parker Duque, your biological father, I'm sure we'll get to meet one of his lawyers next." Then, turning to me, "Parker, this was reckless, I hope you're happy now." The lawyers reference hit me hard. In college our plans were often interrupted by my father's attorneys requesting my *immediate* signature. She still thought of me as that rich, spoiled asshole that admittedly, at the time, I very much was.

"That's not entirely fair Sarah, I'm a real person now," I pleaded. "I don't have family attorneys anymore. I have a mortgage, I worry about paying bills, I work in real estate now." She didn't seem to care at all. "I'm finishing *The Bear!*"

"Are you a writer or are you in real estate?"

"I'm in real estate, but I'm taking a six-month break and it's the first thing I started working on. Chuy is going to proofread it for me."

Chuy shook his head and mouthed, "Nope" to Harper, who laughed.

"Our story? The two brothers, Sam and Jack? You haven't finished that yet?" I could sense she was about to cry.

"Not yet, almost though, I literally stopped this morning. I have it finished in my head; I just have to type it. I'm at the point where Jack and Sam have just run into the bear. The only reason I stopped is because we got here. That's why Chuy was driving, so I could write."

She harrumphed at another failed promise, like I knew she would. She was too smart. "Why are you here?" She sounded exasperated although she looked as beautiful as I'd ever seen her.

"I just drove ma'am." Chuy said with a shrug.

"I think she was asking me, Chuy." I said.

"You *drove*? How old are you, Chuy?" Sarah said, confused.

"Fifteen ma'am."

"Fifteen? And you drove from Atlanta? *You let him drive?* She was looking back at me in even more disbelief.

"He's an incredible driver. He has his learning permit, it's not as bad as it sounds, he's a mature fifteen and a very good driver, I taught him myself." Sarah placed both hands on her hips, she was sizing me up, confident I'd made another questionable judgment call, like the many I'd made in college. Except, how did she know we drove from *Atlanta*?

"When did you start using Ma'am?" I whispered to Chuy amused, "Seriously? Are they teaching you that in school? He shrugged his shoulders.

"Seriously, who is he?" I could tell Sarah was trying to get a better view of Chuy's beautiful legs.

"I told you, my little brother, he drove." I could have said "adopted" little brother to clear things up, but I never used that word in front of Chuy.

Sarah took her eyes off Chuy's legs and focused back on me, "Why are *you* here? You still haven't told me. Why have you waited this long?"

"Technically?" I asked.

"NO, not technically, honestly. Why are you here?"

"Well, if I say that I drove," I turned to Chuy, "How long of a drive was that?"

"About twelve hours Holmes."

"So, if I say we, or I guess Chuy, drove twelve hours it might sound—"

"He's a widower!" Chuy interrupted.

Yes, I was! How did I not think of that? "I just wanted to get away from everything and thought the weather would be nicer up North. It was here or Chicago, I'm glad we chose Saugatuck!"

Sarah looked at me after an awkward silence, "Me too, I guess. Well, we obviously have a lot to discuss, starting with my apology, because this is my mess..." She caught herself before she became emotional, "although this is not the proper venue. Why don't you come over to the house tonight for dinner and we'll talk. Harper will give you directions. Harper, please go home and wait for me, I'll be home after I meet with Mr. Hadley. You and I can talk then...I'm sure you have a lot of questions." She gave Harper a long hug and gave me a nervous glance as she walked back through the door labeled "Private." I looked back at Harper who was smiling.

"A doozy! I'm going to get some mileage out of this, that's for sure. Where are you guys staying?" she asked.

"I thought we'd stay at that white bed and breakfast there by the park. Is that still a bed and breakfast?"

"Yep, curious though, do you have reservations?"

Chuy looked at me and I looked back at my *daughter. My daughter!* "No. I'm afraid it was more of a spontaneous trip. Do you think it's full? Is there another place to stay?"

217

Harper laughed, "What are you, *new*? School just got out. The summer season has started. If you don't have reservations, you don't have a room. You can stay with us though. Mom will flip, but she'll get over it. You probably noticed earlier she doesn't like surprises."

"Bad idea, don't you think?" I said. It was too, I didn't want to surprise Sarah like that.

"Technically, you're family, right? Mom always talks about how important family is, plus, I need a ride home anyway, can you take me?" It appeared to me that Harper inherited her mother's brains and my proclivity to break the rules if you could somehow rationalize it. I was immediately horrified we might have spawned another attorney.

"Of course we can give you a ride, but do you really think she'll be OK with us staying there? That might be a pretty big surprise to get over, don't you think?"

"You really don't have a choice if you want to stay around here. You can drive to Holland tonight if it gets ugly and you're in a pinch."

"What about that cool hotel on the side of the hill where you turn left to go to Oval Beach?"

Harper's answer was a dismissive laugh, ignoring me as she turned to Chuy, "I make my own honey, do you want to see my beehives?" I looked down at the mess around our feet and saw the labels: *Harper's Honey.*

37

AN OLD FRIEND

It was one question after another, with Chuy acting as the interviewer, what grade are you in? Where do you go to school? Do you play sports? What are your hobbies? Etc. It was the greatest car ride of my life. I had a daughter, a funny daughter who was an absolute joy to be around. I missed out on so much, the diaper changing, the first day of school, all the other special little kid stuff, but it didn't matter.

I suppose if I were going to live longer than a week, I might be more upset Sarah didn't tell me, but honestly, I'm not sure I should be. It's embarrassing to admit this, but if you look at the big picture, it might've been a good thing for all involved that I wasn't around then, because I was still growing up myself. From our short car ride, I could gather that neither of us were quite done growing up yet.

When we arrived at her house Harper gave me her key and she, Chuy, and Piper tore around the back to look at her honeybee farm or whatever you call it.

"Don't let Piper get stung!" I shouted after them.

This was awkward, and even though I was beyond curious to see what her life was like it felt creepy to go into Sarah's house alone. Did she have younger kids too? What did her husband look like? Was he home? Did *he* know who Harper's biological father was? I knocked on the door to be safe and waited. I put the key in the door but couldn't bring myself to open it and took the key back out, I was still too nervous. If Sarah's husband was home, it might not be the best ice breaker to let myself in and announce myself as his daughter's father...

I went back to the car to get my bags and my laptop. I figured maybe if I was writing *The Bear* when Sarah came home, it might take the edge off seeing her surprise guest. Maybe she'd start reading it?

As I was walking back to the house the front door opened, then slammed shut faster than it was opened. In the short period of time the door was open I saw a beautiful man in a sweater cape standing there, bathed in pastels. He was tan, skinny and hygiene was apparently of foremost priority, because I could have sworn he sparkled in the sunlight.

"Larry?" I shouted; I couldn't believe it. "Larry, Is that you? It's me, Duque. Parker Duque, from Purdue. Larry!"

The door opened maybe five inches, enough to show his chiseled features. He looked like he was going to cry, "I know who you are. What are you doing here? She wants nothing to do with you. She's *my* wife now Parker." He extended his arm through the opening to show me his wedding band, like he was soaking his fingers in Palmolive.

"Wow! Great to see you too Larry. Can I come in?"

Larry's arm disappeared and he slammed the door in my face. I heard the lock mechanism engage. I took Harper's key back out of my pocket and turned the lock and tried to open the door. I felt a faint resistance like maybe a little kid was trying to hold the door shut. I looked down and saw the unmistakable sole of a Sperry topsider wedged against it and heard a squeal that might resemble a Quaker woman under attack.

"Who... gave... you... a key?" I could hear the strain in his voice.

"Larry, open the door. Are you pushing against it?"

A strained, "Yes" came from behind the door.

"Well then stop already, I'm afraid I'm going to break your arm or something. I know about Harper." The resistance against the door disappeared. I gently pushed the door open and could see Larry shaking, with his back turned to me. He was crying. I would've loved to see the look on Ms. Livingston's face if she could see him "clying" like that.

Larry was Sarah's best friend in college, and a really good friend of mine too. I'd say I'm as jealous as the next guy but I never, not for one second, thought I had anything to worry about with Larry and Sarah. I thought, just like with my brother, that Larry liked dudes but wouldn't act on it. When we were at Purdue the world was still backwards and being gay wasn't really understood or tolerated. I remember meeting Larry's blue-collar family at a tailgate and could tell they definitely weren't the type to accommodate a gay son, so I understood why he wouldn't come out, even to his closest friends.

Larry was about six feet tall with sandy blonde hair, chiseled cheekbones, and a very skinny but athletic build. All the girls in college had massive crushes on him but he never dated any of them or took anyone home after we got drunk at the bars. I mean, if Larry was straight, getting laid would've been a cakewalk. Even as I was trying to force my way in to talk to him, I couldn't believe my luck. Was there a chance I might still be able to get back together with Sarah? Was her husband our gay friend Larry? Could I calm her down enough where it might still be a possibility? Even more important, how much time did I have to calm her down? For the first time since I found out about our little end of the world predicament, I felt energized about living.

"Larry, let's talk, please. There's no reason to cry."

"I knew this day would come! I held her hand while she was giving birth, Parker. I changed Harper's diapers. When she was sick, I stayed awake all night with her, I'm her father. You can't take that away from me. You can't take her away from us."

"She can—"

He interrupted me, "Did you come to take her away? How did you find out?"

"I found out thirty minutes ago at the hardware store, Larry. You seem to be forgetting, I was never told about Harper. I mean, she told me she was pregnant and ending the pregnancy. She didn't tell me she changed her mind. I cried Larry, I full-on *begged her*, but she wouldn't even consider having a baby with me. That's why we broke up, you know that. I should be screaming bloody murder Larry, but I'm not here to do that and I'm not here to take her away from you!" I was just keeping the door open with my foot, not sure if Larry was still pushing against it. "But I am her father and I want to get to know her and be a part of her life. I think you two owe me that. Larry, you know I'll never be able to take away the fact that you were there for them, both of them."

"She had the colic Parker," Larry spit out, he was still crying, "Harper cried for two months straight. It was torture."

"She probably got that from me because after I lost all my money, I did the same thing, except it lasted a year or two longer." He let out a little smile, I had cracked the egg, "Larry, can we sit down and talk about this? Don't you ever watch movies? This two-dad issue is addressed all the time. You're her dad, I can't take that away from you."

He was flashing his beautiful smile at me now and I could see why all the girls at school were crazy about him, "You aren't here with your lawyers to take her away?"

"No."

"OK then. It is nice to see you, it's been a long time. You look different, have you lost weight? Are you working out?"

"Yes actually, but I just quit forever. I was also watching what I ate, but I just quit that forever too."

"Why?"

"It's a long story, but I can sum it up by saying that my wife was just murdered by her lover in a murder-suicide."

"Oh dear." Larry said with a hand to his cheek.

"Yeah, although that kind of situation makes it easier to be a widower."

"I'm so sorry Parker."

"Thanks Larry. If you don't mind, I'd rather not talk about it. Ever."

He looked me straight in the eye, "I completely understand. I would be devastated if somebody took my girls away from me."

My stomach fell like a rock to the floor. I realized with only a week left I'd never get to be with Sarah and Harper as a real family unit, even if ol' Larry was as gay as a three-dollar bill.

A return to ultra-selfishness had been a dream of mine ever since I'd lost

AN OLD FRIEND

it with my fortune. End of the world or not, I had planned on picking it back up, as a hobby, after my big deal closed, so this seemed as fitting an occasion as any. I wanted Sarah back. It had always pissed me off that meatheads and religious fanatics had created an environment where Beau felt he had to hide his sexuality, but now that same environment had my closeted friend married to the only woman I'd ever really loved.

And then I had *another* genius idea, "Larry, could you excuse me for a second," I took out my Hello Kitty cell phone, "I have to make a call."

Piper came back in with me, apparently, she didn't like playing around bees. She laid down onto the floor of the kitchen between me and Larry and went to sleep.

"Why do you seem different, Parker?" Larry asked.

"I've grown up Larry. I got a job, I pay bills, I was forced to become a real person instead of an insecure, arrogant, trust fund baby."

"I have to tell you, when I heard you lost all of your money, my curiosity was piqued. I mean, what in the world could *you* do? Did you even go to class at school? I knew they didn't hire people to spend money or get drunk, and nobody except Sarah believed that writing bullshit you talked about. You were the only aspiring writer I knew that never wrote anything." Larry chuckled, clearly enjoying himself, but it was nothing I didn't deserve, ten times over. "I still don't know what Sarah ever saw in you."

"My money Larry, that's all any girl has ever seen in me."

"Well, that's all you ever showed anybody, was your money. We used to joke about how quickly you would mention your trust fund or that you were a Duque to somebody new."

My heart sank. I can't believe Sarah made fun of me for that. I deserved it, but in fairness, beautiful people don't have to tell others they're special, it's right there to see. When you're not that great looking, and people see you're dating a beautiful girl, they'll keep asking questions until they find out how an imbalance such as this could occur in nature. Then the revelation, "Oh, *he has money.* Puzzle solved."

Over the years I'd convinced myself Sarah wasn't one of the girls looking to get ahead by marrying a rich kid. And now with this revelation I could see the confidence in Larry. All he was worried about was me taking Harper away, not his wife falling for an old flame. How naïve of me to think somebody might automatically see the nice guy I'd turned into instead of the self-centered asshole I used to be. I had earned all this lack of respect myself. I could blame no one else, which is always a terrible situation. I think that I hurt more at that moment than when I found out all of humanity would end.

38

HONEY, I'M HOME!

"Parker! What are you doing here?" Sarah asked as she walked into her own kitchen. Her beautiful green eyes were gently swollen as though she had been crying.

"I didn't mean to surprise you. Harper said we could crash here because all of the—"

"Hah!" Larry laughed, as he slapped both hands on the table like you'd just told him they were selling Gucci at Walmart.

Sarah shot Larry a look, "You and your little brother are welcome to stay here tonight."

"*What?*" Larry chirped.

"Larry, you know everything in town is booked. They drove from Atlanta. We can put them up here tonight and they can stay at Water Street after that."

"First of all, he has a dog," Larry spoke like I wasn't in the room.

Sarah looked at Piper, dead asleep, but sprawled out awkwardly on the kitchen floor, like maybe her lady bits got stung and it felt good to press them against the cold tile, or maybe her lady bits just felt good pressed against the cold tile, but I didn't want to think about it that way. The important part is Piper could sleep in any position, and sleeping dogs are generally low risk propositions for rentals. Sarah looked back at Larry and said nothing, which seemed to be enough.

"Second, I'm storing my office files in the Carriage House right now. I assume you meant the carriage house by Water Street?"

"Larry!" Sarah said sternly.

"Like I said, they can stay at the Carriage House on Water Street," He conceded.

Sarah nodded her head, "Parker, I'm glad you're here because I want to finish our conversation, but first I have to talk to Harper. I think I owe it to her."

"Yes, by all means, where is she?" Larry said as he popped up and away from the table, avoiding Piper like she had hoof and mouth disease.

"Larry, if you don't mind, I'd like to speak to her alone about a decision I made, alone."

"But Sarah, I'm her father," he said looking over at me as he said it, almost taunting.

"Yes, you are Larry, nobody can take that away. Please." I watched Sarah leave the room and my chest ached.

"She cried for months, Parker," I looked back at Larry, who sat back down, smug faced.

"I know, I know. And you changed her diapers." I was deflated. Instead of having been thrust into a new family, I felt like an outsider.

"No dummy, Sarah. You accused her of being a gold digger. Sarah, a gold digger. That's funny. You idiot, she was in love with you, pregnant with your child, and you broke up with her."

"Wasn't she after my money? I never broke up with her. Did she tell you I broke up with her? She flat out left me. Remember I told you, I was the one who wanted to have the baby. She was so against having a baby out of college, I couldn't stop her. It was horrible. *She left me.*"

"Well, when she got back here, she couldn't go through with it. She had Harper and I was right there by her side, like I always was. We fell in love and got married. Maybe if you'd paid less attention to yourself you would've known that her parents own half of this town. They have their fingers in everything, they're loaded. Did you know that? She was never after your money."

226

"She never said a word..."

"Because she's not like you, at all. She doesn't care about money. She never has, that's why I could never figure out what she saw in you. You seemed like a nice guy, but really Parker." It looked like something terrible outside had wrestled his attention away from the condescending speech he was about to deliver, "Oh. My. Gawd! The landscapers left a beautiful little Mexican boy here!"

I craned my neck to see Chuy looking through the patio door into the house.

"That's my little brother, Chuy." I got up to let him in.

"Tell him they missed a huge spot by the pool, and there aren't any bees over there, so I don't want any excuses."

"Larry, did you hear me? He's my *brother*. He's not a landscaper." I walked over to the door and let Chuy in.

"Chuy, this is Harper's dad and a friend of mine from college, Larry Ringer."

Chuy ignored the introduction, "Holmes, she's crying back there. They both are. You should go talk to her." And like a slow train coming into the station he continued, "So if he's Harper's dad, then you're going by Harper's father? Cool. Harper looks just like you Holmes, but in a good way. She's cute actually. Not cute like I would date her though; it would be like banging you." Larry couldn't hide his horror at the prospect of this beautiful miniature landscaper "banging" his princess.

"Chuy, I can't even tell you how wrong that is. And on top of all that wrong, you're her uncle. Larry, I apologize. This is my fault, I've been letting him talk like a sailor." I looked Chuy in the eyes, "It ends now."

"Chill, Holmes. I got you."

I wasn't as upset as I should have been at Chuy's horrifically inappropriate statement. Chuy was, after-all, a teenager in heat, but I also couldn't get my mind off what Larry had just told me; Sarah *loved* me.

Harper and Sarah walked into the house and it was obvious both had been crying. Harper hugged me, which felt indescribably good, then walked over to Larry and sat in his lap.

Sarah looked at me and said, "Your turn. I guess I have some explaining to do. You surprised me at the store, and I want to apologize to the both of you if I didn't handle it very well." Chuy and I shrugged our shoulders. I didn't know what to say. I wasn't expecting her to be so calm.

"Larry, can you and the kids get a pizza tonight?"

"Umm, sure. Where are they going to stay?" He pointed at me and Chuy.

"Chuy can sleep in the guest room and Parker can sleep on the couch in the study."

"We can find something if it's too much, really. Harper said we can get a room in Holland?" I felt like I wasn't Larry's friend anymore, which was weird because we had some *awesome* times at school.

Larry looked at Sarah, who was looking back at him and said, "Nonsense, you two are welcome to stay in our house. Does he speak English?"

Chuy started in, "What the fuck Cracker? I was just—"

"Dad/Larry/ Chuy!" Harper, Sarah, and I chimed in at the same time.

"Color me practical, but none of our landscapers do!" Larry still seemed confused.

"I'm not a landscaper Holmes, I'm a Duque!" Chuy had a soft spot for intermittent conflict, and I suspected this reaction was mostly for the attention it brought.

"You do have very good English!" Larry said.

"You should taste his tacos!" I cracked up as I delivered the line, I felt like it was time to let the air out of this bag. Larry was being an idiot, and Chuy wasn't offended. Sarah and Harper were flabbergasted until Chuy belly laughed with me and said, "Thanks Cracker number two." Everyone laughed, it was a nice break.

"Shall we take a walk and get something to eat?" Sarah was talking to me and I knew she was saying something important, but I was knee deep in how beautiful she was and how glad I was to see her smile again. The best thing was, she was smiling at me.

"What? I'm sorry."

"I said *Let's go!*" She pulled my arm and we started towards the door and despite all the time that'd passed, I felt like we were together again, like nothing had changed, only everything had.

39

JUST LIKE OLD TIMES

As soon as we hit the front porch my mind was racing with what to say first, I had so much I wanted to tell her and so many questions I wanted to ask. Nothing would come out though, my tongue felt like a kielbasa sausage.

It didn't matter, Sarah broke the silence, "I'm going to cry so let's not talk until we're out of sight. Larry will be watching us."

I turned around to see Larry jump behind a curtain in the living room window. I laughed because it struck me as a clumsy reenactment of Ms. Livingston's disappearance after her minion drop kicked me in the nuts.

"Don't look!" She hit me on the arm when she said it, just like she'd done a hundred times before, "Nothing has changed!" Just like everyone else, if you tell me not to look at something, there's a good chance I'm going to look at it.

We walked in silence to the end of the street, and I heard her whimpering. As soon as I looked over, she fell into me and I held her while she cried. I didn't say anything, I was crying too, which sucked because I didn't want to start until I knew what we were crying about. Is she crying because I found out about Harper? I wished we were crying exclusively about our personal situation, but I was crying mostly because I was finally holding Sarah Campbell and it would only be a matter of days before we both turned into space dust.

Like the last uncontrollable glob of toothpaste from a spent tube, Sarah finally managed, "I'm so sorry Parker. I'm so, so, sorry."

"Don't be, please! Sarah, it's OK. I mean it." I was assuming she was apologizing for not telling me about Harper, but she didn't have to say sorry to me for anything, I had already forgiven any wrongdoing on her side, for anything.

"It wasn't fair to you and it wasn't fair to Harper. I got stuck. I got stuck in the lie and then it was too late. It kept getting bigger and bigger and before I knew it, there was no way out. My parents think Larry is Harper's father." She looked up at me, shook her head and panicked, "Larry's parents think he's Harper's father!"

"Sarah," I was trying desperately to avoid an ugly face cry, "today has been the best day of my life." I had to stop and take a deep breath to compose myself. And then I needed another deep breath to compose myself again, I was so happy. "The truth of it is, I was the one that needed to grow up. Had I been around, she probably would've been all screwed up like I was. I would have been a horrible father."

"You would have been a wonderful father Parker. You're so frustrating. Why don't you ever give yourself any credit? After all this time you haven't figured out how to give yourself a break?"

"Do you mean punching a clown in his face?"

"What a horrible thing to do. What on Earth are you talking about?"

"It was a joke I shouldn't have made. I like clowns." I lied.

"OK, try not to punch them, I like them too. We should work on your pessimism."

"Holy Crap, I have been!" I was excited to show her, "You know what you can't stop?"

"Your pessimism?"

"Progress."

"Whoa. Are you feeling OK? That is great for you. I love it!" She was smiling ear to ear, "What did you do with the old Parker?"

"He's long gone. But that's my point. Don't beat yourself up. I think it probably worked out for the best. Do you not remember when I lost my inheritance? I was a wreck."

"That's an understatement."

"I was a wreck like that, *for years*." It was the truth. I wasn't proud of it.

"I don't doubt that. Most people would be, but you adapted. I knew you would. Look what you've done with yourself."

"What do you mean?"

"You drive a pretty fancy car; I assume you've had some level of success."

"Can you believe it? It's still hard for me to believe it actually. It's way more than money. I'm a different person now. I pulled myself together; I feel like I'm a real person now as weird as that sounds. I learned how to fix up buildings, how to buy them, how to run them and all the legal and financial work involved. I'm good at it. The best part is I did it without family money."

"That doesn't surprise me at all" she said, starting to cry again.

"Don't cry, please Sarah. I'm super flexible these days. The timing is perfect. I'm starting my own company, I could visit all the time or even move up here."

It was too late; she was in my arms, which felt good, and she was crying, then sobbing. It was one of the very few times I'd ever seen her so emotional, which is great, because if you haven't noticed by now, I get emotional too sometimes.

"I would like that. For Harper," She said. I was flying. It didn't matter we could be blown to smithereens at any moment. As cheesy as it sounds, for the first time in my life, I felt complete.

There were so many questions I had for her; *what is Harper like? Are you in love with Larry? Why didn't you call me after you decided to keep our baby? Do you want to go have rabbit sex for an hour?*

Even though this was a serious moment I couldn't help myself, I started to get a woody. I think she knew it because she stopped crying and then I knew she knew it when she felt it with her hand and pushed me away. She was laughing and crying, "Parker Duque, you're still the same! Doesn't that thing ever take a break?"

"It's been on a break for a long, long time. You wouldn't believe the break this thing has been on, seriously."

"Tell me about it," she scoffed, "actually, tell it to take another break. Let's grab dinner at Marro's."

"Is that the place I love by the ice cream place? Where they have the garlic rolls with mozzarella on top, soaked in butter?"

"Yes"

"Uh ooh." I said.

"What?"

"You just made it harder," I joked. Actually, walking around with a boner in public made me feel like my father, which helped speed the demise of my unsolicited visitor.

Sarah looked down at what was left of my pup tent and laughed, "OK, seriously, lose that thing. People know me around here."

"Well don't touch it or talk about garlic rolls!"

It was nice to hear her laughing again, even if she insisted on walking ten feet in front of me, disassociating herself from the creepy guy with a boner. I could see she kept in great shape although I decided quickly, I'd better start thinking of my middle school librarian if I wanted to be fit for public consumption by the time we reached Marro's.

40

TABLE FOR TWO

The garlic rolls had been ordered and we were sitting in a booth at Marro's Restaurant downtown. The Italian restaurant had been there forever on Water Street, right in the heart of Saugatuck, near the giant yachts docked along the Kalamazoo. Everyone at the restaurant knew Sarah and we were able to bypass the long wait outside.

"Tell me the truth, why are you here?" It was her first real question.

The question wasn't as easy as it sounded. *To see you Sarah, you're the love of my life. I was kidnapped, my cheating idiot of a wife had been murdered, I had to "kind of" kill two government agents. I've also read an in-depth top-secret file about how aliens are blowing the Earth in two and I thought now was as good a time as any to take a road trip, again, to see you, the love of my life.*

The only way I could express my true feelings about her without appearing super creepy was telling her the end of the world was near. The hitch was, telling her about our impending fate would only wreck everything *for her*, and she was one of the people I wanted to protect the most, especially now.

I desperately wanted to tell her that I'd never gotten over her and thought about her pretty much every day since she left me in front of the Pike House. I also wanted to tell her my heart leapt out of my chest every time I looked in her eyes, but I thought it would probably tip the "creepy" scale off its pedestal.

"Sarah, I know you're married, and this is inappropriate, but I can't keep

233

it to myself. I came to see you." Her eyes grew wide with panic and she gestured to me to stop, but I couldn't. "Please, I have to get this out, I've been through a lot recently and... What's wrong? Why are you looking at me like that?" her panic had turned into the giggles. "What's so funny? I'm about to pour my heart out to you!"

"Parker, do you remember Mimi?" She was still laughing. Her grandmother was right behind me.

"Mimi!" I stood up to greet her, but I think almost anyone can tell you that standing up in a booth doesn't work.

"Oh dearie, don't let me interrupt you, you're the toilet kid, aren't you?"

"Parker Duque Ma'am. It's a pleasure to see you again." All of a sudden I'd turned into a tight-assed Southerner like Chuy.

"Well, nice to see you too. I don't know if she's told you this yet, but she's married with a kid," she said, winking at me afterwards. She was my favorite Campbell other than Sarah. Mimi was sharp as a tack and I loved that she referred to herself as an "Old Broad." She turned toward Sarah, "Sweetheart, I was passing by and Tim Hession told me you were in here with a stranger, which I found too scandalous to pass up, so I thought I'd come in and say hello." She looked at me, then back at Sarah, "I'm glad I did too. Are you coming to dinner tomorrow night?"

"Yes Mimi, can I bring anything?"

"You can bring Sonny here if you want, but it might get ugly if he starts pouring his heart out in front of Larry."

"I'll see you there, Mimi," Sarah got up from the table and gave her a big hug and a kiss on the cheek. Mimi gave me a wink as Sarah was hugging her. I had the feeling she still liked me. On past visits I got along well with both Sarah's mother and grandmother. The Campbell ladies were all blue chip, first class, which made me love Sarah even more.

"The chaos has already started. This is all my fault," Sarah said, tearing up again, putting her head in her hands. I tried to move over to her side of the booth, but she stopped me, "Parker, please don't. I'm married." I went back to my side of the booth feeling lost and waited for her to say something.

After what felt like hours of silence she cracked, "I'm so sorry I didn't call you." She blew her nose which sounded grosser than I expected and continued, "You were so mad I was going to end my pregnancy and I was so mad at you for being such a jerk about losing money you didn't even earn. I thought what we were going through was a little bit more important than your Dad bankrupting his father's company. Obviously, I couldn't end the pregnancy and thank God I didn't; Harper's the best thing I've ever done. After I was done being mad at you, I couldn't believe you weren't calling me. You didn't come for me. I thought you were the one. I loved you and I thought you loved me. Why didn't you call me?"

I was dumbfounded. "Oh my God. I would have had I known it was an option! Do you remember our last conversation? I wanted you to keep the baby and it was a nonstarter for you, we were too young to 'play house' and I couldn't even 'get my head out of my own ass' is I think how you phrased it?"

Sarah laughed a sheepish laugh, "Well, that was an understatement."

"You left me, to abort our baby, I thought that was a pretty good indication you were done with me, and I thought, like every girl before you, you were only attracted to me for my money."

She looked at me with disgust, "I could never understand that. I could tell you a hundred times and you wouldn't believe me. It was maddening when you'd hint around about that after you'd buy me something *I never asked for*. You never understood it wasn't about your money."

I shrugged my shoulders, "I'm not the best-looking guy."

"I've always thought you were beautiful Parker. You made me laugh every day. Nobody could cheer me up or make me laugh like you. You're a wonderful, giving person. Your money had nothing to do with it. I hope you learned that after you lost it."

"Meh..."

"Let me finish please, while I have the courage. I was so embarrassed about getting pregnant, I didn't tell anybody at school. My lie kept getting bigger and bigger. After I left school, Larry visited and saw my big belly and he's been here ever since. People from school would come through the shop from time to time, and I'd ask them about you, but no one knew where you went after graduation or how to get in touch with you. You literally disappeared."

"That was on purpose. I was embarrassed and humiliated. Even guys in my house were mocking me. I still haven't gone back to Purdue since graduation."

"That's funny, me neither, mostly out of fear exposing myself."

"Do you do that a lot?" I couldn't help it.

"Ha, poorly worded. I meant exposing our secret love child and having you find out"

"Are you in love with Larry?"

"It's complicated. I love him, he's an incredible dad, but I'm not 'in love' with him. We have an arrangement. You might have guessed it already because I remember discussing this with you at school, but we were right, he *is* gay, and his family would freak if they knew. We've never had sex." While this fact made me very happy, I thought it best to not point it out.

"This is a small-town Parker, a very conservative small town, and pregnant and unmarried was a big deal around here, it was a horrible situation. You know how conservative my parents are; there was a lot of pressure from them to get married. Why not? Larry could keep his family happy, and I could keep my family happy if we just partnered up. We were already best friends. Even if I could've found your number, I honestly don't think I had the courage to call you. Larry was here for me and proposed. I realize I took the easy way out," she looked me square in the eye, "but I felt like it was my only choice because *he* was here for me."

"You're kidding right? About the "*He* was here for me" part? Because I didn't even know! I would have been here for you, I wanted to be. When I saw my check to the clinic was cashed, I assumed you went through with the procedure."

"When I canceled the procedure, I asked them to keep your money as a donation"

"Oh Sarah, I had no idea. Calling someone after they leave you seemed like harassment to me. I didn't want to be that guy; I was already pathetic enough. I really don't want to fight over it though; we've wasted too much time already. I'm just now finding out you really loved me."

"If you didn't think I loved you, why did you come here now, and come to my store?"

Oh boy. Do I go extra creepy and tell her I'd never stopped loving her? I didn't even know where all this was going, did she want to be with me? Fuck it, it's the end of the world. "It didn't matter whether or not you loved me, I've never stopped loving you. Over the last couple of years, I've become more of an optimist and I guess I thought you would at least remember us fondly, which I know sounds creepy, but—"

"Hah!" she erupted.

"Hah what?"

"Parker Duque. You have never been an optimist."

"You know what you can't stop?"

"Progress. I know, I said I loved it, but that's one saying. It's going to take a lot to convince me you've turned over a new leaf..."

"OK, I can see the merit in that. Anyway, I just went through some rough events over the last couple of days and when that happens to you, you tend to prioritize." I paused and she looked at me, confused.

"Oh. My. God. Are you really a widower? You're not wearing a wedding ring. I assumed you guys made that up, please tell me that part was a lie?"

"It wasn't a lie." I tried to look glum, but I doubt it worked, I was so excited to be with Sarah like this, it pained me to even speak Margot's name.

"I'm sorry to hear about your wife."

"Don't be, now *she* only loved me for my money."

"Oh Parker."

"No, trust me. It's not pessimistic, she told me herself, or rather, I overheard her telling a friend on the phone. She said it disgusted her to have sex with me.

"Aww baby, that's terrible! Your sex is great. Trust me."

"She was folding t-shirts at the Gap when I met her."

"You met her in a Gap?"

"No, my old boss's wife set me up with her. She was a social climber. I met her at an art auction and bought a twelve hundred painting just to impress her, what a desperate fool."

"I'm confused, are you divorced or are you a widower? You don't seem distraught?"

"A widower. She was murdered." Sarah stopped drinking and went white in the face. "By her lover." She spit her wine out all over me and my pizza.

"That was pretty cool. Do you get to do that often?" I wiped the wine off my face.

"Are you messing with me?"

"I wish I was, but I'm not. I was giving a speech at Chuy's school last Thursday and she and her lover had a spat. Her lover shot her in the face because she was going to leave him. Thankfully, he shot himself too. I'd prefer to think of it as a type of natural selection, a culling of the herd if you will."

"I would laugh, but it's too shocking. And gross, and terrible."

"I would cry, but I've moved on, and just for the record, I would've never told you I loved you if you were married to a straight guy and had a kid with him. I'm not that reckless."

"Larry didn't have you fooled?" She laughed.

"He never had me fooled, that's why I was never jealous. He's just like with Beau, it doesn't take a rocket scientist to figure it out."

"He came out to me before we got married, I didn't care. It was an easy solution. I've let him do what he wants. I know he's had a fling or two, but you know Larry, he's timid and very careful not to cause a stir. Like I said, Small—"

"Town. I get it." I looked down at my wine-soaked pizza and back at Sarah, "Not that I don't like pizza with an alcoholic content, but I'm stuffed from the garlic rolls anyway, what do you say we go to that bar on the water across the street?"

"Coral Gables?"

"I think so; remember the place we played pool downstairs? It was Christmas," I asked.

"That's The Crow Bar," She said, "Sure, why not?"

41

I PLAY THE DRUMS

Just like at Marro's, everybody at the Crow Bar knew and adored Sarah. After about five-hundred awkward greetings, we made our way toward the back and settled into a nice booth. Two pitchers, one cover band and several hundred Harper stories later we were feeling pretty loose. I soaked up every story like you'd expect a new dad might. I was so happy it was impossible not to cry, it was very emotional for both of us. I had missed so much, I wanted to know it all and I could tell Sarah enjoyed sharing it with me as much as I loved hearing it.

I could see the guilt she felt weave in and out of her expressions as she told me one funny story after another, most of them charming, some in alarming candor. She elaborated on Larry's reference to Harper having "the colic" where she apparently cried nonstop for months. Sarah told me in what I gathered to be complete honesty, that had I called her during "the colic," she would have offered me full custody.

Apparently, Harper was and has been the unofficial Mayor of Saugatuck since she said her first word, "Hi!" She had little chubby legs, dimples to die for and a smile that would light up the room and make even the coldest tourist laugh. On walks, Harper felt compelled to say "Hi" to literally everyone they passed, which is saying something during tourist season in Saugatuck.

"You said your ex loved you for your money? Do you have money again big shot?"

"A little bit. Not big money, but I earned all of it myself. I thought you didn't care about money?"

"I don't care about other people's money. I have my own money."

"I know, Larry told me. How come you never told me you came from money?"

"I don't. My dad has a decent net worth, but he doesn't have much money and he certainly never gives me any. It's all tied up in real estate around town. The only thing he's sold in the last 30 years was the hardware store and I paid the full market price, too much really."

"He didn't cut you a break?"

"Nope" she said, "He still makes fun of me for paying too much every time something breaks."

"Rough. I remember Pat giving me grief about our toilets."

"*Every* time you came to visit us, I remember, I was horrified. 'I can't be selling three flush toilets young man,' he couldn't let it go." She did a pretty good imitation.

"So, I'm curious, how do you make your money? You couldn't possibly be making any money at that hardware store."

"The hardware store breaks even but I do pretty well selling wood working machinery over the internet."

"*Get out!* I have a wood shop in my garage in Atlanta! Do you mean table saws and lathes and such?" I had noticed how big the building was and how small the hardware shop was. Good lord I was so in love with her it hurt.

"You are a woodworker now?" She seemed impressed.

"I dabble in finish carpentry, I redid all the interior trim in my house."

"We sell Delta, Jet, and Powermatic table saws"

"You sell Powermatic? Could you get better looking? She laughed and was about to say something when we were interrupted.

"Hi Sarah." A very handsome twenty-something year old blonde kid, cute as a puppy dog, was smiling ear to ear at Sarah. *What in the hell? Who is this clown?* I was instantly jealous.

"Hello Michael, you guys sound great! How's life at the nursery?"

"Too good, it'd be nice if we'd slow down a bit, business has been incredible this season. You should come out more; I'd love to see you out there while I'm playing."

Sarah, like most girls, had always had a soft spot for musicians, I know this from experience because when we met, I'd been trying to get her attention for weeks. It wasn't until she saw me sit in with a house band at one of our social functions that I was able to get her attention.

What did he mean, "I'd love to see you out there while I'm playing?" *Motherfucker, am I invisible?* Can't he see *I fathered a child* with this woman? Then I realized he wasn't just a beautiful musician with long blonde hair and an obvious interest in Sarah, he was the *singer* of the band with an obvious interest in Sarah. My jealousy peaked, but then I caught myself. I was older, probably wiser, *self-made*, with more world experience, I didn't need to do anything or say something stupid just because I might be a little jealous.

"I play the drums." I said, knowing full well I haven't played anything but the *air drums* since that social function in college.

"Michael, this is a friend of mine from college, Parker."

"Nice to meet you Sir." Michael extended his hand and squeezed the shit out of mine. Was he posturing? It really wasn't necessary; both of us could see that he could crush me as fast as the fight started. Was he making sure I knew that? Why did he have to go and call me *Sir*? What a *dick*.

"Nice to meet you *Mike*."

"It's Michael."

"Not Mike?"

"I prefer Michael," He said with a fake smile.

Seriously? "OK." I said, happy to get away from the drum talk.

"Parker's so good at the drums. Do you still play?" She asked me, her eyes shining full of hope and admiration.

I knew I should tell the truth, even though it might let her down. "Every chance I get," I lied through my teeth.

"You do?" She was excited.

"Well... Yeah, of course." I said with zero confidence.

Nursery Guy was smirking, he could see through my bullshit, "Why don't you sit in with us for a song?" He was calling me out, taunting me, "C'mon, let's do it. What song do you want to play *Porter*?"

"Parker" Sarah and I corrected him in unison, with her laughing and me returning his smirk. *Motherfucker.* Sarah turned to me as if she'd just given me the greatest gift a guy could ever ask for. I could already see him dropping the "I can't believe *you* dated *that* guy" line the next time they ran into each other. But then I remembered they'd probably never see each other again, and I figured, *you know what? Fuck it.*

"Do you know that song that goes, 'I've got soul, but I'm not a soldier' by the Killers?" I asked.

"Yeah. It's called, *All these things that I have done,* we play it. You think you can play that song?" He laughed a dismissive laugh.

I felt like I could play the shit out of it on the *air drums,* but then I remembered you can't hear mistakes on air drums. *What was I thinking?* Any confidence I had was gone. I was drunk with love and making terrible decisions, this was a bad idea. I needed to bow out, "Yeah, I probably shouldn't."

"Come on little guy, let's see what you got."

I looked at Sarah and she looked at me, she hadn't really stopped smiling since our first pitcher of beer. She mouthed, *"Little guy?"* and laughed. I laughed too, relieved she was on my team, it was silly for me to think this guy was a threat. Sarah looked so beautiful the way she was smiling at me, I didn't want to disappoint her. *Why the fuck wouldn't I play these drums?*

"Fuck it *Mike,* I'm in."

Nursery guy announced me sitting in on the drums, just to make sure everybody within earshot knew I was about to make a fool of myself. The entire crowd stopped what they were doing, this musical experiment had become the car wreck they couldn't turn away from. Nursury Guy basked in the attention and bantered with the band's drummer who had transitioned into the audience, beer in hand, telling him, "Don't get too comfortable." I got settled in and gave him a fake laugh and a thumbs up. He looked back at me and announced to our captivated audience in a doomsday tone, "This is why you don't say, '*I play the drums*' to the lead singer in a rock and roll band."

It didn't matter, I fucking rocked it. And when I say I fucking rocked it, it's only because I *completely fucking rocked the shit out of it.* Granted, I'd picked a song that was pretty easy to play, a song I'd played on the air drums three thousand times in my car, but I fucking rocked it. Sarah was smiling from ear to ear in the front row, singing along and watching *me* the entire time, not Nursury Guy. I couldn't believe how tight I played, it felt so good. I didn't worry about anything, it was perfect.

After they saw I wasn't falling on my face, the crowd got behind me and the entire bar came alive. The energy was incredible, people were singing their hearts out and jumping up and down to the song. Nursery Guy struggled in vain to remain the center of attention, making an valiant, albeit failed attempt to tear off his shirt midsong. The bold move was undercut by his obvious desperation and lack of success, and judging from his bandmate's laughter, it was a bold move he would pay dearly for later.

When the song was over I stood up and screamed, "I PLAY THE DRUMS MOTHERFUCKERS!" and the whole place went nuts screaming back.

When Sarah and I got back to the table our waitress brought a pitcher of beer from the owner and said it was in lieu of compensation for playing with the band.

"I forgot you played the drums. I was so impressed." She started tearing up.

All this incredible momentum, all the fun we'd been having, it was as though it had just hit a brick wall. I mean, I had just rocked the fucking house, I had no idea what happened. I didn't know what to do, "Sarah, why are you crying? We were having so much fun?"

"I'm so confused. I feel like I need to be honest with you. I think about you all the time too. I can't ever get away from you, I see you in Harper every single day and it hurts. I've been holding this secret inside for so long. I could live with the guilt when I believed I was mad at you, but I didn't know I couldn't stay mad at you. Ultimately, I realized I was just making it easier on myself. I'm the one who was wrong and selfish and Parker," she took my hands in hers, "I'm so sorry. I robbed you of 14 years of fatherhood."

I didn't know what to say, I thought we had already talked about all this, but the alcohol seemed to loosen her up a bit.

"I would check up on you all the time." She continued, "When I saw you got married, I was so jealous. The thought of you having children with another woman made me sick to my stomach."

"Sarah, if it helps to apologize you can, but in my mind, you don't have to waste another minute with this guilt, it's not necessary. I'm here now, life is short, let's make the most of the time we've got. There aren't any more secrets, are there?" I asked.

She laughed, "No, I think Harper is or I guess was, my only secret."

I faux wiped the sweat from my brow, "OK, that's good."

She was steeped in wonderful memories, guilt, forgiveness, and alcohol, smiling at me, looking into my eyes, without looking away or saying anything. I loved her and felt like she loved me back.

"What?" I was dying to know what she was thinking about.

"I'd always hoped to find you'd written and published our story or something."

"Are you disappointed?"

"No, I just thought you were a great writer. That's it. There's a Jack Johnson song called, 'Dreams be Dreams,' The chorus makes me think of you every time I hear it."

"How does it go? I'm sure I've heard it. I love Jack Johnson."

"It's the one that starts with the cymbals and then the acoustic guitar."

"You've just described half of his catalog."

"The chorus goes, 'Don't let your dreams, be dreams' except he sings the 'dreams' parts." She sung it for me, and I recognized it. "The song is about not giving up, I think. The chorus is anyway, and that's the part that makes me think of you. When you lost your money, I hoped you wouldn't give up writing."

"I never started; I was faking the writing thing so I could look cool while I lived a life of leisure."

"Never started says who? What about all the stuff you wrote for me? I loved it. I looked forward to your letters over the summer, the little notes you'd leave me were so clever and funny. Are you really writing *The Bear* right now?"

"I *am* writing *The Bear*, I'll say though, I'm halfway through it and I'm not sure it's going to be a *short* story."

"With Little Sammy? You really are?" Her eyes were smiling at the thought, it was nice to see she was excited, "I can't remember the specifics."

"Well, the story has grown a bit I guess, it's about Sammy finding confidence within himself and his relationship with his family. It's about a lot of things really.

"My turn to be honest with you; I had no idea I'd enjoy writing so much."

"Can I read it?"

"Absolutely, but I'm just letting you know now, I highjacked it with some fart jokes. You know I can't help myself."

She looked disappointed, "Parker, what's with the farts? People don't want to read about farts."

"Do you remember Gramps?" There was no way she didn't, "It's part of my life. Just wait until you read it first, it's easy to get through, it's worth it, I promise." I wondered if the world would end before Sarah would get to read it. "Let me proofread what I've done so far, and then you can read it while I finish the rest."

"*I'll* proof it."

"No, I'd be embarrassed, I'm sure it's messed up all over."

"I don't care! You have to let someone read it, that's the first big step, showing it to somebody and opening yourself up to criticism."

"Are you going to criticize it?"

"Ha ha, you know what I mean. See, you're a funny guy. I'm sure it will be great. Let me know when I can read it, I'm dying to get my hands on it."

"I will. I sure wish you'd come sit with me like we used to at Sergeant Preston's."

"Ah. The good old days," She said as she came to my side of the table. She was noticeably drunk and ignoring her "I'm married" schtick. "How's your family?" She was sitting quite close to me; it was very exciting.

"As crazy as ever. My Gramps had a stroke, but he's doing much better. Mom left Dad for a spell, Dad adopted Chuy after that, then Mom took both of them back. Beau is now a divorcee with sole custody of my five-year-old nephew who speaks with a Chinese accent."

"Wow, that's a lot to take in. You mentioned Beau earlier, who is Beau?

"Holy shit, Billy goes by "Beau' now."

"Oh, sweet Billy. I miss him too."

"I forgot you knew him as Billy."

"He has a boy though?"

"If you're asking if he's gay, I can't imagine he's not, but he won't tell me or talk about it and I'm his best friend. He's like Larry without the 'family will disown me' excuse. Our entire family already thinks he is and would be *thrilled* for him if he came out. Honestly, we're all just waiting for Beau."

"Well, I know Larry loves his closed-minded parents and doesn't want to crush them, regardless of what it costs him. I think he feels trapped by his secret as much as I did, we had that in common. His father would have a stroke if Larry came out."

"I think Beau is afraid of butt sex."

Sarah started laughing, "I'm afraid most people are."

I shrugged my shoulders, "I know I am. The only conversation that we've even gotten close to discussing him being gay hovered around how gross butt sex is. So, my very last remaining theory is he's afraid being gay means you have to have butt sex."

"Not true. Do you think all gay men have butt sex?"

Was this a trick question? "Yes?" I answered in an unsure tone, thinking blow jobs didn't count as sex and there weren't many other holes on dudes that would work.

"Parker, that's not a requirement, there are other ways of having fun."

"Wow. I never considered that. I just assumed... So not every gay couple has butt sex?"

"Well in the handbook it says they get kicked out if they don't, so I don't know."

Her answer was as ridiculous as my question, I got it. "And why are we talking about this?" I asked her.

"I have no earthly idea," She was laughing pretty hard, "You're the one who brought up butt sex, not me." After we both stopped laughing, she said, "Chuy seems like a nice kid. He has the most beautiful legs I've ever seen."

"Yeah, he's great. Between me, Beau, and my Mom, we've kind of raised him by committee. Mostly me though, I taught him how to drive you know." She was close enough that I could ever so slyly steal a glance down her shirt and get a peek at the boobs I'd once loved, just sitting there all cute in her bra, unused for 14 years.

"Are you looking down my shirt?" she punched me.

"No," I said, "I wouldn't do that, unless you wanted me to."

She just shook her head, "Hold on, I have to use the ladies' room." I watched her walk away, she looked great. I was so excited to see and be around her I wasn't thinking about dying nearly as much.

I hadn't slept in God knows how long, pounding energy drinks and popping caffeine pills to stay awake, trying to make the most of my last hours on earth. Ever since Dusty filled me in, a vision of the Earth splitting in two had been playing like a tape loop in the background of my mind. Now I was feeling like I might be able to ignore it for a little bit because all I wanted to do was get to know the daughter I never knew I had and of course, have as much bunny rabbit sex as I could with the love of my life.

As I watched Sarah Campbell walk back through the bar towards our booth, love gushed over the rim of my cup. When she saw me staring, she smiled back, possibly a little embarrassed, but still smiling, she was beautiful.

"Where were we?" I asked.

"Chuy's your little brother? Explain that to me again? How does that work?"

"Dad adopted him."

"How did your father adopt Chuy?"

"Illegally, with love and fake documents."

"What?"

"Well, Mom had finally had enough of Dad's antics and kicked him out. Well, you know Dad; he hooked up with this lady in our neighborhood who'd already adopted Chuy on a beach, in Mexico. When they broke up, she left Chuy with Dad and we never saw her again."

"That's crazy. But your Mom took Lucas back."

"And Chuy. Beau hired a high-priced adoption attorney who fabricated some papers and now Chuy is a full-blown illegal Duque. She loves Chuy more than Dad."

"And now he's your driver."

"Only when I'm writing."

"He's lucky to have you in his life," She inched closer to me, "I always thought a guy being a writer was so sexy, so intellectual." There was a slight slur to her words that I hadn't heard in the longest time, she was drunk, and focusing back on my writing. "When we dated over the summer I always looked forward to your letters. Every day I'd run to the mailbox and if there wasn't one, I'd be so sad. They were so funny, and you have such a way with words. I'm sure that you're a great real estater... but I just think you were put on this earth to be an intellectual, sexy writer."

I would've gushed at her compliment, but halfway through my discipline lapsed and I was again looking down her shirt, except she'd taken her bra off in the bathroom. I was staring at a full-on boob, the whole business.

"Are you looking down my shirt you dirty boy?" She smiled and put her hand on my thigh. I took a hundred-dollar bill out of my wallet and put it down on the table. It was time to go.

Walking home she took my hand and we cut through an alley and began kissing like the drunken college idiots we no longer were. We made love against an old garage, standing up. Three pumps, a quiver, and an apology later, our renewed love was consummated.

"That was nice," She said, still curled into me.

I couldn't help but be self-conscious, "Ummm, more for me than you I'm afraid, we'll just have to practice."

"Yes, we have a lot of time to make up for."

"And you have some pruning to do."

"This isn't my house."

I looked at her and then downstairs. She laughed as she finally got my joke, you know your girl is cool if she can laugh about her own overgrown bush.

"As we say in real estate, the grass will grow tall if nobody's using the playground,"

"Parker!" She punched me in the arm and at that point I felt like we would be together for the rest of time.

42

FINALLY, SOME SLEEP

After several hours of blissful sleep, my morning started at the break of dawn with Sarah sneaking into the den where I was sleeping to show me her newly manicured playground. *Five* pumps, a quiver, and an apology later, I had fallen asleep again, only to be awoken by my daughter. Thank GOD I woke up lying on my belly because the resurrection of my sex life had translated into a troubling morning woody.

"Parker."

I stayed on my belly, just like I did growing up, "You could call me Dad if you want." It felt corny to say but I didn't care.

"Hmm, look at me, I've got two dads, like Billy Raniere."

"Well, it's probably a little different—"

"Lighten up Pop!"

"There you go! I like that, very Midwestern. Call me Pop and Larry can be Dad."

"But you're my dad too."

"I like your style kid. Let's go with Pop until the sting wears off for Larry."

"Good plan. You up yet? Wanna hang out?"

"You know I do! Can you do me a favor though? Can you take my keys off the desk there and grab the cooler from the back seat of my car and bring it in?"

"Sure thing Pop."

Sarah had very little for breakfast, so Harper and I volunteered to make a grocery run at Demond's, the little grocery store in Douglas, Saugatuck's kissing cousin of a town, just across the Blue Star Highway. We got bagels and fruit for everyone, but I also took the opportunity to pick up some gems I haven't eaten since I married Margot, it was heaven.

The first thing I bought was Capn' Crunch *"Oops, all berries"* cereal. Are you kidding me? Nothing but the crunch berries? *Oops, I'm in heaven.* Sugary cereal was just the start, our shopping cart looked like a diabetic death trap; donuts, pop tarts, Coke, Oreos, Nutter Butters, basically enough sugar to bring an elephant to its knees.

During our breakfast gathering excursion Harper told me she was nervous about a two-part pom pom tryout that day. She also told me she had a crush on a new boy, which made *me* deathly nervous. That's all she told me though and let me tell you what, trying to get a 14-year-old girl to tell you about her new crush is about as easy as finding Jimmy Hoffa.

I had the feeling there's probably still a lot for me to learn about teenage girls. I was so impressed with the way she carried herself and how many people she knew, basically everyone. It was fun to see, just like with her mother, people lit up when she came around. I watched people go out of their way to come say "Hi" to her. Who knew I could love two people so much? Not me, that's for sure.

When we got back to the house, Sarah and Larry were at the kitchen table having coffee and from the look on Larry's face, an obviously painful talk. Piper was asleep at Sarah's feet. Chuy was safely hidden out of earshot in the study I had slept in the night before.

Larry snapped to as Harper bounced into the room and then into his lap. She could tell he was upset and said, "Don't sweat it Dad. Do you want to practice? One last time before the tryouts?" You should have seen him hop to it. I don't know who was more excited, Larry or Harper.

Sarah whispered to me as she set a speaker and an iPod on the kitchen table, "Wait until you see this."

Britney Spears blasted through the kitchen, "One, two, three," and then words only a teenager could decipher after that. It was high energy dance music and what was happening in front of me was incredible.

I watched Harper slap, cheer, and make her arms like an Egyptian to the music. She was so good I felt ten foot two and bulletproof. My chest heaved with an overwhelming sense of pride, and it was more than I could keep inside, I had tears welling up in my eyes. I never knew the kind of love a parent could feel for their child, but it must be natural because suddenly, I had it by the bucketful. I looked over at Sarah, who was smiling back at me with tears in her eyes. All I could do is put my hand to my chest, as it felt like there was nothing more for me to say. I felt self-conscious about all the "clying" I'd been doing, but none of it could be avoided.

Piper had left the room to escape the noise and Chuy had entered to explore it. I had no idea he was behind me until he whispered in my ear, "Holmes, is that for real?" I turned my attention away from my daughter to see Larry, in his own world, dancing, and clapping. To my surprise, he was better than Harper. *Way* better than Harper. He was lost in himself and his dancing. It was incredibly gay and absolutely wonderful. I thought about the plan I'd set in motion the day before; *this might actually work....*

Larry's tuning forks were ringing like motherfuckers and in an instant all my love for him smothered any agitation I might have felt over his earlier pettiness. I could more than understand his less than pleasant reaction to my showing up, especially now that I had gotten to know the wonderful daughter he thought he'd be losing. It made sense. He'd been a great dad for her in my absence, I appreciated him for that. You could tell Harper loved him dancing there with her, it was spectacular. I know it's probably not feasible, but every teenage girl should have a gay dad too.

And then the music stopped cold. The power went out. If I was a cat, I'd have jumped six feet in the air. Not because I was on my second energy drink, but because I thought I felt the world move under my feet, literally. I wondered whether I was just being emotional, but there was no mistaking it, something had really happened, it was like a miniature earthquake without any shake, just a bump.

"Did you feel that?" Sarah asked me, "Was that an Earthquake?"

"Where are the breakers" I asked, perhaps too frantically. Larry was locked in his dance pose, perfectly still from where the music had left off, like he was a toy that just ran out of batteries. In my mind, all I could see was the image of our big blue marble splitting in two.

"The electrical panel is in the laundry room; I can check it," Sarah said.

"I'll go with you." I ran into the pantry and turned around, "Where is the laundry room?"

"Come with me, spaz," she said, and I followed her to a room off the kitchen and looked in horror as I saw no thrown breakers, the power to the house was out. My chest was white hot. what would happen when the earth splits in two? This was too early, I wanted to scream at the heavens, *I'M NOT DONE YET! PLEASE!*

I didn't know the science—how painful would our demise be? Would every single living creature die an excruciating death? Were we all lobsters in some alien race's boiling water? It was getting harder for me to breath. I ran outside to see if anything was happening. Nothing.

After a good ten minutes or so of white-hot panic, I felt Sarah wrap her arms around me, "What's wrong Parker? Why are you so upset? I can tell something is wrong." Piper could too; she hadn't left my side since the "bump," which freaked me out even more. Animals know when big time major shit is about to go down, it's a scientific fact. When a Tsunami is coming, you won't find a bird or animal anywhere near the shore, they all know well in advance to head to higher ground. They don't see a big wave we can't, *they just know it's coming.*

"Oh, probably just a lack of sleep and me being excited. I guess I'm a little jumpy." I lied.

"Larry asked if we could pick up a generator to take to the school in case their power is out. He can't get in touch with the coaches and the phones are down too. Can you come and help me? I could show you around while we're there." She was smiling a terrific smile, a wonderful, loving smile but I couldn't enjoy it. I was back on the roof of my childhood home, face down on that wet tarp, sliding slowly towards the edge, the fall unavoidable.

"Sure." I felt like crying, but for once in my life I didn't.

43

CAT'S OUT OF THE BAG

I was freaking out the entire way to the hardware store and Sarah could tell something was wrong. As soon as we were in her office Sarah cornered me, "What's wrong?" She started tearing up, she held my arm and looked into my eyes, "I'm moving too fast, aren't I? I was drunk last night but I meant every word I said, did you?"

"Yes."

She still seemed worried, "I missed you so much and this all seems too good to be true. You're leaving, aren't you?" She pulled away, but I pulled her back.

"I will never leave you. I want to spend the rest of my life with you if you'll let me. I want to grow old with you and see what Harper becomes. If we have grandchildren, you can teach me how to change a diaper." I'd wanted to tell her this from the minute I saw her, and I'm glad I got to say it to her, because everything could end at any moment. Neither of our cell phones had signals, everything was out, even the traffic lights were out.

Sarah was smiling again and started to undo my pants when I stopped her, "But we won't be able to. Sarah, we're all going to die, soon. Aliens are about to blow the earth in two. That's what all this is about. What I'm about to tell you sounds crazy as shit, but I'm not crazy."

"What?" She was looking at me, speechless and confused, I had turned into a lunatic that spoke of aliens.

"Where do I start? A jerk from my neighborhood was murdered when he stumbled onto this. CIA agents found out he told me about it before they killed him, so they came for me next. They killed my wife and her lover, but kidnapped me, although I escaped. I made it back to Atlanta, said goodbye to my family and drove up here to see you one last time before the world ends." I felt like my romantic intention, *to see you one last time*, would've received a warmer reception had I not lead this whole thing with *aliens*.

"Where do the aliens fit in?"

"I read a top-secret file that explained it. These orbs came down from the sky and buried themselves in the Earth. They became huge electromagnetic columns that are growing and growing. They took GPS measurements of each column's location and they're perfectly aligned to split the Earth in half when detonated. They say the columns are from aliens."

"Parker, slow down. Look at me and tell me you aren't sick."

"I'm not. I'm not sure I can prove it, but I can try. I have a backpack full of their cash and you can look online to see that my wife and her lover are dead from a murder-suicide and I'll bet you that Brock Martin, the douche bag who told me about it is reported missing too. He's in the trunk of their car. Wait a minute." I dropped my pants to show her the huge bruise and the hole left by the huge hypodermic needle Dusty had jammed into my thigh.

"Ouch, does that hurt?"

"Tremendously, he gave me a charley horse to punish me." I pointed to a smaller bruise, "This is where he injected me with hangover serum to knock me out while we traveled." I pulled my wallet out and handed her the receipt from the "In—N-Out" Burger, "They took me to California, I'd go back tomorrow for more of those burgers if you wanted."

"This is crazy Parker. Let's go through this and fill in some details. Have you seen an alien personally?"

"No." I loved how smart Sarah was. That was a great first question to check if I was nuts.

"Why did the CIA agent want to kill you?"

"Because the jerk from my neighborhood told me about the columns. They didn't want the news to get out and the world to go into a panic."

"So, he killed the jerk, kidnapped you, and killed your wife and her lover, thinking you told her the secret?"

"Well, the agent's four-hundred-pound girlfriend killed Margot and her lover. She planted a note to make it look like a murder-suicide"

"Four hundred pounds?"

"That's my guess, it might have been more. It's misleading though, she was an athlete."

"Why did they kidnap you? Why didn't they just kill you?"

"I gave a speech at Chuy's school on the last day, and he was there waiting to kill me, but he liked my speech so much he didn't want to kill me."

"It must have been a good speech."

"I thought so. Instead, he and his girlfriend drugged me and took me to this cliff top house in Southern California."

"The jerk that told you, how did *he* find out about the columns?"

"He was an insurance guy, working out an insurance claim with a farmer in Iowa. The farm was fenced off, but he stumbled across the farmer's son, who told him about the orb coming out of the sky and turning into one of the columns of metal. I didn't believe a single thing the jerk guy had told me either. It seemed too incredible to believe and I thought he was crazy, just like you think I'm crazy right now. I don't think I really let myself believe it until I read the 'Top Secret' file. That's when I knew this was real. I wish I would have grabbed that file; Beau wouldn't believe me at first either. You just have to trust me."

"His name was Dusty?"

"He went by Dusty; his real name was Denis with one 'n,' but he'd flip out if you called him that. That's why I have my super-bruise," I pointed at my thigh. "He was about five feet tall, really muscular, incredibly quick, and as strong as anyone I've ever met. At first, I honestly thought he might be an alien, but he wasn't. Now Peaches, his girlfriend, she was something else. She was at least six and a half feet tall, impossibly athletic like a sumo wrestler and like I said, probably one biscuit shy of four hundred pounds."

"Peaches?" Sarah asked, *"Dusty and Peaches."*

"Ugliest sex on the planet."

"Where are they now?"

"Umm, without sounding like a smartass, the Pacific Ocean."

"You killed them?"

"No. I mean, I guess, *technically,* I was responsible for their deaths. I would have liked not to, but it was either me or them."

"How do you *technically* kill someone?"

"They were both doing yoga at the edge of the cliff and I pushed Dusty off, then I threw a bag of donuts *just* out of Peaches reach and she lost her balance trying to grab them. I think she jumped to go after them after she lost her balance, but I can't be sure, either way, it was a genius move on my part. So *technically,* I didn't kill her, just wasted a bag of donuts."

"Pushing someone off a cliff sounds like regular killing as opposed to technically killing."

"Fair point, but when I pushed Dusty off the cliff, he only broke his arm. As he was climbing back up, *to kill me,* he said something gross, and I threw up orange juice all over him and the rocks he was holding onto. He lost his grip and took a pretty gnarly line down three hundred feet of rocky cliff."

"Look at me and tell me again you're not crazy."

"You can't make this up. I'm not crazy. Just sad, I can't believe I found you and Harper and now it's going to be over."

"Parker, sweetie. I love you so much. You're so sweet, but you are no optimist."

"Excuse me?" Did she not hear *anything* I just said? This wasn't some bad movie, this was real.

"Those columns were sent by a peaceful race, they're probably here to help us. I believe it with all my heart. You shouldn't assume they're here to kill us."

"What?"

"Don't panic, spaz. Let's go through this because I've thought about something very similar to this."

"What?"

"Our first contact with aliens. I heard a joke about aliens showing up and thinking dogs were in charge because we walked behind them, picking up their poop, and it got me thinking."

"Please." I was upset she wasn't taking me seriously. Sarah had, on many occasions, corrected errant thinking on my part. She was smarter than me, I had no problem admitting that, but there was no correcting this.

"Just hear me out," she said, "We have telescopes that can see for millions of light years away. That means it would take you *millions* of years, if you could travel at the *speed of light,* to get to the limits of where we can see."

"Could you get through this without patronizing me please?"

She smiled, "Sorry, anyway, we haven't seen any evidence of life within our view, right?" I nodded. "For an alien race to have that kind of technology, to travel that great distance in a reasonable amount of time, meaning before they die if they're organic life forms, they'd have to have been around for an incredibly long time, right? I mean we've been around for a long time, look at how advanced we *aren't.* We've got a long way to go before we're even close to traveling at the speed of light and, who knows, we may blow ourselves up beforehand, because I'm not convinced we're a peaceful race just yet."

"You've got a point. One thing I know for sure, if *our* government is in charge, we're screwed."

"There you go. That proves my point. Only a peaceful race can survive that long to invent the kind of technology of delivery and precision you've just described. In just our short lifetimes we've both seen proof humans tend to blow each other up."

"You think the columns are from a peaceful alien race, so they're not here to blow us up."

"*Bingo!*" she said and gave me a kiss.

I felt the weight of the world lifted from my shoulders only to fall right back down all over me. "What if they're just making the Earth into a farm? What if they're going to breed us like cattle and then eat us?"

She smiled at me, "Remember what I said about being a pessimist? Would you drive to Tokyo to eat a steak dinner?"

"If I loved Tokyo steak and we were out of it."

"If they can do what you say, they can probably think of an easier way to get a Tokyo Steak."

She was right. Why in the world would I just automatically assume people I don't even know want to kill me? I felt like a government. I felt like a million bucks actually. I wasn't sure if it was because Sarah had lifted the weight of the world off my shoulders or because she was rubbing my crotch.

"Sarah, if you don't mind, the only thing I'd rather do is to go see my daughter and your gay husband make the pom pom squad." She kept rubbing, who was I kidding, I definitely had time for 7 pumps, a quiver, and an apology. "Did you say you kept your inventory around here?

As Sarah started laughing, the lights in the hardware store came back on. I checked Landon's Hello Kitty phone; it had a signal again. We looked at each other and smiled, her smile more satisfied than mine. She was probably right. The relief was intoxicating. I felt a limberness I never thought my body could know.

"We'll see what becomes of your metal space columns, but let's not waste time worrying about it, we've wasted too much already. We'll get to the high school, but first I'd like to show you where we keep inventory," She winked, patted me on the butt and turned to leave the office.

I was following her out, excited to see Sarah's inventory when I ran into her, she had stopped cold. I laughed and was about to apologize, but I couldn't believe what was happening on the sidewalk in front the store, I smiled, "Holy shit."

44

INTERVENTION?

"Is that Billy?" Sarah shrieked with joy, she loved Beau when he was Billy. It *was* Billy, I never thought he could make it to Saugatuck that fast, but I was thrilled he did.

I nodded yes and reminded her, "Beau." I was still in shock to see him so soon. From what I could tell, he had just come out of the RV behind him. I was looking at him, looking at me, but something was wrong... He was mouthing something important to me.

It could wait. I was so happy to see Landon come out of this fantastic RV, double-parked in front of the hardware store. I laughed with surprise when Gramps sprang out after Landon, then shock as Mom, Dad, and Ms. Livingston followed. I could see Beau had chartered the bus; the uniformed driver was holding the steering wheel like it was the only thing keeping him alive. It's probably a fourteen-hour drive from Atlanta to Saugatuck, I can only imagine what that poor guy had gone through, he looked defeated. Beau signaled the driver, who immediately pulled the bus out of its illegal squat and sped away.

"Landon! I shouted,

He came running at me, "RUNCLE!"

Sarah's face lit up, and I shielded my crotch as he came in for a big hug, thankfully, there was no kick to the nuts, he kept his promise.

"You stop dlinking, kay?"

"What?" I looked at Sarah. I stood back up into a bear hug from my crying mother.

"Hi Mom, what's going on here?" I asked. I felt little hands frisking me and knew Landon was reclaiming Kitty.

"We're here to ask you to stop drinking." My father chimed in. I looked at Beau and it all made sense, he was mouthing the words, *"Go with it."*

"People, I'm not sure what he's told you, but I don't have a drinking problem!" Everyone looked at me, shocked, including Sarah. "Sorry, I know that's what everyone with a drinking problem says. Let's hit 'pause' for a second, we can talk about this after I talk to Beau, although I would like to say thanks for the support, this is impressive for the Duques. On a completely different note, I hope you guys remember Sarah Campbell?"

Mom shrieked and lunged at Sarah, landing her second bear hug. "Of course I remember you; you look exactly the same dear. You know Parker is single now."

"Mom!"

Mom had started and couldn't stop, "She was horrible. Nobody could stand her. Did he tell you about Margot?" Just like Rose, she had been dying to talk trash about Margot.

"No, because she's deceased." I said, thinking most decent people would end the discussion there. I was wrong.

"She was dime piece son, don't listen to your mother," It was Gramps piping in while he and Dad perused the toilet section in the plumbing aisle, "Hell, I'd—"

"Oh wow, Gramps! Thanks for sharing your thoughts, I could tell that was coming from the heart." Beau interrupted Gramps' stream of consciousness, saving the day again.

I turned back to Beau, "Can I talk to you for a second? Sarah, can we use your office?"

Sarah didn't answer, her attention had been commandeered by my ecstatic mother. Mom loved her as much as I did.

Beau explained, once we were inside, "Just go with it! It was the only way I could get everybody up here. It's not a big deal. Mom's the only one taking your drinking problem seriously. Dad's here because Mom is making him."

"I don't have a drinking problem."

"You do now Parker, and I'm asking you to stop. Anywho, tell me right now what's going on with you and Sarah! You two look like a couple, am I reading it wrong? What are you two doing together?"

"We had sex twice last night." I blurted out to him. I wasn't trying to be a pig; I just couldn't wait to tell my best friend everything. Beau knew what I meant, he gave me a warm hug and I returned it, I was so glad my big brother was there with me. It's tough to be scared for your life without your best friend around. I had Chuy but I was there to protect him, just like Beau came here to protect me. I was so happy.

"I'm so happy for you Parker, I thought she was married though."

"She is." I said, eager for him to light up, Beau loves a scandal.

"You homewrecker! Look at you," he shook his head with conflicted approval, "Those are dangerous waters Parker, look what happened to Margot."

"To Larry."

"What happened to Larry? Larry the plumber? Do I know him? Does he own a gun? Spill it!"

"Larry, my friend at Purdue Larry. Sarah is married to *him*. You've drank beer with Larry three or four times."

Beau held his hand to his chest, clutching invisible pearls, "Oh." He was speechless for once. "Larry the dynamite dresser Larry? I think I remember him."

"You do, that's the one. He's married to Sarah and he's gay, they have an arrangement. He helped her—" I stopped myself, Beau didn't know about Harper yet.

"Get out."

"I'm serious." Beau knew *exactly* who Larry was, and I knew Beau had a crush on Larry. My plan was in full-go mode. Fucking genius.

"I just never saw that in him..." Beau pondered the surprise, smiling as subtly as he could.

"Seriously Beau?" I looked him in the eyes, "Larry is single and ready to mingle, and it might be the end of the world? Don't you think everyone should be able to love who they want?"

"Sure, except for the guy who had sex with his golden retriever." He completely missed what I was saying to him.

"Agreed. Except they really don't belong in the same conversation. I'm talking human beings loving human beings, companions, so we don't have to be alone."

Beau sighed and gave me a hug without looking. Was Beau Duque becoming emotional?

"Beau."

"Yes?"

"I also just found out last night that not all gay guys have butt sex."

"Yes they do." Beau said in a dismissive way like I'd just told him most zebras didn't have stripes.

"Nope, it turns out butt sex isn't for everybody and there are other ways to show affection." I could see Beau's wheels turning, mission accomplished. "I'm so glad you brought everybody, I thought it was just going to be you and Landon."

"Yeah, well I'm taking care of Gramps, at least until he recovers from the operation, but I want to be with my family when I die."

"I get it, I'm thrilled to see them except for the intervention thing, but that the best you could do? You could have left Ms. Livingston in Atlanta."

"Given the time constraints, it was the best I could think of," He said, "You're lucky Mom and I love you enough to stop you from drinking your life away."

"Do you think we can change this into something less annoying than an intervention?"

"Sure."

"What should we say?"

"Leave it to me. I'll wing it when we get out there, does it even matter at this point? We're all going to die soon. The entire country just lost power and all the radios went out while we were driving. The radio's working again, but I'm shitting bricks."

"You didn't tell anybody, did you?"

"Heavens no, Mother would be a wreck."

"OK good, I told Sarah and she has a different take on it, and I agree with her. So don't shit your pants just yet, but feel free to take a chance with love— look where it's got me."

"Parker Duque, that's sweet, but we're fucked."

"High school? Late for what?"

"Follow me, Larry will be there." On the way out of Sarah's office I saw a framed baby picture of Harper and couldn't help but smile.

As soon as I walked through the door, my Dad's hand was on my shoulder, "Son, drinking won't take the pain away." He looked at Mom to see if that was good enough, her expression clearly conveyed it wasn't, "I've tried it. You have to face your loss like a man."

Beau was still mouthing, "Go with it" in back of Dad and making a little prayer gesture. Winging it my ass, he was backing out.

"Honey, when was the last time you got drunk?" Mom wasn't going to let this go. I looked at Sarah and then back at Mom.

"Last night, but only because Sarah and I were catching up and reliving old times, not because I was grieving over Margot."

"You got your piece, and you didn't even have to pay for it, Parker! She's history, six feet under, we should celebrate with a drink!" Gramps shouted while picking up a jar of "Harper's Honey" off the front display. I could tell Ms. Livingston was feeling like breaking Gramps' shins, not because I was especially intuitive, but because she had grabbed a long steel crowbar off the wall and was heading his way, slowly.

Ignoring Gramps and his slow-motion assailant, I continued, "And it's time to tell you this intervention was a ruse Beau and I concocted to get you guys to come to Saugatuck for a surprise," I tried to make eye contact with Sarah, but she was now being grilled by Landon, "which shall be revealed later at a time TBD." Nobody was listening. Everyone except Beau and Gramps were watching Ms. Livingston.

I pointed out to Beau that Ms. Livingston was armed and moving towards our Super-nutted Patriarch.

Beau laughed and did nothing, "This should be good, they were both in the war."

Gramps smiled when he spotted the slow-moving danger and barked loudly, "Tiny Genghis!"

Landon abandoned Sarah and ran over to Gramps, who placed him in between his Super-nut and Ms. Livingston's crowbar.

Gramps barked an order in Chinese and Landon struck a defensive posture directly in front of his Super-nut. You should have seen Gramps beaming; this wasn't his first rodeo.

Ms. Livingston went pale at the betrayal, as if her prized number one son had just tooted in front of the Emperor.

I suggested to the casual observer next to me, "This is where you might jump in as her employer."

Beau jogged over, seemingly entertained by the dust-up until he tried to take the crowbar from Ms. Livingston and she wouldn't let go. He spoke curtly in Chinese and she released the crowbar immediately and bowed before him. I felt like Beau would have enjoyed the moment more had the crowbar not been so heavy.

My father walked over to Gramps and whispered in his ear.

"What do you mean we can't drink here?" Gramps said loudly, "We're in Saugatuck, I've been shit canned here more than... I could use a drink right now, my mouth's drier than the bottom of Ghandi's flip flop."

"Didn't you guys just hear me? This was just a ruse to get you up to Saugatuck."

"It's his problem, not mine!" Gramps said to Dad, he was still upset. Landon had left his defensive post at Ms. Livingston's quiet insistence and Gramps moved my father in between his Super-nut and the diminutive Chinese woman.

Beau whispered to me, "If he barks Mandarin and Dad breaks into a defensive pose, I'm going to shit in my drawers."

Gramps continued, "Why can't I drink? I don't have a problem. Have you seen the honeys here?" "This place is what I like to call a target rich environment and I've got the boys back together. Crap, that's the only reason I came, to get drunk and get laid." Gramps was speaking to everybody by way of volume, but he was focused on Ms. Livingston the entire time. I'm 100% sure she didn't appreciate the attention, and I was 100% grateful she was ear-muffing Landon, because otherwise, I'd have to worry about her dropping Gramps with a karate chop to the Super-nut.

"Gramps, you can drink." I said, "And get laid, as long as you promise not to tell us about it."

"See, I told you we could drink!" he said, elbowing my father, "Saugatuck's always good for a party."

"So, you don't feel like you have a problem?" Dad asked without waiting for an answer, "I trust him Felicia; his word is good enough for me. We should leave him alone, that's what we should do." There was silence, general agreement and disinterest filling the air until Dad continued, "Well, it's nice to be back up North. What do you propose we do now, Beau Duque? Should we get some rooms and stay for a couple days?"

"Oh Parker, I still worry about you," Mom said, with nervousness in her voice. "Are you going to be all right?".

"I think so." This time I made eye contact with Sarah and she was smiling back at me. "I think I'm going to be just fine."

"Please stay! I'll figure out the accommodations," Sarah said, "and I would love it if all of you came over to my grandmother's house tonight for dinner. We'll announce the surprise at dinner," Sarah looked at me and gulped. I smiled; *she* was listening.

"What surprise?" Mom asked.

"Parker's intervention was a ruse to get you guys up to Saugatuck. We have a great surprise for you."

"You don't have a drinking problem?" Mom asked me directly.

"Not that I know of."

"Oh, thank God." Mom landed her *third* bear hug.

Gramps asked Sarah, "Does your grandmother look anything like you dear?"

"Crawford Duque!" Mom snapped at Gramps. He ignored her; he was waiting for Sarah's answer to his serious question.

"Nope, she's better looking," Sarah said, always game for fun.

"And absolutely off limits." I added, "This is all great, but we have to head over to the high school to watch Sarah's daughter try out for the pom pom squad. Does anybody want to come?"

A quick and resounding "No" came from Dad, Gramps, and surprisingly, Ms. Livingston.

"Well, I take that back, probably a good place to start the hunt." Gramps had considered out loud, "Can I get a nap in first? I'm as tired as a whore on nickel night."

"We would ALL *love* to come!" my mother said, and you could hear Dad and Ms. Livingston exhale loudly as Landon and Beau high fived.

45

SHE DROP POM

We walked into the gym and there were forty people in the stands. Thirty-eight of them waved to Sarah. This included Larry, who was an absolute hot mess. Decked out in a royal blue and orange velour sweat suit, he was frantically waving at Sarah and I to hurry up. When we *all* started moving towards him as a group, his frantic waving turned into a look of earnest confusion— *until he saw Billy.*

I introduced my family, but Larry was stuck at the end of a double take on Beau, which was only interrupted by his reaction to Landon's "Haroo" and subsequent bow. He turned back to Beau and said calmly, "I'm sorry to stare, you look exactly like Bo Duke from, The *Dukes of Hazard*." He snapped out of it quickly though, dance was his passion, "Sarah you almost missed it!"

The girls were set up on the gym floor below, frozen in identical poses with Harper in the middle. The gym became respectfully silent, and then the only Britney Spears song I knew started blasting. *"One, two, three..."* Boom! They all started dancing their asses off, exactly the same, it was fun to watch. Honestly, it makes a lot more sense if you have a group of girls waving poms, rather than just Larry, Harper, and their goofy smiles in the kitchen. Harper was doing so great, but so was everybody else, so I could see why she was nervous. She looked confident, smiling and locking her arms and doing all that pom pom stuff.

I still wasn't sure what to do if my family figured out Harper's paternity right away. I felt like I was shot out of a cannon when I realized I might have some time left to get to know her. Larry gasped beside me and grabbed his face like somebody had just been emboweled on the gym floor.

"She drop pom." Landon said, pointing. And sure enough, the smile was gone from my little girl's face. She kept at it until there was a chance to pick it back up, which she did, only to drop it again ten seconds later in a choreographed fashion with the rest of the girls.

Larry was beside himself afterwards, which I didn't understand, because I thought she did great. She was one of the better dancers which was yet another attribute, along with her looks and intelligence, that I was glad she inherited from her mother.

After the routine was over, the sophomores and juniors trotted out to shake a leg and Larry bolted from the stands to talk to Harper. Sarah left to go with Larry, which was good, because she still had her wits about her. Larry would need a calm influence, he looked devastated. They came back up to the stands with Harper and my heart broke when I saw she had been crying.

"Ok, we're going to go." Larry said, sounding disappointed.

"What?" I said, "I thought it was two parts?"

Harper looked like she was going to cry, "There are only two openings for the freshman; it's not a big deal. Cheerleading tryouts are next week."

"How old are you Harper?" My mother asked, looking at my father in a, *do you see this?* fashion, but I cut her off.

I was self-conscious about overstepping my boundaries as the brand-new dad, but I hated that she was going to quit, "Harper, can I talk to you for a minute? Alone?" I ignored Larry and Sarah, afraid of either asking me to stop.

To my surprise, she agreed, and no one stopped us. Harper followed me until we were high up on the bleachers, away from the others, "Harper, I thought you were the best one out there. Why are you quitting?"

"Pop, you don't know poms. That was a pretty big mistake."

"You're certainly right about that, I don't know poms, big time. What did your mother say about you leaving?"

"She doesn't care. She isn't big into cheering or dance and she usually lets me do my own thing. She stays out of my way unless it interferes with my studying."

"That's good, she's a cool mom. Listen, all I'm going to say to you is I had a blast watching you dance because it looked like you were really having fun. I would feel horrible for you if this is something you really wanted, and you didn't chase it until it was over."

"It's not a big deal Pop."

"I get the feeling it's a bigger deal than you're letting on. I'll just finish what I was going to say before, it's something that my dad told me when I was young, and I still follow it to this day."

"Land the plane Pop, what is it already?"

"Lord you are my child." I laughed, "It's OK to fail; it is *not* OK to not try."

"That's a double negative; you mean it's OK to fail as long as you try."

"Well, I guess, it kind of takes the drama out of it and that's not the way Dad told me, but you're right. What if everybody blows it on the second part, aren't there two parts?"

"Pop, you know what? You're right."

"Are you serious?"

"Yeah, the next part is tumbling, which I'm good at. Hmm..."

"What?"

"Between you and me, being a cheerleader or a Pom really isn't that big of a deal. It's just an easy way to be popular with the cute guys, I won't die if I don't make the squad."

"Well then," I clapped my hands, "that's all I needed to hear. Forget everything I just said. Let's get out of this joint."

"What about not trying?" She looked at me confused.

"I didn't know about the cute guys angle."

"You and Dad!" She pointed down the stands towards my family, "Is this my new family?"

"Yes."

"Will you guys stay if I finish?"

"You couldn't get me to leave. I'll hold your poms if I have to," I was serious, I would hold poms for her.

"Dorky, but nice," she said as she sauntered down the bleachers. She left me without warning and said something to Larry and he gave me the double thumbs up as I came back down. I got the feeling if Larry and Harper were a two person show, Harper ran it and Larry just did as he was told.

My mother looked like she was going to explode. She was shaking and smiling uncontrollably at me. I assumed she'd just figured out the connection between Harper, Sarah, and me. Like every grandmother, she was very eager to add kids she didn't have to care for to the brood.

Two minutes later, I caught Larry staring at Beau and couldn't help smiling as my plan was coming to fruition. Landon had moved onto my lap. I felt myself floating in happiness, ecstatic to have the whole crazy gang with me to share this exciting new world.

I hadn't thought about what was or wasn't going to happen to us for at least an hour by then, and I owed my newfound optimism to Sarah. *You know what you can't stop? Progress.* I could see my daughter taking the floor to finish what she had started, and I resolved at that point to never slip back into the glass half empty camp again.

46

WHAT TIME IS IT ANYWAY?

Sarah's grandmother, or "Mimi," as everyone called her, lived in a large old house, "up the hill" from downtown Saugatuck. You could still walk to the shops or to Sarah's, but Mimi's house felt like it was in an actual neighborhood, away from the hustle and bustle of the Saugatuck summer tourist season.

I was trying my best to float in a pool of consciousness that was half full, but I found myself slipping off the life raft of optimism Sarah had inflated under me. It wasn't because my entire crazy family was having dinner with Sarah's entire sane family at Mimi's, and it wasn't because my dog Piper hadn't left my side since we got back from try-outs. It was mostly because the sun hadn't gone down like it was supposed to and it still felt like high noon at 8:00 at night.

"Is this messed up, or am I just drunk? Gramps said with a hearty laugh after finishing his beer. Chuy and Harper had formed an attentive audience around him earlier and were cracking up until Gramps said, "Hombre, you might as well get me another beer then. If you can't beat them, join 'em, right? Do they say that in Mexico?" Harper was standing there looking at Gramps with a hairy eyeball when I heard Chuy tell her, "He's not a bad guy. He loves me, he's just lost it a little bit. He had a stroke a while back that turned him into a hillbilly with nice teeth." As she and Chuy walked into the kitchen together I overheard Harper, "Yeah, one time my great-grandfather

272

grabbed poop out of his diaper and threw it at a nurse." She was a Duque.

"Do you think this is related to your well-spaced metal columns?" Sarah asked as she walked up to me, seeming more nervous herself.

"I don't know, what do you think? Almost 8PM and full sun?" I asked back, decidedly more nervous now that the head optimist was wavering as well.

"Well, your brother doesn't seem nervous. Did you ask him to come to Saugatuck?" Beau and Larry had been talking nonstop in ridiculously gay tones since they found each other after the tryout.

"You know I did; it was too perfect. I remembered Larry's infatuation with Billy, and I felt pressed for time. I wonder if we still are." Sarah looked at me, not saying anything and not looking very comfortable. I think her bag of optimistic theories might be vulnerable to surreal weather events.

"Fuck it." I pulled Sarah closer and gave her a kiss. She pushed me away and said under her breath, "Not here! I'm still married. My parents, Mimi."

"Ahh, to him." I pointed to Larry who had his hand on Beau's thigh while telling him a story about the shopping he did in Paris last Christmas. It looked like they were overcompensating and trying to out gay each other. It was very cute, but my money was on Larry.

"I'll make it better," she said, kissing me on the cheek, "later." Sarah walked away into the kitchen. I looked over to see my mother and father who were both giving thumbs up signals. They were so subtle.

The lack of night falling delayed our dinner unintentionally, but after we realized it was getting late, we forged ahead with our dinner plans. Larry and Beau took center stage orchestrating the feast preparations like a gay, yet supposedly straight Vaudeville show. Gramps let out longer and louder sighs every time the show got gayer. Beau didn't care, I wondered if he was letting go because he knew we might die any minute. There was still full sun, and it was past 9:00 by then. The optimism that Sarah had brought to us like a warm blanket felt like a thin sheet.

"Can we talk?" Larry was drunkenly addressing Sarah and me.

Sarah said, "Sure" and I think I nodded my head, but it didn't matter because before I could even put my drink down, I was being led by the arm excitedly into an old porch off the side of the house.

"I'm gay," He said directly to me as soon as we'd settled.

"Come on!"

A smile lit up his face, "and I have a crush on your brother. And I'm sorry for being mean to you Parker. I thought you were here to take Harper away; I realize now you're not." He looked away, then back at the both of us, "Whew! Feels good to get that out!"

Sarah kissed Larry on the cheek and gave him a long hug.

"Parker, I imagine this is a big surprise for you, but I thought since your brother is gay you would be OK with it."

"He is?" I asked, having fun.

"Isn't HE?" Larry didn't seem to be sharing in any of the fun.

"Larry, like you, he's never told me, although it doesn't take a genius to see, he's digging you too. Did he tell you he's a very successful dentist?"

"Serious?" He said as he bit his fist mockingly, "Can I say something else? I'm not blind, I've seen you two flirting." He looked at Sarah, "You have my blessing to cheat on me."

I looked at Sarah and she looked at me and we all started laughing.

Larry stopped laughing, "Sarah, I might be drunk and spilling our deepest secrets right now, but this is only for your ears, OK? Let's be real. I'm not telling my father. He'll beat me and leave me out of his will."

"You don't need his money Larry, you do well for yourself here," She said.

Larry suddenly looked sober, "Yeah but he's circling the damn drain, Sarah and I've endured so much... Seriously though, it's complicated and I don't want to tell him, OK?'

"We'll figure it out together," Sarah said and looked at me.

"Well, consider your secret safe with me buddy." I said,

"Thanks. Do you really think Beau likes me?"

"Color me practical, but it's looking like he does, he's shy though, so he might need encouragement. You will definitely have to make the first move."

Larry mulled it over for a second, "Let's go eat. For some reason I can't wait to get my mouth around one of those kielbasas. They look delicious!" And with that he sauntered out of the room.

Sarah looked at me and I at her, "Did that just happen?" I asked. Sarah leaned into me and gave me a nice kiss. "Let me ask you this," I said, "I know you believe me now because it's broad daylight at 9:30 PM, but did you believe me when I initially told you about Dusty and Peaches?"

"Yes!" she responded like it was a silly question.

"How do I become more like you?" I said, "Because I wouldn't have believed you. It's too crazy of a story."

"You wouldn't have believed me?" she fake punched me on the chest.

"I'm jaded, I guess. I would've thought you lost your marbles."

"We're going to have to work on that," she gave me a quick kiss walked back into the house.

47

DINNER IS SERVED

Mimi's house had a nice, private back yard with a beautifully hardscaped patio that Larry was very proud to have designed for her. The Campbell family gathered most Sundays at Mimi's and had it not been broad daylight, you could tell it would be a magical place to eat at night. There were strings of lights with small round incandescent bulbs strung over the patio where a great big, weathered farm table sat loaded with steak, kielbasa, hamburgers, corn, and Larry and Beau's ad hoc fruit salad. It was a big crowd between the two families, with Sarah's parents keeping mine entertained and Gramps chatting up Mimi well past my comfort level.

Chuy and Harper were seated at the kids' table with Ms. Livingston and Landon. You could tell that Harper had never sat at a kids' table at her great grandmothers, let alone at a kid's table with a semi-mute Chinese woman, but she was handling it well. Remembering where I was less than a week ago with Dusty and Peaches, this seemed like a pretty good outcome, even if the worst was about to happen.

"I would like to make a toast." My grandfather stood up and we all stopped talking, half of us curious, the other half terrified.

"It's an honor to be in the presence of such beautiful women here tonight." Gramps was looking directly at Mimi when he said "beautiful women." *Oh shit*, he had his "Super-nut" back thanks to Beau and Boomer and now he's going to pork my future grandmother in law, *perfect.* Gramps had game.

Like my father and Beau, He was impossibly handsome with a sly grin that could probably crack a coconut open if he tried hard enough. He was still very interested in sex and after his stroke, much too willing to talk about it in public. I knew there would be no way Dad was going to keep Gramps under control, just like the rest of us, he still worshipped the man.

"Speaking for the Duques, I would like to thank the Campbells and our beautiful hostess," Gramps turned and made eyes at Mimi again, "for this wonderful meal. We'd love to return the favor should you ever find yourselves in Atlanta." He stopped again, turning to give his attention back to Mimi, "especially you my dear."

I saw Sarah's father, Mr. Campbell, arch his eyebrows. I think he'd just realized Gramps was on the prowl. He started laughing, his false sense of security was probably based entirely on Gramps and Mimi's age or that she was no longer interested in men. What could Mimi even do? She just had hip replacement surgery. I, on the other hand, was *very* concerned. She looked like her bones would break if she even thought of going coital.

Everyone was waiting for an end to his toast, but Gramps was still locked in on Mimi.

"Gramps, finish it up." I tried to whisper as soft as I could across the table.

"DON'T TELL GRANDPA MONKEY HOW TO PEEL A BANANA!" He hollered back at my general direction, only to immediately slip into a softer cadence, looking directly at Mimi, who was smiling right back at him, "Lord bless this food and the people at this table, Amen"

"Amen," everyone followed with laughter.

The relief on Beau's face after Gramps finished was telling, he was as horrified as I was. My mother and father were making a joke to each other and laughing under their breaths. Dad pointed to Larry and Beau when I caught them laughing and did a disturbingly accurate hand gesture of someone giving a blow job, mouthing *"tonight"* afterwards and pointing to Larry and Beau again.

I tried not to laugh because I didn't want to encourage Dad into another scenario that necessitated more theatrics. I had just polished off an ear of corn and put my napkin down on my plate when I heard a familiar voice rise above the chatter.

"Can I get everybody's attention? I have something to say as well, and this seems as good a time as any." It was Sarah, who was sitting across the table from me and next to Larry, even though he hadn't turned away from Beau the entire night. Once she had everyone's attention, she started up again, "On behalf of the Campbells, I would like to welcome the Duques to Saugatuck again." She started to tear up and seemed like she was looking for the words, "And I want to apologize to you for what I have done to your family." I was going to get up and go over to her, but she noticed and easily stared me back into my seat, which you know, *macho wise*, wasn't exactly a highpoint for me.

"When Parker and I broke up, I was pregnant. He wanted to have the baby and I didn't. I was young and scared, he was going through big changes in his life, and I didn't think I was ready to have a baby." I looked over to the kid's table to see Harper watching her mother intently, knowing she had a starring role. "When I came home, I knew I was wrong, about everything. Harper, you are the best thing that has ever happened to me."

"You got one past the goalie, son! I didn't think you had it in you, Boy!" Gramps burst out, standing up making the touchdown gesture. Mimi looked at Gramps with shock. He fell quickly back into his seat while gesturing his lips were being zipped shut.

Sarah continued, "I was so mad at Parker after we broke up, I didn't want to tell him about Harper, he was such a mess." I felt like it wasn't necessary for all the Duques, even Chuy, to nod their heads in agreement at the, *such a mess* part. *Chuy wasn't even there.*

"After I realized I had no reason to be mad at Parker it was too late, my secret was too big, too complicated. Mimi, I'm sorry to spring this on you. I told Mom and Dad earlier while you were out walking. I've already apologized to Harper and Parker, Mr. and Mrs. Duque, my selfish secret has cheated you out of 14 years of grandparenting and I'm so, so, sorry." Before Sarah could even finish my mother and Mrs. Campbell had left their chairs to join Harper hugging Sarah, surrounding her with love and words of forgiveness. I was still scared to get out of my seat.

Mimi seemed confused, "Sarah honey, what are you saying? I don't understand." Mimi's bad hearing caused her to ignore most conversations, but she could tell this one was a *doozy*.

Everyone was quiet, Sarah cleared her throat before answering, "Parker is Harper's biological father, Mimi. Larry is Harper's Dad, but he was filling in for Parker, who didn't know about Harper." Well, that was scandalous news for an 80 something year old. Mimi's jaw dropped so low I saw her dentures come loose.

"AND I'M GAY" Larry announced while standing up, then looking over to face Harper, saying it again, except calmer, "Harper, I'm gay."

Harper feigned shock, reminding me of the person in the Munch painting, *The Scream*.

Mimi's jaw dropped another inch and her teeth dropped into her potato salad. Without hesitating, she grabbed the dentures and put them in a napkin, turned halfway around for a split second, and BOOM! They were back in. Old people can work their dentures like gunslingers from the Old West. I wouldn't be surprised if she'd spun them on her trigger finger to remove the potato salad before popping them back in.

Gramps turned to me, way too excited, thumbing back at Mimi and whispered in a celebratory manor, *"She wears dentures!"*

I instantly threw up in my mouth. Not because a sweet old woman wears dentures, but because years ago I had a completely one-sided conversation with Gramps about, "BJ's from old birds." He told me that old women with dentures gave the best blow jobs because they didn't have any teeth to get in the way. I threw up then too.

Now I had a mouth full of throw up and a sweet, embarrassed grandma looking lovingly at the toilet kid, her new family member. As her favorite new family member, the last thing I wanted her to think was her denture fiasco caused me to hurl.

I had no idea what to do. Mom, Sarah, and Sarah's mom were still in a three-way hug, and Harper was hugging Larry with Beau waiting to be next. There was a whole hugging party going on and I was stuck there with my mouth full of hurl. I wouldn't, *couldn't* allow myself to think about why

279

Gramps was high fiving my father or even worse why my father *was high fiving him back.* The right thing to do would be to just go ahead and swallow the barf, but if you haven't figured it out by now, doing the right thing has always been a challenge for me if it involves something gross.

After some quick thinking I took a cue from Mimi and picked up my napkin and emptied my mouth into it. It's a good thing I did too, because right after, my father made the universal hip thrust gesture for boning to Gramps and I blew even more chunks into the already burdened napkin. I folded the napkin onto itself, amazed nobody noticed.

"What in herr goin on Runcle Parker-san?" It was Landon staring up at me, trying to hold my hand, "She announce that Harper is Runcle's bastard chird he no take care of." I could tell he was reciting Ms. Livingston's answer, mostly because it was obvious, but also because I could see a smile tainting her otherwise miserable perma-scowl.

I wasn't going to take the bait though, even Ms. Livingston couldn't rain on this parade. "She's your new cousin Landon!" I covered my nuts as I said it, just to be safe.

"Oh boy! How rucky is Randon?" He ran to hug Harper, who hugged her little cousin right back.

"I knew it the minute I saw her. She has your eyes." My mom was in front of me now, posturing for a hug. Apparently, she saw me hurl earlier, "Why don't you get rid of that sweetie?" she said, taking the bulky napkin from me and dropping it in the trash.

"Thanks. I knew it the minute I saw her too, I freaked. I think it's fair to say I didn't handle it with quite the discretion you and Dad pulled off today at the High School..." My attention was instantly diverted, "Hey Dad!" I was trying to scream without raising my voice, "Put that away! There are kids around!" Normally that phrase would send shockwaves of fear through the Duque clan. I'm sure Beau and Mom were relieved to see it was just a big fat joint that Dad was showing Mr. Campbell. Every young person within earshot stopped what they were doing and looked at me.

"False alarm, sorry, nothing to see here folks." I said, shrugging my shoulders as I watched Dad tuck it behind his back. Mr. Campbell and

Dad started laughing again and proceeded to slap each other's backs. Two minutes later they grabbed Mom and Mrs. Campbell from the table to take a "tour of this fine old house." *Who knew the Campbells smoked weed?* I just prayed that Mr. Campbell wouldn't try his favorite toilet joke with my old man.

Sarah walked over to me as we watched our parents walk off into the house and said, "I think they'll get along fine."

"I think you're right." I said, again, hoping for the best.

Sarah and I settled back down at the table with Gramps who was busy sweet-talking Mimi. Ms. Livingston walked Landon and Piper back to Sarah's house and Harper and Chuy walked into town to meet Harper's best friends Grace and Tess at Charlie's Ice Cream.

Ten minutes later, Mimi was telling a story about Harper when *it* happened again. It started with a bump and then for at least thirty seconds it felt like we were on an ever so subtle sideways conveyor belt, like someone was moving the Earth from underneath our feet. Gramps, never one to miss out on an opportunity, took advantage of it by holding Mimi close. I looked at Sarah, was this it?

"Earthquake, it's gotta be." Gramps announced confidently.

Sarah and I each cracked a nervous smile. She squeezed my hand and kissed my cheek to calm me down, but I was a bag of nerves. Beau and Larry left right away, at Beau's insistence, to go back to Sarah's house to check on Landon. I had a feeling Beau was spooked too.

Twenty minutes after the second "bump," night had fallen over Saugatuck. The illuminated patio was as magical as I'd thought it would be, straight out of a magazine. Sarah and I were still seated at the table, comforted by nightfall, with Sarah's optimism growing on each of us. I could see Gramps holding Mimi's hand, whispering something in her ear when I heard Mimi say, "Oh Crawford, you are so bad!"

Sarah's father opened the screen door slowly, cautiously tip toeing to the middle of the patio, followed closely by his wife and my parents, who were also tip toeing for no reason. They all looked up at the stars and after a couple minutes Mr. Campbell said, "Damn Lucas, that's some good weed." They all ran back into the house and we didn't see most of them again for the rest of the night.

Larry and Beau had come back later and were hanging with Sarah and I around the fire pit when Dad literally emerged from the bushes. He wasn't wearing shoes and he wasn't ready to go to bed. I was just glad he didn't have a boner. Dad got everybody high with another huge joint, then disappeared again without warning.

Sarah and Larry were quick to note his departure route, back through the bushes, was in the opposite direction of her parents' house, where he, Mom, and Gramps were spending the night.

48

THE MORNING AFTER

"Do you have any ibuprofen in this house? I asked Sarah, who was still in bed. I had graduated from a couch in the study to Sarah's king size bed and enjoyed the most sleep I'd had since my sleepover with Dusty and Peaches. My head was killing me, Gatorade and ibuprofen were a necessary part of my future.

"If we have some, it would be in the medicine cabinet, but I'd check the expiration date."

"I looked there. What kind of people don't have ibuprofen? Don't you get headaches or a sore muscles?" Was she ignoring me? This little town really was a dream world, it wouldn't surprise me if people here never got headaches.

"I'm going to walk to the drugstore then. Will they be open? It's 10 o'clock. Sarah?"

She was sound asleep. "Love you too," I said as I walked out.

Piper didn't want to come with me, I think she was still spooked, she just stood at the door, which was fine, because I couldn't find her leash. I grabbed Chuy's baseball hat, which fit without adjustment, and noticed it smelled beautiful, if that's even possible.

The weather outside was perfect and seeing strangers on the sidewalks in a world that hadn't blown in two gave me a sense of comfort. The shops were open, people were happy, life was good. Between the fresh air and great memories, my headache had subsided enough for me to duck into my favorite store, Landsharks, and take a minute to laugh at their funny t-shirts.

After I left Landsharks, I walked down Butler Street toward the drug store. Thirty seconds into my walk, a black Suburban with tinted windows drove past me and slowed to a stop. It made me nervous considering what I'd been through. I walked past it and became paranoid the Suburban was following me. I ignored it at first, but then when I turned around, it was following right behind me. I kept asking myself, was it a hillbilly looking for a parking spot or *should I run like a motherfucker?*

I was freaking out, was this going to be a thing for me now? Was this what trauma feels like? Why are those windows so tinted? Why are you driving so slowly? I tried to dismiss it as another sad hillbilly trying to get a parking spot around here, but I was still nervous, I couldn't buy in completely. The Suburban drove past me and pulled into a spot down the block. I felt equal parts relieved and ridiculous once I realized it had stopped "following" me. Those hillbillies were lucky to get a spot. Saugatuck was already full of tourists getting breakfast and shopping before hitting the beach.

As I was walking up the sidewalk towards the black Suburban in its new parking spot, I felt safety in the crowd of people around me. I laughed at myself and looked, out of curiosity, to see the tourists who'd almost made me break into a disemboweled sprint. The passenger door opened, and I stopped laughing. It was Dusty.

49

DUSTY 2.0

The little blonde man sprang out onto the sidewalk in front of me. I stopped dead in my tracks. I could feel my heartbeat in my face; there were people all around us; what was he going to do with me and how was he here? Fuck. How did he survive? *Double Fuck.* Was he one of the aliens who placed the metallic columns around the world? I thought it was funny how his leg came off as he bounced down the cliff. Not really funny ha ha, but funny peculiar. I didn't think legs were supposed to come off like that. I think it was his leg anyway, I knew it wasn't his penis.

"Mr. Duque?" he asked as if he didn't know. To my great relief, the little man wasn't Dusty, he was at least two inches taller and had a slightly skinnier face. This *had* to be Dusty's brother, maybe his twin. They looked so similar they had to be twins, and why not? Psychotic dudes like Dusty always have a twin.

"I'm sorry, who are you looking for?"

"Parker Duque; are you Parker Duque with a 'Q'?"

"Umm, No. You've got the wrong guy I'm afraid," I said nervously, noticing Dusty 2.0 guy wore the same type of jacket Dusty and Peaches wore on *their* murder spree: no letters. Was this his murder spree jacket? I went to walk around him, and a familiar, freakishly strong grip immobilized my arm.

I was about to scream bloody murder when he spoke, "Please step calmly into the car Mr. Duque." His smile was exactly like Dusty's, "You won't be harmed."

"Fuck me running," I sighed, too tired to fight. I climbed into the Suburban, where a dark-haired man with cliché mirrored sunglasses sat in the driver's seat. Dusty 2.0 motioned for me to keep scooting over, which I was more than happy to do myself, but he elected to push me over forcefully and jumped into the back seat next to me. I tried opening my door to make a run for it but couldn't. It's awkward being foiled by kid's door locks.

"OK, what do you guys want..." I couldn't finish my sentence because I no longer cared to. I felt a familiar dizziness. "Oh nah," I slurred, looking down to see *another* giant hypodermic needle in my thigh.

I heard the driver scream, "Bone shot!" and remember thinking, *how do they do that?* before I passed out.

50

DEBRIEFED

When I came to, we were parked two blocks away from where they picked me up in another spot. I looked at my watch and saw the huge hypodermic needle *still* sticking out of my thigh. I pulled the giant syringe, but the needle must have been stuck in my bone. I screamed in horror and pulled harder, it wouldn't come out, "You got it stuck in my bone."

"It's in there good, isn't it? Sorry!"

"Bone shot." The driver said again with an infectious giggle.

I looked at my watch and saw it was *ten-thirty?* "Have I only been out for seven minutes?"

"Here, start drinking this." Dusty 2.0 looked visibly annoyed at the bone shot and the drivers giggling. He handed me a bottled water, "If you don't hydrate, you're going to have what amounts to a world class hangover."

"I'm aware, unfortunately." I downed the water and held my hand out for another.

"I'm agent so and so and we have reason to believe you've murdered two of our finest operatives."

"Agent so and so?"

"You can call me Daryl."

"Daryl, how do you know your two finest operatives are dead? I didn't kill anybody."

"Well, a majestic, seventy-year-old great white shark choked on my girlfriend's neck and washed ashore below the Black Site." Daryl started crying. I looked at the driver.

"This is hard for him" the driver said, motioning to Daryl, "Peaches was his girlfriend and Dusty was his brother. *Twin* brother. He found a mountain goat dry humping his brother's leg."

I decided not to bullshit, "I think you know, anything I did was in self-defense, I wasn't there by my own choosing. And you could make the argument that I didn't actually kill Dusty. I pushed him off a cliff, which he survived, then I threw up on him when he was climbing back up to kill me, and he fell to his death." Daryl looked puzzled. "With Peaches, I threw a bag of delicious off-brand powdered sugar donuts just out of her reach. She jumped off the cliff trying to save the donuts."

"I told you her diet was gonna kill her!" the driver announced from the peanut gallery. He was still looking forward, trying not to laugh, but sporadically letting out tiny little giggles. Daryl looked at his partner in quiet dismay, then lunged forward with a ferocious full palmed slap to the side of his face. The driver held his ear and cowered as he looked ahead in silence.

With his partner's giggles cured. Denis's twin brother Daryl turned back to me, "Technically, you killed them though."

"That's a lot better than killing somebody regular, wouldn't you agree?" I said, trying to be positive, "Peaches killed my wife."

"I know she killed her. I read the Fulton County incident report. It's got *Peaches Wengerd* written all over it. She *loved* doing murder-suicides, *exactly* like that. She convinced your wife to write an "I'm leaving you" letter to him, that's all she needed. The letter makes his death look like a suicide after he kills her in a fit of rage." He was tearing up, lost in admiration, "I'm going to miss my baby."

"Peaches?" I said in genuine disbelief. *What did that morbidly obese woman have that these two brothers wanted more of?* "Daryl, there's something you should know about those two."

"Oh, I know, it seems my brother and I had another thing in common, didn't we? That's why you're not dead right now," he said, looking somewhat disappointed.

"You aren't going to kill me?" I asked.

"No. Oh, good heavens no, and I was just being macho about the '*that's why you're not dead*' part." The driver was nodding his head in agreement. "The government doesn't work that way. Dusty and Peaches went rogue. They were supposed to *apprehend* any possible witnesses and bring them to a DSL, a designated secured location. They've always been terrible with paperwork though, so they decided to just kill people instead. Not to make excuses for them, but leadership *did* tell us it was the end of the world, *for sure,* so it's hard to do paperwork with that in front of you, right?

"What about the people they killed?"

"Meh, they had permission to kill, but *only* if it were an emergency. We have a way to work it out..." Daryl seemed adrift in thought and came back, "Both of them loved killing people but hated paperwork, it's easy to understand the attraction," *it really wasn't,* "I should have known."

"OK, listen, although I only got to know Peaches for a day, I think I can say, honestly, we're both better off, but let's get back to something," when I spoke the hypodermic needle shook, "Can you pull this out? Does this need to be in there?"

"Oh, I'm sorry" he said, and he pulled the monster needle again, nothing. I screamed in pain, which made Daryl panic and pull harder, finally yanking the giant needle out of my leg.

"Jesus!" I screamed again.

"Keep drinking that water." Daryl handed me another bottle of water.

"Did you really have to knock me out for seven minutes to move me two blocks over?"

"Yes," Daryl said, bothered, "It took us a while to find another spot, parking is a bitch around here. I'm sorry you're upset, but it's SOP to control the perp. Plus, obviously I need practice, I've been hitting the bone too much, which is really bad for the perp. You don't want a bone shot, trust me. Keep drinking that water."

"But you just hit my bone, didn't you?"

"I did. I told you I need practice."

"*Bone shot!*" the driver chirped again.

"So, I just got a 'bone shot' for seven, fucking, minutes?" I wanted to scream but thought better of it, "You didn't fly me to California, you drove me around the block. I would have come peacefully!"

"Sorry Mr. Duque, it's practice, it's fun for us *and* its SOP, which means standard operating pro—"

"I know what SOP means."

"You have to remember, we have to find ways to make our job fun just like anybody else, it's not all glamour being in the CIA." The driver slapped his forehead and Daryl flinched, "If we worked for the CIA."

"You aren't planning on doing that again are you?" I asked Daryl, pointing to the new syringe he was holding. He smiled but didn't answer.

"Seriously?" Still no answer. "OK, if you aren't going to kill me what are you here for? How did you find me? I haven't even used a credit card?"

"Remember, I read the murder investigation report from Fulton County? Turns out a 'Parker Duque' had talked to case officer William Roland. Do you know who posted your speech video on YouTube? It was Dusty, he called it, *Parker was right.* I watched it and it was pretty good. I can see why he didn't kill you. He had a rough time as a kid."

"Because of his teeny tiny penis?" I asked, half joking, then terrified Daryl might have a twin teeny tiny penis. I didn't need to pick any more fights.

"I'm not even going to ask you how you know about that." Daryl was unfazed, "Then your daughter here in Saugatuck posted on her Facebook page that she was 'stoked' the *Parker was right* guy from YouTube was her father.

"How did you know I had a daughter?"

Daryl handed me Harper's birth certificate; I was listed as the father. I wanted to have it laminated into a name badge.

"The only thing I couldn't figure out was how you got back to Atlanta?"

"I paid my way onto a charter flight." I felt kind of cool eluding the CIA with at least one part of my plan to stay under the radar.

"You probably paid her, oh, twenty grand to take you and not put you on the passenger list." I must have looked confused. "I'm just having fun; I know how you got home. You paid her with marked government bills. You also took out a loan on your new BMW, and then spent thirty-seven dollars on energy drinks, caffeine pills, and chips at a Chevron. And what road trip wouldn't benefit from an eighteen dollar, economy size tube of KY jelly, purchased just south of Indianapolis." I remembered giving Chuy a twenty at a truck stop in Indy. *Jesus!*

"Oops." I said, nervous to have taken Dusty's slush money without a good excuse. "I didn't have time to go to the bank. I guess you want the rest of it back?"

"No. The government is prepared to call it even if you sign this." He pulled out a one-page non-disclosure agreement. It was an indemnity agreement that didn't hold *an agency to be named later* at fault for anything and forbade me to tell anyone about it or to seek retribution against the U.S. Government in any venue, which was fine. I ended up coming out ahead. Way, way ahead.

"Do I have a choice? You killed my wife and probably took ten years off my life."

"Do you know how much money that is?" he asked. I shrugged, the bag was heavy as hell, but I never counted it. "You took three million dollars."

"You've got my attention." I read the agreement again, "Let me get this straight, I sign this, and you'll leave me alone? Forever?"

"Nope. We'll be watching you although you won't know it. Actually, *we* won't be watching you, but an agent somewhere will be assigned with monitoring your actions for a couple of years. Nothing you can do about that. We're the government after all, we have people to protect."

"From me?" I joked as I signed the papers, "Is that it?"

"No."

He was just staring at me, waiting. I asked him, "What else?"

"Don't you want to know what happened? I'm allowed to de-brief you as part of the deal, but only if you ask."

"What happened?" I asked immediately.

"They say I'm one of the best debriefers in the agency." The driver started cracking up, but this laughter was welcomed by Daryl.

"Tell me! Of course I want to know. You're talking about what happened yesterday with the power going out, the earthquake like bumps, and the extended daylight, right? What's going on? Debrief me."

"Right. We're telling the masses that it was just some sunspots flaring up. We'll get a couple government scientists to verify it and it's over. It's as easy as that. It's amazing what people will believe if it's less scary than the truth.

"What happened to the metal columns?

"They've all disappeared."

"They have?"

"Gone completely. Every last one."

"Do you even know what happened? Because the report I read said those columns were going to split the earth in two. I'm guessing that didn't happen, correct?"

"No, not yet. We know what their intent is though. Government Intelligence has a rock-solid understanding of it, and it doesn't look good." He held up his finger as if to tell me to hold the question I was about to ask, "Let me tell you what happened first. The columns, through a series of electromagnetic pulses, slowed the rotation of the earth. That's why the power went out; the columns were firing as magnets in a coordinated order, like an electric motor does. They slowed the Earth's rotation in its orbit and created a 'knuckle ball' effect."

"Why did they slow the Earth's rotation?"

"I can't tell you that, but I can tell you the end result increased the radius of the Earth's orbit around the Sun."

"This is crazy."

"In other words, it made the Earth circle farther away from the sun." Daryl looked at me, disappointed in my silence and barked to the driver, "Laptop." He held out his hand like a surgeon awaiting a scalpel.

Daryl opened his laptop and showed me an animation of what he'd just described. The Earth rotating peacefully in its orbit around the Sun, then the rotation slowing, causing it to wobble into an orbit a little farther from the Sun and then it started rotating again.

"OK I get it, I got it the first time, but what I don't get is why anybody would want to do that to us?"

"Well, smarty pants..." Daryl stalled as he searched for something on his laptop. He started reading from the laptop, "In addition to the current man-made global warming, in a billion years, the sun will be over ten percent brighter than it is today, and in three billion years the sun's luminosity will increase by over forty percent, creating a runaway greenhouse state which will most likely mean the end of Earth. By increasing the radius of the Earth's orbit around the sun, they've doubled our planet's life expectancy and temporarily solved global warming."

"Get the fuck out! Are you kidding me? So aliens aren't trying to destroy our world, *they're saving it!*"

"Well, I wouldn't go too far. They're not trying to blow it in two."

"So, it turns out this *wasn't* a national security issue?" I was incredulous.

"Oh, Mr. Duque, it was and still *is* a national security issue, if people knew what happened, there'd be anarchy. Extra-terrestrial interference? We can't have that. But no, it doesn't seem like they're trying to blow the world up, although clearly that's an available option for them that we can't stop."

"These aliens have given us more time and fixed the biggest issue facing our planet? That's good, right? Wouldn't all the government 'intelligence' people say that's a *good* thing?"

"Absolutely not. We think they've fixed our planet because they're preparing to harvest us to eat. They're planning on breeding us like cattle and use us as a constant food source for eternity."

The driver turned in disbelief, it seemed as though Daryl had done more debriefing than he was supposed to.

Daryl looked at me and my asshole seized up, I tried to ask another question, but I no longer cared to and struggled to follow why Daryl seemed so hurried. I felt dizzy again and couldn't keep my head up, "Nah—"

"Bone shot!" I heard the driver shout again with excitement.

As gravity wrestled my head towards the floor, I saw *another* giant hypodermic needle sticking out of my leg, then darkness.

51

DETAILS

When I came to, I was lying on my back in a side lawn of a church on Water St. An old couple walked by and looked at me with pained disgust. I couldn't blame them when I realized Daryl had tucked one of my hands inside the front of my pants. Classy. My head was already killing me as I dutifully chugged the two waters Daryl had left me. I was relieved to be done with those two idiots.

Was I a little worried about being farmed and eaten? Not at all. Worst case scenario, they'd take some of us as pets, I'd long envied Piper's life. Maybe I could sleep around some alien's house all day and try to hump the neighbor's pet human when they came over. Still, I wasn't going to be putting too much stock in the government's "intelligence" anytime soon.

The air conditioning of the drug store brought welcomed relief to my aching head. As I walked around the store, I wondered if you could fit any more crap inside a building. It was an old-fashioned drug store that slung every touristy gimmick possible. From "Saugatuck" t-shirts to firecrackers, to root beer floats at the fountain in the back of the store. It was a hangout and the hub of activity for all the kids around town, Harper included. All I needed from that fine institution was a giant-sized Gatorade, four Ibuprofen, and the mercy they could bring me. I spotted the pharmacy section in the middle and as I rounded a corner, I literally ran into Beau.

"You look awful," he said, happy as a lark.

"Good morning to you too." I wasn't sure if it was appropriate to give him shit, but I wasn't about to stop, "Where did you disappear to last night?"

"OK. OK. I need to tell you something, I play for the other team now," he said, with a sheepish grin.

"Beau, that is a complete shock." I hugged him. I was so happy for him, "You deserve to be happy, you're a good person and Larry is a great guy."

"Hey Deluxe, you have to buy these, people know me here—" It was Larry. He stopped cold like a deer in the headlights when he saw me. Maybe it was because he had what looked to be a year's supply of Fleet brand enemas in his basket.

Beau started laughing and I said, "Geez Larry, you OK?" Larry looked at Beau who laughed harder while I reached for them and said, "Why don't you let me get these; I'm dying for some Advil. I've got a headache bigger than Mount Baldie."

"Umm OK." Larry said and handed them over like hot potatoes.

"Listen guys, this doesn't need to be awkward, I'm happy for both of you and glad you're having a good time." I nodded toward the basket of enemas, "This is a good thing."

They both stood there together, beaming. Puppy love. I was happy for Beau, but I needed to break the lovers apart for the time being, "Beau, are you busy right now? I was wondering if you could walk back to Sarah's with me so we could talk about something completely different. In fact, it just happened to me."

"How's she taking it?" Larry asked.

"Umm, taking what?" I was confused.

"Me cheating on her with your brother."

"I think she'll pull through it. I'm trying to provide her with a bit of comfort and distraction myself."

"Thank you, Parker," he said as he gave me a nice hug. "OK, I have to leave, like I said, people know me here." He made a sideways puppy dog face for Beau, "I have to go to the Thandner's house anyway; they're coming in from Chicago this afternoon. I can meet you back at the Carriage House after lunch if you'd like?"

"That sounds great, Lar Bear, don't make me wait too long!" They both had a twinkle in their eyes. It was so sweet, Beau was all smiles after Larry left. *There is someone for everyone.*

"They own a rental house with an adorable little carriage house in the back." Beau offered, then looked at the enemas and back at me, then back at the enemas.

"I don't need to know." I said, "Please. I'm just happy you and Lar Bear have progressed into the nick name stage. Deluxe?"

"I wished you hadn't heard that, it's too embarrassing to explain."

"If it's too embarrassing for you, I'm *great* with not hearing it."

"OK, fine. You know I'd never step foot in the place, but apparently at Subway if you order your sandwich 'deluxe' style, you get three scoops of meat instead of two." He looked at me like I would understand this. I didn't, but was nervous at the meat reference. There was a growing, embarrassed confidence coming over Beau's face until he erupted, "That's fifty percent more meat."

"Oh God." I laughed with him as he grabbed his crotch. "Beau, I don't want to encourage this kind of openness, but I have to tell you, I love the new you. I've always wanted this for you." We hugged a long hug; I didn't care that I had a basket full of enemas.

As we were at the end of our sweet hug Beau whispered in my ear, "And I love butt sex."

"Beau, Deluxe, seriously. I'm very, very happy for you, but there's no reason to share the details."

"But don't you remember we had that whole conversation about butt sex and star muscles? It's actually not that big of a deal."

"Stop!" I extended my enima-free hand up, "Just stop. I'm so glad you love 'butt sex,' I really am, and I'm glad your star muscle is taking it in stride. But again, I'd also really appreciate it if we didn't go that far into the details going forward."

"You should try it. It's really not that big of a deal."

My head was still ringing from the hangover serum Daryl used on me. "We'll take that into consideration," I lied, "but right now I really need you to—"

"Stop with the details, I know," he interrupted.

"Yes, but no, I need you to help me find the ibuprofen before I die."

52

A COMMITMENT

With my bag full of enemas, Beau and I started the short walk to Sarah's house. As we got closer, I noticed Sarah's father was sitting in his car, parked in front. I saw him roll his window up as we approached, which I thought odd, because he was a pretty social guy.

"Hi, Mr. Campbell," I said. He looked at me and reluctantly opened his window.

"Hello, Parker." He was very formal.

There was an awkward silence, which killed me, "You coming in?"

"Nope. We're taking your family to the airport in Grand Rapids. They wanted to stop by and say goodbye to everybody first. They're probably waiting for you in there."

"They're leaving already?" I asked Beau, who shrugged ignorance.

"Yeah, inside boys." Mr. Campbell said before rolling his window back up. I felt like I'd just been shushed away by Sarah's Dad. It was awkward, was he upset with me? There was a lot of big news happening last night. We walked away from Mr. Campbell towards the house.

"He had a boner." Beau said

"What?"

"A huge boner at that. That penis would be getting nowhere near my star muscle, that's for sure."

"Do you have to call it a star muscle?"

"No, not if it bothers you, or makes you want to throw up. It's better than butthole though, don't you think?"

"We don't have to talk about your butthole at all. Ever."

"Oh Parker."

"I won't talk about mine either, just to be fair. Deal?"

"You're being silly. We have over fifty sphincter muscles; they're actually a fascinating part of the body if you consider what they do and how long they're able to retain their resilience. Some are so small you can't even see them." People with medical backgrounds, *even dentists*, are just different than the rest of us because they understand too much. Poor souls: the magic and mystery of the butthole is completely lost on them.

"Beau?"

"Details?"

"Please."

Inside, the whole group was in the kitchen. They had watched the morning news and were attempting to explain sunspots and solar flares to Sarah as she served coffee and muffins. The minute she noticed me staring at her, she made a silly face; she was still the most beautiful woman I had ever seen. I loved her inside-out, if that was such a thing, because it didn't matter if she looked "touched" at the current moment, she was the most beautiful person in the world to me. She was so much more than her physical beauty, her optimism, intelligence, humor, and compassion made every room she walked into a warmer place.

Landon ran to Beau who scooped him up and started assaulting him with kisses. It seemed so out of character for Beau. It was the most affection I'd ever seen him show Landon. It was a wonderful sight to see Beau this happy, but it was a thousand times better to see Landon's face light up while getting the attention. Ms. Livingston looked nervous about her minion enjoying time with his Father. I saw Landon and Ms. Livingston's packed bags stacked neatly by the door.

"Parker, we're going to make like babies and head out." My father said as Beau and I entered the kitchen with Piper behind us, wagging her tail in a furious, Labrador-like manner. Sarah's mom had a smile that matched her glow and I wondered if it was boner related or something.

"Why so soon?" at first, I was disappointed because I wanted them to get to know Harper better, but then I realized *I* wanted to get to know Harper better, so having less competition out of the gate wouldn't be so bad.

"Don't worry Parker, we're coming back next week. We can't wait to spend some time getting to know our precious new addition. Or should I say additions?" Mom had her arm around Harper and gave her a squeeze as she smiled at Sarah. "Chuy's going to stay here until then, if that's OK." I nodded. "We thought we'd take Landon back with us so Beau might spend some time here alone and relax. He's been working so hard lately."

Beau walked over to her and gave her a big hug that seemed to last about two days. When they had finally let go of one another, they were both crying crocodile tears, possibly of the *"You knew I was gay? Yes, I've always known you were gay and it's completely OK"* origin.

"OK," I said, "Are you leaving right now?"

"I think so. Our flight's out of Grand Rapids which I think is an hour away. Do we have enough time?" Dad asked Mrs. Campbell, who was still smiling and not answering, but eventually nodded and said, "Sure." I could tell she had no earthly idea what she'd just affirmed; other than a response was requested of her and *sure* seemed as good a response as any. *Was she stoned?*

"Where's Dad?" Sarah asked. Mom and Dad looked at each other and then at Mrs. Campbell and the three of them started giggling.

Several seconds of confusion filled the air until my Grandfather came out of the bathroom off the kitchen and announced, "He has a boner!" He spoke directly to me with that irresistible sparkle in his eye. "Your old man introduced him to Viagra last night and he's stuck in Bonerville. Can someone get me a glass of water? I lost a lot of fluid last night, heh heh."

Harper threw up into the kitchen sink and Ms. Livingston quickly earmuffed Landon and whisked him out of the room. On the way out I heard Landon ask, "Where Bonerville?"

"Cialis," my Dad corrected Gramps, "Viagra is a one-shot wonder, Cialis is a *commitment*."

Harper bolted out of the kitchen with her hands over her ears screaming,

"Gross!" Chuy grabbed a roll of towels off the counter and followed her upstairs, laughing his ass off.

Sarah looked at me laughing and said, "That's definitely your daughter!" and then over to her mother, "MOM!"

"Honey, your father and I have had more "firsts" in the last twelve hours than we've had in the last twelve years," Mrs. Campbell said, then breaking into a whisper to my parents, "Including doing the pot!" She was as high as a kite. I think they all were. Well, everybody over fifty-five anyway.

Everybody was laughing awkwardly but feeling good, including me. I instantly stopped laughing and feeling good when Mimi came out of the same bathroom Gramps had two minutes ago. She was using a walker.

Gramps walked over, grinning ear to ear, and helped her with her walker

"Mimi!" Sarah was surprised. "I didn't even know you were here!"

"I told you we'd get caught." Gramps whispered, way too loud.

"Crawford, tell me that wasn't worth it?" she whispered back at room volume.

"Are you OK? Did you fall? Why are you using your walker?" Sarah continued.

Out of the corner of my eye I saw Dad giving a fist bump to Gramps and I could feel nausea creeping in.

"I'm fine honey, sweetest pain a woman's ever known. Sarah dear, do you have some ibuprofen? I'm afraid both my hips are sore this morning," she winked at Gramps, "not just the new one." The nausea I could feel creeping in earlier was now riding a horse. Gramps left Dad to whisper in my ear, "That beautiful woman right there is tighter than a gnat's ass stretched over a water barrel."

I held out my bottle of ibuprofen while throwing up in the kitchen sink. I didn't care so much about getting it to Mimi, as I was actually trying to keep Mom from rubbing my back while I hurled, a maternal practice that has absolutely no value.

53

THE UNTHINKABLE

At my request, Beau and Sarah stayed with me in the kitchen after everyone had left. I wanted to give them Daryl's update in private, so I shut the kitchen's swinging door. Sarah put some music on her iPod and set it in the speaker cradle thing and turned around to face me.

"I have something to tell you," she announced.

I wasn't paying attention though. I was thinking how lucky these two were to get debriefed without a huge hypodermic needle in either thigh. Then I thought about Daryl's comment on how I'd be watched. I looked around the kitchen and then back at them, "Can we go outside for a second? I have to talk to both of you."

"Why outside?" Beau asked as I walked past him.

"Please." He followed me out. When we were outside, I told them about the black Suburban, Dusty's twin brother Daryl, and his explanation of what the metal columns did to the Earth's orbit around the Sun.

"I told you!" Sarah said. "That is *incredible* news! People will have one less thing to fight about!"

"What about the sunspots? I thought that was pretty cool. They showed a picture of it on CNN." Beau asked.

"I'm betting big brother might have provided stock footage."

"I told you they weren't going to blow up the planet, did I not?" Sarah repeated.

"You were right. You were right all along. If there was ever a case for optimism, this was it. I'd never even considered what happened could actually be a good thing, that somebody out there might see us as something worth saving."

"Can we stop talking and worrying about this? Forever? It's all too scary. Does Dusty's brother know that we know?" Beau asked nervously, pointing to himself and Sarah.

"No and I want to keep it that way. That's why we came outside to talk about it."

"Do you think my house is bugged?" Sarah seemed concerned.

"Probably not," I said, and I meant it, "Ms. Livingston has been here the whole time; she's like a Kung Fu Warrior. Nobody, and I mean nobody, could sneak up on her to place a bug in here. She's like an ancient, flatulent mist, she's everywhere." I looked around, nervous she might materialize out of nowhere and karate chop me for comparing her to a fart.

"Parker, she's Chinese." Beau corrected me.

"OK, she's like an ancient, flatulent, Chinese warrior."

"I vote we go inside and I second the vote to never talk about either again." Sarah said, "I have something else I want to talk to you about and it's pretty serious." She walked past us into the house.

Beau sat down at the kitchen table and smiled at me like he knew what was coming.

"What?" I asked him.

"Are you going to move here?" Beau asked me.

I looked at Sarah, who stopped opening a cabinet and looked back at us, "Yes, he is, Beau."

"Am I?" I teased. Of course I was, wild horses couldn't stop me.

"I can't move away from my family, Parker, I can't. This is the life that I want for Harper. She has the outdoors up here and knows the entire town. I want her to grow up like I did and have innocent summer crushes on boys from Chicago." *Was that a nod to me?* "I want her heart to flutter when her man rocks the motherfucking house down at the Crow Bar. She just told me this morning she had a crush on a boy visiting from out of town. It's innocent here, Parker, you should want that too." She was getting emotional, over *me*. I got up out of my seat and walked over to her, I had never loved anybody more.

"Of course I will. I shouldn't have joked about it." I looked her in the eye, "If you'll have me, I will move to Saugatuck." Sarah started crying and hugged me without letting go. I hugged her back; it felt so good to really be wanted and loved.

During what I thought was a super special embrace, I heard Beau whisper to Sarah, "*I slept with Larry!*" and I heard Sarah whisper back, "*I slept with your brother!*" I released Sarah to look at my brother and best friend, the gay dentist, fake clapping his hands in an ecstatic yaaaaaaay!

"Is that what you wanted to talk about? Did you two cook this up together? I've always loved it here. I thought maybe we could buy houses and rent them out or I could buy apartments in Holland or Grand Rapids. What do you think?" I was asking Sarah who went back to the cabinet and pulled out a stack of papers and set it down in front of me.

I recognized the title page. She had printed out, and from the looks of it, read and edited what I'd finished of my short story, *The Bear*. I was so embarrassed; I hadn't even read it myself! I thought about how horrible it must have read. I mean, I wrote it on a fifteen-hour, caffeine saturated bender from Atlanta to Saugatuck, while the world was about to blow up underneath my feet! I couldn't believe how personal it was or how I was taking it. I felt like Dusty, with a penis half the size of a pinky finger, skinny dipping in the ocean with the two people I love the most and the tide just went out. I could hardly breathe.

"I loved it!" She said, "I absolutely loved it, and I'm not just saying that because I love you or I'm biased by your cat-like prowess in the sack."

"Really?" I said, able to exhale. "I haven't even read it. You liked it?"

"Chuy read it too" Beau laughed, "He said he was surprised. I think his exact words were, 'I'm surprised, I expected it to suck.'"

"Did you read it?" I asked him

"Obviously, I'm dying to," He looked at Sarah, "it's a tribute to me. I've been busy though." He winked at me as he grabbed it. I let him have the pile of white paper. I was flying. When I was writing *The Bear* I was surprised at how much fun I was having, but that was nothing compared to someone telling you they loved it!

"Oh my God, you are Jack, aren't you? Parker, you *have* to finish this. I'm dying to know how it ends. Is Jack OK?"

"Do you really want to know?" I asked.

"Yes, but don't *tell me*. I want to *read* how it ends. Finish it. You *have* to finish it and you *have* to make it into a book. Parker honey, you said in school it was your dream to be a writer. I don't know if that was the old Parker selling me a line or if you were being sincere. What I do know is that this is great. You can move up here and buy some boring apartments or you could move up here and give writing a try, as long as you move up here, but I think if you have any interest in writing, you should give it a try. I believe in you."

"Well, I have come into some money. Why don't I finish *The Bear* and we'll go from there?"

"Perfect!" She said and gave me a kiss. "I have a song to play for you." She walked back over to her iPod and hit a button. She was right when she said I'd recognize the song right away; it started with soft cymbals, a bass line, and then an acoustic guitar. It was the Jack Johnson song Sarah talked to me about earlier, the one that made her think of me when she heard the chorus. She turned back to us, "Can you believe what happened last night?"

"The sunspots?" I asked, feigning ignorance.

"No, almost every person in both our families got physical last night. Mom, Dad, me, you, Beau, Larry, your mom and dad, Mimi and Gramps!"

I was almost speechless, "Jesus."

"Actually, *Jesus* didn't get laid last night." Beau laughed, "Chuy, Harper, Landon and hopefully Ms. Livingston were all left out of the fun." I could tell he was scanning the kitchen for his bag full of enemas, because he stopped after he saw them in the corner.

And then the world stopped again, not because of some alien intervention, but because I heard a faint scream from upstairs that sounded exactly like Chuy's bumped-my-elbow-but-really-busted-a-nut scream.

"Where are Chuy and Harper?" I barked, panicked, thinking the absolute

worst, remembering what Harper had told Sarah about having a crush on a boy from out of town.

"I think they're upstairs in Harper's room, they've been fooling around up there all morning," Sarah said, using the absolute most unwelcome phrasing a father/brother could imagine. I leapt from my chair to run upstairs, fearing it was already too late. In my panicked, uncoordinated effort, I tripped over Sarah's foot, crashing to the kitchen floor, taking an empty chair out with me.

The gutted, horrific feeling I had inside me popped like a balloon when Harper came running through the kitchen's swinging door, alone, fully clothed, and on the phone. She looked down at me and shrugged before cupping the phone in her hand and whispered excitedly while running in place, *"He called! the boy I was telling you about called, this is him, the cute boy from Chicago!"*

I laid my head back on the ground, exhaled, and laughed. Chuy was just punching a clown in the face alone up there. *Thank you, Jesus.* Sarah was laughing uncontrollably at my wipeout as she lowered herself down to me and kissed me on the forehead. I attempted to get up, but she held me in place until she was sitting cross legged, with my head resting in her lap. My resistance ceased the minute she started running her fingers through my hair, a loving touch I had almost forgotten because it hadn't happened in such a long time.

Piper came over, nestled against me and fell asleep. From our new spot on the floor, Sarah and I watched our daughter agree to meet the mystery boy from Chicago. They would meet later that afternoon at the soda fountain in back of the drug store.

Harper and Beau started jumping up and down afterward, shrilling unintelligible schoolgirl screams, both fueled by the excitement of new boys. Beau was holding my story in his hand, taking care not to lose his place. It was neat to see Harper and Beau celebrating together, I knew Beau would be a wonderful addition to Harper's world just as he had been a wonderful, important, part of mine.

Chuy walked into the room with the zipper of his pants half open and a satisfied grin on his face. Not one to pass up an opportunity to be a wise-ass, he started mock jumping with Beau and Harper, completely unaware of what they were both so excited about.

Just days ago, I had been convinced death was certain, like I was falling down a cliff alongside Dusty and Peaches, with no chance of cheating our fate. I was wrong though. I watched the best day of my life turn into the worst week of my life, and then without slowing down at all, it turned into the best life a guy could ever ask for.

I took the whole scene in and felt a wonderfully deep hum of happiness pressing up against my chest. Was it my tuning forks? I wouldn't bet against it; all I know is it felt impossibly easy to breathe for the first time in a long, long while. I never thought I could be this happy, and I was happy to have been wrong.

With Sarah's hands in my hair and my head comfortably in her lap, my "tuning forks" and the song Sarah had chosen for me were playing in two-part harmony. There *is* someone for everyone. Sarah and Harper sang the chorus together, "Don't let your... dreams, be dreams," it was the most beautiful music I had ever heard. I was finally sure that *this day* was the best fucking day of my life.

Bathed in Sarah's loving touch, I closed my eyes and took a deep breath. She whispered in my ear, so close her warmth tickled, "*You know what you can't stop?*"

54

THE BEAR (RESOLUTION)

CHAPTER SEVEN

SAFE?

The next thing I know, I was in the living room of the big house. Grandma was holding me in her arms, and I could tell that she had been crying and that I hadn't been dreaming. I looked down to see if any part of me had been eaten but I only had little cuts from going through the corn. I started to cry uncontrollably, and she held me tighter in her arms telling me it was "OK." She didn't tell me *Jack* was OK, she just said it was "OK" and "you're safe now, Sam." Didn't she know I didn't care that *I* was OK? All I wanted to know was whether *Jack* was OK. I wanted to ask her if I had killed Jack, but I couldn't because I was really bawling. I kept trying to talk but she just kept shushing me like I was a baby, which was fine because I couldn't get anything out. Every time I tried, I lost my breath and kept crying.

I wanted to tell her that I was just trying to make him play dead like Grandpa had said to do. Nobody can outrun a bear, and that bear wasn't afraid of Jack. Maybe when Jack grows up, but not now. The more I thought about it the harder I cried and the harder I cried the harder my grandma hugged me. It was like I was sinking in quicksand and I couldn't ask for help and the more I tried to ask for help the more I would sink. I felt a hole in the middle of me which made me think my best friend was gone. I saw through the windows there were trucks all over the yard and men with rifles walking around, talking.

I kept thinking about how Jack fell after I hit him with my slingshot and right then I knew why there was a hole in the middle of my heart. I had killed Jack myself, my brother who protected me from Kenny Johnson, from his brother, from Grandpa's farts. I wanted to die and would do anything to change places with Jack.

If you've ever wondered what it feels like to pass out, it's just like going to sleep but faster. Apparently, I passed out *again* because I woke up in the bottom bunk of our room at the farm. It took me a second to remember I was still the boy who killed his brother with a slingshot. I screamed as loud as I could because I didn't know what else to do, I couldn't believe what I'd done. I shouted for Mom which I realized didn't make any sense, but I didn't care, and my Grandma came hurrying in.

"I didn't mean to do it." I was crying but after I was able to get the first couple words out, it became easier to talk, "I was trying to make him play dead. Grandpa said we should play dead. Jack was trying to stare the bear down like Dad did; only the bear wasn't scared. He was going to eat Jack. I wasn't trying to kill him!" and the crying came back big time because I was drowning in guilt and murder.

"Oh Sam, Sam, Sam," Grandma held me tighter, "Jack is OK, he's going to be fine. He has some bad cuts, but they stitched him up. How could *you* have killed him? You sweet, sweet, boy, it's not your fault. Do you feel OK to get up? Your Father and Grandpa are with Jack at the hospital, should we go see him?"

Oh sweet mother Mary, what do you think? Of course I want to go see him! I was just thinking I killed him, it was an incredible shot! You want to talk about bawling? It was like I was trying to set the world record for bawling. You can imagine how bad it feels to kill your brother when you were trying to help him not be killed and how great you would feel after you found out he was actually safe.

My big heart was going too far if you ask me, I couldn't even talk. I wanted to tell her let's go right now but I honestly couldn't say anything I was so relieved. Instead of saying something I just got out of bed and walked towards the door, towards Jack. I noticed that I had my pajamas on now, probably because there was puke all over my old clothes and that's when I realized I must have been out for a while because it was already dark outside.

I was able to stop crying by the time we got into the Lincoln. That's the family car my Grandma drives, but I didn't want to talk. I think Grandma knew it too, because she wasn't asking near half of the questions that I'd have, had she almost got eaten by a bear. Knowing Jack was all right and that Dad was here with him and that I wasn't going to get eaten by a bear made me feel like it was Christmas morning. For real. The only difference was I had no desire to run around like a maniac yelling about the gift I just got like I usually do on Christmas morning.

I asked Grandma about Mom and she said she was probably already at the hospital by now but that she'd called and asked about me. For some reason, I still felt a little bit nervous, and I didn't feel that I could talk about any of it because I was tired of crying. I wondered about my slingshot. Was it just lying there on the ground? I bet one of the guys with the guns picked it up and would probably give it to their kids. Losing a great slingshot that's already broken in would normally set my hair on fire, but the more I thought about it, they could have it.

When we got to the hospital, I saw Dad's truck and I think the combination of relief and my big heart made me start crying like crazy again. All I wanted to do was see Jack, to really know that he was OK and that I didn't kill him. It was an incredible shot after all, and I mean, he fell like a buck does when we go hunting, so how was I to know I didn't kill him?

I was starting to become afraid that he might be mad at me for running or for hitting him with a slingshot pellet (in the head!) before he could stare down that bear. I figured if anyone Jack's size could stare down a bear as big as the one we saw today, it would be Jack. I guess I started doubting whether I needed to knock Jack out with my slingshot because I'm so good at messing things up. I was really nervous that my big heart wouldn't let me explain to Jack why I'd shot him on account of all the bawling I knew I'd be doing. In case you haven't figured it out yet, it's impossible for me to talk when I'm bawling.

We rode up the elevator and walked down a hallway that went on forever; turns out they put Jack at the end of the longest hallway of the entire hospital. Grandma was holding my hand and I wasn't crying, but I wasn't *not* crying, and I knew I was going to start bawling the minute I saw Jack. I wanted to stop and gather myself because I knew everybody would probably be in the room, but I wanted to see Jack and Dad so bad I kept going.

CHAPTER EIGHT

BROTHERS

"Room 419, this is Jack's room," Grandma said softly and kneeled down to wipe my face off. "He had two bad cuts which are bandaged, but don't be scared if you see tubes coming out of one arm, it's a good thing- it's to replace the blood he lost from his cuts. He's safe now, he's going to be just fine, Samuel." My grandmother calls me Samuel sometimes, that is my real name.

I nodded, I wasn't *scared* at all, didn't she know that? Doesn't she know that I have a big heart and that people with big hearts just cry a lot? *She* was the one who looked scared. She had tears in her eyes too.

I walked in and saw Dad sitting with his back facing me. He was watching Jack sleep and holding his hand. Grandpa was talking on the phone in the corner of the room pacing and cussing about something under his breath.

Sure enough, I started bawling when I saw Jack's face, asleep on his pillow. He looked pale and weak like he was about to die, nothing at all like he looked this morning in my room. I was scared all over again and I turned away into my Grandma and tried unsuccessfully to keep my bawling quiet. I wanted to disappear, I wanted to be eaten by a bear, anything. I wanted to do anything but feel like I had killed my brother and best friend which is how I felt seeing Jack like that on his bed, even though I knew I didn't kill him.

Then a feeling I knew well came over me or actually around me. It was my dad's arms holding me and lifting me up. He turned me around and held me tight. World class bawling, I just absolutely lost it. I mean we are talking boogers and all, just an absolute total loss of control because for the first time since I woke up, I felt safe. Dad just let me go too, he didn't try the "shh shh" crap that Grandma was doing, he just kind of squeezed me lightly and put his head up next to mine and held it there. After about four hours of bawling, I came up for air and saw my grandpa standing behind Dad like he was waiting for a turn.

"My little hero!" Grandpa said with a big smile. *What? Huh?* It confused me at first but then I realized he had no idea his "little hero" actually threw up on Jack and then *ran* from the bear, leaving behind a cherry Kool Aide and beef jerky flavored Jack to get eaten. I was glad none of them knew that I ran yet because it was embarrassing. I also knew they would learn eventually, but I hoped they wouldn't be too disappointed in me because I did come back after I realized what I had done. I looked over at Jack, who was waking up on account of all my bawling and I buried my head back into Dad's neck (boogers and all) and started bawling all over again.

After another fifty hours of bawling, I heard Jack say, "Sammy, I'm OK, I'm going to be just fine, you saved my life! Dad, can you put him in the bed?" I saw Dad's eyes and it almost looked like he had been crying too but obviously not nearly as bad as me on account of there were no boogers all over his cheeks. His huge hand covered my entire face as he wiped the tears and boogers off and set me down next to Jack who winced as he moved over to make some room. He had a tube that was coming from a hanging bag and going into his good arm, while his right arm, (his pitching and casting arm) was bandaged above and below his elbow.

"I've got 37 stitches in my arm and side, can you believe it?" he said to me, smiling a little smile, and I knew he was attempting to cheer me up, but it was no use because I just threw my arms around him and started bawling quietly into his shoulder. Obviously, having a little kid with a face full on boogers hugging you and crying all over you is not what you want if you have 37 stitches all over the place.

Jack, as always, was patient though and just grimaced and said, "Sam, Sam, SAM" until Dad went ahead and pulled me off him. I managed to say sorry to Jack in the process. Dad was holding me and was about to say something when Jack looked at Dad and Grandpa and asked, "Can I talk to Sam alone for a second?"

Dad looked at Grandpa, confused, but said "Sure." He put me back into the hospital bed and kissed me and Jack both on the foreheads, which is a new one to me because Dad's not much of a forehead kisser. Mom will take any kind of kiss she can get, but Dad is more of a hugger and a back and thigh slapper.

"Sam, Jack has stitches on his side. You can't hug him, or the stitches will break, Ok?"

"OK" I sniffled, and Dad, Grandpa, and Grandma left the room.

"You don't have to cry anymore Sam, I'm OK. I'm going to be fine. You're a hero today, Sam. You are my hero. I would have been lunch for that son of a bitch had you not knocked me out. That was you, wasn't it? Did you shoot me with your sling shot? Grandpa told me you must have because he found it next to you. He has your slingshot in his back pocket." He turned and pointed to a massive welt on his head. I looked at it and nodded as he smiled back at me. "Let's not do that again, OK?" I laughed and looked down, fighting the urge to cry again.

"Sam," he said again, "I was scared too. It's over now, they're going to get that bear. There are a bunch of guys out there hunting him right now." I nodded my head again because I already knew that. I saw all the trucks were still on Grandpa's lawn when we left for the hospital.

I finally felt like I could talk again because Jack and I had gone through this together. "You aren't mad I shot you? The bear looked like he was going to eat you and I was afraid. I remembered Grandpa said we should play dead. He said no one can outrun a bear. He said we should have played dead. You were trying to stare him down like Dad had done. He was going to eat you!"

I wasn't crying but I could feel the tears coming down my face and looking to Jack for relief or guilt, looking for *something*.

He smiled at me. "I wanted to give you a chance to run away Sam; I wasn't going to let that ugly son of a bitch get the *both* of us. I thought if Dad could do it that I could too, and if that didn't work, I was going to run like hell. Well, when that bear walked up to me Sam, I froze. It stood up again and growled and I didn't know what the hell I was doing. I couldn't move. Did you hear him? He was so tall I shit my pants." Obviously, I started cracking up, and he started laughing too but stopped instantly because of the pain.

He winced again," I'm not kidding, I really shit my pants." At that point he looked at me really serious and pointed his finger at me, "And that's a brother secret. Do you understand me? I mean it." I nodded; it was safe with me *forever*.

"You weren't trying to stare the bear down?"

"I couldn't move, I wasn't trying to stare him down at all, I just froze. He had huge teeth. Did you see his teeth? Did you see him when he stood up? How much taller than me he was?" I *did* see how much taller he was, right before I shot Jack in the head.

Jack was looking at me and I just couldn't stand it any longer, I had to ask him, "Did you *really* poop in your pants?"

He looked at me and smiled, "Yup, I guess that happens to you in really scary situations. I didn't feel it at all, Grandpa told me." I laughed pretty good for the both of us since it hurt Jack's side to laugh and even though I wanted to hug Jack, I just settled on snuggling in next to him. It was good not to cry for a while because after all that crying, my stomach hurt.

Dad came in the room smiling and Mom appeared from behind him like a magic trick. She looked like she had just fallen out of a bawling tree and hit every branch on the way down. She hugged us both but instead of letting up like you are supposed to do when you hug, she just kept hugging. Moms will do that sometimes, especially our mom. Jack eventually had to ask her to stop, and she did.

Pretty soon everybody was in the room and Jack and I told the story of what happened. Neither one of us looked at Grandpa when we talked about riding through the cornfield on the Honda. I knew we probably wouldn't get in trouble for that after what happened today. Hell, we probably could have skinned the cat and not gotten in trouble. It's amazing what almost getting eaten by a bear will cover up.

We talked about walking out of the cornfield and then coming out to find that big son of a bitch just standing there. I was embarrassed when Jack got to the part where I ran and left him to die but he was quick to let me off the hook when he said that I came back for him. He told everyone that he probably would have been an afternoon snack had I not come back.

Mom got upset throughout the whole story but especially when Jack talked about the bear. I was still really embarrassed about throwing up and running, leaving Jack behind to get eaten, especially since everyone knew about it now. Everybody said they were proud of me for saving Jack's life though, which made me feel a little bit better that they weren't concentrating on the embarrassing part. One thing I *was* proud of was that Jack pooped in his pants and that I didn't. I mean, I'm not proud that Jack pooped in his pants, I'm just proud that *I* didn't. I did throw up over the both of us, but I think that you'd agree that it's *much* better than soiling yourself. It did make me think though, if a bear did eat me, would it stop at my butt because there was still poop in there or would it eat my butt too, poop and all? Bears didn't seem gross like that to me though.

Dad picked me up out of Jack's bed when it was time to go. Jack had to stay overnight and get more blood, because most of his had leaked out of the cuts the bear made. I wanted to stay there with him, but Mom must have called it before everyone else because she was the one that got to stay the night in Jack's room. It was great to be with Dad again, and I was looking forward to having him with us the rest of the week for protection. Even though I knew everyone was going to be OK I still felt a little bit scared.

To tell you the truth, I was glad to get out of that room because I was tired of hearing about how I was a hero. I didn't feel like a hero. I was still embarrassed that I ran away and if you ask me, the hero was really Jack. Jack was going to get *eaten* by a bear just to save *me*. Jack didn't even *think* about running away.

When we started driving back to Grandpa's, Dad turned off the radio and said, "Sam, "I am so proud of you. You were so brave today. Jack is alive because of you and your quick thinking." I could feel my big heart starting up again and I hated crying in front of Dad the most, because I wanted to be like him the most and he never cries. I guess it had been building in me the whole time we had been telling the story and just like my tears, I couldn't hold it in anymore.

"*I ran.*" It came out of my mouth without me even trying too, like a hiccup, but Dad didn't hear.

"Sam?"

"*I RAN.*" I said louder, starting to cry. "I ran as fast as I could, and I left Jack there to get eaten." My big heart started to hurt, and I was bawling again, but it felt good to go ahead and get it off my chest and tell Dad. He must not have understood it though, because he was smiling. He pulled the truck over to the side of the road, shut it off, and turned to face me.

"Let's go through this and make sure I have it right. Jack came up with a plan and told you to run, didn't he?" I nodded.

"You did what he told you to do, which is what you should have done, but then you had a better idea, didn't you? You turned around and ran back *towards a bear* to help your brother, didn't you?" He pulled me into his arms and wiped my face off again and I wondered what he was doing with all the boogers that he was wiping off me. I nodded yes.

"Did you know that Jack was trying to stare down a bear when he should have been playing dead?"

"No." I was only half-crying now. "I was going to shoot that son of a bitch in the eye with my slingshot. I didn't think to shoot Jack until I was aiming for the bear and then I remembered what Grandpa had said about playing dead."

I couldn't help to smile because he was making me realize I actually did do something brave! In the end, I *did* save Jack and that more than made up for throwing up or running away. Hell, Jack *shit his pants.* I felt like I had been on the bottom of the pile in football and all of a sudden everyone finally got off of me. I could breathe again, and I didn't want to cry anymore.

316

"Put your hands on my face," He said, taking my hands and placing them on either side of his huge face. Dad usually did that when he wanted us to really listen to him, like when he tells you that you shouldn't take the hooks off his favorite fishing lures and use them to snag carp in Tyler Creek.

"You and your brother mean so much to me," and he stopped, he looked like *he* was going to bawl. Dad's eyes were watering up and he took a deep breath and blew it out through his lips, and I thought, *I need to try that.*

"If anything happened to either of you, I would just die. I wouldn't be able to go on another day without you. We almost lost Jack today, but we didn't because YOU saved him. What YOU did today was as brave and as smart as anything I've ever seen or heard of. And let me tell you right now, Sam Williams, a thousand different things could have happened today before, during, and after your run-in with that bear, and don't you worry about *any* of it except for the fact that *you* saved Jack's life."

He took another breath and blew it through his lips again, "I am so thankful that you two were there together. I am so proud of you to have the smarts to know what to do and the courage to do it. But most of all Sam, I am so proud that you are my son. I love you buddy, and until you have a boy of your own you won't even begin to know how much."

I didn't cry. I felt so good at that moment. All the guilt was gone, and my dad was really proud of me. I can tell you one thing: when your parents are proud of you it's an awfully good feeling. He kissed my forehead and I let go of his face.

"Braver than you actually staring down a bear?" I had to ask.

"Much, much braver Sam, I was scared. I was stupid to think I could take a bear, but I was young, and I thought I was invincible, and I realized when that bear walked up to me and stood up that I had made a huge mistake. I was too scared to run, so I held my ground, and I was lucky the bear wasn't interested. Your Uncle Gary likes to embellish the story and I should have corrected him. I think the bear has tripled in size since it happened."

"Jack was the brave one, he was only trying to save me."

Dad started up the car and looked over to me and said, "Sam, I'm just as proud of Jack as I am of you today and you should be too. But without you, I'm afraid to say he might not be with us. I'm a lucky dad to have such special, brave boys. I feel ten feet tall right now. So does Grandpa."

Grandpa? Wow, this was new territory, I wondered if he was going to let me drive one of his tractors now? Dad never talked like this and it had me feeling really great, really brave, and not embarrassed at all for running away. Because I *did* turn around, and I *did* make an incredible shot which, by the way, I can't believe isn't getting more attention, and I *did* save my brother's life. Not counting animals, this was my first time saving someone's life, which in case you don't know, feels real good.

"They got him." Grandpa said as we walked in the door. "They got your bear, Sam. Big Joe Broughton shot him down by the creek. Big Joe said he's going to stuff him and put him in his bar."

Dad looked at me and I held back the tears. You won't believe this: I was glad it was over, but sad the bear had been killed. I can't explain it, but I was.

Grandpa looked sad though, "He got Buddy, Sam, the bear hurt him pretty bad, and they had to put ol' Buddy down."

Now I was relieved that big ugly bear was dead, and you'd have thought I was out of tears by then, but I started bawling like crazy again because I loved Buddy even though he was a pain in the ass to go fishing with.

Dad took me in his arms as Grandpa left the room. He didn't try to stop me from crying, he just said, "Buddy was a hero today too, Sam."

I knew I had heard a dog bark! Buddy was coming out to go fishing with us! He must have chased the big ugly son of a bitch into the corn or maybe now that I think about it, the bear must have chased buddy into the corn. As big as that bear was, I'm not sure he's ever been afraid of anything except maybe his wife, if he had one, and I could understand that.

Jack came home the next day and we just sat around looking at his stitches, letting them air out while Mom changed the bandages. They were going to be great scars and I would be lying to you if I told you I wasn't a little jealous. Dad and I went fishing every day, sometimes with Grandpa, sometimes just us, and once with Mom. We caught plenty of fish but never caught Big Frank, which was fine because I wouldn't want to catch him without Jack there to see. When it was time to go home, I was glad because it just wasn't the same without Jack or Buddy. Plus I was scared to go out back seeing that I almost got eaten and all.

Then Jack surprised us. "I want to go fishing again before I leave, I don't want to leave here afraid of going fishing at our own farm."

"Me too!" I chimed in, only because I wanted to go fishing with my best friend, although I couldn't imagine not being scared to walk down that road again.

Grandpa beamed, "That's my boys!"

My mom wasn't having it though, "Jack, we have to get home. Your father has to work tomorrow. There will be other trips sweetie." I can guarantee you that Mom didn't want us going back there either.

I looked at my dad, who was looking at Grandpa who sprung up and said, "I'll drive them back, and I'll take them fishing too."

"Settled," Dad said as he looked to my mom who was giving him the evil eye. He kissed her and she just kept looking at him like the shit was going to hit the fan.

"We want to go alone" Jack added and everyone in the room stopped and looked towards him, including me.

"Are you *nuts*?" I asked. I was also thinking about the ride home with Grandpa. If you can imagine, after you almost get eaten by a bear, almost everything seems a little less scary, except riding home with Grandpa. That ought to tell you a lot about riding in the truck with Grandpa.

"They got the bear Sam. I want to go fishing like we always do."

Without saying anything, my dad walked over and gave Jack a kiss on top of his head and then looked to me, "Sam, take your slingshot, would you?"

That night we ate my favorite pizza from the Pizza Hut and went fishing the next morning. I was scared Dad wasn't with us but tried not to show it, because Jack didn't look scared at all. We left the pond around noon because in Jack's case, it's hard to fish with one arm in a sling, and in my case, I was scared as hell another bear was going to walk around every tree and out of every cornfield we came upon. I was getting the farts real bad from the pizza the night before and was convinced that if I heard or saw anything that even looked like a bear I would for sure shit in my pants.

When we got back from fishing we started packing up and Grandpa rode up on his horse Olive, his rifle tied to his saddle. He said he'd been shooting rabbits out back, but I hadn't heard any shots. I wondered if he had been following us in case we ran into another bear, and if he was, I was glad he did. Maybe next summer it will be different.

CHAPTER NINE

ON THE ROAD AGAIN

Throwing our bags in the back of Grandpa's truck, I looked to Jack and asked, "Did you slip him the BEAN-O?"

"It's all gone. I've been slipping it to Grandma all week. She makes Grandpa look like a choir boy. I thought *Dad* would be driving us home." If I hadn't been laughing so hard about Grandma's farts (who knew?), I would have been crying about driving home with Grandpa. He ate the same dinner I did and If he was farting even *half* as bad as me, I knew we'd be goners.

Sure enough, twenty minutes into the drive home my sides began to hurt from eating the delicious Pizza Hut pan pizza with sausage and pepperoni. I felt like I was going to blow up if I didn't let a fart. I knew I'd get cussed at if I did so I thought I'd just go ahead and save it until Grandpa let one of his, because he ate that same pizza too and his farts will cover *anything*.

Well, it seemed like a good enough plan, but nobody told my butt about it and wouldn't you know it? A little fart leaked out without making a noise. I panicked a little and went to turn towards the window and the pressure was too much. Whatever I was holding in was now out. About two seconds went by and as it hit me, I thought of what my dad sometimes says after a stinker, "*goodnight Irene!*" You can't eat a pizza like that and not have spectacular smelling farts the next day.

I waited, terrified, and I looked over at my grandpa, who looked like someone had just punched him in the face. His eyes got wide, and he looked like he was going to cuss me out when Jack elbowed me and leaned forward so Grandpa could see him, "Sorry Grandpa, I can't hold it in. It hurts my stitches too much."

Grandpa just smiled as he rolled down his window and put his hand into Jack's hair, "I guess you get a pass this trip."

I tried to think of how I might be able to ask Jack to cover me for a couple more without grandpa getting wind of it. I ate three whole slices, so you can bet I was literally under a lot of pressure. Just in case you are confused, if you use a saying that you really mean, you can let people know by saying "literally."

I could tell it hurt him to do it, but Jack put his arm around my shoulders, looked at me and smiled as the air cleared. I smiled back and leaned into him a little less worried about things, like what I was going to do about my farts for the rest of the trip, when he leaned down and whispered in my ear, "let 'em rip."

I wondered how many times I would have to save Jack's life before I would ever be able to repay him for everything he does and has done for me. The more I thought about it the sillier I felt, because now I know what Jack and Dad must have known all along: that when someone in your family needs help, you help them, you don't keep score, you help them.

Jack still had his arm around me, I leaned into him and ripped another silent but deadly tearjerker. A minute later he looked at me, cross-eyed and I lost it.

Jack was laughing as hard as his stitches would allow, and begging me to stop laughing but it was too late, I was snorting by that point. The truck smelled horrible but it didn't matter, even Grandpa was laughing, *all bets were off.*

I never felt safer from any bear than I did at that moment.

The End.

About the Author

Parker Duque is married with three kids and lives in Atlanta, GA. He loves doing outdoorsy stuff and spending summers in Michigan with family & friends.

Made in the USA
Columbia, SC
02 August 2021